# THE EDWARDIAN DETECTIVES

## Literary Sleuths of the Edwardian Era

## Edited by Greg Fowlkes

# THE EDWARDIAN DETECTIVES

## Literary Sleuths of the Edwardian Era

© 2012 Resurrected Press
www.ResurrectedPress.com

## Published by Resurrected Press

This classic book was handcrafted by Resurrected Press. Resurrected Press is dedicated to bringing high quality classic books back to the readers who enjoy them. These are not scanned versions of the originals, but, rather, quality checked and edited books meant to be enjoyed!

Please visit ResurrectedPress.com to view our entire catalogue!

ISBN 13: 978-1-937022-50-1

Printed in the United States of America

# FOREWORD

The Victorian Age saw the rise of the detective, both in real life, and in their fictional counterparts. Indeed, the fictional detective, in many ways, preceded the official version. Writers such as Poe, Gaboriau, and Arthur Conan Doyle enjoyed enormous popular success with their tales of the exploits of their sleuths. Sherlock Holmes continues to this day to be the subject of countless movies, television programs, books and stories. But the fictional detective did not die with the passing of Queen Victoria. Indeed, the period between her death and the First World War proved to be an incredibly fruitful one for the creators of fictional sleuths, so much so that at least one critic, Julian Symons, has called it "The First Golden Age of the Short Story." Numerous detectives appeared in the pages of newspapers and magazines such as the Strand and The Saturday Evening Post. Yet today, most of these investigators lie forgotten in obscurity, their exploits long out of print. The intention of this book is to serve as an introduction to the modern reader of these remarkable characters.

The Edwardian age, was a time of change and transition. Whereas the Victorian age had been marked by the power of steam, the advent of the railroad, the introduction of gaslight, in the Edwardian age we begin to see the use of electricity and the telephone, the replacement of the horse and carriage with the automobile, and the first primitive airplanes. An industrial economy was replacing that based on agriculture. Wealth was no longer based on land but on securities and trade.

It was also a time of political unrest and upheaval. It was an age of anarchists and assassins. Rebellion and nationalism rocked the Balkans. Socialism was suppressed by force in Russia. The Ottoman and Austro-Hungarian Empires were on their last legs ready to fragment at the seams. Women were seeking the vote and the middle class was seeking a say in running their lives and their countries. The neat, tidy, and orderly world of the Victorians was slowly preparing to collapse, a collapse that would finally occur as an aftermath of the First World War.

With this change, came a change in the crimes the detectives investigated, and in the detectives themselves. Swindles and securities fraud were as likely to be the subject as the theft of fabulous jewelry. Murders were often petty, involving not the elite, but the middle and lower classes, with the motivation being a matter of a few hundred pounds rather than the inheritance of grand estates worth millions. Espionage and crimes intending to destabilize governments were increasingly the focus of the stories.

The detectives changed as well. Where as the Victorian sleuth tended to be an intellectual working behind the scenes, the Edwardian detective was often much more flamboyant, their activities played out in full view of the press. Indeed, for several of the characters, the newspaperman or woman has become an active participant in the process of investigation.

The detectives of the Edwardian era tended towards the unusual rather than the realistic. Readers of the time were looking to be entertained. One of the reasons that the short story form was so popular was that it could be read in a magazine or newspaper on the commute to and from work. There was little time to develop character or go into an elaborate plot. Instead, what was desired was a puzzle where the clues were all laid out for the reader and then summed up at the end of the story with a brilliant flash of deduction.

The sleuths presented in this collection are a varied lot. They include an Austrian policeman, a more or less conventional detective, an English priest, a blind man, a lecturer in medical jurisprudence, a man who solves crimes sitting at a table in an ABC tea room, a master of disguise, an English Lady who joined Scotland Yard to prove the innocence of her fiancée, and an American polymath who is a master of all subjects. They have little in common except for the fact that they are able to solve crimes in extraordinary fashion, that and the fact that they were all enormously popular in their day.

Technically, the Edwardian age ran from only from 1901 to 1910, but for the purpose of this book it has been expanded to include the period from the turn of the century until the beginning of the First World War. This seems fair, as there was very little difference between the years 1911-1914 and the decade preceding. One of the detectives, Arthur Morrison's Martin Hewitt, began his career in print before the beginning of this period, but continued to appear during it. Several of the detectives, notably R. Austin Freeman's Dr. John Thorndyke and G. K, Chesterton's Father Brown had long and distinguished careers that lasted well into the ensuing decades. For the most part, though, they remained fashionable only for the brief time of the era or a few years after. In the case of Jacques Futrelle's Van Dusen, his career was cut tragically short when Futrelle went down with the Titanic.

Resurrected Press is proud to bring the reader this collection of stories and hopes that it will serve as an introduction to this important, but long neglected period in the history of detective fiction. For those interested, suggestions for further reading are included in the introductions to each of the stories.

Greg Fowlkes
Editor-In-Chief
Resurrected Press
www.ResurrectedPress.com

# Resurrected Press Classic Mystery Catalogue

**E. C. Bentley**
*Trent's Last Case: The Woman in Black*

**Ernest Bramah**
*Max Carrados Resurrected:*
*The Detective Stories of Max Carrados*

**Agatha Christie**
*The Secret Adversary*
*The Mysterious Affair at Styles*

**Octavus Roy Cohen**
*Midnight*

**Freeman Wills Croft**
*The Ponson Case*
*The Pit Prop Syndicate*

**J. S. Fletcher**
*The Herapath Property*
*The Rayner-Slade Amalgamation*
*The Chestermarke Instinct*
*The Paradise Mystery*
*Dead Men's Money*
*The Middle of Things*
*Ravensdene Court*
*Scarhaven Keep*
*The Orange-Yellow Diamond*
*The Middle Temple Murder*
*The Tallyrand Maxim*
*The Borough Treasurer*
*In the Mayor's Parlour*
*The Saftey Pin*

## R. Austin Freeman
*The Mystery of 31 New Inn from the Dr. Thorndyke Series*
*John Thorndyke's Cases from the Dr. Thorndyke Series*
*The Red Thumb Mark from The Dr. Thorndyke Series*
*The Eye of Osiris from The Dr. Thorndyke Series*
*A Silent Witness from the Dr. John Thorndyke Series*
*The Cat's Eye from the Dr. John Thorndyke Series*
*Helen Vardon's Confession: A Dr. John Thorndyke Story*
*As a Thief in the Night: A Dr. John Thorndyke Story*
*Mr. Pottermack's Oversight: A Dr. John Thorndyke Story*
*Dr. Thorndyke Intervenes: A Dr. John Thorndyke Story*
*The Singing Bone: The Adventures of Dr. Thorndyke*
*The Stoneware Monkey: A Dr. John Thorndyke Story*
*The Great Portrait Mystery, and Other Stories: A Collection of Dr.
John Thorndyke and Other Stories*
*The Penrose Mystery: A Dr. John Thorndyke Story*
*The Uttermost Farthing: A Savant's Vendetta*

## Arthur Griffiths
*The Passenger From Calais*
*The Rome Express*

## Fergus Hume
*The Mystery of a Hansom Cab*
*The Green Mummy*
*The Silent House*
*The Secret Passage*

## Edgar Jepson
*The Loudwater Mystery*

## A. E. W. Mason
*At the Villa Rose*

## A. A. Milne
*The Red House Mystery*

## Baroness Emma Orczy
*The Old Man in the Corner*

## Edgar Allan Poe
*The Detective Stories of Edgar Allan Poe*

**Arthur J. Rees**
*The Hampstead Mystery*
*The Shrieking Pit*
*The Hand In The Dark*
*The Moon Rock*
*The Mystery of the Downs*

**Mary Roberts Rinehart**
*Sight Unseen and The Confession*

**Dorothy L. Sayers**
*Whose Body?*

**Sir William Magnay**
*The Hunt Ball Mystery*

**Mabel and Paul Thorne**
*The Sheridan Road Mystery*

**Louis Tracy**
*The Strange Case of Mortimer Fenley*
*The Albert Gate Mystery*
*The Bartlett Mystery*
*The Postmaster's Daughter*
*The House of Peril*
*The Sandling Case: What Would You Have Done?*

**Charles Edmonds Walk**
*The Paternoster Ruby*

**John R. Watson**
*The Mystery of the Downs*
*The Hampstead Mystery*

**Edgar Wallace**
*The Daffodil Mystery*
*The Crimson Circle*

# TABLE OF CONTENTS

# THE CASE OF LAKER, ABSCONDED

## BY ARTHUR MORRISON

ARTHUR MORRISON

**ORIGINALLY PUBLISHED 1896**

# The Case of Laker, Absconded

### By Arthur Morrison

## Martin Hewitt, Detective

One of the more popular detectives in this period was Martin Hewitt, the creation of Arthur Morrison. Unlike many of his contemporaries, there was little unusual or flamboyant about Hewitt. He was a kind of an inversion of Sherlock Holmes, ordinary looking, short instead of lean and tall, and generally good natured. His detective style was less flamboyant than other fictional detectives of the period, solving crimes through leg work and keen observation followed by intelligent deduction rather than the mental gymnastics commonly exhibited. The crimes he faced also tended to be less exotic, the work of small time crooks rather than arch criminals.

Morrison had grown up in the rough and tumble world of London's East End, and had a familiarity both from his youth and from his experiences as a newspaperman on the *Evening Globe*. He wrote about this side of life in a number of novels including *Tales of Mean Streets* and *A Child of the Jago* which were well received at the time. He used this background when writing his detective fiction, and as a result his stories tend to be less fanciful and more realistic in tone than those of Conan Doyle.

Hewitt began his career in the late 1890's and continued on until the early 1900's, rather a shorter period than many of the detectives. This is due, in part, to Morrison essentially retiring from writing on the eve of World War I to devote himself to the collecting of Japanese prints and paintings.

More stories featuring Martin Hewitt may be found in Resurrected Press's collections *Martin Hewitt Resurrected*.

# THE CASE OF LAKER, ABSCONDED

There were several of the larger London banks and insurance offices from which Hewitt held a sort of general retainer as detective adviser, in fulfilment of which he was regularly consulted as to the measures to be taken in different cases of fraud, forgery, theft, and so forth, which it might be the misfortune of the particular firms to encounter. The more important and intricate of these cases were placed in his hands entirely, with separate commissions, in the usual way. One of the most important companies of the sort was the General Guarantee Society, an insurance corporation which, among other risks, took those of the integrity of secretaries, clerks, and cashiers. In the case of a cash-box elopement on the part of any person guaranteed by the society, the directors were naturally anxious for a speedy capture of the culprit, and more especially of the booty, before too much of it was spent, in order to lighten the claim upon their funds, and in work of this sort Hewitt was at times engaged, either in general advice and direction or in the actual pursuit of the plunder and the plunderer.

Arriving at his office a little later than usual one morning, Hewitt found an urgent message awaiting him from the General Guarantee Society, requesting his attention to a robbery which had taken place on the previous day. He had gleaned some hint of the case from the morning paper, wherein appeared a short paragraph, which ran thus:

*SERIOUS BANK ROBBERY.—In the course of yesterday a clerk employed by Messrs Liddle, Neal & Liddle, the well-known bankers, disappeared, having in his possession a large sum of money, the property of his employers—a sum reported to be rather over £15,000. It would seem that he had been entrusted to collect the money in his capacity of 'walk-clerk' from various other banks and trading concerns during the morning, but failed to return at the usual time. A large number of the notes which he received had been cashed at the Bank of England before suspicion was aroused. We understand that Detective-Inspector Plummer, of Scotland Yard, has the case in hand.*

The clerk, whose name was Charles William Laker, had, it appeared from the message, been guaranteed in the usual way by the General Guarantee Society, and Hewitt's presence at the office was at once desired in order that steps might quickly be taken for the man's apprehension and in the recovery, at any rate, of as much of the booty as possible.

A smart hansom brought Hewitt to Threadneedle Street in a bare quarter of an hour, and there a few minutes' talk with the manager, Mr Lyster, put him in possession of the main facts of the case, which appeared to be simple. Charles William Laker was twenty-five years of age, and had been in the employ of Messrs Liddle, Neal & Liddle for something more than seven years—since he left school, in fact—and until the previous day there had been nothing in his conduct to complain of. His duties as walk-clerk consisted in making a certain round, beginning at about half-past ten each morning. There were a certain number of the more important banks between which and Messrs Liddle, Neal & Liddle there were daily transactions, and a few smaller semi-private banks and merchant firms acting as financial agents with whom there was business intercourse of less importance and regularity; and each of these, as necessary, he visited in turn, collecting cash due on bills and other instruments of a like nature. He carried a wallet, fastened securely to his person by a chain, and this wallet contained the bills and the cash. Usually at the end of his round, when all his bills had been converted into cash, the wallet held very large sums. His work and responsibilities, in fine, were those common to walk-clerks in all banks.

On the day of the robbery he had started out as usual—possibly a little earlier than was customary—and the bills and other securities in his possession represented considerably more than £15,000. It had been ascertained that he had called in the usual way at each establishment on the round, and had transacted his business at the last place by about a quarter-past one, being then, without doubt, in possession of cash to the full value of the bills negotiated. After that, Mr Lyster said, yesterday's report was that nothing more had been heard of him. But this morning there had been a message to the effect that he had been traced out of the country—to Calais, at least, it was thought. The directors of the society wished Hewitt to take the case in hand personally and at once, with a view of recovering what was possible from the plunder by way of salvage; also, of course, of finding Laker, for it is an important moral gain to guarantee societies, as an example, if a thief is caught and punished. Therefore Hewitt and Mr Lyster, as soon as might be, made for Messrs Liddle, Neal & Liddle's, that the investigation might be begun.

The bank premises were quite near—in Leadenhall Street. Having arrived there, Hewitt and Mr Lyster made their way to the firm's private rooms. As they were passing an outer waiting-room, Hewitt noticed two women. One, the elder, in widow's weeds, was sitting with her head bowed in her hand over a small writing-table. Her face was not visible, but her whole attitude was that of a person overcome with unbearable grief; and she sobbed quietly. The other was a young woman of twenty-two or twenty-three. Her thick black veil revealed no more than that her features were small and regular and that her face was pale and drawn. She stood with a hand on the elder woman's shoulder, and she quickly turned her head away as the two men entered.

Mr Neal, one of the partners, received them in his own room. 'Good-morning, Mr Hewitt,' he said, when Mr Lyster had introduced the detective. 'This is a serious business—very. I think I am sorrier for Laker himself than for anybody else, ourselves included—or, at any rate, I am sorrier for his mother. She is waiting now to see Mr Liddle, as soon as he arrives—Mr Liddle has known the family for a long time. Miss Shaw is with her, too, poor girl. She is a governess, or something of that sort, and I believe she and Laker were engaged to be married. It's all very sad.'

'Inspector Plummer, I understand,' Hewitt remarked, 'has the affair in hand, on behalf of the police?'

'Yes,' Mr Neal replied; 'in fact, he's here now, going through the contents of Laker's desk, and so forth; he thinks it possible Laker may have had accomplices. Will you see him?'

'Presently. Inspector Plummer and I are old friends. We met last, I think, in the case of the Stanway cameo, some months ago. But, first, will you tell me how long Laker has been a walk-clerk?'

'Barely four months, although he has been with us altogether seven years. He was promoted to the walk soon after the beginning of the year.'

'Do you know anything of his habits—what he used to do in his spare time, and so forth?'

'Not a great deal. He went in for boating, I believe, though I have heard it whispered that he had one or two more expensive tastes—expensive, that is, for a young man in his position,' Mr Neal explained, with a dignified wave of the hand that he peculiarly affected. He was a stout old gentleman, and the gesture suited him.

'You have had no reason to suspect him of dishonesty before, I take it?'

'Oh, no. He made a wrong return once, I believe, that went for some time undetected, but it turned out, after all, to be a clerical error—a mere clerical error.'

'Do you know anything of his associates out of the office?'

'No, how should I? I believe Inspector Plummer has been making inquiries as to that, however, of the other clerks. Here he is, by the bye, I expect. Come in!'

It was Plummer who had knocked, and he came in at Mr Neal's call. He was a middle-sized, small-eyed, impenetrable-looking man, as yet of no great reputation in the force. Some of my readers may remember his connection with that case, so long a public mystery, that I have elsewhere fully set forth and explained under the title of 'The Stanway Cameo Mystery'. Plummer carried his billy-cock hat in one hand and a few papers in the other. He gave Hewitt good-morning, placed his hat on a chair, and spread the papers on the table.

'There's not a great deal here,' he said, 'but one thing's plain—Laker had been betting. See here, and here, and here'— he took a few letters from the bundle in his hand—'two letters from a bookmaker about settling—wonder he trusted a clerk—

several telegrams from tipsters, and a letter from some friend—
only signed by initials—asking Laker to put a sovereign on a
horse for the friend "with his own". I'll keep these, I think. It
may be worth while to see that friend, if we can find him. Ah, we
often find it's betting, don't we, Mr Hewitt? Meanwhile, there's
no news from France yet.'

'You are sure that is where he is gone?' asked Hewitt.

'Well, I'll tell you what we've done as yet. First, of course, I
went round to all the banks. There was nothing to be got from
that. The cashiers all knew him by sight, and one was a personal
friend of his. He had called as usual, said nothing in particular,
cashed his bills in the ordinary way, and finished up at the
Eastern Consolidated Bank at about a quarter-past one. So far
there was nothing whatever. But I had started two or three men
meanwhile making inquiries at the railway stations, and so on. I
had scarcely left the Eastern Consolidated when one of them
came after me with news. He had tried Palmer's Tourist Office,
although that seemed an unlikely place, and there struck the
track.'

'Had he been there?'

'Not only had he been there, but he had taken a tourist ticket
for France. It was quite a smart move, in a way. You see it was
the sort of ticket that lets you do pretty well what you like; you
have the choice of two or three different routes to begin with,
and you can break your journey where you please, and make all
sorts of variations. So that a man with a ticket like that, and a
few hours' start, could twist about on some remote branch route,
and strike off in another direction altogether, with a new ticket,
from some out-of-the-way place, while we were carefully sorting
out and inquiring along the different routes he *might* have
taken. Not half a bad move for a new hand; but he made one bad
mistake, as new hands always do—as old hands do, in fact, very
often. He was fool enough to give his own name, C. Laker!
Although that didn't matter much, as the description was
enough to fix him.

There he was, wallet and all, just as he had come from the
Eastern Consolidated Bank. He went straight from there to
Palmer's, by the bye, and probably in a cab. We judge that by the
time. He left the Eastern Consolidated at a quarter-past one,
and was at Palmer's by twenty-five-past—ten minutes. The clerk

at Palmer's remembered the time because he was anxious to get out to his lunch, and kept looking at the clock, expecting another clerk in to relieve him. Laker didn't take much in the way of luggage, I fancy. We inquired carefully at the stations, and got the porters to remember the passengers for whom they had been carrying luggage, but none appeared to have had any dealings with our man. That, of course, is as one would expect. He'd take as little as possible with him, and buy what he wanted on the way, or when he'd reached his hiding-place. Of course, I wired to Calais (it was a Dover to Calais route ticket) and sent a couple of smart men off by the 8.15 mail from Charing Cross. I expect we shall hear from them in the course of the day. I am being kept in London in view of something expected at headquarters, or I should have been off myself.'

'That is all, then, up to the present? Have you anything else in view?'

'That', all I've absolutely ascertained at present. As for what I'm going to do'—a slight smile curled Plummer's lip—' well, I shall see. I've a thing or two in my mind.'

Hewitt smiled slightly himself; he recognized Plummer's touch of professional jealousy. 'Very well,' he said, rising, 'I'll make an inquiry or two for myself at once. Perhaps, Mr Neal, you'll allow one of your clerks to show me the banks, in their regular order, at which Laker called yesterday. I think I'll begin at the beginning.'

Mr Neal offered to place at Hewitt's disposal anything or anybody the bank contained, and the conference broke up. As Hewitt, with the clerk, came through the rooms separating Mr Neal's sanctum from the outer office, he fancied he saw the two veiled women leaving by a side door.

The first bank was quite close to Liddle, Neal & Liddle's. There the cashier who had dealt with Laker the day before remembered nothing in particular about the interview. Many other walk-clerks had called during the morning, as they did every morning, and the only circumstances of the visit that he could say anything definite about were those recorded in figures in the books. He did not know Laker's name till Plummer had mentioned it in making inquiries on the previous afternoon. As far as he could remember, Laker behaved much as usual, though really he did not notice much; he looked chiefly at the bills. He described Laker in a way that corresponded with the photograph that Hewitt had borrowed from the bank; a young man with a brown moustache and ordinary-looking fairly regular face, dressing much as other clerks dressed—tall hat, black cutaway coat, and so on. The numbers of the notes handed over had already been given to Inspector Plummer, and these Hewitt did not trouble about.

The next bank was in Cornhill, and here the cashier was a personal friend of Laker's—at any rate, an acquaintance—and he remembered a little more. Laker's manner had been quite as usual, he said; certainly he did not seem preoccupied or excited in his manner. He spoke for a moment or two—of being on the river on Sunday, and so on—and left in his usual way.

'Can you remember *everything* he said?' Hewitt asked. 'If you can tell me, I should like to know exactly what he did and said to the smallest particular.'

'Well, he saw me a little distance off—I was behind there, at one of the desks—and raised his hand to me, and said, "How d'ye do?" I came across and took his bills, and dealt with them in the usual way. He had a new umbrella lying on the counter—rather a handsome umbrella—and I made a remark about the handle. He took it up to show me, and told me it was a present he had just received from a friend. It was a gorse-root handle, with two silver bands, one with his monogram, C.W.L. I said it was a very nice handle, and asked him whether it was fine in his district on Sunday. He said he had been up the river, and it was very fine there. And I think that was all.'

'Thank you. Now about this umbrella. Did he carry it rolled? Can you describe it in detail?'

'Well, I've told you about the handle, and the rest was much as usual, I think; it wasn't rolled—just napping loosely, you know. It was rather an odd-shaped handle, though. I'll try and sketch it, if you like, as well as I can remember.' He did so, and Hewitt saw in the result rough indications of a gnarled crook, with one silver band near the end, and another, with the monogram, a few inches down the handle. Hewitt put the sketch in his pocket, and bade the cashier good-day.

At the next bank the story was the same as at the first— there was nothing remembered but the usual routine. Hewitt and the clerk turned down a narrow paved court, and through into Lombard Street for the next visit. The bank—that of Buller, Clayton, Ladds & Co.—was just at the corner at the end of the court, and the imposing stone entrance-porch was being made larger and more imposing still, the way being almost blocked by ladders and scaffold-poles. Here there was only the usual tale, and so on through the whole walk. The cashiers knew Laker only by sight, and that not always very distinctly. The calls of walk-clerks were such matters of routine that little note was taken of the persons of the clerks themselves, who were called by the names of their firms, if they were called by any names at all. Laker had behaved much as usual, so far as the cashiers could remember, and when finally the Eastern Consolidated was left behind, nothing more had been learnt than the chat about Laker's new umbrella.

Hewitt had taken leave of Mr Neal's clerk, and was stepping into a hansom, when he noticed a veiled woman in widow's weeds hailing another hansom a little way behind. He recognized the figure again, and said to the driver: 'Drive fast to Palmer's Tourist Office, but keep your eye on that cab behind, and tell me presently if it is following us.'

The cabman drove off, and after passing one or two turnings, opened the lid above Hewitt's head, and said: 'That there other keb *is* a-follerin' us, sir, an' keepin' about even distance all along.'

'All right; that's what I wanted to know. Palmer's now.' At Palmer's the clerk who had attended to Laker remembered him very well and described him. He also remembered the wallet, and *thought* he remembered the umbrella—was practically sure of it, in fact, upon reflection. He had no record of the name given, but remembered it distinctly to be Laker. As a matter of fact, names were never asked in such a transaction, but in this case Laker appeared to be ignorant of the usual procedure, as well as in a great hurry, and asked for the ticket and gave his name all in one breath, probably assuming that the name would be required.

Hewitt got back to his cab, and started for Charing Cross. The cabman once more lifted the lid and informed him that the hansom with the veiled woman in it was again following, having waited while Hewitt had visited Palmer's. At Charing Cross Hewitt discharged his cab and walked straight to the lost property office. The man in charge knew him very well, for his business had carried him there frequently before.

'I fancy an umbrella was lost in the station yesterday,' Hewitt said. 'It was a new umbrella, silk, with a gnarled gorse-root handle and two silver bands, something like this sketch. There was a monogram on the lower band—"C. W. L." were the letters. Has it been brought here?'

'There was two or three yesterday,' the man said; 'let's see.' He took the sketch and retired to a corner of his room. 'Oh, yes—here it is, I think; isn't this it? Do you claim it?' 'Well, not exactly that, but I think I'll take a look at it, if you'll let me. By the way, I see it's rolled up. Was it found like that?'

'No; the chap rolled it up what found it—porter he was. It's a fad of his, rolling up umbrellas close and neat, and he's rather proud of it. He often looks as though he'd like to take a man's umbrella away and roll it up for him when it's a bit clumsy done. Rum fad, eh?'

'Yes; everybody has his little fad, though. Where was this found—close by here?'

'Yes, sir; just there, almost opposite this window, in the little corner.'

'About two o'clock?'

'Ah, about that time, more or less.'

Hewitt took the umbrella up, unfastened the band, and shook the silk out loose. Then he opened it, and as he did so a small scrap of paper fell from inside it. Hewitt pounced on it like lightning. Then, after examining the umbrella thoroughly, inside and out, he handed it back to the man, who had not observed the incident of the scrap of paper.

'That will do, thanks,' he said. 'I only wanted to take a peep at it—just a small matter connected with a little case of mine. Good-morning.'

He turned suddenly and saw, gazing at him with a terrified expression from a door behind, the face of the woman who had followed him in the cab. The veil was lifted, and he caught but a mere glance of the face ere it was suddenly withdrawn. He stood for a moment to allow the woman time to retreat, and then left the station and walked toward his office, close by.

Scarcely thirty yards along the Strand he met Plummer. 'I'm going to make some much closer inquiries all down the line as far as Dover,' Plummer said. 'They wire from Calais that they have no clue as yet, and I mean to make quite sure, if I can, that Laker hasn't quietly slipped off the line somewhere between here and Dover. There's one very peculiar thing,' Plummer added confidentially. 'Did you see the two women who were waiting to see a member of the firm at Liddle, Neal & Liddle's?'

'Yes. Laker's mother and his *fiancée*, I was told.'

'That's right. Well, do you know that girl—Shaw her name is—has been shadowing me ever since I left the Bank. Of course I spotted it from the beginning—these amateurs don't know how to follow anybody—and, as a matter of fact, she's just inside that jeweller's shop door behind me now, pretending to look at the things in the window. But it's odd, isn't it?'

'Well,' Hewitt replied, 'of course it's not a thing to be neglected. If you'll look very carefully at the corner of Villiers Street, without appearing to stare, I think you will possibly observe some signs of Laker's mother. She's shadowing *me*.'

Plummer looked casually in the direction indicated, and then immediately turned his eyes in another direction.

'I see her,' he said; 'she's just taking a look round the corner. That's a thing not to be be ignored. Of course, the Lakers' house is being watched—we set a man on it at once, yesterday. But I'll put some one on now to watch Miss Shaw's place too. I'll telephone through to Liddle's—probably they'll be able to say where it is. And the women themselves must be watched, too. As a matter of fact, I had a notion that Laker wasn't alone in it. And it's just possible, you know, that he has sent an accomplice off with his tourist ticket to lead us a dance while he looks after himself in another direction. Have you done anything?'

'Well,' Hewitt replied, with a faint reproduction of the secretive smile with which Plummer had met an inquiry of his earlier in the morning, 'I've been to the station here, and I've found Laker's umbrella in the lost property office.'

'Oh! Then probably he *has* gone. I'll bear that in mind, and perhaps have a word with the lost property man.'

Plummer made for the station and Hewitt for his office. He mounted the stairs and reached his door just as I myself, who had been disappointed in not finding him in, was leaving. I had called with the idea of taking Hewitt to lunch with me at my club, but he declined lunch. 'I have an important case in hand,' he said. 'Look here, Brett. See this scrap of paper. You know the types of the different newspapers—which is this?'

He handed me a small piece of paper. It was part of a cutting containing an advertisement, which had been torn in half.

> *oast. You 1st. Then to-*
> *3rd L. No.197 red bl. straight*
> *time.*

'I *think*,' I said, 'this is from the *Daily Chronicle*, judging by the paper. It is plainly from the "agony column", but all the papers use pretty much the same type for these advertisements, except the *Times*. If it were not torn I could tell you at once, because the *Chronicle* columns are rather narrow.'

'Never mind—I'll send for them all.' He rang, and sent Kerrett for a copy of each morning paper of the previous day. Then he took from a large wardrobe cupboard a decent but well-worn and rather roughened tall hat. Also a coat a little worn and shiny on the collar. He exchanged these for his own hat and coat, and then substituted an old necktie for his own clean white one, and encased his legs in mud-spotted leggings. This done, he produced a very large and thick pocket-book, fastened by a broad elastic band, and said, 'Well, what do you think of this? Will it do for Queen's taxes, or sanitary inspection, or the gas, or the water-supply?'

'Very well indeed, I should say,' I replied. 'What's the case?'

'Oh, I'll tell you all about that when it's over—no time now. Oh, here you are, Kerrett. By the bye, Kerrett, I'm going out presently by the back way. Wait for about ten minutes or a quarter of an hour after I am gone, and then just go across the road and speak to that lady in black, with the veil, who is waiting in that little foot-passage opposite. Say Mr Martin Hewitt sends his compliments, and he advises her not to wait, as he has already left his office by another door, and has been gone some little time. That's all; it would be a pity to keep the poor woman waiting all day for nothing. Now the papers. *Daily News, Standard, Telegraph, Chronicle*—yes, here it is, in the *Chronicle*'

The whole advertisement read thus:

> *YOB.—H.R. Shop roast. You 1st. Then to-*

*night. O2. 2nd top 3rd L. No.197 red bl. straight
mon. One at a time.*

'What's this,' I asked, 'a cryptogram?'

'I'll see,' Hewitt answered. 'But I won't tell you anything about it till afterwards, so you get your lunch. Kerrett, bring the directory.'

This was all I actually saw of this case myself, and I have written the rest in its proper order from Hewitt's information, as I have written some other cases entirely.

To resume at the point where, for the time, I lost sight of the matter. Hewitt left by the back way and stopped an empty cab as it passed. 'Abney Park Cemetery' was his direction to the driver. In little more than twenty minutes the cab was branching off down the Essex Road on its way to Stoke Newington, and in twenty minutes more Hewitt stopped it in Church Street, Stoke Newington. He walked through a street or two, and then down another, the houses of which he scanned carefully as he passed. Opposite one which stood by itself he stopped, and, making a pretence of consulting and arranging his large pocket-book, he took a good look at the house. It was rather larger, neater, and more pretentious than the others in the street, and it had a natty little coach-house just visible up the side entrance. There were red blinds hung with heavy lace in the front windows, and behind one of these blinds Hewitt was able to catch the glint of a heavy gas chandelier.

He stepped briskly up the front steps and knocked sharply at the door. 'Mr Merston?' he asked, pocket-book in hand, when a neat parlourmaid opened the door.

'Yes.'

'Ah!' Hewitt stepped into the hall and pulled off his hat; 'it's only the meter. There's been a deal of gas running away somewhere here, and I'm just looking to see if the meters are right. Where is it?'

The girl hesitated. 'I'll—I'll ask master,' she said.

'Very well. I don't want to take it away, you know—only to give it a tap or two, and so on.'

The girl retired to the back of the hall, and without taking her eyes off Martin Hewitt, gave his message to some invisible person in a back room, whence came a growling reply of 'All right'.

Hewitt followed the girl to the basement, apparently looking straight before him, but in reality taking in every detail of the place. The gas meter was in a very large lumber cupboard under the kitchen stairs. The girl opened the door and lit a candle. The meter stood on the floor, which was littered with hampers and boxes and odd sheets of brown paper. But a thing that at once arrested Hewitt's attention was a garment of some sort of bright blue cloth, with large brass buttons, which was lying in a tumbled heap in a corner, and appeared to be the only thing in the place that was not covered with dust. Nevertheless, Hewitt took no apparent notice of it, but stooped down and solemnly tapped the meter three times with his pencil, and listened with great gravity, placing his ear to the top. Then he shook his head and tapped again. At length he said:

'It's a bit doubtful. I'll just get you to light the gas in the kitchen a moment. Keep your hand to the burner, and when I call out shut it off *at once*; see?'

The girl turned and entered the kitchen, and Hewitt immediately seized the blue coat—for a coat it was. It had a dull red piping in the seams, and was of the swallowtail pattern—livery coat, in fact. He held it for a moment before him, examining its pattern and colour, and then rolled it up and flung it again into the corner.

'Right!' he called to the servant. 'Shut off!'

The girl emerged from the kitchen as he left the cupboard.

'Well,' she asked, 'are you satisfied now?'

'Quite satisfied, thank you,' Hewitt replied.

'Is it all right?' she continued, jerking her hand toward the cupboard.

'Well, no, it isn't; there's something wrong there, and I'm glad I came. You can tell Mr Merston, if you like, that I expect his gas bill will be a good deal less next quarter.' And there was a suspicion of a chuckle in Hewitt's voice as he crossed the hall to leave. For a gas inspector is pleased when he finds at length what he has been searching for.

Things had fallen out better than Hewitt had dared to expect. He saw the key of the whole mystery in that blue coat; for it was the uniform coat of the hall porters at one of the banks that he had visited in the morning, though which one he could not for the moment remember. He entered the nearest post-office and despatched a telegram to Plummer, giving certain directions and asking the inspector to meet him; then he hailed the first available cab and hurried toward the City.

At Lombard Street he alighted, and looked in at the door of each bank till he came to Buller, Clayton, Ladds & Co.'s. This was the bank he wanted. In the other banks the hall porters wore mulberry coats, brick-dust coats, brown coats, and what not, but here, behind the ladders and scaffold poles which obscured the entrance, he could see a man in a blue coat, with dull red piping and brass buttons. He sprang up the steps, pushed open the inner swing door, and finally satisfied himself by a closer view of the coat, to the wearer's astonishment. Then he regained the pavement and walked the whole length of the bank premises in front, afterwards turning up the paved passage at the side, deep in thought. The bank had no windows or doors on the side next the court, and the two adjoining houses were old and supported in place by wooden shores. Both were empty, and a great board announced that tenders would be received in a month's time for the purchase of the old materials of which they were constructed; also that some part of the site would be let on a long building lease.

Hewitt looked up at the grimy fronts of the old buildings. The windows were crusted thick with dirt—all except the bottom window of the house nearer the bank, which was fairly clean, and seemed to have been quite lately washed. The door, too, of this house was cleaner than that of the other, though the paint was worn. Hewitt reached and fingered a hook driven into the left-hand doorpost about six feet from the ground. It was new, and not at all rusted; also a tiny splinter had been displaced when the hook was driven in, and clean wood showed at the spot.

Having observed these things, Hewitt stepped back and read at the bottom of the big board the name, 'Winsor & Weekes, Surveyors and Auctioneers, Abchurch Lane'. Then he stepped into Lombard Street.

Two hansoms pulled up near the post-office, and out of the first stepped Inspector Plummer and another man. This man and the two who alighted from the second hansom were unmistakably plain-clothes constables—their air, gait, and boots proclaimed it.

'What's all this?' demanded Plummer, as Hewitt approached.

'You'll soon see, I think. But, first, have you put the watch on No. 197, Hackworth Road?'

'Yes; nobody will get away from there alone.'

'Very good. I am going into Abchurch Lane for a few minutes. Leave your men out here, but just go round into the court by Buller, Clayton & Ladds's, and keep your eye on the first door on the left. I think we'll find something soon. Did you get rid of Miss Shaw?'

'No, she's behind now, and Mrs Laker's with her. They met in the Strand, and came after us in another cab. Rare fun, eh! They think we're pretty green! It's quite handy, too. So long as they keep behind me it saves all trouble of watching *them*.' And Inspector Plummer chuckled and winked.

'Very good. You don't mind keeping your eye on that door, do you? I'll be back very soon,' and with that Hewitt turned off into Abchurch Lane.

At Winsor & Weekes's information was not difficult to obtain. The houses were destined to come down very shortly, but a week or so ago an office and a cellar in one of them was let temporarily to a Mr Westley. He brought no references; indeed, as he paid a fortnight's rent in advance, he was not asked for any, considering the circumstances of the case. He was opening a London branch for a large firm of cider merchants, he said, and just wanted a rough office and a cool cellar to store samples in for a few weeks till the permanent premises were ready. There was another key, and no doubt the premises might be entered if there were any special need for such a course. Martin Hewitt gave such excellent reasons that Winsor & Weekes's managing clerk immediately produced the key and accompanied Hewitt to the spot.

'I think you'd better have your men handy,' Hewitt remarked to Plummer when they reached the door, and a whistle quickly brought the men over.

The key was inserted in the lock and turned, but the door would not open; the bolt was fastened at the bottom. Hewitt stooped and looked under the door.

'It's a drop bolt,' he said. 'Probably the man who left last let it fall loose, and then banged the door, so that it fell into its place. I must try my best with a wire or a piece of string.'

A wire was brought, and with some manoeuvring Hewitt contrived to pass it round the bolt, and lift it little by little, steadying it with the blade of a pocket-knife. When at length the bolt was raised out of the hole, the knife-blade was slipped under it, and the door swung open.

They entered. The door of the little office just inside stood open, but in the office there was nothing, except a board a couple of feet long in a corner. Hewitt stepped across and lifted this, turning it downward face toward Plummer. On it, in fresh white paint on a black ground, were painted the words:

*"BULLER, CLAYTON, LADDS & CO.,*
*TEMPORARY ENTRANCE."*

Hewitt turned to Winsor & Weekes's clerk and asked, 'The man who took this room called himself Westley, didn't he?'

'Yes.'

'Youngish man, clean-shaven, and well-dressed?'

'Yes, he was.'

'I fancy,' Hewitt said, turning to Plummer, 'I *fancy* an old friend of yours is in this—Mr Sam Gunter.'

'What, the "Hoxton Yob"?'

'I think it's possible he's been Mr Westley for a bit, and somebody else for another bit. But let's come to the cellar.'

Winsor & Weekes's clerk led the way down a steep flight of steps into a dark underground corridor, wherein they lighted their way with many successive matches. Soon the cellar corridor made a turn to the right, and as the party passed the turn, there came from the end of the passage before them a fearful yell.

'Help! help! Open the door! I'm going mad—mad! O my God!'

And there was a sound of desperate beating from the inside of the cellar door at the extreme end. The men stopped, startled.

'Come,' said Hewitt, 'more matches!' and he rushed to the door. It was fastened with a bar and padlock.

'Let me out, for God's sake!' came the voice, sick and hoarse, from the inside. 'Let me out!'

'All right!' Hewitt shouted. 'We have come for you. Wait a moment.'

The voice sank into a sort of sobbing croon, and Hewitt tried several keys from his own bunch on the padlock. None fitted. He drew from his pocket the wire he had used for the bolt of the front door, straightened it out, and made a sharp bend at the end.

'Hold a match close,' he ordered shortly, and one of the men obeyed. Three or four attempts were necessary, and several different bendings of the wire were effected, but in the end Hewitt picked the lock, and flung open the door.

From within a ghastly figure fell forward among them fainting, and knocked out the matches.

'Hullo!' cried Plummer. 'Hold up! Who are you?'

'Let's get him up into the open,' said Hewitt. 'He can't tell you who he is for a bit, but I believe he's Laker.'

'Laker! What, here?'

'I think so. Steady up the steps. Don't bump him. He's pretty sore already, I expect.'

Truly the man was a pitiable sight. His hair and face were caked in dust and blood, and his finger-nails were torn and bleeding. Water was sent for at once, and brandy.

'Well,' said Plummer hazily, looking first at the unconscious prisoner and then at Hewitt, 'but what about the swag?'

'You'll have to find that yourself,' Hewitt replied. 'I think my share of the case is about finished. I only act for the Guarantee Society, you know, and if Laker's proved innocent——'

'Innocent! How?'

'Well, this is what took place, as near as I can figure it. You'd better undo his collar, I think'—this to the men. 'What I believe has happened is this. There has been a very clever and carefully prepared conspiracy here, and Laker has not been the criminal, but the victim.'

'Been robbed himself, you mean? But how? Where?'

'Yesterday morning, before he had been to more than three banks—here, in fact.'

'But then how? You're all wrong. We *know* he made the whole round, and did all the collection. And then Palmer's office, and all, and the umbrella; why—'

The man lay still unconscious. 'Don't raise his head,' Hewitt said. 'And one of you had best fetch a doctor. He's had a terrible shock.' Then turning to Plummer he went on, 'As to *how* they managed the job, I'll tell you what I think. First it struck some very clever person that a deal of money might be got by robbing a walk-clerk from a bank. This clever person was one of a clever gang of thieves—perhaps the Hoxton Row gang, as I think I hinted. Now you know quite as well as I do that such a gang will spend any amount of time over a job that promises a big haul, and that for such a job they can always command the necessary capital. There are many most respectable persons living in good style in the suburbs whose chief business lies in financing such ventures, and taking the chief share of the proceeds. Well, this is their plan, carefully and intelligently carried out. They watch Laker, observe the round he takes, and his habits. They find that there is only one of the clerks with whom he does business that he is much acquainted with, and that this clerk is in a bank which is commonly second in Laker's round. The sharpest man among them—and I don't think there's a man in London could do this as well as young Sam Gunter—studies Laker's dress and habits just as an actor studies a character. They take this office and cellar, as we have seen, *because it is next door to a bank whose front entrance is being altered*—a fact which Laker must know from his daily visits. The smart man—Gunter, let us say, and I have other reasons for believing it to be he—makes up precisely like Laker, false moustache, dress, and everything, and waits here with the rest of the gang. One of the gang is dressed in a blue coat with brass buttons, like a hall-porter in Buller's bank. Do you see?'

'Yes, I think so. It's pretty clear now.'

'A confederate watches at the top of the court, and the moment Laker turns in from Cornhill—having already been, mind, at the only bank where he was so well known that the disguised thief would not have passed muster—as soon as he turns in from Cornhill, I say, a signal is given, and that board'— pointing to that with the white letters—'is hung on the hook in the doorpost. The sham porter stands beside it, and as Laker approaches says, "This way in, sir, this morning. The front way's shut for the alterations". Laker suspecting nothing, and supposing that the firm have made a temporary entrance

through the empty house, enters. He is seized when well along
the corridor, the board is taken down and the door shut.
Probably he is stunned by a blow on the head—see the blood
now. They take his wallet and all the cash he has already
collected. Gunter takes the wallet and also the umbrella, since it
has Laker's initials, and is therefore distinctive. He simply
completes the walk in the character of Laker, beginning with
Buller, Clayton & Ladds's just round the corner. It is nothing
but routine work, which is quickly done, and nobody notices him
particularly—it is the bills they examine. Meanwhile this
unfortunate fellow is locked up in the cellar here, right at the
end of the underground corridor, where he can never make
himself heard in the street, and where next him are only the
empty cellars of the deserted house next door. The thieves shut
the front door and vanish. The rest is plain. Gunter, having
completed the round, and bagged some £15,000 or more, spends
a few pounds in a tourist ticket at Palmer's as a blind, being
careful to give Laker's name. He leaves the umbrella at Charing
Cross in a conspicuous place right opposite the lost property
office, where it is sure to be seen, and so completes his false
trail.'

'Then who are the people at 197, Hackworth Road?'

'The capitalist lives there—the financier, and probably the
directing spirit of the whole thing. Merston's the name he goes
by there, and I've no doubt he cuts a very imposing figure in
chapel every Sunday. He'll be worth picking up—this isn't the
first thing he's been in, I'll warrant.'

'But—but what about Laker's mother and Miss Shaw?'

'Well, what? The poor women are nearly out of their minds
with terror and shame, that's all, but though they may think
Laker a criminal, they'll never desert him. They've been
following us about with a feeble, vague sort of hope of being able
to baffle us in some way or help him if we caught him, or
something, poor things. Did you ever hear of a real woman who'd
desert a son or a lover merely because he was a criminal? But
here's the doctor. When he's attended to him will you let your
men take Laker home? I must hurry and report to the
Guarantee Society, I think.'

'But,' said the perplexed Plummer, 'where did you get your clue? You must have had a tip from some one, you know—you can't have done it by clairvoyance. What gave you the tip?'

'The *Daily Chronicle*.'

'The *what*?'

'The *Daily Chronicle*. Just take a look at the "agony column" in yesterday morning's issue, and read the message to "Yob"—to Gunter, in fact. That's all.'

By this time a cab was waiting in Lombard Street, and two of Plummer's men, under the doctor's directions, carried Laker to it. No sooner, however, were they in the court than the two watching women threw themselves hysterically upon Laker, and it was long before they could be persuaded that he was not being taken to gaol. The mother shrieked aloud, 'My boy—my boy! Don't take him! Oh, don't take him! They've killed my boy! Look at his head—oh, his head!' and wrestled desperately with the men, while Hewitt attempted to soothe her, and promised to allow her to go in the cab with her son if she would only be quiet. The younger woman made no noise, but she held one of Laker's limp hands in both hers.

Hewitt and I dined together that evening, and he gave me a full account of the occurrences which I have here set down. Still, when he was finished I was not able to see clearly by what process of reasoning he had arrived at the conclusions that gave him the key to the mystery, nor did I understand the 'agony column' message, and I said so.

'In the beginning,' Hewitt explained, 'the thing that struck me as curious was the fact that Laker was said to have given his own name at Palmer's in buying his ticket. Now, the first thing the greenest and newest criminal thinks of is changing his name, so that the giving of his own name seemed unlikely to begin with. Still, he *might* have made such a mistake, as Plummer suggested when he said that criminals usually make a mistake somewhere—as they do, in fact. Still, it was the least likely mistake I could think of—especially as he actually didn't wait to be asked for his name, but blurted it out when it wasn't really wanted. And it was conjoined with another rather curious mistake, or what would have been a mistake, if the thief were Laker. Why should he conspicuously display his wallet—such a distinctive article—for the clerk to see and note? Why rather had he not got rid of it before showing himself? Suppose it should be somebody personating Laker? In any case I determined not to be prejudiced by what I had heard of Laker's betting. A man may bet without being a thief.

'But, again, supposing it *were* Laker? Might he not have given his name, and displayed his wallet, and so on, while buying a ticket for France, in order to draw pursuit after himself in that direction while he made off in another, in another name, and disguised? Each supposition was plausible. And, in either case, it might happen that whoever was laying this trail would probably lay it a little farther. Charing Cross was the next point, and there I went. I already had it from Plummer that Laker had not been recognized there. Perhaps the trail had been laid in some other manner. Something left behind with Laker's name on it, perhaps? I at once thought of the umbrella with his monogram, and, making a long shot, asked for it at the lost property office, as you know. The guess was lucky: In the umbrella, as you know, I found the scrap of paper. That, I judged, had fallen in from the hand of the man carrying the umbrella. He had torn the paper in half in order to fling it away, and one piece had fallen into the loosely flapping umbrella. It is a thing that will often happen with an omnibus ticket, as you may have noticed. Also, it was proved that the umbrella *was* unrolled when found, and rolled immediately after. So here was a piece of paper dropped by the person who had brought the umbrella to Charing Cross and left it. I got the whole advertisement, as you remember, and I studied it. "Yob" is back-slang for "boy", and is often used in nicknames to denote a young smooth-faced thief. Gunter, the man I suspect, as a matter of fact, is known as the "Hoxton Yob". The message, then, was addressed to some one known by such a nickname. Next, "H.R. shop roast". Now, in thieves' slang, to "roast" a thing or a person is to watch it or him. They call any place a shop—notably, a thieves' den. So that this meant that some resort—perhaps the "Hoxton Row shop"—was watched. "You 1st then to-night" would be clearer, perhaps, when the rest was understood. I thought a little over the rest, and it struck me that it must be a direction to some other house, since one was warned of as being watched. Besides, there was the number, 197, and "red bl.", which would be extremely likely to mean "red blinds ", by way of clearly distinguishing the house. And then the plan of the thing was plain. You have noticed, probably, that the map of London which accompanies the Post Office Directory is divided, for convenience of reference, into numbered squares?'

'Yes. The squares are denoted by letters along the top margin and figures down the side. So that if you consult the directory, and find a place marked as being in D 5, for instance, you find vertical divisions D, and run your finger down it till it intersects horizontal division 5, and there you are.'

'Precisely. I got my Post Office Directory, and looked for "O 2". It was in North London, and took in parts of Abney Park Cemetery and Clissold Park; "2nd top" was the next sign. Very well, I counted the second street intersecting the top of the square—counting, in the usual way, from the left. That was Lordship Road. Then "3rd L". From the point where Lordship Road crossed the top of the square, I ran my finger down the road till it came to "3rd L", or, in other words, the third turning on the left—Hackworth Road. So there we were, unless my guesses were altogether wrong. "Straight mon" probably meant "straight moniker"—that is to say, the proper name, a thief's *real* name, in contradistinction to that he may assume. I turned over the directory till I found Hackworth Road, and found that No. 197 was inhabited by a Mr Merston. From the whole thing I judged this. There was to have been a meeting at the "H.R. shop", but that was found, at the last moment, to be watched by the police for some purpose, so that another appointment was made for this house in the suburbs. "You 1st. Then to-night"— the person addressed was to come first, and the others in the evening. They were to ask for the householder's "straight moniker"—Mr Merston. And they were to come one at a time.

'Now, then, what was this? What theory would fit it? Suppose this were a robbery, directed from afar by the advertiser. Suppose, on the day before the robbery, it was found that the place fixed for division of spoils were watched. Suppose that the principal thereupon advertised (as had already been agreed in case of emergency) in these terms. The principal in the actual robbery—the "Yob" addressed—was to go first with the booty. The others were to come after, one at a time. Anyway, the thing was good enough to follow a little further, and I determined to try No. 197 Hackworth Road. I have told you what I found there, and how it opened my eyes. I went, of course, merely on chance, to see what I might chance to see. But luck favoured, and I happened on that coat—brought back rolled up, on the evening after the robbery, doubtless by the thief who had used it, and flung carelessly into the handiest cupboard. *That* was this gang's mistake.'

'Well, I congratulate you,' I said. 'I hope they'll catch the rascals.'

'I rather think they will, now they know where to look. They can scarcely miss Merston, anyway. There has been very little to go upon in this case, but I stuck to the thread, however slight, and it brought me through. The rest of the case, of course, is Plummer's. It was a peculiarity of my commission that I could equally well fulfil it by catching the man with all the plunder, or by proving him innocent. Having done the latter, my work was at an end, but I left it where Plummer will be able to finish the job handsomely.'

Plummer did. Sam Gunter, Merston, and one accomplice were taken—the first and last were well known to the police—and were identified by Laker. Merston, as Hewitt had suspected, had kept the lion's share for himself, so that altogether, with what was recovered from him and the other two, nearly £11,000 was saved for Messrs Liddle, Neal & Liddle. Merston, when taken, was in the act of packing up to take a holiday abroad, and there cash his notes, which were found, neatly packed in separate thousands, in his portmanteau. As Hewitt had predicted, his gas bill *was* considerably less next quarter, for less than half-way through it he began a term in gaol.

As for Laker, he was reinstated, of course, with an increase of salary by way of compensation for his broken head. He had passed a terrible twenty-six hours in the cellar, unfed and unheard. Several times he had become insensible, and again and again he had thrown himself madly against the door, shouting and tearing at it, till he fell back exhausted, with broken nails and bleeding fingers. For some hours before the arrival of his rescuers he had been sitting in a sort of stupor, from which he was suddenly aroused by the sound of voices and footsteps. He was in bed for a week, and required a rest of a month in addition before he could resume his duties. Then he was quietly lectured by Mr Neal as to betting, and, I believe, dropped that practice in consequence. I am told that he is 'at the counter' now—a considerable promotion.

# THE FENCHURCH
# STREET MYSTERY
## BY BARONESS EMMUSKA ORCZY

"The old man in the corner."

## ORIGINALLY PUBLISHED IN 1908

# The Fenchurch Street Mystery

## By Baroness Emmuska Orczy

The Old Man in the Corner is perhaps one of the most singular detectives ever to appear in print. One of the school of "arm chair" detectives, except that the chair he inhabited was in the corner of an Aerated Bread Company tea room on Norfolk Street, he based his deduction solely on what he read in the newspaper accounts of the crime with the occasional visit to a court room to hear testimony in person. He never felt the need to reveal his solutions to the police, confiding only to young Polly Burton, a newspaper woman who often stopped in at the same A.B.C. tea room.

The form of the stories was always the same. The "Old Man" would go over the particulars of some gruesome and baffling crime, Miss Burton would comment, and then the "Old Man" would expound on his solution, which usually depended on some obvious point that the police had completely neglected. As the police were never informed, and the alleged criminals never brought to justice, the accuracy of the "old Man's" deductions are never verified, but the reader is left with the impression that the solution is so obvious it must be true.

Like much of the detective fiction of the period, the entertainment value of the stories lie more in the cleverness of the crime, and the even more clever solution than on characterizations. Still, these stories were extremely popular at the time and *The Old Man in the Corner* is considered one of the classics of detective ficiton.

The first "Old Man" stories appeared in the *Royal Magazine* in 1901 and 1902 and were later published in book form in three collections, *The Case of Miss Elliot*(1905), *The Old Man in the Corner*(1909), and *Unravelled Knots* (1926). *The Fenchurch Street Mystery* was the first story in the series and serves to introduce the characters.

The author, the Baroness Emma Orczy, is better known for her many historical novels, in particular *The Scarlet Pimpernel* and subsequent books in the series. More stories featuring the "Old Man" may be found in the Resurrected Press edition of *The Old Man in the Corner*.

# THE FENCHURCH STREET MYSTERY

## I - The Fenchurch Street Mystery

The man in the corner pushed aside his glass, and leant across the table.

"Mysteries!" he commented. "There is no such thing as a mystery in connection with any crime, provided intelligence is brought to bear upon its investigation."

Very much astonished Polly Burton looked over the top of her newspaper, and fixed a pair of very severe, coldly inquiring brown eyes upon him.

She had disapproved of the man from the instant when he shuffled across the shop and sat down opposite to her, at the same marble-topped table which already held her large coffee (3d.), her roll and butter (2d.), and plate of tongue (6d.).

Now this particular corner, this very same table, that special view of the magnificent marble hall—known as the Norfolk

Street branch of the Aerated Bread Company's depots—were Polly's own corner, table, and view. Here she had partaken of eleven pennyworth of luncheon and one pennyworth of daily information ever since that glorious never-to-be-forgotten day when she was enrolled on the staff of the *Evening Observer* (we'll call it that, if you please), and became a member of that illustrious and world-famed organization known as the British Press.

She was a personality, was Miss Burton of the *Evening Observer*. Her cards were printed thus:

---

### Miss Mary J. Burton.

*Evening Observer.*

---

She had interviewed Miss Ellen Terry and the Bishop of Madagascar, Mr. Seymour Hicks and the Chief Commissioner of Police. She had been present at the last Marlborough House garden party—in the cloak-room, that is to say, where she caught sight of Lady Thingummy's hat, Miss What-you-may-call's sunshade, and of various other things modistical or fashionable, all of which were duly described under the heading "Royalty and Dress" in the early afternoon edition of the *Evening Observer*.

(The article itself is signed M.J.B., and is to be found in the files of that leading halfpennyworth.)

For these reasons—and for various others, too—Polly felt irate with the man in the corner, and told him so with her eyes, as plainly as any pair of brown eyes can speak.

She had been reading an article in the *Daily Telegraph*. The article was palpitatingly interesting. Had Polly been commenting audibly upon it? Certain it is that the man over there had spoken in direct answer to her thoughts.

She looked at him and frowned; the next moment she smiled. Miss Burton (of the *Evening Observer)* had a keen sense of humour, which two years' association with the British Press had not succeeded in destroying, and the appearance of the man was sufficient to tickle the most ultra-morose fancy. Polly thought to herself that she had never seen any one so pale, so thin, with such funny light-coloured hair, brushed very smoothly across the top of a very obviously bald crown. He looked so timid and nervous as he fidgeted incessantly with a piece of string; his long, lean, and trembling fingers tying and untying it into knots of wonderful and complicated proportions.

Having carefully studied every detail of the quaint personality Polly felt more amiable.

"And yet," she remarked kindly but authoritatively, "this article, in an otherwise well-informed journal, will tell you that, even within the last year, no fewer than six crimes have completely baffled the police, and the perpetrators of them are still at large."

"Pardon me," he said gently, "I never for a moment ventured to suggest that there were no mysteries to the *police*; I merely remarked that there were none where intelligence was brought to bear upon the investigation of crime."

"Not even in the Fenchurch Street *mystery*. I suppose," she asked sarcastically.

"Least of all in the so-called Fenchurch Street *mystery*," he replied quietly.

Now the Fenchurch Street mystery, as that extraordinary crime had popularly been called, had puzzled—as Polly well knew—the brains of every thinking man and woman for the last twelve months. It had puzzled her not inconsiderably; she had been interested, fascinated; she had studied the case, formed her own theories, thought about it all often and often, had even written one or two letters to the Press on the subject— suggesting, arguing, hinting at possibilities and probabilities, adducing proofs which other amateur detectives were equally ready to refute. The attitude of that timid man in the corner, therefore, was peculiarly exasperating, and she retorted with sarcasm destined to completely annihilate her self-complacent interlocutor.

"What a pity it is, in that case, that you do not offer your priceless services to our misguided though well-meaning police."

"Isn't it?" he replied with perfect good-humour. "Well, you know, for one thing I doubt if they would accept them; and in the second place my inclinations and my duty would—were I to become an active member of the detective force—nearly always be in direct conflict. As often as not my sympathies go to the criminal who is clever and astute enough to lead our entire police force by the nose.

"I don't know how much of the case you remember," he went on quietly. "It certainly, at first, began even to puzzle me. On the 12th of last December a woman, poorly dressed, but with an unmistakable air of having seen better days, gave information at Scotland Yard of the disappearance of her husband, William Kershaw, of no occupation, and apparently of no fixed abode. She was accompanied by a friend—a fat, oily-looking German—and between them they told a tale which set the police immediately on the move.

"It appears that on the 10th of December, at about three o'clock in the afternoon, Karl Mueller, the German, called on his friend, William Kershaw, for the purpose of collecting a small debt—some ten pounds or so—which the latter owed him. On arriving at the squalid lodging in Charlotte Street, Fitzroy Square, he found William Kershaw in a wild state of excitement, and his wife in tears. Mueller attempted to state the object of his visit, but Kershaw, with wild gestures, waved him aside, and— in his own words—flabbergasted him by asking him point-blank for another loan of two pounds, which sum, he declared, would be the means of a speedy fortune for himself and the friend who would help him in his need.

"After a quarter of an hour spent in obscure hints, Kershaw, finding the cautious German obdurate, decided to let him into the secret plan, which, he averred, would place thousands into their hands."

Instinctively Polly had put down her paper; the mild stranger, with his nervous air and timid, watery eyes, had a peculiar way of telling his tale, which somehow fascinated her.

"I don't know," he resumed, "if you remember the story which the German told to the police, and which was corroborated in every detail by the wife or widow. Briefly it was this: Some thirty years previously, Kershaw, then twenty years of age, and a medical student at one of the London hospitals, had a chum named Barker, with whom he roomed, together with another.

"The latter, so it appears, brought home one evening a very considerable sum of money, which he had won on the turf, and the following morning he was found murdered in his bed. Kershaw, fortunately for himself, was able to prove a conclusive *alibi*; he had spent the night on duty at the hospital; as for Barker, he had disappeared, that is to say, as far as the police were concerned, but not as far as the watchful eyes of his friend Kershaw were able to spy—at least, so the latter said. Barker very cleverly contrived to get away out of the country, and, after sundry vicissitudes, finally settled down at Vladivostok, in Eastern Siberia, where, under the assumed name of Smethurst, he built up an enormous fortune by trading in furs.

"Now, mind you, every one knows Smethurst, the Siberian millionaire. Kershaw's story that he had once been called Barker, and had committed a murder thirty years ago, was never proved, was it? I am merely telling you what Kershaw said to his friend the German and to his wife on that memorable afternoon of December the 10th.

"According to him Smethurst had made one gigantic mistake in his clever career—he had on four occasions written to his late friend, William Kershaw. Two of these letters had no bearing on the case, since they were written more than twenty-five years ago, and Kershaw, moreover, had lost them—so he said—long ago. According to him, however, the first of these letters was written when Smethurst, alias Barker, had spent all the money he had obtained from the crime, and found himself destitute in New York.

"Kershaw, then in fairly prosperous circumstances, sent him a L10 note for the sake of old times. The second, when the tables had turned, and Kershaw had begun to go downhill, Smethurst, as he then already called himself, sent his whilom friend L50. After that, as Mueller gathered, Kershaw had made sundry demands on Smethurst's ever-increasing purse, and had accompanied these demands by various threats, which, considering the distant country in which the millionaire lived, were worse than futile.

"But now the climax had come, and Kershaw, after a final moment of hesitation, handed over to his German friend the two last letters purporting to have been written by Smethurst, and which, if you remember, played such an important part in the mysterious story of this extraordinary crime. I have a copy of both these letters here," added the man in the corner, as he took out a piece of paper from a very worn-out pocket-book, and, unfolding it very deliberately, he began to read:—

*"'Sir,—Your preposterous demands for money are wholly unwarrantable. I have already helped you quite as much as you deserve. However, for the sake of old times, and because you once helped me when I was in a terrible difficulty, I am willing to once more let you impose upon my good nature. A friend of mine here, a Russian merchant, to whom I have sold my business, starts in a few days for an extended tour to many European and Asiatic ports in his yacht, and has invited me to accompany him as far as England. Being tired of foreign parts, and desirous of seeing the old country once again after thirty years' absence, I have decided to accept his invitation. I don't know when we may actually be in Europe, but I promise you that as soon as we touch a suitable port I will write to you again, making an appointment for you to see me in London. But remember that if your demands are too preposterous I will not for a moment listen to them, and that I am the last man in the world to submit to persistent and unwarrantable blackmail.*

*'I am, sir,*
*'Yours truly,        '*
*Francis Smethurst.'*

"The second letter was dated from Southampton," continued the old man in the corner calmly, "and, curiously enough, was the only letter which Kershaw professed to have received from Smethurst of which he had kept the envelope, and which was dated. It was quite brief," he added, referring once more to his piece of paper.

*"'Dear Sir,—Referring to my letter of a few weeks ago, I wish to inform you that the Tsarskoe Selo will touch at Tilbury on Tuesday next, the 10th. I shall land there, and immediately go up to London by the first train I can get. If you like, you may meet me at Fenchurch Street Station, in the first-class waiting-room,*

*in the late afternoon. Since I surmise that after thirty years'*
*absence my face may not be familiar to you, I may as well tell you*
*that you will recognize me by a heavy Astrakhan fur coat, which I*
*shall wear, together with a cap of the same. You may then*
*introduce yourself to me, and I will personally listen to what you*
*may have to say.*
    *'Yours faithfully,*
    *'Francis Smethurst.'*

"It was this last letter which had caused William Kershaw's
excitement and his wife's tears. In the German's own words, he
was walking up and down the room like a wild beast,
gesticulating wildly, and muttering sundry exclamations. Mrs.
Kershaw, however, was full of apprehension. She mistrusted the
man from foreign parts—who, according to her husband's story,
had already one crime upon his conscience—who might, she
feared, risk another, in order to be rid of a dangerous enemy.
Woman-like, she thought the scheme a dishonourable one, for
the law, she knew, is severe on the blackmailer.

"The assignation might be a cunning trap, in any case it was
a curious one; why, she argued, did not Smethurst elect to see
Kershaw at his hotel the following day? A thousand whys and
wherefores made her anxious, but the fat German had been won
over by Kershaw's visions of untold gold, held tantalisingly
before his eyes. He had lent the necessary L2, with which his
friend intended to tidy himself up a bit before he went to meet
his friend the millionaire. Half an hour afterwards Kershaw had
left his lodgings, and that was the last the unfortunate woman
saw of her husband, or Mueller, the German, of his friend.

"Anxiously his wife waited that night, but he did not return;
the next day she seems to have spent in making purposeless and
futile inquiries about the neighbourhood of Fenchurch Street;
and on the 12th she went to Scotland Yard, gave what
particulars she knew, and placed in the hands of the police the
two letters written by Smethurst."

## II - A Millionaire in the Dock

The man in the corner had finished his glass of milk. His watery blue eyes looked across at Miss Polly Burton's eager little face, from which all traces of severity had now been chased away by an obvious and intense excitement.

"It was only on the 31st," he resumed after a while, "that a body, decomposed past all recognition, was found by two lightermen in the bottom of a disused barge. She had been moored at one time at the foot of one of those dark flights of steps which lead down between tall warehouses to the river in the East End of London. I have a photograph of the place here," he added, selecting one out of his pocket, and placing it before Polly.

"The actual barge, you see, had already been removed when I took this snapshot, but you will realize what a perfect place this alley is for the purpose of one man cutting another's throat in comfort, and without fear of detection. The body, as I said, was decomposed beyond all recognition; it had probably been there eleven days, but sundry articles, such as a silver ring and a tie pin, were recognizable, and were identified by Mrs. Kershaw as belonging to her husband.

"She, of course, was loud in denouncing Smethurst, and the police had no doubt a very strong case against him, for two days after the discovery of the body in the barge, the Siberian millionaire, as he was already popularly called by enterprising interviewers, was arrested in his luxurious suite of rooms at the Hotel Cecil.

"To confess the truth, at this point I was not a little puzzled. Mrs. Kershaw's story and Smethurst's letters had both found their way into the papers, and following my usual method— mind you, I am only an amateur, I try to reason out a case for the love of the thing—I sought about for a motive for the crime, which the police declared Smethurst had committed. To effectually get rid of a dangerous blackmailer was the generally accepted theory. Well! did it ever strike you how paltry that motive really was?"

Miss Polly had to confess, however, that it had never struck her in that light.

"Surely a man who had succeeded in building up an immense fortune by his own individual efforts, was not the sort of fool to believe that he had anything to fear from a man like Kershaw. He must have *known* that Kershaw held no damning proofs against him—not enough to hang him, anyway. Have you ever seen Smethurst?" he added, as he once more fumbled in his pocket-book.

Polly replied that she had seen Smethurst's picture in the illustrated papers at the time. Then he added, placing a small photograph before her:

"What strikes you most about the face?"

"Well, I think its strange, astonished expression, due to the total absence of eyebrows, and the funny foreign cut of the hair."

"So close that it almost looks as if it had been shaved. Exactly. That is what struck me most when I elbowed my way into the court that morning and first caught sight of the millionaire in the dock. He was a tall, soldierly-looking man, upright in stature, his face very bronzed and tanned. He wore neither moustache nor beard, his hair was cropped quite close to his head, like a Frenchman's; but, of course, what was so very remarkable about him was that total absence of eyebrows and even eyelashes, which gave the face such a peculiar appearance—as you say, a perpetually astonished look.

"He seemed, however, wonderfully calm; he had been accommodated with a chair in the dock—being a millionaire— and chatted pleasantly with his lawyer, Sir Arthur Inglewood, in the intervals between the calling of the several witnesses for the prosecution; whilst during the examination of these witnesses he sat quite placidly, with his head shaded by his hand.

"Mueller and Mrs. Kershaw repeated the story which they had already told to the police. I think you said that you were not able, owing to pressure of work, to go to the court that day, and hear the case, so perhaps you have no recollection of Mrs. Kershaw. No? Ah, well! Here is a snapshot I managed to get of her once. That is her. Exactly as she stood in the box—over-dressed—in elaborate crape, with a bonnet which once had contained pink roses, and to which a remnant of pink petals still clung obtrusively amidst the deep black.

"She would not look at the prisoner, and turned her head resolutely towards the magistrate. I fancy she had been fond of that vagabond husband of hers: an enormous wedding-ring encircled her finger, and that, too, was swathed in black. She firmly believed that Kershaw's murderer sat there in the dock, and she literally flaunted her grief before him.

"I was indescribably sorry for her. As for Mueller, he was just fat, oily, pompous, conscious of his own importance as a witness; his fat fingers, covered with brass rings, gripped the two incriminating letters, which he had identified. They were his passports, as it were, to a delightful land of importance and notoriety. Sir Arthur Inglewood, I think, disappointed him by stating that he had no questions to ask of him. Mueller had been brimful of answers, ready with the most perfect indictment, the most elaborate accusations against the bloated millionaire who had decoyed his dear friend Kershaw, and murdered him in Heaven knows what an out-of-the-way corner of the East End.

"After this, however, the excitement grew apace. Mueller had been dismissed, and had retired from the court altogether, leading away Mrs. Kershaw, who had completely broken down.

"Constable D 21 was giving evidence as to the arrest in the meanwhile. The prisoner, he said, had seemed completely taken by surprise, not understanding the cause or history of the accusation against him; however, when put in full possession of the facts, and realizing, no doubt, the absolute futility of any resistance, he had quietly enough followed the constable into the cab. No one at the fashionable and crowded Hotel Cecil had even suspected that anything unusual had occurred.

"Then a gigantic sigh of expectancy came from every one of the spectators. The 'fun' was about to begin. James Buckland, a porter at Fenchurch Street railway station, had just sworn to tell all the truth, etc. After all, it did not amount to much. He said that at six o'clock in the afternoon of December the 10th, in the midst of one of the densest fogs he ever remembers, the 5.5 from Tilbury steamed into the station, being just about an hour late. He was on the arrival platform, and was hailed by a passenger in a first-class carriage. He could see very little of him beyond an enormous black fur coat and a travelling cap of fur also.

"The passenger had a quantity of luggage, all marked F.S., and he directed James Buckland to place it all upon a four-wheel cab, with the exception of a small hand-bag, which he carried himself. Having seen that all his luggage was safely bestowed, the stranger in the fur coat paid the porter, and, telling the cabman to wait until he returned, he walked away in the direction of the waiting-rooms, still carrying his small hand-bag.

"'I stayed for a bit,' added James Buckland, 'talking to the driver about the fog and that; then I went about my business, seein' that the local from Southend 'ad been signalled.'

"The prosecution insisted most strongly upon the hour when the stranger in the fur coat, having seen to his luggage, walked away towards the waiting-rooms. The porter was emphatic. 'It was not a minute later than 6.15,' he averred.

"Sir Arthur Inglewood still had no questions to ask, and the driver of the cab was called.

"He corroborated the evidence of James Buckland as to the hour when the gentleman in the fur coat had engaged him, and having filled his cab in and out with luggage, had told him to wait. And cabby did wait. He waited in the dense fog—until he was tired, until he seriously thought of depositing all the luggage in the lost property office, and of looking out for another fare—waited until at last, at a quarter before nine, whom should he see walking hurriedly towards his cab but the gentleman in the fur coat and cap, who got in quickly and told the driver to take him at once to the Hotel Cecil. This, cabby declared, had occurred at a quarter before nine. Still Sir Arthur Inglewood made no comment, and Mr. Francis Smethurst, in the crowded, stuffy court, had calmly dropped to sleep.

"The next witness, Constable Thomas Taylor, had noticed a shabbily dressed individual, with shaggy hair and beard, loafing about the station and waiting-rooms in the afternoon of December the 10th. He seemed to be watching the arrival platform of the Tilbury and Southend trains.

"Two separate and independent witnesses, cleverly unearthed by the police, had seen this same shabbily dressed individual stroll into the first-class waiting-room at about 6.15 on Wednesday, December the 10th, and go straight up to a gentleman in a heavy fur coat and cap, who had also just come into the room. The two talked together for a while; no one heard what they said, but presently they walked off together. No one seemed to know in which direction.

"Francis Smethurst was rousing himself from his apathy; he whispered to his lawyer, who nodded with a bland smile of encouragement. The employes of the Hotel Cecil gave evidence as to the arrival of Mr. Smethurst at about 9.30 p.m. on Wednesday, December the 10th, in a cab, with a quantity of luggage; and this closed the case for the prosecution.

"Everybody in that court already *saw* Smethurst mounting the gallows. It was uninterested curiosity which caused the elegant audience to wait and hear what Sir Arthur Inglewood had to say. He, of course, is the most fashionable man in the law at the present moment. His lolling attitudes, his drawling speech, are quite the rage, and imitated by the gilded youth of society.

"Even at this moment, when the Siberian millionaire's neck literally and metaphorically hung in the balance, an expectant titter went round the fair spectators as Sir Arthur stretched out his long loose limbs and lounged across the table. He waited to make his effect—Sir Arthur is a born actor—and there is no doubt that he made it, when in his slowest, most drawly tones he said quietly;

"'With regard to this alleged murder of one William Kershaw, on Wednesday, December the 10th, between 6.15 and 8.45 p.m., your Honour, I now propose to call two witnesses, who saw this same William Kershaw alive on Tuesday afternoon, December the 16th, that is to say, six days after the supposed murder.'

"It was as if a bombshell had exploded in the court. Even his Honour was aghast, and I am sure the lady next to me only recovered from the shock of the surprise in order to wonder whether she need put off her dinner party after all.

"As for me," added the man in the corner, with that strange mixture of nervousness and self-complacency which had set Miss Polly Burton wondering, "well, you see, *I* had made up my mind long ago where the hitch lay in this particular case, and I was not so surprised as some of the others.

"Perhaps you remember the wonderful development of the case, which so completely mystified the police—and in fact everybody except myself. Torriani and a waiter at his hotel in the Commercial Road both deposed that at about 3.30 p.m. on December the 10th a shabbily dressed individual lolled into the coffee-room and ordered some tea. He was pleasant enough and talkative, told the waiter that his name was William Kershaw, that very soon all London would be talking about him, as he was about, through an unexpected stroke of good fortune, to become a very rich man, and so on, and so on, nonsense without end.

"When he had finished his tea he lolled out again, but no sooner had he disappeared down a turning of the road than the waiter discovered an old umbrella, left behind accidentally by the shabby, talkative individual. As is the custom in his highly respectable restaurant, Signor Torriani put the umbrella carefully away in his office, on the chance of his customer calling to claim it when he had discovered his loss. And sure enough nearly a week later, on Tuesday, the 16th, at about 1 p.m., the same shabbily dressed individual called and asked for his umbrella. He had some lunch, and chatted once again to the waiter. Signor Torriani and the waiter gave a description of William Kershaw, which coincided exactly with that given by Mrs. Kershaw of her husband.

"Oddly enough he seemed to be a very absent-minded sort of person, for on this second occasion, no sooner had he left than the waiter found a pocket-book in the coffee-room, underneath the table. It contained sundry letters and bills, all addressed to William Kershaw. This pocket-book was produced, and Karl Mueller, who had returned to the court, easily identified it as having belonged to his dear and lamented friend 'Villiam.'

"This was the first blow to the case against the accused. It was a pretty stiff one, you will admit. Already it had begun to collapse like a house of cards. Still, there was the assignation, and the undisputed meeting between Smethurst and Kershaw, and those two and a half hours of a foggy evening to satisfactorily account for."

The man in the corner made a long pause, keeping the girl on tenterhooks. He had fidgeted with his bit of string till there was not an inch of it free from the most complicated and elaborate knots.

"I assure you," he resumed at last, "that at that very moment the whole mystery was, to me, as clear as daylight. I only marvelled how his Honour could waste his time and mine by putting what he thought were searching questions to the accused relating to his past. Francis Smethurst, who had quite shaken off his somnolence, spoke with a curious nasal twang, and with an almost imperceptible soupcon of foreign accent, He calmly denied Kershaw's version of his past; declared that he had never been called Barker, and had certainly never been mixed up in any murder case thirty years ago.

"'But you knew this man Kershaw,' persisted his Honour, 'since you wrote to him?'

"'Pardon me, your Honour,' said the accused quietly, 'I have never, to my knowledge, seen this man Kershaw, and I can swear that I never wrote to him.'

"'Never wrote to him?' retorted his Honour warningly. 'That is a strange assertion to make when I have two of your letters to him in my hands at the present moment.'

"'I never wrote those letters, your Honour,' persisted the accused quietly, 'they are not in my handwriting.'

"'Which we can easily prove,' came in Sir Arthur Inglewood's drawly tones, as he handed up a packet to his Honour; 'here are a number of letters written by my client since he has landed in this country, and some of which were written under my very eyes.'

"As Sir Arthur Inglewood had said, this could be easily proved, and the prisoner, at his Honour's request, scribbled a few lines, together with his signature, several times upon a sheet of note-paper. It was easy to read upon the magistrate's astounded countenance, that there was not the slightest similarity in the two handwritings.

"A fresh mystery had cropped up. Who, then, had made the assignation with William Kershaw at Fenchurch Street railway station? The prisoner gave a fairly satisfactory account of the employment of his time since his landing in England.

"'I came over on the *Tsarskoe Selo*,' he said, 'a yacht belonging to a friend of mine. When we arrived at the mouth of the Thames there was such a dense fog that it was twenty-four hours before it was thought safe for me to land. My friend, who is a Russian, would not land at all; he was regularly frightened at this land of fogs. He was going on to Madeira immediately.

"'I actually landed on Tuesday, the 10th, and took a train at once for town. I did see to my luggage and a cab, as the porter and driver told your Honour; then I tried to find my way to a refreshment-room, where I could get a glass of wine. I drifted into the waiting-room, and there I was accosted by a shabbily dressed individual, who began telling me a piteous tale. Who he was I do not know. He *said* he was an old soldier who had served

his country faithfully, and then been left to starve. He begged of
me to accompany him to his lodgings, where I could see his wife
and starving children, and verify the truth and piteousness of
his tale.

"'Well, your Honour,' added the prisoner with noble
frankness, 'it was my first day in the old country. I had come
back after thirty years with my pockets full of gold, and this was
the first sad tale I had heard; but I am a business man, and did
not want to be exactly "done" in the eye. I followed my man
through the fog, out into the streets. He walked silently by my
side for a time. I had not a notion where I was.

"'Suddenly I turned to him with some question, and realized
in a moment that my gentleman had given me the slip. Finding,
probably, that I would not part with my money till I *had* seen
the starving wife and children, he left me to my fate, and went in
search of more willing bait.

"'The place where I found myself was dismal and deserted. I
could see no trace of cab or omnibus. I retraced my steps and
tried to find my way back to the station, only to find myself in
worse and more deserted neighbourhoods. I became hopelessly
lost and fogged. I don't wonder that two and a half hours elapsed
while I thus wandered on in the dark and deserted streets; my
sole astonishment is that I ever found the station at all that
night, or rather close to it a policeman, who showed me the way.'

"'But how do you account for Kershaw knowing all your
movements?' still persisted his Honour, 'and his knowing the
exact date of your arrival in England? How do you account for
these two letters, in fact?'

"'I cannot account for it or them, your Honour,' replied the
prisoner quietly. 'I have proved to you, have I not, that I never
wrote those letters, and that the man—er—Kershaw is his
name?—was not murdered by me?'

"'Can you tell me of anyone here or abroad who might have
heard of your movements, and of the date of your arrival?'

"'My late employes at Vladivostok, of course, knew of my
departure, but none of them could have written these letters,
since none of them know a word of English.'

"'Then you can throw no light upon these mysterious letters?
You cannot help the police in any way towards the clearing up of
this strange affair?'

"'The affair is as mysterious to me as to your Honour, and to the police of this country.'

"Francis Smethurst was discharged, of course; there was no semblance of evidence against him sufficient to commit him for trial. The two overwhelming points of his defence which had completely routed the prosecution were, firstly, the proof that he had never written the letters making the assignation, and secondly, the fact that the man supposed to have been murdered on the 10th was seen to be alive and well on the 16th. But then, who in the world was the mysterious individual who had apprised Kershaw of the movements of Smethurst, the millionaire?"

## III - HIS DEDUCTION

The man in the corner cocked his funny thin head on one side and looked at Polly; then he took up his beloved bit of string and deliberately untied every knot he had made in it. When it was quite smooth he laid it out upon the table.

"I will take you, if you like, point by point along the line of reasoning which I followed myself, and which will inevitably lead you, as it led me, to the only possible solution of the mystery.

"First take this point," he said with nervous restlessness, once more taking up his bit of string, and forming with each point raised a series of knots which would have shamed a navigating instructor, "obviously it was *impossible* for Kershaw not to have been acquainted with Smethurst, since he was fully apprised of the latter's arrival in England by two letters. Now it was clear to me from the first that *no one* could have written those two letters except Smethurst. You will argue that those letters were proved not to have been written by the man in the dock. Exactly. Remember, Kershaw was a careless man—he had lost both envelopes. To him they were insignificant. Now it was never *disproved* that those letters were written by Smethurst."

"But—" suggested Polly.

"Wait a minute," he interrupted, while knot number two appeared upon the scene, "it was proved that six days after the murder, William Kershaw was alive, and visited the Torriani

Hotel, where already he was known, and where he conveniently left a pocket-book behind, so that there should be no mistake as to his identity; but it was never questioned where Mr. Francis Smethurst, the millionaire, happened to spend that very same afternoon."

"Surely, you don't mean?" gasped the girl.

"One moment, please," he added triumphantly. "How did it come about that the landlord of the Torriani Hotel was brought into court at all? How did Sir Arthur Inglewood, or rather his client, know that William Kershaw had on those two memorable occasions visited the hotel, and that its landlord could bring such convincing evidence forward that would for ever exonerate the millionaire from the imputation of murder?"

"Surely," I argued, "the usual means, the police—"

"The police had kept the whole affair very dark until the arrest at the Hotel Cecil. They did not put into the papers the usual: 'If anyone happens to know of the whereabouts, etc. etc'. Had the landlord of that hotel heard of the disappearance of Kershaw through the usual channels, he would have put himself in communication with the police. Sir Arthur Inglewood produced him. How did Sir Arthur Inglewood come on his track?"

"Surely, you don't mean?"

"Point number four," he resumed imperturbably, "Mrs. Kershaw was never requested to produce a specimen of her husband's handwriting. Why? Because the police, clever as you say they are, never started on the right tack. They believed William Kershaw to have been murdered; they looked for William Kershaw.

"On December the 31st, what was presumed to be the body of William Kershaw was found by two lightermen: I have shown you a photograph of the place where it was found. Dark and deserted it is in all conscience, is it not? Just the place where a bully and a coward would decoy an unsuspecting stranger, murder him first, then rob him of his valuables, his papers, his very identity, and leave him there to rot. The body was found in a disused barge which had been moored some time against the wall, at the foot of these steps. It was in the last stages of decomposition, and, of course, could not be identified; but the police would have it that it was the body of William Kershaw.

"It never entered their heads that it was the body of *Francis Smethurst, and that William Kershaw was his murderer.*

"Ah! it was cleverly, artistically conceived! Kershaw is a genius. Think of it all! His disguise! Kershaw had a shaggy beard, hair, and moustache. He shaved up to his very eyebrows! No wonder that even his wife did not recognize him across the court; and remember she never saw much of his face while he stood in the dock. Kershaw was shabby, slouchy, he stooped. Smethurst, the millionaire, might have served in the Prussian army.

"Then that lovely trait about going to revisit the Torriani Hotel. Just a few days' grace, in order to purchase moustache and beard and wig, exactly similar to what he had himself shaved off. Making up to look like himself! Splendid! Then leaving the pocket-book behind! He! he! he! Kershaw was not murdered! Of course not. He called at the Torriani Hotel six days after the murder, whilst Mr. Smethurst, the millionaire, hobnobbed in the park with duchesses! Hang such a man! Fie!"

He fumbled for his hat. With nervous, trembling fingers he held it deferentially in his hand whilst he rose from the table. Polly watched him as he strode up to the desk, and paid twopence for his glass of milk and his bun. Soon he disappeared through the shop, whilst she still found herself hopelessly bewildered, with a number of snap-shot photographs before her, still staring at a long piece of string, smothered from end to end in a series of knots, as bewildering, as irritating, as puzzling as the man who had lately sat in the corner.

# THE CRIME OF THE FRENCH CAFÉ

## BY NICHOLAS CARTER

ORIGINALLY PUBLISHED IN 1893

EDITOR'S NOTES:

# THE CRIME OF THE FRENCH CAFÉ

### BY NICHOLAS CARTER

Nick Carter proved to be one of the longest lived detective characters in fiction. Originally appearing in the dime novel *The Old Detective's Pupil; or, The Mysterious Crime of Madison Square in* 1886, Carter would appear in a pulp magazines and a variety of other formats such as radio and films, eventually being transformed into a spy in the 1960's with the last story appearing in 1990. Many of the early stories were published in the Street & Smith magazine *Nick Carter Weekly* which later became *Detective Story Magazine.*

The original Nick Carter was an American detective operating in New York, and the stories, as fitting their venue, were as full of action as they were of detection. He was assisted in many of his adventures by his son Chick.

The authorship of stories were always attributed to Nick Carter with many of them being told as a first person narrative. Though the authorship was never explicitly stated number of different writers are believed to have been responsible for the stories in this period, starting with John R. Coryell, and including Frederick Day, Thomas Harbaugh, and Eugene Sawyer.

# THE CRIME OF THE FRENCH CAFÉ

## Chapter I. Private Dining-Room "B."

There is a well-known French restaurant in the "Tenderloin" district which provides its patrons with small but elegantly appointed private dining-rooms.

The restaurant occupies a corner house; and, though its reputation is not strictly first-class in some respects, its cook is an artist, and its wine cellar as good as the best.

It has two entrances, and the one on the side street is not well lighted at night.

At half-past seven o'clock one evening Nick Carter was standing about fifty yards from this side door.

The detective had shadowed a man to a house on the side street, and was waiting for him to come out.

The case was a robbery of no great importance, but Nick had taken it to oblige a personal friend, who wished to have the business managed quietly. This affair would not be worth mentioning, except that it led Nick to one of the most peculiar and interesting criminal puzzles that he had ever come across in all his varied experience.

While Nick waited for his man he saw a closed carriage stop before the side door of the restaurant.

Almost immediately a waiter, bare-headed and wearing his white apron, came hurriedly out of the side door and got into the carriage, which instantly moved away at a rapid rate.

This incident struck Nick as being very peculiar. The waiter had acted like a man who was running away.

As he crossed the sidewalk he glanced hastily from side to side, as if afraid of being seen, and perhaps stopped.

It looked as if the waiter might have robbed one of the restaurant's patrons, or possibly its proprietor. If Nick had had no business on his hands he would have followed that carriage.

As it happened, however, the man for whom the detective was watching appeared at that moment.

Nick was obliged to follow him, but he knew that he would not have to go far, for Chick was waiting on Sixth avenue, and it was in that direction that the thief turned.

So it happened that within ten minutes Nick was able to turn this case over to his famous assistant, and return to clear up the mystery of the queer incident which he had chanced to observe.

Nick would not have been surprised to find the restaurant in an uproar, but it was as quiet as usual. He entered by the side door, ascended a flight of stairs, and came to a sort of office with a desk and a register.

It was the custom of the place that guests should put down their names as in a hotel before being assigned to a private dining-room.

There was nobody in sight.

The hall led toward the front of the building, and there were three rooms on the side of it toward the street.

All the doors were open and the rooms were empty. Nick glanced into these rooms, and then turned toward the desk. As he did so he saw a waiter coming down the stairs from the floor above.

This man was known by the name of Gaspard. He was the head waiter, and was on duty in the lower hall.

"Ah, Gaspard," said Nick, "who's your waiter on this floor to-night?"

Gaspard looked at Nick anxiously. He did not, of course, know who the detective really was, but he remembered him as one who had assisted the police in a case in which that house had been concerned about two years before.

"Jean Corbut," replied Gaspard. "I hope nothing is wrong."

"That remains to be seen," said Nick. "What sort of a man is this Corbut?"

"A little man," answered Gaspard, "and very thin. He has long, black hair, and mustaches pointed like two needles."

"Have you sent him out for anything?"

"Oh, no; he is here."

"Where?"

"In one of the rooms at the front. We have parties in A and B."

"You go and find him," said Nick. "I want to see him right away."

Gaspard went to the front of the house. A hall branched off at right angles with that in which Nick was standing. On the second hall were three rooms, A, B and C.

Room C was next the avenue. The other two had windows on an open space between two wings of the building. Nick glanced at the register, and saw that "R.M. Clark and wife" had been assigned to room A, and "John Jones and wife" to room B. Room C was vacant.

The detective had barely time to note these entries on the book when Gaspard came running back.

His face was as white as paper, and his lips were working as if he were saying something, but not a sound came from them.

He was struck dumb with fright. Whatever it was that he had seen must have been horrible, to judge from the man's trembling limbs and distorted face.

Nick had seen people in that condition before, and he did not waste time trying to get any information out of Gaspard.

Instead, he seized the frightened fellow by the shoulder and pushed him along toward the front of the house.

Gaspard made a feeble resistance. Evidently he did not want to see again the sight which had so terrified him.

But he was powerless in Nick's grasp. In five seconds they stood before the open door of room B.

The door was open, and there was a bright glare of gas within.

It shone upon the table, where a rich repast lay untasted. It illumined the gaudy furnishings of the room and the costly pictures upon the walls.

It shone, too, upon a beautiful face, rigid and perfectly white, except for a horrible stain of black and red upon the temple.

The face was that of a woman of twenty-five years. She had very abundant hair of a light corn color, which clustered in little curls around her forehead, and was gathered behind in a great mass of plaited braids.

She reclined in a large easy-chair, in a natural attitude, but the pallid face, the fixed and glassy eyes, and the grim wound upon the temple announced, in unmistakable terms, the presence of death.

Nick drew a long breath and set his lips together firmly. He had felt that something was wrong in that house. The waiter who had run across the sidewalk and got into that carriage had borne a guilty secret with him, as the detective's experienced eye had instantly perceived.

But this was a good deal worse than Nick had expected. He had looked for a robbery, or, perhaps, a secret and bloody quarrel between two of the waiters, but not for a murder such as this.

One glance at the woman showed her to be elegant in dress and of a refined appearance.

She could have had nothing in common with the missing Corbut, unless, indeed, he was other than he seemed.

Certainly, whatever was Corbut's connection with the crime, there was another person, at least, as intimately concerned in it. And he, too, had fled.

Where was the man who had brought this woman to this house? How was it possible to account for his absence except by the conclusion that he was the murderer?

That was the first and most natural explanation. Whether it was the true one or not, the man must be found.

Nick turned to Gaspard. The head waiter had sunk down on a chair by the table and seemed prostrated.

From previous experience Nick knew Gaspard to be a man without nerve, and he was not surprised to find him prostrated by this sudden shock.

There was a bottle of champagne standing in ice beside the table. The detective opened it and made Gaspard drink a glass of the sparkling liquor.

It put a little heart into the man, and he was able to answer questions.

Nick, meanwhile, closed the door of the room. Apparently the tragedy was known only to Gaspard and himself and to the guilty authors of it.

"Did you see this woman when she came in?" asked Nick.

"No."

"Who showed her and the man with her to this room?"

"Corbut."

"Who waited on them?"

"Corbut."

"Who waited on the people in room A?"

"Corbut."

"They are gone, I suppose?"

"Yes; I looked in there before I came in here."

"Did you see any of these people?"

"I saw the two men."

"How did that happen?"

"One of them came out into the hall to call Corbut, who had not answered the bell quick enough."

"Which one was that?"

"The man in room A."

"How do you know?"

"Because I saw the other man, later, coming out of room B."

"This room?"

"Yes."

"You are sure of that?"

"Perfectly."

"Did he see you?"'

"I think not. I was standing right at the corner of the two halls. The man came out and glanced around, but I stepped back quickly, because we do not like to appear to spy upon our guests. He did not see me."

"What did he do?"

"He went out the front way. I supposed the lady went with him, for I was sure that I heard the rustling of her dress."

"Where was Corbut then?"

"In room A."

"How long did he stay there?"

"Only a minute. I went back to the desk, and then was called by a waiter upstairs. Just as I turned to go I saw Corbut coming through the hall."

"Did you speak to him?"

"Yes; I called to him to stay by the desk while I went upstairs."

"Did he answer?"

"Yes; he said 'very well.'"

"And that's the last you saw of him?"

"Yes."

"All right; so much for Corbut. Now for the two men. Would you know them?"

"Not the man in room A. I didn't notice him particularly."

"But how about the man who came out of this room? He's the one we're after."

"I would know him," said Gaspard, slowly. "Yes; I feel sure that I could identify him."

"That's good. Now for the crime itself. Go back to the desk and ring for a messenger. When he comes, send him here. Don't let anybody else come, and don't say a word to anybody about this affair."

Gaspard, with a very pale face, went back to his desk.

Nick remained alone with the beautiful dead.

### Chapter II. Gaspard Spots His Man.

A revolver lay on the carpet just where it would have been if it had dropped from the woman's right hand.

Its position suggested the possibility of suicide, and there was, at the first glance, nothing to contradict that theory, except the conduct of Corbut and the man who had registered as John Jones.

It might be that the woman had committed suicide, and the men had fled for fear of being implicated in the affair.

Nick examined this side of the case at once.

The pistol had evidently been held only a few inches from the woman's head when it was fired.

Her white flesh showed the marks of the powder.

The bullet had passed straight through the head.

The revolver carried a long thirty-two cartridge. Three of the five chambers were loaded.

One of them contained an empty shell, on which the hammer rested. The fatal bullet had doubtless come from this chamber, for the shell had been recently discharged.

In the fifth chamber was an old shell, which had apparently been carried under the hammer for safety, as is quite common.

The woman had a purse containing about twenty dollars, but no cards or other things which might lead to identification.

Her ears had been pierced for earrings, but she seemed not to have worn them recently. She had no watch.

There was one plain gold ring on the third finger of her right hand, and there was a deep mark showing that she had worn another, but that ring was gone.

How recently it had been removed was, of course, beyond discovery. There was no sign that it had been violently torn away.

When Nick had proceeded thus far with his investigation the messenger boy arrived. The detective sent messages to his assistants, Chick and Patsy.

He then notified a coroner, who came about ten o'clock and took charge of the body.

A minute examination failed to reveal any marks upon the clothing which might assist in establishing the woman's identity.

Nick then left the restaurant, taking Gaspard with him. Inspector Mclaughlin's men were by this time on hand, and they took charge of the house, under Nick's direction.

At seven o'clock in the morning Nick received a message from Patsy, who had been directed to find the cabman in whose cab Corbut had fled.

Patsy had located the cabman at his home on West Thirty-second street. The man's name was Harrigan.

Nick took Gaspard with him and went to the house where Harrigan boarded.

"I got on to him easy enough," said Patsy, whom they found outside the house. "I found the policeman who was on that beat last night, and got him to give me a list of all the night-hawks he'd seen around there up to eight o'clock of the evening.

"Then I began to chase up the fellows on that list. The second man put me on to Harrigan. He remembered seeing him get the job, but couldn't tell what sort of a man hired him.

"I guess there's no doubt that he's the man, but I haven't questioned him yet. He's in there asleep."

Nick passed himself off as a friend of Harrigan's, and was directed with Patsy to the man's room.

They went in without being invited, after having tried in vain to get an answer to their pounding on his door.

The cabman was snoring in a heavy slumber.

"From what I heard," said Patsy, "Harrigan had a very large skate on last night. He's sleeping it off."

Nick shook the man unmercifully, and at last he sat up in bed.

"What t' 'ell?" said he, looking about him wildly. "Who are youse, an' wha's the row?"

As the quickest way to sober the man, Nick showed his shield. It acted like a cold shower-bath.

"Say, what was it I done?" gasped Harrigan. "'S' help me, I dunno nothing about it. I had a load on me last night, an' I ain't responsible."

Patsy laughed.

"There's no charge against you," said Nick; "I only want to ask you a few questions."

Harrigan sank back on the pillow with a gasp of relief.

"Gimme that water-pitcher," he said; "me t'roat's full o' cobwebs."

He drank about a quart of water, and then declared himself ready for a cross-examination. Nick sized him up for a decent sort of fellow; and saw no reason to doubt that he was telling the truth when he answered the questions that were put to him.

It appeared that he had been on Seventh avenue, near the French restaurant, from a little after six to about half-past seven on the previous evening.

At the latter hour a man had engaged his cab. He had taken it to the side door of the restaurant, and the waiter had got in. The man who hired the cab was already inside.

He had driven them somewhere on Fifty-seventh street, or it might be Fifty-eighth. He couldn't remember exactly.

The two men got out together. He didn't know what had become of them.

His fare was paid all right. Then he had a couple more drinks, and the next thing he knew he was at the stable where he had hired the cab.

Of course he didn't confess this in so many words, but Nick understood the facts well enough.

That was absolutely all that Harrigan knew about the case.

"Would you recognize the man who hired your cab if you saw him again?" asked Nick.

"Oh, sure," said Harrigan. "I wasn't so very full. I had me wits about me. Say, you ain't going to do me dirt an' git me license taken away? I was all right. I didn't do any harm."

Nick assured Harrigan that if he acted right in this case his license would be safe, and then left the man to his slumbers.

"Not very promising, is it, my boy?" said Nick to Patsy, as they went downstairs. "We've lost the trail as soon as we struck it."

"Do you think he's giving it to us straight?"

"Yes; he doesn't know where he took the men nor what became of them after they left his cab."

"It's a pity he had such a jag. He'd have been the best witness in the case."

Nick smiled.

"If he hadn't been drunk he wouldn't have had anything to do with the case," he said.

"What do you mean?"

"Why, it's clear enough. This man that we want saw Harrigan on that cab while the man was on his way to the restaurant with the woman. Then when it became necessary to get Corbut out of the way, he remembered the drunken cabman, and hired him."

"I don't see how you know that."

"A man would rather have a sober driver than a drunken one, wouldn't he?"

"Yes."

"Well, the man who told you he saw Harrigan get the job was sober, wasn't he?"

"Yes."

"Then why didn't the man take his cab? Because he wanted a drunken driver, who wouldn't be sharp enough to get on to any queer business.

"But he wouldn't have tried to find a drunken cabman just by luck, and he wouldn't have taken a sober one. Therefore he had seen Harrigan and hoped to find him in the same place.

"That's part of the plot. Now, then, you go to Chick, who's watching the body of the woman. I'm going to take Gaspard uptown and have a look at that part of the city where Harrigan left his passengers."

Nick and Gaspard went to the Thirty-third street station of the Sixth avenue elevated road.

They walked to the edge of the platform on the uptown end.

Suddenly Gaspard gave a violent start. He uttered an exclamation of surprise and pointed across the tracks.

"What is it?" cried Nick.

"The man who was in room B!" exclaimed Gaspard. "I am sure of it!"

At that instant a downtown train rushed into the station, cutting off Nick's view.

And a half-second later an uptown train pulled in on their side. Nick pushed open a gate before the train had fairly stopped. He dragged Gaspard after him.

The gateman tried to stop them, but Nick pushed the fellow in the car so violently that he sat down on the floor.

Then the detective pulled the other gate open, and, still dragging Gaspard, sprang down in the space between the tracks.

The other train was just starting. Nick leaped up and opened one of the gates.

Gaspard stood trembling. Excitement and terror rendered him incapable of action.

Nick reached down, and, seizing the man by the shoulders, lifted him up to the platform of the car as if he had been a child of ten.

"Look back," cried the detective, pushing Gaspard to the other side of the car. "Is your man still at the station?"

Two or three men were there, having, apparently, just missed the train.

It seemed possible that the criminal—if such he was—had seen Gaspard point, and had been shrewd enough not to board the car.

But Gaspard looked back and declared that his man was not there.

"Good," said Nick. "He must be on the train. We have him sure."

## Chapter III. John Jones.

"I want you!" whispered Nick.

How many luckless criminals have been startled by those words! How many have seen the prison or the gallows rise before them at the sound!

In this case, however, the words seemed to produce less than the ordinary effect.

The man to whom they were addressed turned suddenly toward the detective, but did not shrink or tremble.

"I beg your pardon," said he; "I didn't quite understand what you said."

The man's coolness made Nick even more in doubt about Gaspard's identification.

After boarding the train they had walked through it hurriedly, and in the car next the engine Gaspard had clutched Nick's arm, whispering:

"There is your man!"

The person indicated was well-dressed, rather good-looking, and about thirty-five years old. There was nothing particularly striking about his appearance.

It would have been easy to have found dozens of such men on lower Broadway any day.

Nick feared a mistake. But Gaspard was sure.

"I never forget a face," he said. "That is the man whom I saw coming out of room B. That is the murderer."

The man was standing up and holding on to one of the straps. His profile was turned to them.

Nick waited until he turned and showed his full face. The detective was bound to give Gaspard every chance to change his mind.

But he remained firm, and at last Nick approached the accused and suddenly whispered the terrifying words in his ear.

Having done so, he was obliged to carry it through. Therefore, when the stranger asked Nick to repeat what he had said, the detective, in a low voice, inaudible to anybody else in the car, told him what the accusation was.

"This is ridiculous," said the man. "I read the story of this affair in the papers this morning, but I am not connected with it in any way. If you arrest me, you must be prepared to take the consequences."

"I guess we can manage the affair quietly," said Nick, "and give you no trouble at all. I suppose you were going downtown to business?"

"Yes."

"Well, I will go along, too, if you don't mind."

"By all means," said the man, and he looked much relieved.

"I understand what your duty is," he continued. "Since this imported French jackass has made this charge, of course you'll have to look into it. Come down to the office and make some inquiries, and then go up to my flat. I was at home last evening after eight o'clock.

"What did you do before that?"

"I had dinner with my wife, and then put her aboard a train. She's gone away on a visit."

"Where has she gone?"

"No, sir; none of that. I don't propose to have a detective go flying after her to scare her to death. She keeps out of this mess, if I have any say about it."

"But if you're arrested she'll hear about it and come back to the city."

"I'm not going to be arrested. You're too sensible a man to do such a thing. I can see that.

"Here we are. We get off at Franklin street. My place of business is just a little way up the street, toward Broadway."

They left the train. Nick was beginning to feel that a mistake had been made. This man's easy manner and perfect confidence were hard to square with the idea of his guilt.

"By the way," said the suspect, as they descended the stairs, "I forgot to give you my card."

He handed it to Nick as he spoke, and the detective read this:

*MR. JOHN JONES.*
*ALLEN, MORSE & JONES,*
*Electrical Fixtures,*
*The "Sunlight" Lamp.*

"What did I tell you!" exclaimed Gaspard, who was looking over Nick's shoulder. "It is the name that was on the register. He is the man."

But Nick took a different view. He was of the opinion that Mr. Jones had presented very strong evidence of his complete innocence.

Anybody else might have signed himself "John Jones," but the real John Jones, never!

It would be mighty hard to convince a jury that a man meditating murder had recorded his correct name for the benefit of the police.

The coincidence was certainly astonishing, but it was in Jones' favor.

They walked over to the office of Allen, Morse & Jones.

Mr. Allen was there.

"Good-morning, Mr. Allen," said Jones, "My name has got me into trouble again."

"How is that?"

"Did you read about that French restaurant murder last night?"

"Well, I glanced at the story in one of the papers."

"This Frenchman here is a waiter in the place. He saw me in an elevated train just now, and told this other man, who is a detective, that I was the party who took that woman to the restaurant.

"That was bad enough, but when they found out what my name was, they convicted me immediately. It appears that the visitor to the restaurant signed the very uncommon name of John Jones on the books."

"Why, what the devil!" exclaimed Allen, looking wrathfully at poor Gaspard, who was shaking in his shoes. "Don't you know that this is a serious matter? What do you mean?"

"He is the man," cried Gaspard. "If I were dying, I would swear with my last breath that he is the man."

"But who's the woman?" asked Allen, turning to Nick. "And what has she to do with my partner?"

"That I cannot say," replied Nick; "she has not been identified."

"Then you have absolutely nothing to go upon except this fellow's word?"

"Nothing."

"Why, this is nonsense."

"Perhaps so," said Nick, "but you will admit that I would be false to my duty if I did not make an investigation."

"Investigate all you wish," laughed Jones. "But don't bother me any more than you have to. This is my busy day."

"I'm going right away," said Nick. "All I want of you is that you will give me your address, and meet me at your home in the latter part of the afternoon."

"Very well," said Jones, and he scribbled on a piece of paper. "I'll be there at half-past four o'clock."

Nick thanked Mr. Jones for his courtesy, and immediately withdrew. But he did not go far.

In a convenient doorway he wrote a note to Chick, on the back of the scrap of paper which Jones had given him, and sealed it in an envelope.

Then he sent Gaspard with it to Chick, who was on the lookout in the undertaker's room, where the body lay.

Having dispatched this message, Nick changed his disguise and kept watch over the establishment of Allen, Morse & Jones.

Nothing of importance happened until a little after noon, when a reply came from Chick.

Translated from the detective's cipher, it read as follows:

"The address is that of a good flat house. Jones lives there with his wife.

"They have been there only about two months. Nobody in the house knows anything about them.

"They had one servant, who was taken sick about two weeks ago and carried to a hospital, where she died.

"Since then they have lived absolutely alone. There was nobody in the house who had seen Mrs. Jones' face. She always wore a heavy veil.

"The only description I could get tallied with that of the body. The principal point was the hair.

"I have just found a woman who saw Mr. and Mrs. Jones go out yesterday afternoon. She remembers Mrs. Jones' dress. The description agrees with that found on the corpse.

"Jones carried an alligator-skin traveling-bag. Nobody saw either of them come back to the house, but Jones evidently slept there.

"I shall take the woman who saw them go out to the room where the body lies.

"Will send Patsy down with the result of this effort at identification. I believe it will show the woman to be Mrs. Jones. I send this that you may have warning."

"CHICK."

Nick read this note and then glanced across the street toward the office of Allen, Morse & Jones.

Through the window he could see Jones calmly writing a letter. Could it be possible that this man was guilty of so hideous a crime?

Half an hour passed, and then came the second message, as follows:

"Identified as Mrs. Jones."

### Chapter IV. All Sorts Of Identifications.

"I am sorry to tell you, Mr. Jones, that the body of the woman murdered last night has been identified as that of your wife."

So spoke Nick, and this time Jones' calmness was not proof against the surprise.

"It can't be possible!" he exclaimed, leaping from his chair.

"I am so informed," said Nick, "and I must place you under arrest."

"But there is some infernal mistake here," said the accused. "I know that my wife is all right. This must be somebody else."

"A lady living in the same house with you has recognized the body."

"I don't care if she has. Nobody in that house knows my wife."

"Is there anybody in the city who does know her?"

"I can't think of anybody."

"How about the grocer with whom you traded?"

"Our servant attended to all that till she was taken sick. Since then I've done what little there was to do. We've eaten most of our meals at restaurants."

"What restaurants?"

"Oh, all around. There's the Alcazar, for instance, where we have sometimes dined together."

"Does the head waiter there know her?"

"I suppose he would remember her face. He doesn't know the name."

"All right. I'll have him look at the body."

"But, man, you're going to let me look at it, aren't you?" exclaimed Jones. "That would settle it, I should think."

"I'll take you there now, and we will try to get somebody from the Alcazar at the same time."

Nick took the prisoner at once to the Alcazar. The head waiter remembered Jones' face. He had seen him dining with a lady who had beautiful light hair.

The three went to the undertaker's rooms.

Nick watched Jones narrowly as he approached the body. He started violently at the first sight of it. Then he became calm.

"The hair is wonderfully like," he said, "but there is no resemblance between the two faces."

"That is true, gentlemen," said the head waiter; "this is not the lady."

"On the contrary," said a voice close beside them, "I believe that this lady was your wife, Mr. Jones."

All the color went out of Jones' face as he turned quickly toward the man who had spoken.

"Ah, Mr. Gottlieb," he said, "I am surprised to hear you say that."

"Mr. Gottlieb is the grocer from whom the Joneses bought their supplies," said Chick, who had advanced to Nick's side.

"I was not aware that you had ever seen my wife," said Jones, looking searchingly at the grocer.

"I never saw her plainly," said Gottlieb. "She came into my store once or twice, but always closely veiled. So I cannot be sure; and, of course, if you insist that this is not your wife's body, I must be mistaken."

"You are mistaken, sir," said Jones, coldly.

He turned to Nick.

"Mr. Gottlieb has sealed my doom for the present," he said, with a smile. "I am ready to go with you."

Nick took his prisoner to Police Headquarters.

The detective had meanwhile sent Patsy in quest of Harrigan, the coachman.

Jones was taken into the superintendent's room, and a dozen other men were assembled there, waiting for the arrival of the cabman.

Harrigan was very nervous when he appeared.

"Youse fellies are tryin' to do me out o' my license," said he; "but I'm tellin' yer I was all right last night. I wasn't half so paralyzed as youse t'ink I was. Show me your man and I'll identify him."

Harrigan was led into the superintendent's room. When he saw how many men were there he seemed to be a great deal taken aback.

But he put a bold face on the matter, and promptly advanced, saying:

"This is the man."

Nick made a gesture of disappointment, and then he laughed, and the superintendent with him.

The man whom Harrigan had selected was Chick.

It was evident that the cabman was going upon pure guesswork. Being sharply questioned, he confessed that he had no idea how his "fare" of the previous night looked.

"I'll give it to youse dead straight," said he, at last; "I don't know whether the mug was white or black. Say, he might have been a Chinee."

"I believe that fellow is faking," said the sergeant to Nick, as Harrigan left the room.

"No; he's straight enough, I guess," said Nick. "He's not the sort of man who would have been let into a game of this kind."

Nick then proceeded to question the prisoner in the presence of Chick and the superintendent.

His answers were straightforward enough, but they threw little light upon the affair.

The only subject which he refused to discuss was the whereabouts of his wife. When questioned about her, he invariably declined to speak.

"She's gone on a little pleasure trip," he said, "and I want her to enjoy it. This affair will be all over when she gets back. She'll never hear of it, where she is, and that's as it should be."

Nick returned to his house, where he was informed that a visitor was waiting for him.

He found a gentleman somewhat under forty years of age, and apparently in prosperous circumstances, pacing the study floor.

The visitor was evidently greatly excited about something, for his hands trembled and he started nervously when Nick entered.

"Mr. Carter," he said, anxiously, "can I trust you fully?"

Nick laughed.

"I shan't do anything to prevent it," he said.

"Will you swear to keep what I shall tell you a secret?"

"No, sir; I will not."

The man made a despairing gesture.

"I supposed that your business was always strictly confidential," he said.

"So it is, but I take no oaths."

"I didn't mean that exactly, but—but—"

The man hesitated, stammered, and was unable to proceed.

"Come, sir," said Nick; "be calm. Tell me plainly what you want me to do for you."

"It isn't for me; it's for a—for a friend of mine."

"Very well; what can I do for your friend?"

"He is accused of a terrible crime, of which he is entirely innocent. I want you to save him."

"I have been asked to do that many times."

"And you have always succeeded?"

"Oh, no; in several cases the persons have been hanged."

The visitor shuddered violently.

"I had heard," he said, "that you never failed to find the guilty persons and to save the innocent."

"That is the truth. It has been my good fortune to leave no case unsettled."

"But you said that these innocent persons had been hanged."

"They were hanged," said Nick, "but they were not innocent. Their friends assured me that the persons were entirely guiltless, but it was not true.

"And therefore," Nick continued, looking straight into the man's eyes, "I should advise you to be very sure of your friend's innocence before you put the case in my hands."

The visitor looked very much relieved.

"I'm perfectly sure of it," he cried. "My friend had nothing to do with this case."

"I'm glad to hear it. Who is he?"

"The man who has been arrested in this restaurant murder case."

"John Jones?"

"That is the name he has given to the police."

"But isn't that his right name?"

"I—I don't know," stammered the visitor.

"He must be a very particular friend of yours, since you don't know what his name is!"

"I never saw him in my life."

"Look here, Mr.—"

"Hammond is my name."

"Well, Mr. Hammond, your statements don't hang together. You began by saying that this man was your friend."

"I didn't mean that exactly, but I sympathize with him. It must be terrible to be arrested for such a crime and to find the evidence growing stronger in spite of your innocence."

"How do you know that he is innocent?"

Before Hammond could reply there came a knock at the door. Nick answered it.

"Come in, Gaspard," he said, throwing the door wide open.

"You sent for me, and—Good God! who is this?"

"You know him, then?"

"Yes, yes, I know him," cried Gaspard; "he is the man who was in room A last night."

## Chapter V. Patsy's Tip.

Gaspard's declaration produced a stunning effect upon Hammond.

At first he seemed thunderstruck. There was a look in his face which made Nick say to himself, "It isn't true."

But whether the accusation was true or false, Nick knew at once that Hammond recognized Gaspard.

Yet he couldn't be a regular visitor to the place, because Gaspard had said that he had never seen either of the two men before the fatal evening.

Therefore, as Hammond had recognized Gaspard, he must be the man who was in room A, because the man in room B had not seen the head waiter, according to Gaspard's story.

Hammond, after the first shock of surprise, recovered his nerve wonderfully.

He calmly took a chair and sat there in deep thought for nearly five minutes. He paid no attention to questions.

Finally he looked up and said:

"I don't know why I should deny it to you. There is no charge against the man in room A."

"None whatever," said Nick. "He is wanted merely as a witness."

"It occurred to me that you might have some theory of a conspiracy in which both men were concerned."

"I never thought of it."

"Then I am not to be put under arrest?"

"Certainly not, unless some new evidence appears, and I do not expect it."

"Very well; I was the man in room A."

"And who was the lady?"

"I decline to mention her name. She has nothing to do with this case. You will easily understand that I do not wish to bring a lady's name into a tragedy of this kind."

"I can understand that. Now tell me why you feel so sure of this man Jones' innocence."

"Will you promise to keep me out of this affair as much as you can?"

"Why do you wish it? What are you afraid of?"

"Well," said Hammond, looking very much embarrassed, "I'm a married man, very respectable sort of a fellow; and the lady with whom I dined was not my wife. It's all right, you know. My wife is not a jealous woman. But the thing would not look well in print."

"I won't make this public if I can help it, Mr. Hammond. Not that I have much sympathy for you. You shouldn't have been there. But the publicity would annoy your wife, and do nobody any good."

"Thank you," said Hammond, with a grim smile; "now I will tell my story. There is very little to tell.

"We arrived before the other party. We heard them go into room B.

"By and by, I went out into the hall to find the waiter, who didn't answer my ring. I saw this man," pointing to Gaspard, "at the desk, and should have spoken to him, but just then the waiter hove in sight at the end of the hall.

"So I went back. Just as I was closing the door of our room, I heard the man come out of room B.

"I didn't see him, but I know that he went down the front stairs, for I heard his footsteps, and also heard the door shut.

"The waiter came in and finally went out again. We. were just ready to leave the place when we heard the pistol-shot in the other room.

"Then we got out of the house just as fast as we could. It was cowardly, perhaps, but I knew that something terrible had happened, and I didn't want to be mixed up in it.

"Of course I wanted to keep the lady out of it, too, and— and—well, you can see that there were many reasons why I should have decided to make tracks."

"You know that the man was not in room B when the shot was fired?" said Nick.

"I'm sure of it."

"He might have come back."

"No; the front door makes a loud noise when it is shut I should have heard him if he had come in that way. And if he had come the other way this man would have seen him."

"You didn't see him at all, did you?"

"No."

"So you can't say whether Jones was the man?"

"No; but I'm sure he wasn't the murderer."

"You think it was suicide?"

"I'm sure of it. How could it have been anything else? The woman was alone."

"There might have been somebody else in the room."

"No; our waiter told us that the party consisted of only two."

"You mean Corbut?"

"I believe that's his name—the fellow who disappeared."

"How do you account for his disappearance?"

"I don't; but perhaps he was afraid of being mixed up in the affair. He may have a record which won't permit him to go before the police, even as a witness."

"How could he have got that cab?"

"I've thought a good deal about that. It was mentioned in the papers. I believe he may have slipped out the front way, called the cab, and then gone back to get something.

"Perhaps he went back for his clothes but didn't dare to take them."

"And how about the cabman's story of the man who engaged the cab?"

"The cabman's a liar. That's plain enough."

"I'm afraid he is. Now, Mr. Hammond, could either Corbut or this man Gaspard have got into room B without your knowing it?"

"Easily. Great heavens, I never thought of that! One of them may be the murderer!"

Gaspard, at these words, turned as white as a sheet.

He was so frightened that his English—which was usually very fluent—deserted him, and he mumbled protestations of innocence in his mother tongue.

"Thank you, Mr. Hammond," said Nick, without appearing to notice Gaspard's distress. "I have no more questions to ask, but I would be obliged to you if you would wait here a few minutes for me."

Nick went into another room, where he knew that Patsy was waiting.

A set of signals is arranged in Nick's house, by which he always knows when one of his staff gets in.

"Patsy," said Nick, "there's a fellow up stairs whom you'll have to shadow."

"Gaspard?"

"No; a man who calls himself Hammond. Gaspard has identified him as the man who was in room A."

"Look here," said Patsy, "am I a farmer, or is the man Gaspard the greatest living identifier?"

"What do you mean?"

"Why, it strikes me that he picked out his men a good deal too easy. If it's all straight, I'd like the loan of his luck for a few days.

"That identification on the elevated station looked to me like a fake. I don't believe he ever intended that you should get hold of the man.

"In my opinion, he's simply running around identifying everybody he sees."

"But this man Hammond admits it."

"Is he telling the truth?"

"No," said Nick, with a peculiar smile, "I don't believe he is."

"Well, then, Gaspard's a liar, and if he's lied here, he may have done the same thing in Jones' case."

Nick looked shrewdly at his youthful assistant. He is very fond of this bright boy, and gives him every chance to develop his theories in those cases in which he is employed.

"Come, my lad," said the famous detective, "tell me what has set you against Gaspard."

"He's going to skip."

"Is that so? Well, this is serious."

"It's a fact. I got it from one of the men in the restaurant. My man was told of it by Corbut."

"Corbut?"

"Yes; and there's another suspicious circumstance. There's a Frenchwoman who is going to give little old New York the shake at the same time as Gaspard. They're going back to sunny France together.

"Now, nobody knows this but the man I talked with. Gaspard thinks that Corbut was the only one who knew it.

"So it was for Gaspard's interest, in case he really did this job, and lifted some valuable plunder off that woman, to get Corbut out of the way.

"Did he pay Corbut to skip first? And is he now identifying Tom, Dick and Harry for the purpose of bothering us and keeping us busy till he can light out?"

"It's worth looking into," said Nick. "At any rate, you stick to Gaspard. I'll put somebody else onto Hammond."

## Chapter VI. Mrs. John Jones.

Nothing of great importance occurred in the case until the next afternoon when Nick was at Police Headquarters.

He was talking with Superintendent Byrnes.

"The identification of that woman gets stronger all the time," said the superintendent. "I'm beginning to think that she is really the wife of our prisoner."

"It looks so," said Nick.

At that moment a card was brought in. The superintendent looked at it and whistled softly.

Then he handed the card to Nick, who read the name. The two men exchanged glances, and both smiled.

"Mrs. John Jones," said Nick; "well, this puts a new face on the matter."

"It's a great case," was the reply. "I'm mighty glad you happened to be on the scene at once."

He turned to the officer who had brought the card, and directed that Mrs. Jones should be admitted immediately.

A pretty young woman entered. She was of about the same height as the unfortunate victim of the tragedy in the restaurant, and much like her in build.

The faces did not resemble each other in outline, but the coloring was similar. There was a faint resemblance in the large, light blue eyes.

The hair was of the same peculiar shade, and nearly as luxuriant. But nobody would ever have mistaken one woman for the other, after a fair look at their faces.

The costumes, however, were positively identical. Mrs. John Jones, to all appearances, wore the very same clothes as Nick had seen upon the woman in room B.

Mrs. Jones was evidently very nervous, but she made a fine attempt to control herself.

"You have my husband under arrest, I believe," she said. "And he is accused, they say, of killing me."

She tried to smile, but it was rather a ghastly effort.

The superintendent motioned the woman to a seat.

"Mr. John Jones is here," he said, "and he is suspected of murder."

"I have read about it," replied the woman. "There certainly appeared to be evidence against him, but of course you must be aware that I know him to be innocent."

"How?"

"Because I was with him when the crime was committed. At half-past seven o'clock of that evening we were walking toward the Grand Central Depot.

"We had dined in our flat. The people who say they saw us go out tell the truth.

"But we came back. It was my intention to take an afternoon train, but I decided to wait.

"So we came back and had dinner. Nobody saw us go in or out of the flat.

"After dinner we walked to the depot, and I took the eight-ten train for my home in Maysville, ten miles from Albany.

"I arrived in Albany Wednesday morning, and remained there with friends throughout the day and night. Then I went to Maysville, where I heard the news, and came back at once."

The superintendent touched his bell. Two minutes later John Jones was brought into the room.

"Amy!" exclaimed he. "How came you here?"

He ran up to her, and they greeted each other affectionately. The woman, who had controlled herself up to this point, burst into tears. Jones turned in wrath toward Nick.

"Haven't we had enough of this infernal nonsense?" he exclaimed. "You have raised the devil with my business and scared my wife into a fit. Now let me out, and arrest the Ameer of Afghanistan. He had more to do with this affair than I did."

Nick did not reply, but he made a secret sign to the superintendent.

"You are at liberty, Mr. Jones," said Byrnes, calmly. "I regret that it was necessary to detain you so long."

"I have no complaint to make against you," said Jones. "It was that man's work, and he shall pay for it."

He scowled at Nick, and then, after bowing to the superintendent, walked out of the room with his wife on his arm.

"Shall I call a man?" asked Byrnes.

"If you please," said Nick. "My force is pretty busy."

"Musgrave!" said the superintendent.

A man appeared so suddenly that he seemed to come out of the wall.

"Shadow the couple that has just left here," said Byrnes. "You are under Mr. Carter's orders until dismissed by him."

Musgrave turned to Nick.

"I have no special instructions," said Nick, "except that you keep your eyes on the woman."

The officer saluted, and vanished almost as quickly as he had come in.

At half-past seven o'clock that evening Musgrave was on guard outside the flat, the address of which had been given to Nick by Jones.

An old man selling papers came along the street, calling "Extra!" in a cracked voice.

Musgrave bought a paper.

"Well," said the newsman, in Nick Carter's voice, "what have you to report?"

"From headquarters they went to an employment agency on Sixth avenue. They engaged a colored girl as a servant.

"They then came straight here, and the girl followed them. Mr. and Mrs. Jones have not been out since."

"Are you sure of that?"

"Perfectly. There is no way to get out of that house from the rear."

"How about the fire-escape?"

"There is only that one on the side which you can see. The little yard back of the house is walled in by buildings."

"So Mr. and Mrs. Jones must be inside?"

"Yes."

"And the girl?"

"She is out. She has been going on errands half a dozen times, but usually to the grocer's or the butcher's around the corner. I don't know where she has gone this time. She's been out about a quarter of an hour."

"All right. I'm going over there."

Nick changed his disguise to that in which Jones had seen him. He did it in the hall of the flat house, while waiting for the door to be opened in answer to his ring.

Jones met him on the upper landing.

"Look here," said Jones, when he recognized Nick, "isn't this going a little too far? What do you want now?"

"I would like to ask Mrs. Jones a few questions if you have no objections."

"I object very seriously."

"Will you ask her if she is willing to see me?"

"No; I won't."

"Then I shall have to use my authority."

"Don't do that. Come now, be a good fellow. Amy is sick with all this worry. She's just gone to bed. Let her alone until to-morrow."

"I will," said Nick. "Good-night."

He descended the stairs and rejoined Musgrave, who was standing in a dark place on the opposite side of the street.

"Have you seen a light in that window?" asked Nick, pointing to the flat.

"No."

"Then Jones lied to me a minute ago when he said that his wife had just gone to bed. That window is in the principal bedroom of the flat."

"There's been no light there."

"Then they've fooled you, Musgrave."

"What do you mean?"

"I mean that Mrs. Jones is out."

"It can't be possible."

"It's true. She's gone out disguised as her own servant."

"I can't believe it. Why, the girl's black as your hat."

"That's why they engaged her, in my opinion. It made the trick easier. A black face is a good disguise. But I'm going to be sure about it."

"How?"

"I'm going to see whether the colored girl is in the flat."

"How can you get in?"

"I'm going down the air shaft. The servant's room opens on that shaft. They'll have made her go in there so that her light won't show, as it would if she were in the kitchen."

Nick went to an engine-house near by, where he secured a coil of knotted rope.

He wished to make his investigations secretly, so as not to put Jones on his guard. It would not have been safe to get into the flat by the ordinary methods.

By using the fire escape of the building next door to the flat house, Nick got to the roof.

The top of the air shaft was covered with a framework, in which large panes of glass were set.

Nick removed one of them. Then he made his rope fast, and crept through the space where the glass had been.

The Jones' flat was next to the top, so Nick had a short descent.

But there was an awful stretch of empty air under him as he hung there.

The shaft went to the basement floor, about seventy feet below the level of the window which opened into the room occupied by the Jones' new servant.

He found that window readily. One glance through it was enough to satisfy him.

There sat the colored girl, reading a book. Nick's suspicions had been correct.

Naturally he did not delay very long in the air shaft. He had a hard climb to make, hand over hand, to the roof.

The instant that his eyes rested on the girl, he began the ascent.

He had gone up less than six feet when the rope suddenly gave way, and he found himself plunging downward through the shaft.

### Chapter VII. The Wardrobe Of Gaspard's Friend.

Nick Carter is hard to kill. A good many crooks have tried to put him out of the world, and a fair percentage of them have lost their own lives in the attempt without inflicting any injury upon Nick.

He is a man of resources, and that's what saves him. When one thing fails him, he finds something else to take its place.

And so, when that rope gave way, he took the next best thing.

That happened to be the sill of the window of Mr. Jones' bath-room. Nick seized it with a grip of iron as he shot downward.

The strain on his arms was something awful, but he held on. His fingers gripped the wood till they dented it.

In two seconds he had scrambled through the window into Jones' flat.

It was done so noiselessly that the colored servant in the room directly opposite, across the narrow shaft, was not disturbed in her reading.

From the bath-room Nick made his way to the hall, and thence to the parlor, where Mr. Jones—to judge by the light in the window observed by Musgrave—had decided to spend the evening.

Mr. Jones was not visible when Nick looked into the room.

The bedroom adjoining was also empty.

Nick ran through the flat, but saw nobody. He returned to the parlor, and there stood Mr. Jones under the chandelier.

"Well, upon my word!" exclaimed Jones, "how did you get here?"

"I might ask you the same," said Nick, "but it isn't worth while."

"I've been here all the time."

"Except when you were on the roof."

"Nonsense! What should I be doing on the roof."

"It wasn't what you were doing; it was what you were undoing that bothered me. You were undoing the knot with which I fastened my rope before I descended your air shaft to get a peep at your servant."

"Nonsense again, Mr. Carter. How could I get to the roof?"

"I'll show you just how it was done. In the first place, you saw me coming back to the house, and you guessed what I was going to do.

"You went into this room," and Nick dragged Jones into a sort of closet adjoining the parlor, "and you got out of that window onto the fire escape.

"That led you to the roof, and the rest was simple. You saw me go down, and you tried to make me go down farther and a good deal faster. But you failed, and the game's up. Now come to headquarters again."

"What for?"

"For trying to kill me. That's the charge against you. And I haven't got through with you on that other matter."

"But for heaven's sake pity my wife!"

"What's the matter with her?"

"She will be crazy when she gets back and finds me gone."

"One of my men will tell her where you are. Why did you lie to me about her going out? I've a great mind to place her, too, under arrest."

"You can't do it. It's no crime to dodge a detective. I admit that she did it, but for a very innocent purpose. She has gone to see our lawyer."

"Very well; I will attend to that later. Now, come with me."

Nick took Jones to the street. Musgrave got a policeman, and Jones was put in his care.

Musgrave remained on the watch for Mrs. Jones, while Nick went to get a report from Patsy, who was shadowing Gaspard.

Jones' last words to Nick were these:

"I am a victim of circumstances. I had nothing to do with the murder in the restaurant, nor with any attempt upon your life.

You are doing me a grave injustice. If you were not as blind as a bat you would see who the real criminals are."

These words were pronounced in a calm and steady tone, and it cannot be denied that they produced a great effect upon Nick.

"If it should prove that I have wronged you," he said, "I will repay you for the injury to the limit of your demand."

And the detective did a lot of hard thinking while he was walking toward Gaspard's lodgings, where he expected to meet Patsy.

Certainly if Jones ever succeeded in establishing his innocence he would have won a friend in Nick Carter, whose good will is worth a fortune to any man.

Nick found Patsy outside the house where Gaspard lodged.

"I'm dead onto this fellow," said the youth. "He's just about ready to flit. He's bought lots of stuff to-day, and is flush with money.

"A man just went in there with a suit of clothes. Two delivery wagons from dry goods stores have been here. I suppose that the stuff they brought belongs to the woman who is going with Gaspard."

"Have you seen her?"

"No; she has kept mighty dark."

"Hello! what's this?"

Nick drew Patsy more closely into the shadow of the steps by which they were standing.

A carriage rumbled over the pavement and stopped before the door of Gaspard's lodging-house.

"Upon my word," said Nick, "it's my old friend Harrigan on the box. The way people keep bobbing up in this case is something wonderful."

"Perhaps the woman's in the cab," whispered Patsy.

On the contrary, the cab was empty.

Harrigan got off the box and rang the bell.

Nick heard him ask for Gaspard Lebeau. Gaspard was summoned.

"I've two trunks for you," said Harrigan.

"For me?" asked Gaspard.

"Yes; a young woman hired me to bring them, and she said it would be all right. You'd pay the price."

"What sort of a woman?"

"A very gallus French siren with a big white hat and a black plume as long as the tail of me horse."

"All right," said Gaspard, promptly; "bring in the trunks."

They were carried up the stairs to Gaspard's room.

Harrigan mounted the box and drove away.

"Follow him," said Nick. "Bring him back here in about half an hour."

Patsy darted away in pursuit of the cab.

Nick walked up to the door of Gaspard's house and rang the bell.

He was directed to the Frenchman's room.

Gaspard was examining the two trunks. He looked very much embarrassed at the sight of Nick.

"What's all this, Gaspard?" asked the detective. "I hear you're going back to France."

"I? Oh, no. New York suits me much better."

"But what are these trunks doing here?"

Gaspard looked particularly foolish.

"They are the property of a friend—a lady. To tell the truth, I hope to marry her. A charming girl, monsieur; and innocent as a dove."

"Why does she send her trunks here?"

"Ah, that I do not know. It was not agreed upon."

"Have you any idea what is in them?"

"Her wardrobe. Ah, she is extravagant. She buys many dresses. But then, what would you have? When one is young and beautiful—"

Gaspard finished his sentence with a sweep of the arms.

"They are heavy," said Nick, lifting one of the trunks and setting it crosswise on a lounge.

He took a bunch of keys from his pocket. Gaspard seemed aghast.

"You would not open it?" he cried.

"Perhaps it won't be necessary," said Nick. "This may answer."

He drew a knife from his pocket and opened one of the blades, which was sharpened like a very large nut-pick.

With a sudden movement, he struck this into the bottom of the trunk, and then withdrew it.

A dark red stream followed the blade when it was withdrawn. The end of the trunk projected over the side of the couch, and the red fluid dripped upon the carpet.

"My God!" exclaimed Gaspard. "It is blood!"

"So it would seem," said Nick, quietly.

He set the trunk upon the floor and snapped back the lock with a skeleton key.

Then he threw open the lid and revealed a mass of excelsior and scraps of newspapers.

This being torn away disclosed a dead and ghastly face—the face of unfortunate Corbut, the waiter.

## Chapter VIII. Tracing The Trunks.

Corbut's body had been cut in two. Only half was in the trunk which Nick had opened.

The other half was not, however, far away. It was in the other trunk.

Both trunks contained considerable blood, but they had been neatly lined with rubber cloth, apparently taken from a rubber blanket and a man's heavy waterproof coat.

It was so fitted that the trunks, when closed, were water-tight.

"The neatest job I ever saw," said Nick. "Come, Gaspard, tell the story."

"I swear to you," cried Gaspard, "that I know nothing about it."

At this moment Patsy rapped on the door. He had brought back Harrigan.

"Come in!" said Nick; and they both entered.

"Holy mother!" shrieked Harrigan, when he saw the open trunks. "So help me, gentlemen, I don't know nothing about this business. I ain't in it. I'm tellin' yer straight. Youse don't believe I had anything to do wid this, do yer?"

"You brought the trunks here," said Nick.

"Lemme tell youse all about it," cried Harrigan, who was so anxious to tell that he couldn't talk fast enough. "De French leddy struck me on me old place. You know. Where I was de odder night.

"She talked a kind o' dago, but I tumbled to what she was a-givin' me. This was about half-past seven o'clock.

"'Meet me,' says she, 'in an hour.' An' she give me street an' number.

"It was West Fifty-seventh street; but dere ain't no such number. Dere's nuttin' but a high board fence.

"But that didn't make no difference, 'cause when I got dere, her jiblets was a-standing on der sidewalk, waitin' for me.

"'Drive over ter de corner,' says she, 'and' turn round an' come back.'

"I did it, an' when I got dare, she showed me dese two trunks. I hadn't seen 'em before.

"Den she give me dis mug's address, an' two bones for me fare, an' tole me ter come down here, which I did, an' I wish ter —— I hadn't; see?"

"That's a pretty good story, Harrigan," said Nick. "Patsy, get a policeman to stay here with Gaspard."

Patsy brought the blue-coat in a few minutes.

"Now, we'll go up to Fifty-seventh street," said Nick.

Half an hour later they had found the place where, as Harrigan claimed, "de French leddy" had delivered the trunks to him.

"I t'ought o' course she'd been fired out o' some boardin'-house," said Harrigan. "Dere's a hash-mill dere on der right. I had an idea she'd been trun out o' dere."

Nick meanwhile had been examining the sidewalk with the aid of his dark lantern.

"Clever work," he said. "There are no marks on the sidewalk. The trunks were not dragged. That woman must be pretty strong. You say you didn't see the trunks when you first drove up?"

"No."

"Then they couldn't have been here. Where were they? Not in any of these houses. She couldn't have got them out quick enough. Then they must have been behind that fence."

There was a little gate in the fence, which Nick opened as he spoke.

"Ah, here we have tracks," he said. "It's all clear enough now. The trunks were brought across this vacant lot from one of the houses facing the other street."

The lot is the width of three flat houses, which stand behind it. There are no gates in the fence between the yards of the houses and the lot, but Nick found a wide board that could be pulled off and replaced without much trouble.

Passing through the opening made by taking away this board, he found himself in the yard of the middle house.

"The trunks came from here," he said. "They were lowered down in the dumb waiter to the cellar and then carried through the lot to Fifty-seventh street.

"I'll leave the rest of this job to you, Patsy. Find out all you can and have as many witnesses as you can get together, at the superintendent's office to-morrow afternoon, at three o'clock. We're going to have a special examination into this case."

The special examination began promptly at the hour named by Nick.

All the persons hitherto mentioned in connection with the case—except, of course, the two victims—were present. There were also several witnesses whom Patsy had secured.

"The case which I have made out," said Nick, "is perfectly clear. It begins with Gaspard's identification of the prisoner, Jones.

"We know that he was at the restaurant when the crime was committed. His name is on the books.

"In some way, which I am not now prepared to fully explain, the waiter, Corbut, obtained a knowledge of the crime. It was necessary for the criminal to get Corbut out of the way.

"I saw Corbut get into a cab at the door of the restaurant. The driver, Harrigan, testified to taking him and another man to a point on West Fifty-seventh street. He was not sure of the exact spot, but he fixed the locality in a general way.

"From that point all trace of Corbut was lost for a time. At last his body was found.

"I succeeded in tracing the body back to a place near the spot where Harrigan last saw Corbut alive.

"I discovered that the body had been removed from a flat house on West Fifty-eighth street.

"My assistant, Patsy, questioned the people in that house. He learned that the third flat had been occupied by a couple who lived very quietly.

"The man was often away. I now desire to ask the witness, Eliza Harris, who lives in that house, when she last saw the man in question—the man who rented that third flat."

A bright-eyed little woman arose at this, and said:

"I see him now. There he is!"

She pointed to John Jones.

"He wore a false beard," she continued, "but I know him. And there's the woman."

She stretched out her hand toward Mrs. Jones.

"To their flat," Nick continued, "as I have every reason to believe, Corbut was taken by Jones on that night, and there he was murdered and his body cut in two.

"It was placed in the trunks. Jones intended, probably, to remove it next day, but his arrest prevented.

"Of course it was necessary to get the body out of the way very soon. But Jones was too closely watched. That work had to be done by the woman, and she did it exceedingly well."

Nick told how Musgrave had been duped.

"Now," he continued, "nothing remains but to clear up the details of the crime in the restaurant. I shall proceed to state exactly how it was done."

At this moment Jones, who had previously remained perfectly calm, uttered a horrible groan, and half arose to his feet. He sank back fainting.

And then came a surprising incident, for which even the shrewd superintendent of police had been wholly unprepared.

A pale-faced man, who had been sitting beside Nick, arose and cried, in a voice that trembled with emotion:

"Stop! Stop! I can bear this no longer!"

It was Hammond, the man who begged Nick to save Jones.

While Nick had been speaking, Hammond's eyes had been fixed upon Jones' face. He had watched the agony of fear growing upon the wretched man and gradually overcoming him.

And when the burden became too great for the accused to bear, Hammond also reached the limit of his endurance.

"I can't stand it," he cried. "You shall not torture this innocent man any longer."

"What do you mean?" asked the superintendent.

"This is what I mean. The fear of disgrace has kept me silent too long. Now I will confess everything. Do you think I will sit here and let an innocent man be condemned and his wife put to torture to save me from the just punishment of my fault?

"Never! Listen to me. It was I who took that unhappy woman to the place where she met her death. It was I who wrote that name in the register.

"I! I, and not that innocent man, was her companion. The waiter, Gaspard, is mistaken.

"I am the man who was in room B!"

## Chapter IX. Hammond's Story.

The effect of this statement can hardly be exaggerated.

It shook the very foundation of the case against the prisoner. If Gaspard's identification could be disproved, it seemed almost sure that Jones was saved.

Even though it could be shown beyond a doubt that Corbut had been murdered in a flat which was rented by Jones, that would not prove that Jones had done it.

The murderer was evidently the man who had ridden in the cab with Corbut. And Harrigan, the only witness, had failed to recognize Jones as that man.

The suspicion must instantly arise that a plot had been carefully laid, with the purpose of putting the crime upon Jones.

Some enemy had signed his name on the register, and the same cruel wretch had decoyed Corbut to the vacant flat and murdered him there. It was easy to suppose that the criminal knew the flat to be empty and had obtained a key.

It might have been by this secret enemy's connivance that the trunks were removed and sent to Gaspard.

But if Hammond was the wretch who had done all this, why had he confessed?

All these and many other thoughts must have rushed through the mind of the superintendent, in the pause which followed Hammond's declaration.

Byrnes looked at Nick for an explanation.

"This is an extraordinary statement, Mr. Hammond," said Nick. "Have you any evidence to support it?"

"I have ample evidence. I was seen in the company of the woman now dead, not fifty yards from the restaurant on the night when she met her death. I can call one of the most prominent and respected men in this city to prove that. The Rev. Elliot Sandford is the man."

This name produced a great impression.

"Why has he kept silence?" asked Nick.

"He promised me that he would do so as long as his conscience would permit. I called upon him on the morning after the crime.

"He believed me when I asserted my innocence. He agreed to be silent for the sake of my family."

"But who is the dead woman?" asked Nick.

"I have not the least idea."

"You did not know her!"

"No. Let me tell the full story. It was a chance acquaintance. I met her on the street that afternoon.

"I was walking behind her on Twenty-third street. You know what wonderful hair she had. I was admiring it.

"Suddenly I saw her drop a little purse. I picked it up and handed it to her, and somehow we fell into conversation.

"Her manner mystified me. Sometimes she seemed to be laboring under some secret grief which nearly drove her to tears. In another moment she would be apparently as merry as a schoolgirl.

"She showed no reserve whatever, but something in her manner warned me that she was a lady, and I did not presume upon her confidence.

"We walked together a long while, and at last we found ourselves near that restaurant. How we came there I do not know. I paid no attention to where we were going. T was too much fascinated by my companion.

"Suddenly she said: 'It is late and I am hungry. Let us go to dinner.'

"I thought it a strange thing to say, but I was glad enough to comply. We went into that restaurant because it was right before us.

"I signed the first name that came into my head, and then Corbut showed us into the private dining-room.

"I ordered a dinner, but before it was served, I began to be a good deal surprised at my companion's behavior. She paced up and down the room, and every now and then she listened at the door which was between us and room A.

"'I have all a woman's curiosity,' she said, 'I'd like to hear what those people are saying over their dinner.'

"I tried to make her sit down, and playfully took hold of her. Then I made a discovery which frightened me.

"The woman had a pistol in her pocket.

"Suddenly she turned upon me and exclaimed:

"'What shall we do after dinner? I'll tell you what I'd like. I want to go to the theater. Let's see something real funny. Yes, I must go. You run out now and get the tickets. There's a place just down the street where they're sold. You can get back before your dinner is cold.'

"Of course, it was perfectly plain that she was trying to get rid of me. Well, I had no objection. That pistol had scared me badly. I didn't want to be mixed up in a scandal.

"So I took my hat and cleared out. But once on the street, my courage came back, and also my curiosity. I wanted to know more of that strange woman.

"I bought the theater tickets and hurried back. I opened the door of room B.

"You know what I saw. She sat there dead, with the pistol by her side. She had committed suicide.

"I rushed out with the intention of calling for help, but fear overcame me. I looked around into the hall. This man Gaspard was at the desk.

"I dared not summon him. I turned and ran."

Hammond ceased, and a sigh ran around the room. Nick could read relief in all the faces. The mystery was solved. The innocent man was no longer to suffer under unjust suspicion.

That was what could be seen in the faces. Hammond's words had the ring of truth. Neither the superintendent nor Nick nor any other person there doubted a single statement of his story.

"When Gaspard identified me as the man in room A," Hammond continued, "I thought I saw a chance to save Mr. Jones very easily, and so I told a falsehood."

"It was a foolish thing to do," said Nick. "The truth is always best. If we had known at the outset what we know now, Mr. Jones might have been spared a great deal of trouble. Since the woman committed suicide—"

"Hold on!" cried the superintendent. "How do you account for the murder of Corbut?"

"He must have found the body and robbed it. Probably he took some money and a diamond ring. There was the mark of a ring on her finger, but the ring was gone.

"Corbut fled with these things. He engaged Harrigan's cab. He was decoyed to that flat by some woman, probably, who knew that nobody was in it, and was there murdered.

"Of course, neither Mr. nor Mrs. Jones had anything to do with it. Now, if Mr. Jones would only explain how he happened to be at that restaurant, the case would be clear. We know positively that he was there."

A great light of hope had shone in Jones' face while Hammond was telling his story, and when Nick added his explanation of Corbut's death, the prisoner nearly laughed for joy.

"It's true I was there," he said. "My wife and I dined in room A, and—"

"Fool!" exclaimed the woman, in a terrible voice. "Don't you see that this is a trap?"

In her wild excitement, she covered Jones' mouth with her hand to prevent his speaking further.

"That is true," said Nick. "It was a trap, and the wretch has fallen into it. Jones, you have put the halter around your neck."

"No! It is a lie!" exclaimed Jones, freeing himself from the woman's grasp. "I tell you that I was in room A. The crime, if there was a crime, was committed in room B."

"No, it wasn't," said Nick. "It was committed in room A."

## Chapter X. The True Story Of Mrs. John Jones.

Jones fell back into his chair. The woman bit her lip till the blood spurted out.

Then suddenly the color left her face. She sat up, staring straight before her, and she did not move during the explanation which Nick gave.

While he was speaking, the detective watched her narrowly. Certainly she was meditating some remarkable action. He wondered what it could be.

"Yes," said Nick, turning to the superintendent, "we have at last straightened out the matter of those two rooms and their occupants.

"As to the spot where the crime was committed, I have not been in doubt from the first.

"You will remember that the fatal wound was visible on both the woman's temples. The bullet passed entirely through her head.

"But where was the bullet? That was the question which I asked myself at once.

"I could not find it in room B, where the body lay. Then I tried room A, with no better success.

"At this point Chick took up the hunt, and carried it to the end. The bullet was in neither room. It was just between them.

"You remember that there was a door which I found fastened upon both sides.

"Chick opened that door, and in its framework, the wood of which was old and soft, he found the bullet.

"The mark was covered when the door was shut. Therefore the door must have been open when the shot was fired.

"The position of the bullet shows that the shot was fired from room A. Then the woman, for some reason, had got into that room. She had unlocked the door on her side and had managed to induce the persons on the other side to slip their bolt.

"Now, why did she do this? Of course there is only one answer. Jealousy was her motive. The man in room A was her husband.

"I have satisfied myself of that. She must have known that he was going to dine in that house with another woman.

"It is clear that she made the acquaintance of Hammond because she was determined to get into that restaurant, and women are not admitted alone.

"The dropping of the purse was, of course, a very simple trick. She had noticed Hammond behind her, and as he was evidently a gentleman, she decided to use him for her purpose.

"You have heard how she led him to the restaurant. Of course it was only by chance that they got the room next to that in which her husband was.

"Hammond has told how she listened to the voices, and how she got rid of him.

"What followed can be easily understood. She got into room A. She drew her pistol and attempted to shoot either her faithless husband or his companion.

"Jones disarmed her and shot her with her own pistol.

"Then he carried her into room B, and put her in that chair.

"At that moment Corbut entered, for the door of room B was not locked.

"In some way they bribed him to keep silence. They sent him into room A, where he locked the connecting door on that side.

"Jones fastened it on the side of room B and fled. It was then that Gaspard saw him coming out of room B. And that's what mixed the case so badly.

"It gave us the wrong arrangement of men in those rooms. That was the only reason why I ever doubted Jones' guilt. I was convinced that the man who had brought the woman to the house was not the man who had shot her.

"You did not know, Mr. Hammond, that when you told me, in my house, that you were the man in room A, that you practically confessed to being the murderer."

At these words, Hammond gave a dry and painful gasp. He saw what an escape he had had.

"As to the two women," Nick continued, "it is easy to read the secret.

"Jones had two wives. The real wife, now dead, lived in the flat the address of which Jones gave me. This woman lived in the Fifty-eighth street flat, where Corbut was murdered.

"Jones divided his time between them. He really loved this one and wished to be rid of the other.

"His true wife surprised his secret at last, and it led her to her death.

"That night after the murder the plan was formed by which this woman was to personate the other. The striking similarity in the hair, which was the most conspicuous beauty of each, suggested the plot.

"Perhaps Jones had thought of such a thing long before. That may have led him to keep his real wife practically unknown in this city, while he was frequently seen with this woman.

"As to the dresses, this woman, who is a very clever dressmaker, as I am told, doubtless had time to copy the other's costume in the night and the day following the crime.

"She did most of the work in Albany, where she went as soon as possible. Then wearing the duplicate dress, she went to her friends in Maysville, and afterward came here.

"Is it all plain now?"

"It is clear as a bell, Mr. Carter," said the superintendent.

"Wait a moment!"

It was the woman's voice. She spoke calmly, and looked straight into Nick's face.

"You have made one grave error," she said. "It was not John who killed that woman; it was I.

"She tried to shoot him, and I wrenched the pistol from her hand. I shot her dead.

"The plot was all mine. It was I who bribed Corbut. It was I who killed him.

"John brought him to our flat. I sent my husband away, and when he returned a few minutes later, Corbut was dead. John had no guilty hand in either crime.

"He fainted at the sight of Corbut's body. When he came to himself, the body was no longer to be seen. I had put it into the trunks. It was I who afterward sent them to Gaspard.

"These crimes I committed for love of this man. I had been his wife for five years, and for three of them I did not know he had another.

"And when I found it out, I did not do as this woman did. I simply loved him more.

"I love him still, and because I love him I tell the truth to save him. Yes, more, because I love him, I will shed more blood. He shall not see me imprisoned or condemned to death. I will spare him that pain."

As she spoke, she drew a little ornamental dagger from her dress. It was a mere toy. Nobody would have supposed it to be a deadly weapon.

However, Nick sprang forward to prevent her from doing herself an injury.

He was too late. She plunged the dagger into her brain.

So firm and true was her hand that the slender blade pierced the thin bone of her right temple, and was driven in until the hilt made an impression on her white skin like a seal upon wax.

Jones uttered a scream of horror at this sight. He, too, had attempted to stay her hand, but had been too slow.

As she fell, he plucked the dagger from the wound and attempted to drive it into his own brain. But Nick caught his arm and wrested the blood-stained weapon from him.

Deprived thus of the means for ending his life, Jones fell upon his knees before the woman and covered her hands with kisses, nor could he be taken away, until the hands were chilled by death.

And that was the strange end of the affair. The woman's confession, though it may not have been true, will doubtless save Jones' life.

At the time of this writing the district attorney is of the opinion that a plea of murder in the second degree had better be accepted. There is no indication that the prisoner will fight the case.

So Jones will spend his days in prison, though he will escape the death chair.

A word should be added about the witness, Gaspard. He has been cleared of all reproach, and has sailed for France with his bride.

# THE MAN WITH THE
# NAILED SHOES
## BY R. AUSTIN FREEMAN

R. Austin Freeman

## ORIGINALLY PUBLISHED IN 1909

# THE MAN WITH THE NAILED SHOES

### BY R. AUSTIN FREEMAN

Long before such television shows as "Bones", "CSI" and "Quincy, M.E." there was Dr. John Thorndyke. Thorndyke is both a medical doctor and a barrister. In addition, he is a lecturer in Medical Jurisprudence at the medical school of St. Margaret's Hospital. Unlike most of the fictional detectives of the era, he solves his cases not with a superior intellect, though he is certainly brilliant in his field, but through the application of science, science that is thoroughly grounded in reality.

Thorndyke's creator, R. Austin Freeman, was himself a doctor, and was familiar with the latest scientific techniques. It is said that he never included anything in his books unless he, himself, had performed the experiment. This attention to detail makes the science in the stories seem much more modern than it actually is, and the reader must remind himself that these stories were actually written beginning in the early 1900's.

Thorndyke first appeared in the novel *The Red Thumbmark* which centers on the doctor refuting the evidence of a fingerprint found at a crime scene to prove the innocence of his client. Later adventures involve such forensic staples as plaster casts of footprints, racial analysis of hairs, the identification of microorganisms to trace the origins of sand, and chemical analysis of dust to determine a person's occupation. Much of the work centers about establishing the identities of bodies or arriving at the time of death. Thorndyke continued his work for nearly forty years in short stories and novels, with parts of the last novel being written in a bomb shelter during World War II.

"The Man With Nailed Boots" appears in the collection John Thorndyke's Cases. As in all of the Thorndyke stories, it is told from the viewpoint of another person, in this case, Dr. Jervis, a one time medical student of Thorndyke's who was to become a lifelong assistant to the doctor.

More adventures featuring Dr. Thorndyke may be found in the collections *John Thorndyke's Cases* and *The Singing Bone* and in the novels *The Red Thumbmark, The Eye of Osiris, The Mystery of 31 New Inn, A Silent Witness, A Cat's Eye* and *Helen Vardon's Confession.*

# THE MAN WITH THE NAILED SHOES

There are, I suppose, few places even on the East Coast of England more lonely and remote than the village of Little Sundersley and the country that surrounds it. Far from any railway, and some miles distant from any considerable town, it remains an outpost of civilization, in which primitive manners and customs and old-world tradition linger on into an age that has elsewhere forgotten them. In the summer, it is true, a small contingent of visitors, adventurous in spirit, though mostly of sedate and solitary habits, make their appearance to swell its meagre population, and impart to the wide stretches of smooth sand that fringe its shores a fleeting air of life and sober gaiety; but in late September—the season of the year in which I made its acquaintance—its pasture-lands lie desolate, the rugged paths along the cliffs are seldom trodden by human foot, and the sands are a desert waste on which, for days together, no footprint appears save that left by some passing sea-bird.

I had been assured by my medical agent, Mr. Turcival, that I should find the practice of which I was now taking charge 'an exceedingly soft billet, and suitable for a studious man;' and certainly he had not misled me, for the patients were, in fact, so few that I was quite concerned for my principal, and rather dull for want of work. Hence, when my friend John Thorndyke, the well-known medico-legal expert, proposed to come down and stay with me for a weekend and perhaps a few days beyond, I hailed the proposal with delight, and welcomed him with open arms.

"You certainly don't seem to be overworked, Jervis," he remarked, as we turned out of the gate after tea, on the day of his arrival, for a stroll on the shore. "Is this a new practice, or an old one in a state of senile decay?"

"Why, the fact is," I answered, "there is virtually no practice. Cooper—my principal—has been here about six years, and as he has private means he has never made any serious effort to build one up; and the other man, Dr. Burrows, being uncommonly keen, and the people very conservative, Cooper has never really got his foot in. However, it doesn't seem to trouble him."

"Well, if he is satisfied, I suppose you are," said Thorndyke, with a smile. "You are getting a seaside holiday, and being paid for it. But I didn't know you were as near to the sea as this."

We were entering, as he spoke, an artificial gap-way cut through the low cliff, forming a steep cart-track down to the shore. It was locally known as Sundersley Gap, and was used principally, when used at all, by the farmers' carts which came down to gather seaweed after a gale.

"What a magnificent stretch of sand!" continued Thorndyke, as we reached the bottom, and stood looking out seaward across the deserted beach. "There is something very majestic and solemn in a great expanse of sandy shore when the tide is out, and I know of nothing which is capable of conveying the impression of solitude so completely. The smooth, unbroken surface not only displays itself untenanted for the moment, but it offers convincing testimony that it has lain thus undisturbed through a considerable lapse of time. Here, for instance, we have clear evidence that for several days only two pairs of feet besides our own have trodden this gap."

"How do you arrive at the 'several days'?" I asked.

"In the simplest manner possible," he replied. "The moon is now in the third quarter, and the tides are consequently neap-tides. You can see quite plainly the two lines of seaweed and jetsam which indicate the high-water marks of the spring-tides and the neap-tides respectively. The strip of comparatively dry sand between them, over which the water has not risen for several days, is, as you see, marked by only two sets of footprints, and those footprints will not be completely obliterated by the sea until the next spring-tide—nearly a week from to-day."

"Yes, I see now, and the thing appears obvious enough when one has heard the explanation. But it is really rather odd that no one should have passed through this gap for days, and then that four persons should have come here within quite a short interval of one another."

"What makes you think they have done so?" Thorndyke asked.

"Well," I replied, "both of these sets of footprints appear to be quite fresh, and to have been made about the same time."

"Not at the same time, Jervis," rejoined Thorndyke. "There is certainly an interval of several hours between them, though precisely how many hours we cannot judge, since there has been so little wind lately to disturb them; but the fisherman unquestionably passed here not more than three hours ago, and I should say probably within an hour; whereas the other man—who seems to have come up from a boat to fetch something of considerable weight—returned through the gap certainly not less, and probably more, than four hours ago."

I gazed at my friend in blank astonishment, for these events befell in the days before I had joined him as his assistant, and his special knowledge and powers of inference were not then fully appreciated by me.

"It is clear, Thorndyke," I said, "that footprints have a very different meaning to you from what they have for me. I don't see in the least how you have reached any of these conclusions."

"I suppose not," was the reply; "but, you see, special knowledge of this kind is the stock-in-trade of the medical jurist, and has to be acquired by special study, though the present example is one of the greatest simplicity. But let us consider it point by point; and first we will take this set of footprints which I have inferred to be a fisherman's. Note their enormous size. They should be the footprints of a giant. But the length of the stride shows that they were made by a rather short man. Then observe the massiveness of the soles, and the fact that there are no nails in them. Note also the peculiar clumsy tread—the deep toe and heel marks, as if the walker had wooden legs, or fixed ankles and knees. From that character we can safely infer high boots of thick, rigid leather, so that we can diagnose high boots, massive and stiff, with nailless soles, and many sizes too large for the wearer. But the only boot that answers this description is the fisherman's thigh-boot—made of enormous size to enable him to wear in the winter two or three pairs of thick knitted stockings, one over the other. Now look at the other footprints; there is a double track, you see, one set coming from the sea and one going towards it. As the man (who was bow-legged and turned his toes in) has trodden in his own footprints, it is obvious that he came from the sea, and returned to it. But observe the difference in the two sets of prints; the returning ones are much deeper than the others, and the stride much shorter. Evidently he was carrying something when he returned, and that something was very heavy. Moreover, we can see, by the greater depth of the toe impressions, that he was stooping forward as he walked, and so probably carried the weight on his back. Is that quite clear?"

"Perfectly," I replied. "But how do you arrive at the interval of time between the visits of the two men?"

"That also is quite simple. The tide is now about halfway out; it is thus about three hours since high water. Now, the fisherman walked just about the neap-tide, high-water mark, sometimes above it and sometimes below. But none of his footprints have been obliterated; therefore he passed after high water—that is, less than three hours ago; and since his footprints are all equally distinct, he could not have passed when the sand was very wet. Therefore he probably passed less than an hour ago. The other man's footprints, on the other hand, reach only to the neap-tide, high-water mark, where they end abruptly. The sea has washed over the remainder of the tracks and obliterated them. Therefore he passed not less than three hours and not more than four days ago—probably within twenty-four hours."

As Thorndyke concluded his demonstration the sound of voices was borne to us from above, mingled with the tramping of feet, and immediately afterwards a very singular party appeared at the head of the gap descending towards the shore. First came a short burly fisherman clad in oilskins and sou'-wester, clumping along awkwardly in his great sea-boots, then the local police-sergeant in company with my professional rival Dr. Burrows, while the rear of the procession was brought up by two constables carrying a stretcher. As he reached the bottom of the gap the fisherman, who was evidently acting as guide, turned along the shore, retracing his own tracks, and the procession followed in his wake.

"A surgeon, a stretcher, two constables, and a police-sergeant," observed Thorndyke. "What does that suggest to your mind, Jervis?"

"A fall from the cliff," I replied, "or a body washed up on the shore."

"Probably," he rejoined; "but we may as well walk in that direction."

We turned to follow the retreating procession, and as we strode along the smooth surface left by the retiring tide Thorndyke resumed: "The subject of footprints has always interested me deeply for two reasons. First, the evidence furnished by footprints is constantly being brought forward, and is often of cardinal importance; and, secondly, the whole subject is capable of really systematic and scientific treatment. In the main the data are anatomical, but age, sex, occupation, health, and disease all give their various indications. Clearly, for instance, the footprints of an old man will differ from those of a young man of the same height, and I need not point out to you that those of a person suffering from locomotor ataxia or paralysis agitans would be quite unmistakable."

"Yes, I see that plainly enough," I said.

"Here, now," he continued, "is a case in point." He halted to point with his stick at a row of footprints that appeared suddenly above high-water mark, and having proceeded a short distance, crossed the line again, and vanished where the waves had washed over them. They were easily distinguished from any of the others by the clear impressions of circular rubber heels.

"Do you see anything remarkable about them?" he asked.

"I notice that they are considerably deeper than our own," I answered.

"Yes, and the boots are about the same size as ours, whereas the stride is considerably shorter—quite a short stride, in fact. Now there is a pretty constant ratio between the length of the foot and the length of the leg, between the length of leg and the height of the person, and between the stature and the length of stride. A long foot means a long leg, a tall man, and a long stride. But here we have a long foot and a short stride. What do you make of that?" He laid down his stick—a smooth partridge cane, one side of which was marked by small lines into inches and feet—beside the footprints to demonstrate the discrepancy.

"The depth of the footprints shows that he was a much heavier man than either of us," I suggested; "perhaps he was unusually fat."

"Yes," said Thorndyke, "that seems to be the explanation. The carrying of a dead weight shortens the stride, and fat is practically a dead weight. The conclusion is that he was about five feet ten inches high, and excessively fat." He picked up his cane, and we resumed our walk, keeping an eye on the procession ahead until it had disappeared round a curve in the coast-line, when we mended our pace somewhat. Presently we reached a small headland, and, turning the shoulder of cliff, came full upon the party which had preceded us. The men had halted in a narrow bay, and now stood looking down at a prostrate figure beside which the surgeon was kneeling.

"We were wrong, you see," observed Thorndyke. "He has not fallen over the cliff, nor has he been washed up by the sea. He is lying above high-water mark, and those footprints that we have been examining appear to be his."

As we approached, the sergeant turned and held up his hand.

"I'll ask you not to walk round the body just now, gentlemen," he said. "There seems to have been foul play here, and I want to be clear about the tracks before anyone crosses them."

Acknowledging this caution, we advanced to where the constables were standing, and looked down with some curiosity at the dead man. He was a tall, frail-looking man, thin to the point of emaciation, and appeared to be about thirty-five years of age. He lay in an easy posture, with half-closed eyes and a placid expression that contrasted strangely enough with the tragic circumstances of his death.

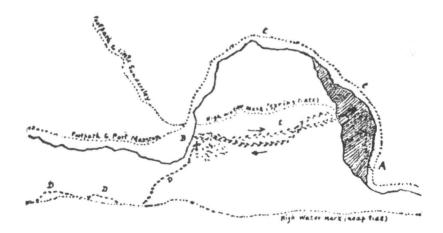

"It is a clear case of murder," said Dr. Burrows, dusting the sand from his knees as he stood up. "There is a deep knife-wound above the heart, which must have caused death almost instantaneously."

"How long should you say he has been dead, Doctor?" asked the sergeant.

"Twelve hours at least," was the reply. "He is quite cold and stiff."

"Twelve hours, eh?" repeated the officer. "That would bring it to about six o'clock this morning."

"I won't commit myself to a definite time," said Dr. Burrows hastily. "I only say not less than twelve hours. It might have been considerably more."

"Ah!" said the sergeant. "Well, he made a pretty good fight for his life, to all appearances." He nodded at the sand, which for some feet around the body bore the deeply indented marks of feet, as though a furious struggle had taken place. "It's a mighty queer affair," pursued the sergeant, addressing Dr. Burrows. "There seems to have been only one man in it—there is only one set of footprints besides those of the deceased—and we've got to find out who he is; and I reckon there won't be much trouble about that, seeing the kind of trade-marks he has left behind him."

"No," agreed the surgeon; "there ought not to be much trouble in identifying those boots. He would seem to be a labourer, judging by the hob-nails."

"No, sir; not a labourer," dissented the sergeant. "The foot is too small, for one thing; and then the nails are not regular hob-nails. They're a good deal smaller; and a labourer's boots would have the nails all round the edges, and there would be iron tips on the heels, and probably on the toes too. Now these have got no tips, and the nails are arranged in a pattern on the soles and heels. They are probably shooting-boots or sporting shoes of some kind." He strode to and fro with his notebook in his hand, writing down hasty memoranda, and stooping to scrutinize the impressions in the sand. The surgeon also busied himself in noting down the facts concerning which he would have to give evidence, while Thorndyke regarded in silence and with an air of intense preoccupation the footprints around the body which remained to testify to the circumstances of the crime.

"It is pretty clear, up to a certain point," the sergeant observed, as he concluded his investigations, "how the affair happened, and it is pretty clear, too, that the murder was premeditated. You see, Doctor, the deceased gentleman, Mr.

Hearn, was apparently walking home from Port Marston; we saw his footprints along the shore—those rubber heels make them easy to identify—and he didn't go down Sundersley Gap. He probably meant to climb up the cliff by that little track that you see there, which the people about here call the Shepherd's Path. Now the murderer must have known that he was coming, and waited upon the cliff to keep a lookout. When he saw Mr. Hearn enter the bay, he came down the path and attacked him, and, after a tough struggle, succeeded in stabbing him. Then he turned and went back up the path. You can see the double track between the path and the place where the struggle took place, and the footprints going to the path are on top of those coming from it."

"If you follow the tracks," said Dr. Burrows, "you ought to be able to see where the murderer went to."

"I'm afraid not," replied the sergeant. "There are no marks on the path itself—the rock is too hard, and so is the ground above, I fear. But I'll go over it carefully all the same."

The investigations being so far concluded, the body was lifted on to the stretcher, and the cortege, consisting of the bearers, the Doctor, and the fisherman, moved off towards the Gap, while the sergeant, having civilly wished us "Good-evening," scrambled up the Shepherd's Path, and vanished above.

"A very smart officer that," said Thorndyke. "I should like to know what he wrote in his notebook."

"His account of the circumstances of the murder seemed a very reasonable one," I said.

"Very. He noted the plain and essential facts, and drew the natural conclusions from them. But there are some very singular features in this case; so singular that I am disposed to make a few notes for my own information."

He stooped over the place where the body had lain, and having narrowly examined the sand there and in the place where the dead man's feet had rested, drew out his notebook and made a memorandum. He next made a rapid sketch-plan of the bay, marking the position of the body and the various impressions in the sand, and then, following the double track leading from and to the Shepherd's Path, scrutinized the footprints with the deepest attention, making copious notes and sketches in his book.

"We may as well go up by the Shepherd's Path," said Thorndyke. "I think we are equal to the climb, and there may be visible traces of the murderer after all. The rock is only a sandstone, and not a very hard one either."

We approached the foot of the little rugged track which zigzagged up the face of the cliff, and, stooping down among the stiff, dry herbage, examined the surface. Here, at the bottom of the path, where the rock was softened by the weather, there were several distinct impressions on the crumbling surface of the murderer's nailed boots, though they were somewhat confused by the tracks of the sergeant, whose boots were heavily nailed. But as we ascended the marks became rather less distinct, and at quite a short distance from the foot of the cliff we lost them altogether, though we had no difficulty in following the more recent traces of the sergeant's passage up the path.

When we reached the top of the cliff we paused to scan the path that ran along its edge, but here, too, although the sergeant's heavy boots had left quite visible impressions on the ground, there were no signs of any other feet. At a little distance the sagacious officer himself was pursuing his investigations, walking backwards and forwards with his body bent double, and his eyes fixed on the ground.

"Not a trace of him anywhere," said he, straightening himself up as we approached. "I was afraid there wouldn't be after all this dry weather. I shall have to try a different tack. This is a small place, and if those boots belong to anyone living here they'll be sure to be known."

"The deceased gentleman—Mr. Hearn, I think you called him," said Thorndyke as we turned towards the village—"is he a native of the locality?"

"Oh no, sir," replied the officer. "He is almost a stranger. He has only been here about three weeks; but, you know, in a little place like this a man soon gets to be known—and his business, too, for that matter," he added, with a smile.

"What was his business, then?" asked Thorndyke.

"Pleasure, I believe. He was down here for a holiday, though it's a good way past the season; but, then, he had a friend living here, and that makes a difference. Mr. Draper up at the Poplars was an old friend of his, I understand. I am going to call on him now."

We walked on along the footpath that led towards the village, but had only proceeded two or three hundred yards when a loud hail drew our attention to a man running across a field towards us from the direction of the cliff.

"Why, here is Mr. Draper himself," exclaimed the sergeant, stopping short and waving his hand. "I expect he has heard the news already."

Thorndyke and I also halted, and with some curiosity watched the approach of this new party to the tragedy. As the stranger drew near we saw that he was a tall, athletic-looking man of about forty, dressed in a Norfolk knickerbocker suit, and having the appearance of an ordinary country gentleman, excepting that he carried in his hand, in place of a walking-stick, the staff of a butterfly-net, the folding ring and bag of which partly projected from his pocket.

"Is it true, Sergeant?" he exclaimed as he came up to us, panting from his exertions. "About Mr. Hearn, I mean. There is a rumour that he has been found dead on the beach."

"It's quite true, sir, I am sorry to say; and, what is worse, he has been murdered."

"My God! you don't say so!"

He turned towards us a face that must ordinarily have been jovial enough, but was now white and scared and, after a brief pause, he exclaimed:

"Murdered! Good God! Poor old Hearn! How did it happen, Sergeant? and when? and is there any clue to the murderer?"

"We can't say for certain when it happened," replied the sergeant, "and as to the question of clues, I was just coming up to call on you."

"On me!" exclaimed Draper, with a startled glance at the officer. "What for?"

"Well, we should like to know something about Mr. Hearn— who he was, and whether he had any enemies, and so forth; anything, in fact, that would give as a hint where to look for the murderer. And you are the only person in the place who knew him at all intimately."

Mr Draper's pallid face turned a shade paler, and he glanced about him with an obviously embarrassed air.

"I'm afraid." he began in a hesitating manner, "I'm afraid I shan't be able to help you much. I didn't know much about his affairs. You see he was—well—only a casual acquaintance—"

"Well," interrupted the sergeant, "you can tell us who and what he was, and where he lived, and so forth. We'll find out the rest if you give us the start."

"I see," said Draper. "Yes, I expect you will." His eyes glanced restlessly to and fro, and he added presently: "You must come up to-morrow, and have a talk with me about him, and I'll see what I can remember."

"I'd rather come this evening," said the sergeant firmly.

"Not this evening," pleaded Draper. "I'm feeling rather—this affair, you know, has upset me. I couldn't give proper attention—"

His sentence petered out into a hesitating mumble, and the officer looked at him in evident surprise at his nervous, embarrassed manner. His own attitude, however, was perfectly firm, though polite.

"I don't like pressing you, sir," said he, "but time is precious—we'll have to go single file here; this pond is a public nuisance. They ought to bank it up at this end. After you, sir."

The pond to which the sergeant alluded had evidently extended at one time right across the path, but now, thanks to the dry weather, a narrow isthmus of half-dried mud traversed the morass, and along this Mr. Draper proceeded to pick his way. The sergeant was about to follow, when suddenly he stopped short with his eyes riveted upon the muddy track. A single glance showed me the cause of his surprise, for on the stiff, putty-like surface, standing out with the sharp distinctness of a wax mould, were the fresh footprints of the man who had just passed, each footprint displaying on its sole the impression of stud-nails arranged in a diamond-shaped pattern, and on its heel a group of similar nails arranged in a cross.

The sergeant hesitated for only a moment, in which he turned a quick startled glance upon us; then he followed, walking gingerly along the edge of the path as if to avoid treading in his predecessor's footprints. Instinctively we did the same, following closely, and anxiously awaiting the next development of the tragedy. For a minute or two we all proceeded in silence, the sergeant being evidently at a loss how to act, and Mr. Draper busy with his own thoughts. At length the former spoke.

"You think, Mr. Draper, you would rather that I looked in on you to-morrow about this affair?"

"Much rather, if you wouldn't mind," was the eager reply.

"Then, in that case," said the sergeant, looking at his watch, "as I've got a good deal to see to this evening, I'll leave you here, and make my way to the station."

With a farewell flourish of his hand he climbed over a stile, and when, a few moments later, I caught a glimpse of him through an opening in the hedge, he was running across the meadow like a hare.

The departure of the police-officer was apparently a great relief to Mr. Draper, who at once fell back and began to talk with us.

"You are Dr. Jervis, I think," said he. "I saw you coming out of Dr. Cooper's house yesterday. We know everything that is happening in the village, you see." He laughed nervously, and added: "But I don't know your friend."

I introduced Thorndyke, at the mention of whose name our new acquaintance knitted his brows, and glanced inquisitively at my friend.

"Thorndyke," he repeated; "the name seems familiar to me. Are you in the Law, sir?"

Thorndyke admitted the impeachment, and our companion, having again bestowed on him a look full of curiosity, continued: "This horrible affair will interest you, no doubt, from a professional point of view. You were present when my poor friend's body was found, I think?"

"No," replied Thorndyke; "we came up afterwards, when they were removing it."

Our companion then proceeded to question as about the murder, but received from Thorndyke only the most general and ambiguous replies. Nor was there time to go into the matter at length, for the footpath presently emerged on to the road close to Mr. Draper's house.

"You will excuse my not asking you in to-night," said he, "but you will understand that I am not in much form for visitors just now."

We assured him that we fully understood, and, having wished him "Good-evening," pursued our way towards the village.

"The sergeant is off to get a warrant, I suppose," I observed.

"Yes; and mighty anxious lest his man should be off before he can execute it. But he is fishing in deeper waters than he thinks, Jervis. This is a very singular and complicated case; one of the strangest, in fact, that I have ever met. I shall follow its development with deep interest."

"The sergeant seems pretty cocksure, all the same," I said.

"He is not to blame for that," replied Thorndyke. "He is acting on the obvious appearances, which is the proper thing to do in the first place. Perhaps his notebook contains more than I think it does. But we shall see."

When we entered the village I stopped to settle some business with the chemist, who acted as Dr. Cooper's dispenser, suggesting to Thorndyke that he should walk on to the house; but when I emerged from the shop some ten minutes later he was waiting outside, with a smallish brown-paper parcel under each arm. Of one of these parcels I insisted on relieving him, in spite of his protests, but when he at length handed it to me its weight completely took me by surprise.

"I should have let them send this home on a barrow," I remarked.

"So I should have done," he replied, "only I did not wish to draw attention to my purchase, or give my address."

Accepting this hint I refrained from making any inquiries as to the nature of the contents (although I must confess to considerable curiosity on the subject), and on arriving home I assisted him to deposit the two mysterious parcels in his room.

When I came downstairs a disagreeable surprise awaited me. Hitherto the long evenings had been spent by me in solitary and undisturbed enjoyment of Dr. Cooper's excellent library, but to-night a perverse fate decreed that I must wander abroad, because, forsooth, a preposterous farmer, who resided in a hamlet five miles distant, had chosen the evening of my guest's arrival to dislocate his bucolic elbow. I half hoped that Thorndyke would offer to accompany me, but he made no such suggestion, and in fact seemed by no means afflicted at the prospect of my absence.

"I have plenty to occupy me while you are away," he said cheerfully; and with this assurance to comfort me I mounted my bicycle and rode off somewhat sulkily along the dark road.

My visit occupied in all a trifle under two hours, and when I reached home, ravenously hungry and heated by my ride, half-past nine had struck, and the village had begun to settle down for the night.

"Sergeant Payne is a-waiting in the surgery, sir," the housemaid announced as I entered the hall.

"Confound Sergeant Payne!" I exclaimed. "Is Dr. Thorndyke with him?"

"No, sir," replied the grinning damsel. "Dr. Thorndyke is hout."

"Hout!" I repeated (my surprise leading to unintentional mimicry).

"Yes, sir. He went hout soon after you, sir, on his bicycle. He had a basket strapped on to it—leastways a hamper—and he borrowed a basin and a kitchen-spoon from the cook."

I stared at the girl in astonishment. The ways of John Thorndyke were, indeed, beyond all understanding.

"Well, let me have some dinner or supper at once," I said, "and I will see what the sergeant wants."

The officer rose as I entered the surgery, and, laying his helmet on the table, approached me with an air of secrecy and importance.

"Well, sir," said he, "the fat's in the fire. I've arrested Mr. Draper, and I've got him locked up in the court-house. But I wish it had been someone else."

"So does he, I expect," I remarked.

"You see, sir," continued the sergeant, "we all like Mr. Draper. He's been among us a matter of seven years, and he's like one of ourselves. However, what I've come about is this; it seems the gentleman who was with you this evening is Dr. Thorndyke, the great expert. Now Mr. Draper seems to have heard about him, as most of us have, and he is very anxious for him to take up the defence. Do you think he would consent?"

"I expect so," I answered, remembering Thorndyke's keen interest in the case; "but I will ask him when he comes in."

"Thank you, sir," said the sergeant. "And perhaps you wouldn't mind stepping round to the court-house presently yourself. He looks uncommon queer, does Mr. Draper, and no wonder, so I'd like you to take a look at him, and if you could bring Dr. Thorndyke with you, he'd like it, and so should I, for, I assure you, sir, that although a conviction would mean a step up the ladder for me, I'd be glad enough to find that I'd made a mistake."

I was just showing my visitor out when a bicycle swept in through the open gate, and Thorndyke dismounted at the door, revealing a square hamper—evidently abstracted from the surgery—strapped on to a carrier at the back. I conveyed the sergeant's request to him at once, and asked if he was willing to take up the case.

"As to taking up the defence," he replied, "I will consider the matter; but in any case I will come up and see the prisoner."

With this the sergeant departed, and Thorndyke, having unstrapped the hamper with as much care as if it contained a collection of priceless porcelain, bore it tenderly up to his bedroom; whence he appeared, after a considerable interval, smilingly apologetic for the delay.

"I thought you were dressing for dinner," I grumbled as he took his seat at the table.

"No," he replied. "I have been considering this murder. Really it is a most singular case, and promises to be uncommonly complicated, too."

"Then I assume that you will undertake the defence?"

"I shall if Draper gives a reasonably straightforward account of himself."

It appeared that this condition was likely to be fulfilled, for when we arrived at the court-house (where the prisoner was accommodated in a spare office, under rather free-and-easy conditions considering the nature of the charge) we found Mr. Draper in an eminently communicative frame of mind.

"I want you, Dr. Thorndyke, to undertake my defence in this terrible affair, because I feel confident that you will be able to clear me. And I promise you that there shall be no reservation or concealment on my part of anything that you ought to know."

"Very well," said Thorndyke. "By the way, I see you have changed your shoes."

"Yes, the sergeant took possession of those I was wearing. He said something about comparing them with some footprints, but there can't be any footprints like those shoes here in Sundersley. The nails are fixed in the soles in quite a peculiar pattern. I had them made in Edinburgh."

"Have you more than one pair?"

"No. I have no other nailed boots."

"That is important," said Thorndyke. "And now I judge that you have something to tell us that bears on this crime. Am I right?"

"Yes. There is something that I am afraid it is necessary for you to know, although it is very painful to me to revive memories of my past that I had hoped were buried for ever. But perhaps, after all, it may not be necessary for these confidences to be revealed to anyone but yourself."

"I hope not," said Thorndyke; "and if it is not necessary you may rely upon me not to allow any of your secrets to leak out. But you are wise to tell me everything that may in any way bear upon the case."

At this juncture, seeing that confidential matters were about to be discussed, I rose and prepared to withdraw; but Draper waved me back into my chair.

"You need not go away, Dr. Jervis," he said. "It is through you that I have the benefit of Dr. Thorndyke's help, and I know that you doctors can be trusted to keep your own counsel and your clients' secrets. And now for some confessions of mine. In the first place, it is my painful duty to tell you that I am a discharged convict—an 'old lag,' as the cant phrase has it."

He coloured a dusky red as he made this statement, and glanced furtively at Thorndyke to observe its effect. But he might as well have looked at a wooden figure-head or a stone mask as at my friend's immovable visage; and when his communication had been acknowledged by a slight nod, he proceeded:

"The history of my wrong-doing is the history of hundreds of others. I was a clerk in a bank, and getting on as well as I could expect in that not very progressive avocation, when I had the misfortune to make four very undesirable acquaintances. They were all young men, though rather older than myself, and were close friends, forming a sort of little community or club. They were not what is usually described as 'fast.' They were quite sober and decently-behaved young follows, but they were very decidedly addicted to gambling in a small way, and they soon infected me. Before long I was the keenest gambler of them all. Cards, billiards, pool, and various forms of betting began to be the chief pleasures of my life, and not only was the bulk of my scanty salary often consumed in the inevitable losses, but presently I found myself considerably in debt, without any visible means of discharging my liabilities. It is true that my four friends were my chief—in fact, almost my only—creditors, but still, the debts existed, and had to be paid.

"Now these four friends of mine—named respectively Leach, Pitford, Hearn, and Jezzard—were uncommonly clever men, though the full extent of their cleverness was not appreciated by me until too late. And I, too, was clever in my way, and a most undesirable way it was, for I possessed the fatal gift of imitating handwriting and signatures with the most remarkable accuracy. So perfect were my copies that the writers themselves were frequently unable to distinguish their own signatures from my imitations, and many a time was my skill invoked by some of my companions to play off practical jokes upon the others. But these jests were strictly confined to our own little set, for my four friends were most careful and anxious that my dangerous accomplishment should not become known to outsiders.

"And now follows the consequence which you have no doubt foreseen. My debts, though small, were accumulating, and I saw no prospect of being able to pay them. Then, one night, Jezzard made a proposition. We had been playing bridge at his rooms, and once more my ill luck had caused me to increase my debt. I scribbled out an IOU, and pushed it across the table to Jezzard, who picked it up with a very wry face, and pocketed it.

"'Look here, Ted,' he said presently, 'this paper is all very well, but, you know, I can't pay my debts with it. My creditors demand hard cash.'

"'I'm very sorry,' I replied, 'but I can't help it.'

"'Yes, you can,' said he, 'and I'll tell you how.' He then propounded a scheme which I at first rejected with indignation, but which, when the others backed him up, I at last allowed myself to be talked into, and actually put into execution. I contrived, by taking advantage of the carelessness of some of my superiors at the bank, to get possession of some blank cheque forms, which I filled up with small amounts—not more than two or three pounds—and signed with careful imitations of the signatures of some of our clients. Jezzard got some stamps made for stamping on the account numbers, and when this had been done I handed over to him the whole collection of forged cheques in settlement of my debts to all of my four companions.

"The cheques were duly presented—by whom I do not know; and although, to my dismay, the modest sums for which I had drawn them had been skilfully altered into quite considerable amounts, they were all paid without demur excepting one. That one, which had been altered from three pounds to thirty-nine, was drawn upon an account which was already slightly overdrawn. The cashier became suspicious; the cheque was impounded, and the client communicated with. Then, of course, the mine exploded. Not only was this particular forgery detected, but inquiries were set afoot which soon brought to light the others. Presently circumstances, which I need not describe, threw some suspicion on me. I at once lost my nerve, and finally made a full confession.

"The inevitable prosecution followed. It was not conducted vindictively. Still, I had actually committed the forgeries, and though I endeavoured to cast a part of the blame on to the shoulders of my treacherous confederates, I did not succeed. Jezzard, it is true, was arrested, but was discharged for lack of evidence, and, consequently, the whole burden of the forgery fell upon me. The jury, of course, convicted me, and I was sentenced to seven years' penal servitude.

"During the time that I was in prison an uncle of mine died in Canada, and by the provisions of his will I inherited the whole of his very considerable property, so that when the time arrived for my release, I came out of prison, not only free, but comparatively rich. I at once dropped my own name, and, assuming that of Alfred Draper, began to look about for some quiet spot in which I might spend the rest of my days in peace, and with little chance of my identity being discovered. Such a place I found in Sundersley, and here I have lived for the last seven years, liked and respected, I think, by my neighbours, who have little suspected that they were harbouring in their midst a convicted felon.

"All this time I had neither seen nor heard anything of my four confederates, and I hoped and believed that they had passed completely out of my life. But they had not. Only a month ago I met them once more, to my sorrow, and from the day of that meeting all the peace and security of my quiet existence at Sundersley have vanished. Like evil spirits they have stolen into my life, changing my happiness into bitter misery, filling my days with dark forebodings and my nights with terror."

Here Mr. Draper paused, and seemed to sink into a gloomy reverie.

"Under what circumstances did you meet these men?" Thorndyke asked.

"Ah!" exclaimed Draper, arousing with sudden excitement, "the circumstances were very singular and suspicious. I had gone over to Eastwich for the day to do some shopping. About eleven o'clock in the forenoon I was making some purchases in a shop when I noticed two men looking in the window, or rather pretending to do so, whilst they conversed earnestly. They were smartly dressed, in a horsy fashion, and looked like well-to-do farmers, as they might very naturally have been since it was market-day. But it seemed to me that their faces were familiar to me. I looked at them more attentively, and then it suddenly dawned upon me, most unpleasantly, that they resembled Leach and Jezzard. And yet they were not quite like. The resemblance was there, but the differences were greater than the lapse of time would account for. Moreover, the man who resembled Jezzard had a rather large mole on the left cheek just under the eye, while the other man had an eyeglass stuck in one eye, and wore a waxed moustache, whereas Leach had always been clean-shaven, and had never used an eyeglass.

"As I was speculating upon the resemblance they looked up, and caught my intent and inquisitive eye, whereupon they moved away from the window; and when, having completed my purchases, I came out into the street, they were nowhere to be seen.

"That evening, as I was walking by the river outside the town before returning to the station, I overtook a yacht which was being towed down-stream. Three men were walking ahead on the bank with a long tow-line, and one man stood in the cockpit steering. As I approached, and was reading the name Otter on the stern, the man at the helm looked round, and with a start of surprise I recognized my old acquaintance Hearn. The recognition, however, was not mutual, for I had grown a beard in the interval, and I passed on without appearing to notice him; but when I overtook the other three men, and recognized, as I had feared, the other three members of the gang, I must have looked rather hard at Jezzard, for he suddenly halted, and exclaimed: 'Why, it's our old friend Ted! Our long-lost and lamented brother!' He held out his hand with effusive cordiality, and began to make inquiries as to my welfare; but I cut him short with the remark that I was not proposing to renew the acquaintance, and, turning off on to a footpath that led away from the river, strode off without looking back.

"Naturally this meeting exercised my mind a good deal, and when I thought of the two men whom I had seen in the town, I could hardly believe that their likeness to my quondam friends was a mere coincidence. And yet when I had met Leach and Jezzard by the river, I had found them little altered, and had particularly noticed that Jezzard had no mole on his face, and that Leach was clean-shaven as of old.

"But a day or two later all my doubts were resolved by a paragraph in the local paper. It appeared that on the day of my visit to Eastwich a number of forged cheques had been cashed at the three banks. They had been presented by three well-dressed, horsy-looking men who looked like well-to-do farmers. One of them had a mole on the left cheek, another was distinguished by a waxed moustache and a single eyeglass, while the description of the third I did not recognize. None of the cheques had been drawn for large amounts, though the total sum obtained by the forgers was nearly four hundred pounds; but the most interesting point was that the cheque-forms had been manufactured by photographic process, and the water-mark skilfully, though not quite perfectly, imitated. Evidently the swindlers were clever and careful men, and willing to take a good deal of trouble for the sake of security, and the result of their precautions was that the police could make no guess as to their identity.

"The very next day, happening to walk over to Port Marston, I came upon the Otter lying moored alongside the quay in the harbour. As soon as I recognized the yacht, I turned quickly and walked away, but a minute later I ran into Leach and Jezzard, who were returning to their craft. Jezzard greeted me with an air of surprise. 'What! Still hanging about here, Ted—' he exclaimed. 'That is not discreet of you, dear boy. I should earnestly advise you to clear out.'

"'What do you mean—' I asked.

"'Tut, tut!' said he. 'We read the papers like other people, and we know now what business took you to Eastwich. But it's foolish of you to hang about the neighbourhood where you might be spotted at any moment.'

"The implied accusation took me aback so completely that I stood staring at him in speechless astonishment, and at that unlucky moment a tradesman, from whom I had ordered some house-linen, passed along the quay. Seeing me, he stopped and touched his hat.

"'Beg pardon, Mr. Draper,' said he, 'but I shall be sending my cart up to Sundersley to-morrow morning if that will do for you.'

"I said that it would, and as the man turned away, Jezzard's face broke out into a cunning smile.

"So you are Mr. Draper, of Sundersley, now, are you—' said he. 'Well, I hope you won't be too proud to come and look in on your old friends. We shall be staying here for some time.'

"That same night Hearn made his appearance at my house. He had come as an emissary from the gang, to ask me to do some work for them—to execute some forgeries, in fact. Of course I refused, and pretty bluntly, too, whereupon Hearn began to throw out vague hints as to what might happen if I made enemies of the gang, and to utter veiled, but quite intelligible, threats. You will say that I was an idiot not to send him packing, and threaten to hand over the whole gang to the police; but I was never a man of strong nerve, and I don't mind admitting that I was mortally afraid of that cunning devil, Jezzard.

"The next thing that happened was that Hearn came and took lodgings in Sundersley, and, in spite of my efforts to avoid him, he haunted me continually. The yacht, too, had evidently settled down for some time at a berth in the harbour, for I heard that a local smack-boy had been engaged as a deck-hand; and I frequently encountered Jezzard and the other members of the gang, who all professed to believe that I had committed the Eastwich forgeries. One day I was foolish enough to allow myself to be lured on to the yacht for a few minutes, and when I would have gone ashore, I found that the shore ropes had been cast off, and that the vessel was already moving out of the harbour. At first I was furious, but the three scoundrels were so jovial and good-natured, and so delighted with the joke of taking me for a sail against my will, that I presently cooled down, and having changed into a pair of rubber-soled shoes (so that I should not make dents in the smooth deck with my hobnails), bore a hand at sailing the yacht, and spent quite a pleasant day.

"From that time I found myself gradually drifting back into a state of intimacy with these agreeable scoundrels, and daily becoming more and more afraid of them. In a moment of imbecility I mentioned what I had seen from the shop-window at Eastwich, and, though they passed the matter off with a joke, I could see that they were mightily disturbed by it. Their efforts to induce me to join them were redoubled, and Hearn took to calling almost daily at my house—usually with documents and signatures which he tried to persuade me to copy.

"A few evenings ago he made a new and startling proposition. We were walking in my garden, and he had been urging me once more to rejoin the gang—unsuccessfully, I need not say. Presently he sat down on a seat against a yew-hedge at the bottom of the garden, and, after an interval of silence, said suddenly:

"'Then you absolutely refuse to go in with us—'

"'Of course I do,' I replied. 'Why should I mix myself up with a gang of crooks when I have ample means and a decent position—'

"'Of course,' he agreed, 'you'd be a fool if you did. But, you see, you know all about this Eastwich job, to say nothing of our other little exploits, and you gave us away once before. Consequently, you can take it from me that, now Jezzard has run you to earth, he won't leave you in peace until you have given us some kind of a hold on you. You know too much, you see, and as long as you have a clean sheet you are a standing menace to us. That is the position. You know it, and Jezzard knows it, and he is a desperate man, and as cunning as the devil.'

"'I know that,' I said gloomily.

"'Very well,' continued Hearn. 'Now I'm going to make you an offer. Promise me a small annuity—you can easily afford it—or pay me a substantial sum down, and I will set you free for ever from Jezzard and the others.'

"'How will you do that—' I asked.

"'Very simply,' he replied. 'I am sick of them all, and sick of this risky, uncertain mode of life. Now I am ready to clean off my own slate and set you free at the same time; but I must have some means of livelihood in view.'

"'You mean that you will turn King's evidence—' I asked.

"'Yes, if you will pay me a couple of hundred a year, or, say, two thousand down on the conviction of the gang.'

"I was so taken aback that for some time I made no reply, and as I sat considering this amazing proposition, the silence was suddenly broken by a suppressed sneeze from the other side of the hedge.

"Hearn and I started to our feet. Immediately hurried footsteps were heard in the lane outside the hedge. We raced up the garden to the gate and out through a side alley, but when we reached the lane there was not a soul in sight. We made a brief and fruitless search in the immediate neighbourhood, and then turned back to the house. Hearn was deathly pale and very agitated, and I must confess that I was a good deal upset by the incident.

"'This is devilish awkward,' said Hearn.

"'It is rather,' I admitted; 'but I expect it was only some inquisitive yokel.'

"'I don't feel so sure of that,' said he. 'At any rate, we were stark lunatics to sit up against a hedge to talk secrets.'

"He paced the garden with me for some time in gloomy silence, and presently, after a brief request that I would think over his proposal, took himself off.

"I did not see him again until I met him last night on the yacht. Pitford called on me in the morning, and invited me to come and dine with them. I at first declined, for my housekeeper was going to spend the evening with her sister at Eastwich, and stay there for the night, and I did not much like leaving the house empty. However, I agreed eventually, stipulating that I should be allowed to come home early, and I accordingly went. Hearn and Pitford were waiting in the boat by the steps—for the yacht had been moved out to a buoy—and we went on board and spent a very pleasant and lively evening. Pitford put me ashore at ten o'clock, and I walked straight home, and went to bed. Hearn would have come with me, but the others insisted on his remaining, saying that they had some matters of business to discuss."

"Which way did you walk home?" asked Thorndyke.

"I came through the town, and along the main road."

"And that is all you know about this affair?"

"Absolutely all," replied Draper. "I have now admitted you to secrets of my past life that I had hoped never to have to reveal to any human creature, and I still have some faint hope that it may not be necessary for you to divulge what I have told you."

"Your secrets shall not be revealed unless it is absolutely indispensable that they should be," said Thorndyke; "but you are placing your life in my hands, and you must leave me perfectly free to act as I think best."

With this he gathered his notes together, and we took our departure.

"A very singular history, this, Jervis," he said, when, having wished the sergeant "Good-night," we stepped out on to the dark road. "What do you think of it?"

"I hardly know what to think," I answered, "but, on the whole, it seems rather against Draper than otherwise. He admits that he is an old criminal, and it appears that he was being persecuted and blackmailed by the man Hearn. It is true that he represents Jezzard as being the leading spirit and prime mover in the persecution, but we have only his word for that. Hearn was in lodgings near him, and was undoubtedly taking the most active part in the business, and it is quite possible, and indeed probable, that Hearn was the actual deus ex machina."

Thorndyke nodded. "Yes," he said, "that is certainly the line the prosecution will take if we allow the story to become known. Ha! what is this? We are going to have some rain."

"Yes, and wind too. We are in for an autumn gale, I think."

"And that," said Thorndyke, "may turn out to be an important factor in our case."

"How can the weather affect your case?" I asked in some surprise. But, as the rain suddenly descended in a pelting shower, my companion broke into a run, leaving my question unanswered.

On the following morning, which was fair and sunny after the stormy night, Dr. Burrows called for my friend. He was on his way to the extemporized mortuary to make the post-mortem examination of the murdered man's body. Thorndyke, having notified the coroner that he was watching the case on behalf of the accused, had been authorized to be present at the autopsy; but the authorization did not include me, and, as Dr. Burrows did not issue any invitation, I was not able to be present. I met them, however, as they were returning, and it seemed to me that Dr. Burrows appeared a little huffy.

"Your friend," said he, in a rather injured tone, "is really the most outrageous stickler for forms and ceremonies that I have ever met."

Thorndyke looked at him with an amused twinkle, and chuckled indulgently.

"Here was a body," Dr. Burrows continued irritably, "found under circumstances clearly indicative of murder, and bearing a knife-wound that nearly divided the arch of the aorta; in spite of which, I assure you that Dr. Thorndyke insisted on weighing the body, and examining every organ—lungs, liver, stomach, and brain—yes, actually the brain!—as if there had been no clue whatever to the cause of death. And then, as a climax, he insisted on sending the contents of the stomach in a jar, sealed with our respective seals, in charge of a special messenger, to Professor Copland, for analysis and report. I thought he was going to demand an examination for the tubercle bacillus, but he didn't; which," concluded Dr. Burrows, suddenly becoming sourly facetious, "was an oversight, for, after all, the fellow may have died of consumption."

Thorndyke chuckled again, and I murmured that the precautions appeared to have been somewhat excessive.

"Not at all," was the smiling response. "You are losing sight of our function. We are the expert and impartial umpires, and it is our business to ascertain, with scientific accuracy, the cause of death. The prima facie appearances in this case suggest that the deceased was murdered by Draper, and that is the hypothesis advanced. But that is no concern of ours. It is not our function to confirm an hypothesis suggested by outside circumstances, but rather, on the contrary, to make certain that no other explanation is possible. And that is my invariable practice. No matter how glaringly obvious the appearances may be, I refuse to take anything for granted."

Dr. Burrows received this statement with a grunt of dissent, but the arrival of his dogcart put a stop to further discussion.

Thorndyke was not subpoenaed for the inquest. Dr. Burrows and the sergeant having been present immediately after the finding of the body, his evidence was not considered necessary, and, moreover, he was known to be watching the case in the interests of the accused. Like myself, therefore, he was present as a spectator, but as a highly interested one, for he took very complete shorthand notes of the whole of the evidence and the coroner's comments.

I shall not describe the proceedings in detail. The jury, having been taken to view the body, trooped into the room on tiptoe, looking pale and awe-stricken, and took their seats; and thereafter, from time to time, directed glances of furtive curiosity at Draper as he stood, pallid and haggard, confronting the court, with a burly rural constable on either side.

The medical evidence was taken first. Dr. Burrows, having been sworn, began, with sarcastic emphasis, to describe the condition of the lungs and liver, until he was interrupted by the coroner.

"Is all this necessary?" the latter inquired. "I mean, is it material to the subject of the inquiry?"

"I should say not," replied Dr. Burrows. "It appears to me to be quite irrelevant, but Dr. Thorndyke, who is watching the case for the defence, thought it necessary."

"I think," said the coroner, "you had better give us only the facts that are material. The jury want you to tell them what you consider to have been the cause of death. They don't want a lecture on pathology."

"The cause of death," said Dr. Burrows, "was a penetrating wound of the chest, apparently inflicted with a large knife. The weapon entered between the second and third ribs on the left side close to the sternum or breast-bone. It wounded the left lung, and partially divided both the pulmonary artery and the aorta—the two principal arteries of the body."

"Was this injury alone sufficient to cause death?" the coroner asked.

"Yes," was the reply; "and death from injury to these great vessels would be practically instantaneous."

"Could the injury have been self-inflicted?"

"So far as the position and nature of the wound are concerned," replied the witness, "self-infliction would be quite possible. But since death would follow in a few seconds at the most, the weapon would be found either in the wound, or grasped in the hand, or, at least, quite close to the body. But in this case no weapon was found at all, and the wound must therefore certainly have been homicidal."

"Did you see the body before it was moved?"

"Yes. It was lying on its back, with the arms extended and the legs nearly straight; and the sand in the neighbourhood of the body was trampled as if a furious struggle had taken place."

"Did you notice anything remarkable about the footprints in the sand?"

"I did," replied Dr. Burrows. "They were the footprints of two persons only. One of these was evidently the deceased, whose footmarks could be easily identified by the circular rubber heels. The other footprints were those of a person—apparently a man—who wore shoes, or boots, the soles of which were studded with nails; and these nails were arranged in a very peculiar and unusual manner, for those on the soles formed a lozenge or diamond shape, and those on the heel were set out in the form of a cross."

"Have you ever seen shoes or boots with the nails arranged in this manner?"

"Yes. I have seen a pair of shoes which I am informed belong to the accused; the nails in them are arranged as I have described."

"Would you say that the footprints of which you have spoken were made by those shoes?"

"No; I could not say that. I can only say that, to the best of my belief, the pattern on the shoes is similar to that in the footprints."

This was the sum of Dr. Burrows' evidence, and to all of it Thorndyke listened with an immovable countenance, though with the closest attention. Equally attentive was the accused man, though not equally impassive; indeed, so great was his agitation that presently one of the constables asked permission to get him a chair.

The next witness was Arthur Jezzard. He testified that he had viewed the body, and identified it as that of Charles Hearn; that he had been acquainted with deceased for some years, but knew practically nothing of his affairs. At the time of his death deceased was lodging in the village.

"Why did he leave the yacht?" the coroner inquired. "Was there any kind of disagreement!"

"Not in the least," replied Jezzard. "He grew tired of the confinement of the yacht, and came to live ashore for a change. But we were the best of friends, and he intended to come with us when we sailed."

"When did you see him last?"

"On the night before the body was found—that is, last Monday. He had been dining on the yacht, and we put him ashore about midnight. He said as we were rowing him ashore that he intended to walk home along the sands as the tide was out. He went up the stone steps by the watch-house, and turned at the top to wish us good-night. That was the last time I saw him alive."

"Do you know anything of the relations between the accused and the deceased?" the coroner asked.

"Very little," replied Jezzard. "Mr. Draper was introduced to us by the deceased about a month ago. I believe they had been acquainted some years, and they appeared to be on excellent terms. There was no indication of any quarrel or disagreement between them."

"What time did the accused leave the yacht on the night of the murder?"

"About ten o'clock. He said that he wanted to get home early, as his housekeeper was away and he did not like the house to be left with no one in it."

This was the whole of Jezzard's evidence, and was confirmed by that of Leach and Pitford. Then, when the fisherman had deposed to the discovery of the body, the sergeant was called, and stepped forward, grasping a carpet-bag, and looking as uncomfortable as if he had been the accused instead of a witness. He described the circumstances under which he saw the body, giving the exact time and place with official precision.

"You have heard Dr. Burrows' description of the footprints?" the coroner inquired.

"Yes. There were two sets. One set were evidently made by deceased. They showed that he entered St. Bridget's Bay from the direction of Port Marston. He had been walking along the shore just about high-water mark, sometimes above and sometimes below. Where he had walked below high-water mark the footprints had of course been washed away by the sea."

"How far back did you trace the footprints of deceased?"

"About two-thirds of the way to Sundersley Gap. Then they disappeared below high-water mark. Later in the evening I walked from the Gap into Port Marston, but could not find any further traces of deceased. He must have walked between the tide-marks all the way from Port Marston to beyond Sundersley. When these footprints entered St. Bridget's Bay they became mixed up with the footprints of another man, and the shore was trampled for a space of a dozen yards as if a furious struggle had taken place. The strange man's tracks came down from the Shepherd's Path, and went up it again; but, owing to the hardness of the ground from the dry weather, the tracks disappeared a short distance up the path, and I could not find them again."

"What were these strange footprints like?" inquired the coroner.

"They were very peculiar," replied the sergeant. "They were made by shoes armed with smallish hob-nails, which were arranged in a diamond-shaped pattern on the soles and in a cross on the heels. I measured the footprints carefully, and made a drawing of each foot at the time." Here the sergeant produced a long notebook of funereal aspect, and, having opened it at a marked place, handed it to the coroner, who examined it attentively, and then passed it on to the jury. From the jury it was presently transferred to Thorndyke, and, looking over his shoulder, I saw a very workmanlike sketch of a pair of footprints with the principal dimensions inserted.

Thorndyke surveyed the drawing critically, jotted down a few brief notes, and returned the sergeant's notebook to the coroner, who, as he took it, turned once more to the officer.

"Have you any clue, sergeant, to the person who made these footprints?" he asked.

By way of reply the sergeant opened his carpet-bag, and, extracting therefrom a pair of smart but stoutly made shoes, laid them on the table.

"Those shoes," he said, "are the property of the accused; he was wearing them when I arrested him. They appear to correspond exactly to the footprints of the murderer. The measurements are the same, and the nails with which they are studded are arranged in a similar pattern."

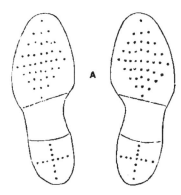

"Would you swear that the footprints were made with these shoes?" asked the coroner.

"No, sir, I would not," was the decided answer. "I would only swear to the similarity of size and pattern."

"Had you ever seen these shoes before you made the drawing?"

"No, sir," replied the sergeant; and he then related the incident of the footprints in the soft earth by the pond which led him to make the arrest.

The coroner gazed reflectively at the shoes which he held in his hand, and from them to the drawing; then, passing them to the foreman of the jury, he remarked:

"Well, gentlemen, it is not for me to tell you whether these shoes answer to the description given by Dr. Burrows and the sergeant, or whether they resemble the drawing which, as you have heard, was made by the officer on the spot and before he had seen the shoes; that is a matter for you to decide. Meanwhile, there is another question that we must consider." He turned to the sergeant and asked: "Have you made any inquiries as to the movements of the accused on the night of the murder?"

"I have," replied the sergeant, "and I find that, on that night, the accused was alone in the house, his housekeeper having gone over to Eastwich. Two men saw him in the town about ten o'clock, apparently walking in the direction of Sundersley."

This concluded the sergeant's evidence, and when one or two more witnesses had been examined without eliciting any fresh facts, the coroner briefly recapitulated the evidence, and requested the jury to consider their verdict. Thereupon a solemn hush fell upon the court, broken only by the whispers of the jurymen, as they consulted together; and the spectators gazed in awed expectancy from the accused to the whispering jury. I glanced at Draper, sitting huddled in his chair, his clammy face as pale as that of the corpse in the mortuary hard by, his hands tremulous and restless; and, scoundrel as I believed him to be, I could not but pity the abject misery that was written large all over him, from his damp hair to his incessantly shifting feet.

The jury took but a short time to consider their verdict. At the end of five minutes the foreman announced that they were agreed, and, in answer to the coroner's formal inquiry, stood up and replied:

"We find that the deceased met his death by being stabbed in the chest by the accused man, Alfred Draper."

"That is a verdict of wilful murder," said the coroner, and he entered it accordingly in his notes. The Court now rose. The spectators reluctantly trooped out, the jurymen stood up and stretched themselves, and the two constables, under the guidance of the sergeant, carried the wretched Draper in a fainting condition to a closed fly that was waiting outside.

"I was not greatly impressed by the activity of the defence," I remarked maliciously as we walked home.

Thorndyke smiled. "You surely did not expect me to cast my pearls of forensic learning before a coroner's jury," said he.

"I expected that you would have something to say on behalf of your client," I replied. "As it was, his accusers had it all their own way."

"And why not?" he asked. "Of what concern to us is the verdict of the coroner's jury?"

"It would have seemed more decent to make some sort of defence," I replied.

"My dear Jervis," he rejoined, "you do not seem to appreciate the great virtue of what Lord Beaconsfield so felicitously called 'a policy of masterly inactivity'; and yet that is one of the great lessons that a medical training impresses on the student."

"That may be so," said I. "But the result, up to the present, of your masterly policy is that a verdict of wilful murder stands against your client, and I don't see what other verdict the jury could have found."

"Neither do I," said Thorndyke.

I had written to my principal, Dr. Cooper, describing the stirring events that were taking place in the village, and had received a reply from him instructing me to place the house at Thorndyke's disposal, and to give him every facility for his work. In accordance with which edict my colleague took possession of a well-lighted, disused stable-loft, and announced his intention of moving his things into it. Now, as these "things" included the mysterious contents of the hamper that the housemaid had seen, I was possessed with a consuming desire to be present at the "flitting," and I do not mind confessing that I purposely lurked about the stairs in the hopes of thus picking up a few crumbs of information.

But Thorndyke was one too many for me. A misbegotten infant in the village having been seized with inopportune convulsions, I was compelled, most reluctantly, to hasten to its relief; and I returned only in time to find Thorndyke in the act of locking the door of the loft.

"A nice light, roomy place to work in," he remarked, as he descended the steps, slipping the key into his pocket.

"Yes," I replied, and added boldly: "What do you intend to do up there?"

"Work up the case for the defence," he replied, "and, as I have now heard all that the prosecution have to say, I shall be able to forge ahead."

This was vague enough, but I consoled myself with the reflection that in a very few days I should, in common with the rest of the world, be in possession of the results of his mysterious proceedings. For, in view of the approaching assizes, preparations were being made to push the case through the magistrate's court as quickly as possible in order to obtain a committal in time for the ensuing sessions. Draper had, of course, been already charged before a justice of the peace and evidence of arrest taken, and it was expected that the adjourned hearing would commence before the local magistrates on the fifth day after the inquest.

The events of these five days kept me in a positive ferment of curiosity. In the first place an inspector of the Criminal Investigation Department came down and browsed about the place in company with the sergeant. Then Mr. Bashfield, who was to conduct the prosecution, came and took up his abode at the "Cat and Chicken." But the most surprising visitor was Thorndyke's laboratory assistant, Polton, who appeared one evening with a large trunk and a sailor's hammock, and announced that he was going to take up his quarters in the loft.

As to Thorndyke himself, his proceedings were beyond speculation. From time to time he made mysterious appearances at the windows of the loft, usually arrayed in what looked suspiciously like a nightshirt. Sometimes I would see him holding a negative up to the light, at others manipulating a photographic printing-frame; and once I observed him with a paintbrush and a large gallipot; on which I turned away in despair, and nearly collided with the inspector.

"Dr. Thorndyke is staying with you, I hear," said the latter, gazing earnestly at my colleague's back, which was presented for his inspection at the window.

"Yes," I answered. "Those are his temporary premises."

"That is where he does his bedevilments, I suppose?" the officer suggested.

"He conducts his experiments there," I corrected haughtily.

"That's what I mean," said the inspector; and, as Thorndyke at this moment turned and opened the window, our visitor began to ascend the steps.

"I've just called to ask if I could have a few words with you, Doctor," said the inspector, as he reached the door.

"Certainly," Thorndyke replied blandly. "If you will go down and wait with Dr. Jervis, I will be with you in five minutes."

The officer came down the steps grinning, and I thought I heard him murmur "Sold!" But this may have been an illusion. However, Thorndyke presently emerged, and he and the officer strode away into the shrubbery. What the inspector's business was, or whether he had any business at all, I never learned; but the incident seemed to throw some light on the presence of Polton and the sailor's hammock. And this reference to Polton reminds me of a very singular change that took place about this time in the habits of this usually staid and sedate little man; who, abandoning the somewhat clerical style of dress that he ordinarily affected, broke out into a semi-nautical costume, in which he would sally forth every morning in the direction of Port Marston. And there, on more than one occasion, I saw him leaning against a post by the harbour, or lounging outside a waterside tavern in earnest and amicable conversation with sundry nautical characters.

On the afternoon of the day before the opening of the proceedings we had two new visitors. One of them, a grey-haired spectacled man, was a stranger to me, and for some reason I failed to recall his name, Copland, though I was sure I had heard it before. The other was Anstey, the barrister who usually worked with Thorndyke in cases that went into Court. I saw very little of either of them, however, for they retired almost immediately to the loft, where, with short intervals for meals, they remained for the rest of the day, and, I believe, far into the night. Thorndyke requested me not to mention the names of his visitors to anyone, and at the same time apologized for the secrecy of his proceedings.

"But you are a doctor, Jervis," he concluded, "and you know what professional confidences are; and you will understand how greatly it is in our favour that we know exactly what the prosecution can do, while they are absolutely in the dark as to our line of defence."

I assured him that I fully understood his position, and with this assurance he retired, evidently relieved, to the council chamber.

The proceedings, which opened on the following day, and at which I was present throughout, need not be described in detail. The evidence for the prosecution was, of course, mainly a repetition of that given at the inquest. Mr. Bashfield's opening statement, however, I shall give at length, inasmuch as it summarized very clearly the whole of the case against the prisoner.

"The case that is now before the Court," said the counsel, "involves a charge of wilful murder against the prisoner Alfred Draper, and the facts, in so far as they are known, are briefly these: On the night of Monday, the 27th of September, the deceased, Charles Hearn, dined with some friends on board the yacht Otter. About midnight he came ashore, and proceeded to walk towards Sundersley along the beach. As he entered St. Bridget's Bay, a man, who appears to have been lying in wait, and who came down the Shepherd's Path, met him, and a deadly struggle seems to have taken place. The deceased received a wound of a kind calculated to cause almost instantaneous death, and apparently fell down dead.

"And now, what was the motive of this terrible crime? It was not robbery, for nothing appears to have been taken from the corpse. Money and valuables were found, as far as is known, intact. Nor, clearly, was it a case of a casual affray. We are, consequently, driven to the conclusion that the motive was a personal one, a motive of interest or revenge, and with this view the time, the place, and the evident deliberateness of the murder are in full agreement.

"So much for the motive. The next question is, Who was the perpetrator of this shocking crime? And the answer to that question is given in a very singular and dramatic circumstance, a circumstance that illustrates once more the amazing lack of precaution shown by persons who commit such crimes. The murderer was wearing a very remarkable pair of shoes, and those shoes left very remarkable footprints in the smooth sand, and those footprints were seen and examined by a very acute and painstaking police-officer, Sergeant Payne, whose evidence you will hear presently. The sergeant not only examined the footprints, he made careful drawings of them on the spot—on the spot, mind you, not from memory—and he made very exact measurements of them, which he duly noted down. And from those drawings and those measurements, those tell-tale shoes have been identified, and are here for your inspection.

"And now, who is the owner of those very singular, those almost unique shoes? I have said that the motive of this murder must have been a personal one, and, behold! the owner of those shoes happens to be the one person in the whole of this district who could have had a motive for compassing the murdered man's death. Those shoes belong to, and were taken from the foot of, the prisoner, Alfred Draper, and the prisoner, Alfred Draper, is the only person living in this neighbourhood who was acquainted with the deceased.

"It has been stated in evidence at the inquest that the relations of these two men, the prisoner and the deceased, were entirely friendly; but I shall prove to you that they were not so friendly as has been supposed. I shall prove to you, by the evidence of the prisoner's housekeeper, that the deceased was often an unwelcome visitor at the house, that the prisoner often denied himself when he was really at home and disengaged, and, in short, that he appeared constantly to shun and avoid the deceased.

"One more question and I have finished. Where was the prisoner on the night of the murder? The answer is that he was in a house little more than half a mile from the scene of the crime. And who was with him in that house? Who was there to observe and testify to his going forth and his coming home? No one. He was alone in the house. On that night, of all nights, he was alone. Not a soul was there to rouse at the creak of a door or the tread of a shoe—to tell as whether he slept or whether he stole forth in the dead of the night.

"Such are the facts of this case. I believe that they are not disputed, and I assert that, taken together, they are susceptible of only one explanation, which is that the prisoner, Alfred Draper, is the man who murdered the deceased, Charles Hearn."

Immediately on the conclusion of this address, the witnesses were called, and the evidence given was identical with that at the inquest. The only new witness for the prosecution was Draper's housekeeper, and her evidence fully bore out Mr. Bashfield's statement. The sergeant's account of the footprints was listened to with breathless interest, and at its conclusion the presiding magistrate—a retired solicitor, once well known in criminal practice—put a question which interested me as showing how clearly Thorndyke had foreseen the course of events, recalling, as it did, his remark on the night when we were caught in the rain.

"Did you," the magistrate asked, "take these shoes down to the beach and compare them with the actual footprints?"

"I obtained the shoes at night," replied the sergeant, "and I took them down to the shore at daybreak the next morning. But, unfortunately, there had been a storm in the night, and the footprints were almost obliterated by the wind and rain."

When the sergeant had stepped down, Mr. Bashfield announced that that was the case for the prosecution. He then resumed his seat, turning an inquisitive eye on Anstey and Thorndyke.

The former immediately rose and opened the case for the defence with a brief statement.

"The learned counsel for the prosecution," said he, "has told us that the facts now in the possession of the Court admit of but one explanation—that of the guilt of the accused. That may or may not be; but I shall now proceed to lay before the Court certain fresh facts—facts, I may say, of the most singular and startling character, which will, I think, lead to a very different conclusion. I shall say no more, but call the witnesses forthwith, and let the evidence speak for itself."

The first witness for the defence was Thorndyke; and as he entered the box I observed Polton take up a position close behind him with a large wicker trunk. Having been sworn, and requested by Anstey to tell the Court what he knew about the case, he commenced without preamble:

"About half-past four in the afternoon of the 28th of September I walked down Sundersley Gap with Dr. Jervis. Our attention was attracted by certain footprints in the sand, particularly those of a man who had landed from a boat, had walked up the Gap, and presently returned, apparently to the boat.

"As we were standing there Sergeant Payne and Dr. Burrows passed down the Gap with two constables carrying a stretcher. We followed at a distance, and as we walked along the shore we encountered another set of footprints—those which the sergeant has described as the footprints of the deceased. We examined these carefully, and endeavoured to frame a description of the person by whom they had been made."

"And did your description agree with the characters of the deceased?" the magistrate asked.

"Not in the least," replied Thorndyke, whereupon the magistrate, the inspector, and Mr. Bashfield laughed long and heartily.

"When we turned into St. Bridget's Bay, I saw the body of deceased lying on the sand close to the cliff. The sand all round was covered with footprints, as if a prolonged, fierce struggle had taken place. There were two sets of footprints, one set being apparently those of the deceased and the other those of a man with nailed shoes of a very peculiar and conspicuous pattern. The incredible folly that the wearing of such shoes indicated caused me to look more closely at the footprints, and then I made the surprising discovery that there had in reality been no struggle; that, in fact, the two sets of footprints had been made at different times."

"At different times!" the magistrate exclaimed in astonishment.

"Yes. The interval between them may have been one of hours or one only of seconds, but the undoubted fact is that the two sets of footprints were made, not simultaneously, but in succession."

"But how did you arrive at that fact?" the magistrate asked.

"It was very obvious when one looked," said Thorndyke. "The marks of the deceased man's shoes showed that he repeatedly trod in his own footprints; but never in a single instance did he tread in the footprints of the other man, although they covered the same area. The man with the nailed shoes, on the contrary, not only trod in his own footprints, but with equal frequency in those of the deceased. Moreover, when the body was removed, I observed that the footprints in the sand on which it was lying were exclusively those of the deceased. There was not a sign of any nail-marked footprint under the corpse, although there were many close around it. It was evident, therefore, that the footprints of the deceased were made first and those of the nailed shoes afterwards."

As Thorndyke paused the magistrate rubbed his nose thoughtfully, and the inspector gazed at the witness with a puzzled frown.

"The singularity of this fact," my colleague resumed, "made me look at the footprints yet more critically, and then I made another discovery. There was a double track of the nailed shoes, leading apparently from and back to the Shepherd's Path. But on examining these tracks more closely, I was astonished to find that the man who had made them had been walking backwards; that, in fact, he had walked backwards from the body to the Shepherd's Path, had ascended it for a short distance, had turned round, and returned, still walking backwards, to the face of the cliff near the corpse, and there the tracks vanished altogether. On the sand at this spot were some small, inconspicuous marks which might have been made by the end of a rope, and there were also a few small fragments which had fallen from the cliff above. Observing these, I examined the surface of the cliff, and at one spot, about six feet above the beach, I found a freshly rubbed spot on which were parallel scratches such as might have been made by the nailed sole of a boot. I then ascended the Shepherd's Path, and examined the cliff from above, and here I found on the extreme edge a rather deep indentation, such as would be made by a taut rope, and, on lying down and looking over, I could see, some five feet from the top, another rubbed spot with very distinct parallel scratches."

"You appear to infer," said the chairman, "that this man performed these astonishing evolutions and was then hauled up the cliff?"

"That is what the appearances suggested," replied Thorndyke.

The chairman pursed up his lips, raised his eyebrows, and glanced doubtfully at his brother magistrates. Then, with a resigned air, he bowed to the witness to indicate that he was listening.

"That same night," Thorndyke resumed, "I cycled down to the shore, through the Gap, with a supply of plaster of Paris, and proceeded to take plaster moulds of the more important of the footprints." (Here the magistrates, the inspector, and Mr. Bashfield with one accord sat up at attention; Sergeant Payne swore quite audibly; and I experienced a sudden illumination respecting a certain basin and kitchen spoon which had so puzzled me on the night of Thorndyke's arrival.) "As I thought that liquid plaster might confuse or even obliterate the prints in sand, I filled up the respective footprints with dry plaster, pressed it down lightly, and then cautiously poured water on to it. The moulds, which are excellent impressions, of course show the appearance of the boots which made the footprints, and from these moulds I have prepared casts which reproduce the footprints themselves.

"The first mould that I made was that of one of the tracks from the boat up to the Gap, and of this I shall speak presently. I next made a mould of one of the footprints which have been described as those of the deceased."

"Have been described!" exclaimed the chairman. "The deceased was certainly there, and there were no other footprints, so, if they were not his, he must have flown to where he was found."

"I will call them the footprints of the deceased," replied Thorndyke imperturbably. "I took a mould of one of them, and with it, on the same mould, one of my own footprints. Here is the mould, and here is a cast from it." (He turned and took them from the triumphant Polton, who had tenderly lifted them out of the trunk in readiness.) "On looking at the cast, it will be seen that the appearances are not such as would be expected. The deceased was five feet nine inches high, but was very thin and light, weighing only nine stone six pounds, as I ascertained by weighing the body, whereas I am five feet eleven and weigh nearly thirteen stone. But yet the footprint of the deceased is nearly twice as deep as mine—that is to say, the lighter man has sunk into the sand nearly twice as deeply as the heavier man."

The magistrates were now deeply attentive. They were no longer simply listening to the despised utterances of a mere scientific expert. The cast lay before them with the two footprints side by side; the evidence appealed to their own senses and was proportionately convincing.

"This is very singular," said the chairman; "but perhaps you can explain the discrepancy?"

"I think I can," replied Thorndyke; "but I should prefer to place all the facts before you first."

"Undoubtedly that would be better," the chairman agreed. "Pray proceed."

"There was another remarkable peculiarity about these footprints," Thorndyke continued, "and that was their distance apart—the length of the stride, in fact. I measured the steps carefully from heel to heel, and found them only nineteen and a half inches. But a man of Hearn's height would have an ordinary stride of about thirty-six inches—more if he was walking fast. Walking with a stride of nineteen and a half inches he would look as if his legs were tied together.

"I next proceeded to the Bay, and took two moulds from the footprints of the man with the nailed shoes, a right and a left. Here is a cast from the mould, and it shows very clearly that the man was walking backwards."

"How does it show that?" asked the magistrate.

"There are several distinctive points. For instance, the absence of the usual 'kick off' at the toe, the slight drag behind the heel, showing the direction in which the foot was lifted, and the undisturbed impression of the sole."

"You have spoken of moulds and casts. What is the difference between them?"

"A mould is a direct, and therefore reversed, impression. A cast is the impression of a mould, and therefore a facsimile of the object. If I pour liquid plaster on a coin, when it sets I have a mould, a sunk impression, of the coin. If I pour melted wax into the mould I obtain a cast, a facsimile of the coin. A footprint is a mould of the foot. A mould of the footprint is a cast of the foot, and a cast from the mould reproduces the footprint."

"Thank you," said the magistrate. "Then your moulds from these two footprints are really facsimiles of the murderer's shoes, and can be compared with these shoes which have been put in evidence?"

"Yes, and when we compare them they demonstrate a very important fact."

"What is that?"

"It is that the prisoner's shoes were not the shoes that made those footprints." A buzz of astonishment ran through the court, but Thorndyke continued stolidly: "The prisoner's shoes were not in my possession, so I went on to Barker's pond, on the clay margin of which I had seen footprints actually made by the prisoner. I took moulds of those footprints, and compared them with these from the sand. There are several important differences, which you will see if you compare them. To facilitate the comparison I have made transparent photographs of both sets of moulds to the same scale. Now, if we put the photograph of the mould of the prisoner's right shoe over that of the murderer's right shoe, and hold the two superposed photographs up to the light, we cannot make the two pictures coincide. They are exactly of the same length, but the shoes are of different shape. Moreover, if we put one of the nails in one photograph over the corresponding nail in the other photograph, we cannot make the rest of the nails coincide. But the most conclusive fact of all—from which there is no possible escape—is that the number of nails in the two shoes is not the same. In the sole of the prisoner's right shoe there are forty nails; in that of the murderer there are forty-one. The murderer has one nail too many."

There was a deathly silence in the court as the magistrates and Mr. Bashfield pored over the moulds and the prisoner's shoes, and examined the photographs against the light. Then the chairman asked: "Are these all the facts, or have you something more to tell us?" He was evidently anxious to get the key to this riddle.

"There is more evidence, your Worship," said Anstey. "The witness examined the body of deceased." Then, turning to Thorndyke, he asked:

"You were present at the post-mortem examination?"

"I was."

"Did you form any opinion as to the cause of death?"

"Yes. I came to the conclusion that death was occasioned by an overdose of morphia."

A universal gasp of amazement greeted this statement. Then the presiding magistrate protested breathlessly:

"But there was a wound, which we have been told was capable of causing instantaneous death. Was that not the case?"

"There was undoubtedly such a wound," replied Thorndyke. "But when that wound was inflicted the deceased had already been dead from a quarter to half an hour."

"This is incredible!" exclaimed the magistrate. "But, no doubt, you can give us your reasons for this amazing conclusion?"

"My opinion," said Thorndyke, "was based on several facts. In the first place, a wound inflicted on a living body gapes rather widely, owing to the retraction of the living skin. The skin of a dead body does not retract, and the wound, consequently, does not gape. This wound gaped very slightly, showing that death was recent, I should say, within half an hour. Then a wound on the living body becomes filled with blood, and blood is shed freely on the clothing. But the wound on the deceased contained only a little blood-clot. There was hardly any blood on the clothing, and I had already noticed that there was none on the sand where the body had lain."

"And you consider this quite conclusive?" the magistrate asked doubtfully.

"I do," answered Thorndyke. "But there was other evidence which was beyond all question. The weapon had partially divided both the aorta and the pulmonary artery—the main arteries of the body. Now, during life, these great vessels are full of blood at a high internal pressure, whereas after death they become almost empty. It follows that, if this wound had been inflicted during life, the cavity in which those vessels lie would have become filled with blood. As a matter of fact, it contained practically no blood, only the merest oozing from some small veins, so that it is certain that the wound was inflicted after death. The presence and nature of the poison I ascertained by analyzing certain secretions from the body, and the analysis enabled me to judge that the quantity of the poison was large; but the contents of the stomach were sent to Professor Copland for more exact examination."

"Is the result of Professor Copland's analysis known?" the magistrate asked Anstey.

"The professor is here, your Worship," replied Anstey, "and is prepared to swear to having obtained over one grain of morphia from the contents of the stomach; and as this, which is in itself a poisonous dose, is only the unabsorbed residue of what was actually swallowed, the total quantity taken must have been very large indeed."

"Thank you," said the magistrate. "And now, Dr. Thorndyke, if you have given us all the facts, perhaps you will tell us what conclusions you have drawn from them."

"The facts which I have stated," said Thorndyke, "appear to me to indicate the following sequence of events. The deceased died about midnight on September 27, from the effects of a poisonous dose of morphia, how or by whom administered I offer no opinion. I think that his body was conveyed in a boat to Sundersley Gap. The boat probably contained three men, of whom one remained in charge of it, one walked up the Gap and along the cliff towards St. Bridget's Bay, and the third, having put on the shoes of the deceased, carried the body along the shore to the Bay. This would account for the great depth and short stride of the tracks that have been spoken of as those of the deceased. Having reached the Bay, I believe that this man laid the corpse down on his tracks, and then trampled the sand in the neighbourhood. He next took off deceased's shoes and put them on the corpse; then he put on a pair of boots or shoes which he had been carrying—perhaps hung round his neck—and which had been prepared with nails to imitate Draper's shoes. In these shoes he again trampled over the area near the corpse. Then he walked backwards to the Shepherd's Path, and from it again, still backwards, to the face of the cliff. Here his accomplice had lowered a rope, by which he climbed up to the top. At the top he took off the nailed shoes, and the two men walked back to the Gap, where the man who had carried the rope took his confederate on his back, and carried him down to the boat to avoid leaving the tracks of stockinged feet. The tracks that I saw at the Gap certainly indicated that the man was carrying something very heavy when he returned to the boat."

"But why should the man have climbed a rope up the cliff when he could have walked up the Shepherd's Path?" the magistrate asked.

"Because," replied Thorndyke, "there would then have been a set of tracks leading out of the Bay without a corresponding set leading into it; and this would have instantly suggested to a smart police-officer—such as Sergeant Payne—a landing from a boat."

"Your explanation is highly ingenious," said the magistrate, "and appears to cover all the very remarkable facts. Have you anything more to tell us?"

"No, your Worship," was the reply, "excepting" (here he took from Polton the last pair of moulds and passed them up to the magistrate) "that you will probably find these moulds of importance presently."

As Thorndyke stepped from the box—for there was no cross-examination—the magistrates scrutinized the moulds with an air of perplexity; but they were too discreet to make any remark.

When the evidence of Professor Copland (which showed that an unquestionably lethal dose of morphia must have been swallowed) had been taken, the clerk called out the—to me—unfamiliar name of Jacob Gummer. Thereupon an enormous pair of brown dreadnought trousers, from the upper end of which a smack-boy's head and shoulders protruded, walked into the witness-box.

Jacob admitted at the outset that he was a smack-master's apprentice, and that he bad been "hired out" by his master to one Mr. Jezzard as deck-hand and cabin-boy of the yacht Otter.

"Now, Gummer," said Anstey, "do you remember the prisoner coming on board the yacht?"

"Yes. He has been on board twice. The first time was about a month ago. He went for a sail with us then. The second time was on the night when Mr. Hearn was murdered."

"Do you remember what sort of boots the prisoner was wearing the first time he came?"

"Yes. They were shoes with a lot of nails in the soles. I remember them because Mr. Jezzard made him take them off and put on a canvas pair."

"What was done with the nailed shoes?"

"Mr. Jezzard took 'em below to the cabin."

"And did Mr. Jezzard come up on deck again directly?"

"No. He stayed down in the cabin about ten minutes."

"Do you remember a parcel being delivered on board from a London boot-maker?"

"Yes. The postman brought it about four or five days after Mr. Draper had been on board. It was labelled 'Walker Bros., Boot and Shoe Makers, London.' Mr. Jezzard took a pair of shoes from it, for I saw them on the locker in the cabin the same day."

"Did you ever see him wear them?"

"No. I never see 'em again."

"Have you ever heard sounds of hammering on the yacht?"

"Yes. The night after the parcel came I was on the quay alongside, and I heard someone a-hammering in the cabin."

"What did the hammering sound like?"

"It sounded like a cobbler a-hammering in nails."

"Have you ever seen any boot-nails on the yacht?"

"Yes. When I was a-clearin' up the cabin the next mornin', I found a hobnail on the floor in a corner by the locker."

"Were you on board on the night when Mr. Hearn died?"

"Yes. I'd been ashore, but I came aboard about half-past nine."

"Did you see Mr. Hearn go ashore?"

"I see him leave the yacht. I had turned into my bunk and gone to sleep, when Mr. Jezzard calls down to me: 'We're putting Mr. Hearn ashore,' says he; 'and then,' he says, 'we're a-going for an hour's fishing. You needn't sit up,' he says, and with that he shuts the scuttle. Then I got up and slid back the scuttle and put my head out, and I see Mr. Jezzard and Mr. Leach a-helpin' Mr. Hearn acrost the deck. Mr. Hearn he looked as if he was drunk. They got him into the boat—and a rare job they had—and Mr. Pitford, what was in the boat already, he pushed off. And then I popped my head in again, 'cause I didn't want them to see me."

"Did they row to the steps?"

"No. I put my head out again when they were gone, and I heard 'em row round the yacht, and then pull out towards the mouth of the harbour. I couldn't see the boat, 'cause it was a very dark night."

"Very well. Now I am going to ask you about another matter. Do you know anyone of the name of Polton?"

"Yes," replied Gummer, turning a dusky red. "I've just found out his real name. I thought he was called Simmons."

"Tell us what you know about him," said Anstey, with a mischievous smile.

"Well," said the boy, with a ferocious scowl at the bland and smiling Polton, "one day he come down to the yacht when the gentlemen had gone ashore. I believe he'd seen 'em go. And he offers me ten shillin' to let him see all the boots and shoes we'd got on board. I didn't see no harm, so I turns out the whole lot in the cabin for him to look at. While he was lookin' at 'em he asks me to fetch a pair of mine from the fo'c'sle, so I fetches 'em. When I come back he was pitchin' the boots and shoes back into the locker. Then, presently, he nips off, and when he was gone I looked over the shoes, and then I found there was a pair missing. They was an old pair of Mr. Jezzard's, and what made him nick 'em is more than I can understand."

"Would you know those shoes if you saw them!"

"Yes, I should," replied the lad.

"Are these the pair?" Anstey handed the boy a pair of dilapidated canvas shoes, which he seized eagerly.

"Yes, these is the ones what he stole!" he exclaimed.

Anstey took them back from the boy's reluctant hands, and passed them up to the magistrate's desk. "I think," said he, "that if your Worship will compare these shoes with the last pair of moulds, you will have no doubt that these are the shoes which made the footprints from the sea to Sundersley Gap and back again."

The magistrates together compared the shoes and the moulds amidst a breathless silence. At length the chairman laid them down on the desk.

"It is impossible to doubt it," said he. "The broken heel and the tear in the rubber sole, with the remains of the chequered pattern, make the identity practically certain."

As the chairman made this statement I involuntarily glanced round to the place where Jezzard was sitting. But he was not there; neither he, nor Pitford, nor Leach. Taking advantage of the preoccupation of the Court, they had quietly slipped out of the door. But I was not the only person who had noted their absence. The inspector and the sergeant were already in earnest consultation, and a minute later they, too, hurriedly departed.

The proceedings now speedily came to an end. After a brief discussion with his brother-magistrates, the chairman addressed the Court.

"The remarkable and I may say startling evidence, which has been heard in this court to-day, if it has not fixed the guilt of this crime on any individual, has, at any rate, made it clear to our satisfaction that the prisoner is not the guilty person, and he is accordingly discharged. Mr. Draper, I have great pleasure in informing you that you are at liberty to leave the court, and that you do so entirely clear of all suspicion; and I congratulate you very heartily on the skill and ingenuity of your legal advisers, but for which the decision of the Court would, I am afraid, have been very different."

That evening, lawyers, witnesses, and the jubilant and grateful client gathered round a truly festive board to dine, and fight over again the battle of the day. But we were scarcely halfway through our meal when, to the indignation of the servants, Sergeant Payne burst breathlessly into the room.

"They've gone, sir!" he exclaimed, addressing Thorndyke. "They've given us the slip for good."

"Why, how can that be?" asked Thorndyke.

"They're dead, sir! All three of them!"

"Dead!" we all exclaimed.

"Yes. They made a burst for the yacht when they left the court, and they got on board and put out to sea at once, hoping, no doubt, to get clear as the light was just failing. But they were in such a hurry that they did not see a steam trawler that was entering, and was hidden by the pier. Then, just at the entrance, as the yacht was creeping out, the trawler hit her amidships, and fairly cut her in two. The three men were in the water in an instant, and were swept away in the eddy behind the north pier; and before any boat could put out to them they had all gone under. Jezzard's body came up on the beach just as I was coming away."

We were all silent and a little awed, but if any of us felt regret at the catastrophe, it was at the thought that three such cold-blooded villains should have made so easy an exit; and to one of us, at least, the news came as a blessed relief.

# THE BLUE CROSS
## BY G. K. CHESTERTON

G. K. Chesterton

# ORIGINALLY PUBLISHED IN 1910

# THE BLUE CROSS
## BY G. K. CHESTERTON

Father Brown, the creation of the noted author G. K. Chesterton, was a most unlikely detective. He s described as a short, stumpy Catholic priest, with shapeless clothes and a large umbrella. Originally the parish priest of Cobhole, Essex, he later made his base in London. His character is based on Father John O'Connor of Bradford who Chesterton knew well.

His methods, too, differed from those of his contemporaries. Rather than being based on the analysis of clues and logical deduction, he used intuition and his knowledge of "human evil" based on his experience as a priest and confessor. Despite, or perhaps because of, his background as a priest, Father Brown always emphasizes the rational.

Father Brown first appeared in the story "The Blue Cross" in *The Story Teller* September 1910, with several subsequent issues also containing stories. The first collection of stories, The Innocence of Father Brown appeared in 1911, and was followed by four more collections, the last of which was first published in 1935.

G. K. Chesterton was a well known writer, novelist, poet, philosopher and all round man of letters who was well respected during his lifetime and is still greatly admired by many people. He was a writer and columnist for *The Daily News* and the *Illustrated London News,* as well as a contributor to *The Encyclopedia Britannica*

The Father Brown character has appeared in numerous movies and television programs including the BBC's Mystery series. More stories featuring Father Brown may be found in the Resurrected Press editions of *The Innocence and Wisdon of Father Brown.*

# THE BLUE CROSS

Between the silver ribbon of morning and the green glittering ribbon of sea, the boat touched Harwich and let loose a swarm of folk like flies, among whom the man we must follow was by no means conspicuous—nor wished to be. There was nothing notable about him, except a slight contrast between the holiday gaiety of his clothes and the official gravity of his face. His clothes included a slight, pale grey jacket, a white waistcoat, and a silver straw hat with a grey-blue ribbon. His lean face was dark by contrast, and ended in a curt black beard that looked Spanish and suggested an Elizabethan ruff. He was smoking a cigarette with the seriousness of an idler. There was nothing about him to indicate the fact that the grey jacket covered a loaded revolver, that the white waistcoat covered a police card, or that the straw hat covered one of the most powerful intellects in Europe. For this was Valentin himself, the head of the Paris police and the most famous investigator of the world; and he was coming from Brussels to London to make the greatest arrest of the century.

Flambeau was in England. The police of three countries had tracked the great criminal at last from Ghent to Brussels, from Brussels to the Hook of Holland; and it was conjectured that he would take some advantage of the unfamiliarity and confusion of the Eucharistic Congress, then taking place in London. Probably he would travel as some minor clerk or secretary connected with it; but, of course, Valentin could not be certain; nobody could be certain about Flambeau.

It is many years now since this colossus of crime suddenly ceased keeping the world in a turmoil; and when he ceased, as they said after the death of Roland, there was a great quiet upon the earth. But in his best days (I mean, of course, his worst) Flambeau was a figure as statuesque and international as the Kaiser. Almost every morning the daily paper announced that he had escaped the consequences of one extraordinary crime by committing another. He was a Gascon of gigantic stature and bodily daring; and the wildest tales were told of his outbursts of athletic humour; how he turned the juge d'instruction upside down and stood him on his head, "to clear his mind"; how he ran down the Rue de Rivoli with a policeman under each arm. It is due to him to say that his fantastic physical strength was generally employed in such bloodless though undignified scenes; his real crimes were chiefly those of ingenious and wholesale robbery. But each of his thefts was almost a new sin, and would make a story by itself. It was he who ran the great Tyrolean Dairy Company in London, with no dairies, no cows, no carts, no milk, but with some thousand subscribers. These he served by the simple operation of moving the little milk cans outside people's doors to the doors of his own customers. It was he who had kept up an unaccountable and close correspondence with a young lady whose whole letter-bag was intercepted, by the extraordinary trick of photographing his messages infinitesimally small upon the slides of a microscope. A sweeping simplicity, however, marked many of his experiments. It is said that he once repainted all the numbers in a street in the dead of night merely to divert one traveller into a trap. It is quite certain that he invented a portable pillar-box, which he put up at corners in quiet suburbs on the chance of strangers dropping postal orders into it. Lastly, he was known to be a startling acrobat; despite his huge figure, he could leap like a grasshopper and melt into the tree-tops like a monkey. Hence the great Valentin, when he set out to find Flambeau, was perfectly aware that his adventures would not end when he had found him.

But how was he to find him? On this the great Valentin's ideas were still in process of settlement.

There was one thing which Flambeau, with all his dexterity of disguise, could not cover, and that was his singular height. If Valentin's quick eye had caught a tall apple-woman, a tall grenadier, or even a tolerably tall duchess, he might have arrested them on the spot. But all along his train there was nobody that could be a disguised Flambeau, any more than a cat could be a disguised giraffe. About the people on the boat he had already satisfied himself; and the people picked up at Harwich or on the journey limited themselves with certainty to six. There was a short railway official travelling up to the terminus, three fairly short market gardeners picked up two stations afterwards, one very short widow lady going up from a small Essex town, and a very short Roman Catholic priest going up from a small Essex village. When it came to the last case, Valentin gave it up and almost laughed. The little priest was so much the essence of those Eastern flats; he had a face as round and dull as a Norfolk dumpling; he had eyes as empty as the North Sea; he had several brown paper parcels, which he was quite incapable of collecting. The Eucharistic Congress had doubtless sucked out of their local stagnation many such creatures, blind and helpless, like moles disinterred. Valentin was a sceptic in the severe style of France, and could have no love for priests. But he could have pity for them, and this one might have provoked pity in anybody. He had a large, shabby umbrella, which constantly fell on the floor. He did not seem to know which was the right end of his return ticket. He explained with a moon-calf simplicity to everybody in the carriage that he had to be careful, because he had something made of real silver "with blue stones" in one of his brown-paper parcels. His quaint blending of Essex flatness with saintly simplicity continuously amused the Frenchman till the priest arrived (somehow) at Tottenham with all his parcels, and came back for his umbrella. When he did the last, Valentin even had the good nature to warn him not to take care of the silver by telling everybody about it. But to whomever he talked, Valentin kept his eye open for someone else; he looked out steadily for anyone, rich or poor, male or female, who was well up to six feet; for Flambeau was four inches above it.

He alighted at Liverpool Street, however, quite conscientiously secure that he had not missed the criminal so far. He then went to Scotland Yard to regularise his position and arrange for help in case of need; he then lit another cigarette and went for a long stroll in the streets of London. As he was walking in the streets and squares beyond Victoria, he paused suddenly and stood. It was a quaint, quiet square, very typical of London, full of an accidental stillness. The tall, flat houses round looked at once prosperous and uninhabited; the square of shrubbery in the centre looked as deserted as a green Pacific islet. One of the four sides was much higher than the rest, like a dais; and the line of this side was broken by one of London's admirable accidents—a restaurant that looked as if it had strayed from Soho. It was an unreasonably attractive object, with dwarf plants in pots and long, striped blinds of lemon yellow and white. It stood specially high above the street, and in the usual patchwork way of London, a flight of steps from the

street ran up to meet the front door almost as a fire-escape
might run up to a first-floor window. Valentin stood and smoked
in front of the yellow-white blinds and considered them long.

The most incredible thing about miracles is that they
happen. A few clouds in heaven do come together into the
staring shape of one human eye. A tree does stand up in the
landscape of a doubtful journey in the exact and elaborate shape
of a note of interrogation. I have seen both these things myself
within the last few days. Nelson does die in the instant of
victory; and a man named Williams does quite accidentally
murder a man named Williamson; it sounds like a sort of
infanticide. In short, there is in life an element of elfin
coincidence which people reckoning on the prosaic may
perpetually miss. As it has been well expressed in the paradox of
Poe, wisdom should reckon on the unforeseen.

Aristide Valentin was unfathomably French; and the French
intelligence is intelligence specially and solely. He was not "a
thinking machine"; for that is a brainless phrase of modern
fatalism and materialism. A machine only is a machine because
it cannot think. But he was a thinking man, and a plain man at
the same time. All his wonderful successes, that looked like
conjuring, had been gained by plodding logic, by clear and
commonplace French thought. The French electrify the world not
by starting any paradox, they electrify it by carrying out a
truism. They carry a truism so far—as in the French Revolution.
But exactly because Valentin understood reason, he understood
the limits of reason. Only a man who knows nothing of motors
talks of motoring without petrol; only a man who knows nothing
of reason talks of reasoning without strong, undisputed first
principles. Here he had no strong first principles. Flambeau had
been missed at Harwich; and if he was in London at all, he
might be anything from a tall tramp on Wimbledon Common to a
tall toast-master at the Hotel Metropole. In such a naked state of
nescience, Valentin had a view and a method of his own.

In such cases he reckoned on the unforeseen. In such cases,
when he could not follow the train of the reasonable, he coldly
and carefully followed the train of the unreasonable. Instead of
going to the right places—banks, police stations, rendezvous—he
systematically went to the wrong places; knocked at every empty
house, turned down every cul de sac, went up every lane blocked

with rubbish, went round every crescent that led him uselessly out of the way. He defended this crazy course quite logically. He said that if one had a clue this was the worst way; but if one had no clue at all it was the best, because there was just the chance that any oddity that caught the eye of the pursuer might be the same that had caught the eye of the pursued. Somewhere a man must begin, and it had better be just where another man might stop. Something about that flight of steps up to the shop, something about the quietude and quaintness of the restaurant, roused all the detective's rare romantic fancy and made him resolve to strike at random. He went up the steps, and sitting down at a table by the window, asked for a cup of black coffee.

It was half-way through the morning, and he had not breakfasted; the slight litter of other breakfasts stood about on the table to remind him of his hunger; and adding a poached egg to his order, he proceeded musingly to shake some white sugar into his coffee, thinking all the time about Flambeau. He remembered how Flambeau had escaped, once by a pair of nail scissors, and once by a house on fire; once by having to pay for an unstamped letter, and once by getting people to look through a telescope at a comet that might destroy the world. He thought his detective brain as good as the criminal's, which was true. But he fully realised the disadvantage. "The criminal is the creative artist; the detective only the critic," he said with a sour smile, and lifted his coffee cup to his lips slowly, and put it down very quickly. He had put salt in it.

He looked at the vessel from which the silvery powder had come; it was certainly a sugar-basin; as unmistakably meant for sugar as a champagne-bottle for champagne. He wondered why they should keep salt in it. He looked to see if there were any more orthodox vessels. Yes; there were two salt-cellars quite full. Perhaps there was some speciality in the condiment in the salt-cellars. He tasted it; it was sugar. Then he looked round at the restaurant with a refreshed air of interest, to see if there were any other traces of that singular artistic taste which puts the sugar in the salt-cellars and the salt in the sugar-basin. Except for an odd splash of some dark fluid on one of the white-papered walls, the whole place appeared neat, cheerful and ordinary. He rang the bell for the waiter.

When that official hurried up, fuzzy-haired and somewhat blear-eyed at that early hour, the detective (who was not without an appreciation of the simpler forms of humour) asked him to taste the sugar and see if it was up to the high reputation of the hotel. The result was that the waiter yawned suddenly and woke up.

"Do you play this delicate joke on your customers every morning?" inquired Valentin. "Does changing the salt and sugar never pall on you as a jest?"

The waiter, when this irony grew clearer, stammeringly assured him that the establishment had certainly no such intention; it must be a most curious mistake. He picked up the sugar-basin and looked at it; he picked up the salt-cellar and looked at that, his face growing more and more bewildered. At last he abruptly excused himself, and hurrying away, returned in a few seconds with the proprietor. The proprietor also examined the sugar-basin and then the salt-cellar; the proprietor also looked bewildered.

Suddenly the waiter seemed to grow inarticulate with a rush of words.

"I zink," he stuttered eagerly, "I zink it is those two clergymen."

"What two clergymen?"

"The two clergymen," said the waiter, "that threw soup at the wall."

"Threw soup at the wall?" repeated Valentin, feeling sure this must be some singular Italian metaphor.

"Yes, yes," said the attendant excitedly, and pointed at the dark splash on the white paper; "threw it over there on the wall."

Valentin looked his query at the proprietor, who came to his rescue with fuller reports.

"Yes, sir," he said, "it's quite true, though I don't suppose it has anything to do with the sugar and salt. Two clergymen came in and drank soup here very early, as soon as the shutters were taken down. They were both very quiet, respectable people; one of them paid the bill and went out; the other, who seemed a slower coach altogether, was some minutes longer getting his things together. But he went at last. Only, the instant before he stepped into the street he deliberately picked up his cup, which he had only half emptied, and threw the soup slap on the wall. I was in the back room myself, and so was the waiter; so I could only rush out in time to find the wall splashed and the shop empty. It don't do any particular damage, but it was confounded cheek; and I tried to catch the men in the street. They were too far off though; I only noticed they went round the next corner into Carstairs Street."

The detective was on his feet, hat settled and stick in hand. He had already decided that in the universal darkness of his mind he could only follow the first odd finger that pointed; and this finger was odd enough. Paying his bill and clashing the glass doors behind him, he was soon swinging round into the other street.

It was fortunate that even in such fevered moments his eye was cool and quick. Something in a shop-front went by him like a mere flash; yet he went back to look at it. The shop was a popular greengrocer and fruiterer's, an array of goods set out in the open air and plainly ticketed with their names and prices. In the two most prominent compartments were two heaps, of oranges and of nuts respectively. On the heap of nuts lay a scrap of cardboard, on which was written in bold, blue chalk, "Best tangerine oranges, two a penny." On the oranges was the equally clear and exact description, "Finest Brazil nuts, 4d. a lb." M. Valentin looked at these two placards and fancied he had met this highly subtle form of humour before, and that somewhat recently. He drew the attention of the red-faced fruiterer, who was looking rather sullenly up and down the street, to this inaccuracy in his advertisements. The fruiterer said nothing, but sharply put each card into its proper place. The detective, leaning elegantly on his walking-cane, continued to scrutinise the shop. At last he said, "Pray excuse my apparent irrelevance, my good sir, but I should like to ask you a question in experimental psychology and the association of ideas."

The red-faced shopman regarded him with an eye of menace; but he continued gaily, swinging his cane, "Why," he pursued, "why are two tickets wrongly placed in a greengrocer's shop like a shovel hat that has come to London for a holiday? Or, in case I do not make myself clear, what is the mystical association which connects the idea of nuts marked as oranges with the idea of two clergymen, one tall and the other short?"

The eyes of the tradesman stood out of his head like a snail's; he really seemed for an instant likely to fling himself upon the stranger. At last he stammered angrily: "I don't know what you 'ave to do with it, but if you're one of their friends, you can tell 'em from me that I'll knock their silly 'eads off, parsons or no parsons, if they upset my apples again."

"Indeed?" asked the detective, with great sympathy. "Did they upset your apples?"

"One of 'em did," said the heated shopman; "rolled 'em all over the street. I'd 'ave caught the fool but for havin' to pick 'em up."

"Which way did these parsons go?" asked Valentin.

"Up that second road on the left-hand side, and then across the square," said the other promptly.

"Thanks," replied Valentin, and vanished like a fairy. On the other side of the second square he found a policeman, and said: "This is urgent, constable; have you seen two clergymen in shovel hats?"

The policeman began to chuckle heavily. "I 'ave, sir; and if you arst me, one of 'em was drunk. He stood in the middle of the road that bewildered that—"

"Which way did they go?" snapped Valentin.

"They took one of them yellow buses over there," answered the man; "them that go to Hampstead."

Valentin produced his official card and said very rapidly: "Call up two of your men to come with me in pursuit," and crossed the road with such contagious energy that the ponderous policeman was moved to almost agile obedience. In a minute and a half the French detective was joined on the opposite pavement by an inspector and a man in plain clothes.

"Well, sir," began the former, with smiling importance, "and what may—?"

Valentin pointed suddenly with his cane. "I'll tell you on the top of that omnibus," he said, and was darting and dodging across the tangle of the traffic. When all three sank panting on the top seats of the yellow vehicle, the inspector said: "We could go four times as quick in a taxi."

"Quite true," replied their leader placidly, "if we only had an idea of where we were going."

"Well, where are you going?" asked the other, staring.

Valentin smoked frowningly for a few seconds; then, removing his cigarette, he said: "If you know what a man's doing, get in front of him; but if you want to guess what he's doing, keep behind him. Stray when he strays; stop when he stops; travel as slowly as he. Then you may see what he saw and may act as he acted. All we can do is to keep our eyes skinned for a queer thing."

"What sort of queer thing do you mean?" asked the inspector.

"Any sort of queer thing," answered Valentin, and relapsed into obstinate silence.

The yellow omnibus crawled up the northern roads for what seemed like hours on end; the great detective would not explain further, and perhaps his assistants felt a silent and growing doubt of his errand. Perhaps, also, they felt a silent and growing desire for lunch, for the hours crept long past the normal luncheon hour, and the long roads of the North London suburbs seemed to shoot out into length after length like an infernal telescope. It was one of those journeys on which a man perpetually feels that now at last he must have come to the end of the universe, and then finds he has only come to the beginning of Tufnell Park. London died away in draggled taverns and dreary scrubs, and then was unaccountably born again in blazing high streets and blatant hotels. It was like passing through thirteen separate vulgar cities all just touching each other. But though the winter twilight was already threatening the road ahead of them, the Parisian detective still sat silent and watchful, eyeing the frontage of the streets that slid by on either side. By the time they had left Camden Town behind, the policemen were nearly asleep; at least, they gave something like a jump as Valentin leapt erect, struck a hand on each man's shoulder, and shouted to the driver to stop.

They tumbled down the steps into the road without realising why they had been dislodged; when they looked round for enlightenment they found Valentin triumphantly pointing his finger towards a window on the left side of the road. It was a large window, forming part of the long facade of a gilt and palatial public-house; it was the part reserved for respectable dining, and labelled "Restaurant." This window, like all the rest along the frontage of the hotel, was of frosted and figured glass;

but in the middle of it was a big, black smash, like a star in the ice.

"Our cue at last," cried Valentin, waving his stick; "the place with the broken window."

"What window? What cue?" asked his principal assistant. "Why, what proof is there that this has anything to do with them?"

Valentin almost broke his bamboo stick with rage.

"Proof!" he cried. "Good God! the man is looking for proof! Why, of course, the chances are twenty to one that it has nothing to do with them. But what else can we do? Don't you see we must either follow one wild possibility or else go home to bed?" He banged his way into the restaurant, followed by his companions, and they were soon seated at a late luncheon at a little table, and looked at the star of smashed glass from the inside. Not that it was very informative to them even then.

"Got your window broken, I see," said Valentin to the waiter as he paid the bill.

"Yes, sir," answered the attendant, bending busily over the change, to which Valentin silently added an enormous tip. The waiter straightened himself with mild but unmistakable animation.

"Ah, yes, sir," he said. "Very odd thing, that, sir."

"Indeed?" Tell us about it," said the detective with careless curiosity.

"Well, two gents in black came in," said the waiter; "two of those foreign parsons that are running about. They had a cheap and quiet little lunch, and one of them paid for it and went out. The other was just going out to join him when I looked at my change again and found he'd paid me more than three times too much. 'Here,' I says to the chap who was nearly out of the door, 'you've paid too much.' 'Oh,' he says, very cool, 'have we?' 'Yes,' I says, and picks up the bill to show him. Well, that was a knock-out."

"What do you mean?" asked his interlocutor.

"Well, I'd have sworn on seven Bibles that I'd put 4s. on that bill. But now I saw I'd put 14s., as plain as paint."

"Well?" cried Valentin, moving slowly, but with burning eyes, "and then?"

"The parson at the door he says all serene, 'Sorry to confuse your accounts, but it'll pay for the window.' 'What window?' I says. 'The one I'm going to break,' he says, and smashed that blessed pane with his umbrella."

All three inquirers made an exclamation; and the inspector said under his breath, "Are we after escaped lunatics?" The waiter went on with some relish for the ridiculous story:

"I was so knocked silly for a second, I couldn't do anything. The man marched out of the place and joined his friend just round the corner. Then they went so quick up Bullock Street that I couldn't catch them, though I ran round the bars to do it."

"Bullock Street," said the detective, and shot up that thoroughfare as quickly as the strange couple he pursued.

Their journey now took them through bare brick ways like tunnels; streets with few lights and even with few windows; streets that seemed built out of the blank backs of everything and everywhere. Dusk was deepening, and it was not easy even for the London policemen to guess in what exact direction they were treading. The inspector, however, was pretty certain that they would eventually strike some part of Hampstead Heath. Abruptly one bulging gas-lit window broke the blue twilight like a bull's-eye lantern; and Valentin stopped an instant before a little garish sweetstuff shop. After an instant's hesitation he went in; he stood amid the gaudy colours of the confectionery with entire gravity and bought thirteen chocolate cigars with a certain care. He was clearly preparing an opening; but he did not need one.

An angular, elderly young woman in the shop had regarded his elegant appearance with a merely automatic inquiry; but when she saw the door behind him blocked with the blue uniform of the inspector, her eyes seemed to wake up.

"Oh," she said, "if you've come about that parcel, I've sent it off already."

"Parcel?" repeated Valentin; and it was his turn to look inquiring.

"I mean the parcel the gentleman left—the clergyman gentleman."

"For goodness' sake," said Valentin, leaning forward with his first real confession of eagerness, "for Heaven's sake tell us what happened exactly."

"Well," said the woman a little doubtfully, "the clergymen came in about half an hour ago and bought some peppermints and talked a bit, and then went off towards the Heath. But a second after, one of them runs back into the shop and says, 'Have I left a parcel!' Well, I looked everywhere and couldn't see one; so he says, 'Never mind; but if it should turn up, please post it to this address,' and he left me the address and a shilling for my trouble. And sure enough, though I thought I'd looked everywhere, I found he'd left a brown paper parcel, so I posted it to the place he said. I can't remember the address now; it was somewhere in Westminster. But as the thing seemed so important, I thought perhaps the police had come about it."

"So they have," said Valentin shortly. "Is Hampstead Heath near here?"

"Straight on for fifteen minutes," said the woman, "and you'll come right out on the open." Valentin sprang out of the shop and began to run. The other detectives followed him at a reluctant trot.

The street they threaded was so narrow and shut in by shadows that when they came out unexpectedly into the void common and vast sky they were startled to find the evening still so light and clear. A perfect dome of peacock-green sank into gold amid the blackening trees and the dark violet distances. The glowing green tint was just deep enough to pick out in points of crystal one or two stars. All that was left of the daylight lay in a golden glitter across the edge of Hampstead and that popular hollow which is called the Vale of Health. The holiday makers who roam this region had not wholly dispersed; a few couples sat shapelessly on benches; and here and there a distant girl still shrieked in one of the swings. The glory of heaven deepened and darkened around the sublime vulgarity of man; and standing on the slope and looking across the valley, Valentin beheld the thing which he sought.

Among the black and breaking groups in that distance was one especially black which did not break—a group of two figures clerically clad. Though they seemed as small as insects, Valentin could see that one of them was much smaller than the other. Though the other had a student's stoop and an inconspicuous manner, he could see that the man was well over six feet high. He shut his teeth and went forward, whirling his stick impatiently. By the time he had substantially diminished the distance and magnified the two black figures as in a vast microscope, he had perceived something else; something which startled him, and yet which he had somehow expected. Whoever was the tall priest, there could be no doubt about the identity of the short one. It was his friend of the Harwich train, the stumpy little cure of Essex whom he had warned about his brown paper parcels.

Now, so far as this went, everything fitted in finally and rationally enough. Valentin had learned by his inquiries that morning that a Father Brown from Essex was bringing up a silver cross with sapphires, a relic of considerable value, to show some of the foreign priests at the congress. This undoubtedly was the "silver with blue stones"; and Father Brown undoubtedly was the little greenhorn in the train. Now there was nothing wonderful about the fact that what Valentin had found out Flambeau had also found out; Flambeau found out everything. Also there was nothing wonderful in the fact that when Flambeau heard of a sapphire cross he should try to steal it; that was the most natural thing in all natural history. And most certainly there was nothing wonderful about the fact that Flambeau should have it all his own way with such a silly sheep as the man with the umbrella and the parcels. He was the sort of man whom anybody could lead on a string to the North Pole; it was not surprising that an actor like Flambeau, dressed as another priest, could lead him to Hampstead Heath. So far the crime seemed clear enough; and while the detective pitied the priest for his helplessness, he almost despised Flambeau for condescending to so gullible a victim. But when Valentin thought of all that had happened in between, of all that had led him to his triumph, he racked his brains for the smallest rhyme or reason in it. What had the stealing of a blue-and-silver cross from a priest from Essex to do with chucking soup at wall paper? What had it to do with calling nuts oranges, or with paying for windows first and breaking them afterwards? He had come to the end of his chase; yet somehow he had missed the middle of it. When he failed (which was seldom), he had usually grasped the clue, but nevertheless missed the criminal. Here he had grasped the criminal, but still he could not grasp the clue.

The two figures that they followed were crawling like black flies across the huge green contour of a hill. They were evidently sunk in conversation, and perhaps did not notice where they were going; but they were certainly going to the wilder and more silent heights of the Heath. As their pursuers gained on them, the latter had to use the undignified attitudes of the deer-stalker, to crouch behind clumps of trees and even to crawl prostrate in deep grass. By these ungainly ingenuities the hunters even came close enough to the quarry to hear the murmur of the discussion, but no word could be distinguished except the word "reason" recurring frequently in a high and almost childish voice. Once over an abrupt dip of land and a dense tangle of thickets, the detectives actually lost the two figures they were following. They did not find the trail again for an agonising ten minutes, and then it led round the brow of a great dome of hill overlooking an amphitheatre of rich and desolate sunset scenery. Under a tree in this commanding yet neglected spot was an old ramshackle wooden seat. On this seat sat the two priests still in serious speech together. The gorgeous green and gold still clung to the darkening horizon; but the dome above was turning slowly from peacock-green to peacock-blue, and the stars detached themselves more and more like solid jewels. Mutely motioning to his followers, Valentin contrived to creep up behind the big branching tree, and, standing there in deathly silence, heard the words of the strange priests for the first time.

After he had listened for a minute and a half, he was gripped by a devilish doubt. Perhaps he had dragged the two English policemen to the wastes of a nocturnal heath on an errand no saner than seeking figs on its thistles. For the two priests were talking exactly like priests, piously, with learning and leisure, about the most aerial enigmas of theology. The little Essex priest spoke the more simply, with his round face turned to the strengthening stars; the other talked with his head bowed, as if he were not even worthy to look at them. But no more innocently clerical conversation could have been heard in any white Italian cloister or black Spanish cathedral.

The first he heard was the tail of one of Father Brown's sentences, which ended: "... what they really meant in the Middle Ages by the heavens being incorruptible."

The taller priest nodded his bowed head and said:

"Ah, yes, these modern infidels appeal to their reason; but who can look at those millions of worlds and not feel that there may well be wonderful universes above us where reason is utterly unreasonable?"

"No," said the other priest; "reason is always reasonable, even in the last limbo, in the lost borderland of things. I know that people charge the Church with lowering reason, but it is just the other way. Alone on earth, the Church makes reason really supreme. Alone on earth, the Church affirms that God himself is bound by reason."

The other priest raised his austere face to the spangled sky and said:

"Yet who knows if in that infinite universe—?"

"Only infinite physically," said the little priest, turning sharply in his seat, "not infinite in the sense of escaping from the laws of truth."

Valentin behind his tree was tearing his fingernails with silent fury. He seemed almost to hear the sniggers of the English detectives whom he had brought so far on a fantastic guess only to listen to the metaphysical gossip of two mild old parsons. In his impatience he lost the equally elaborate answer of the tall cleric, and when he listened again it was again Father Brown who was speaking:

"Reason and justice grip the remotest and the loneliest star. Look at those stars. Don't they look as if they were single diamonds and sapphires? Well, you can imagine any mad botany or geology you please. Think of forests of adamant with leaves of brilliants. Think the moon is a blue moon, a single elephantine sapphire. But don't fancy that all that frantic astronomy would make the smallest difference to the reason and justice of conduct. On plains of opal, under cliffs cut out of pearl, you would still find a notice-board, 'Thou shalt not steal.'"

Valentin was just in the act of rising from his rigid and crouching attitude and creeping away as softly as might be, felled by the one great folly of his life. But something in the very silence of the tall priest made him stop until the latter spoke. When at last he did speak, he said simply, his head bowed and his hands on his knees:

"Well, I think that other worlds may perhaps rise higher than our reason. The mystery of heaven is unfathomable, and I for one can only bow my head."

Then, with brow yet bent and without changing by the faintest shade his attitude or voice, he added:

"Just hand over that sapphire cross of yours, will you? We're all alone here, and I could pull you to pieces like a straw doll."

The utterly unaltered voice and attitude added a strange violence to that shocking change of speech. But the guarder of the relic only seemed to turn his head by the smallest section of the compass. He seemed still to have a somewhat foolish face turned to the stars. Perhaps he had not understood. Or, perhaps, he had understood and sat rigid with terror.

"Yes," said the tall priest, in the same low voice and in the same still posture, "yes, I am Flambeau."

Then, after a pause, he said:

"Come, will you give me that cross?"

"No," said the other, and the monosyllable had an odd sound.

Flambeau suddenly flung off all his pontifical pretensions. The great robber leaned back in his seat and laughed low but long.

"No," he cried, "you won't give it me, you proud prelate. You won't give it me, you little celibate simpleton. Shall I tell you why you won't give it me? Because I've got it already in my own breast-pocket."

The small man from Essex turned what seemed to be a dazed face in the dusk, and said, with the timid eagerness of "The Private Secretary":

"Are—are you sure?"

Flambeau yelled with delight.

"Really, you're as good as a three-act farce," he cried. "Yes, you turnip, I am quite sure. I had the sense to make a duplicate of the right parcel, and now, my friend, you've got the duplicate and I've got the jewels. An old dodge, Father Brown—a very old dodge."

"Yes," said Father Brown, and passed his hand through his hair with the same strange vagueness of manner. "Yes, I've heard of it before."

The colossus of crime leaned over to the little rustic priest with a sort of sudden interest.

"You have heard of it?" he asked. "Where have you heard of it?"

"Well, I mustn't tell you his name, of course," said the little man simply. "He was a penitent, you know. He had lived prosperously for about twenty years entirely on duplicate brown paper parcels. And so, you see, when I began to suspect you, I thought of this poor chap's way of doing it at once."

"Began to suspect me?" repeated the outlaw with increased intensity. "Did you really have the gumption to suspect me just because I brought you up to this bare part of the heath?"

"No, no," said Brown with an air of apology. "You see, I suspected you when we first met. It's that little bulge up the sleeve where you people have the spiked bracelet."

"How in Tartarus," cried Flambeau, "did you ever hear of the spiked bracelet?"

"Oh, one's little flock, you know!" said Father Brown, arching his eyebrows rather blankly. "When I was a curate in Hartlepool, there were three of them with spiked bracelets. So, as I suspected you from the first, don't you see, I made sure that the cross should go safe, anyhow. I'm afraid I watched you, you know. So at last I saw you change the parcels. Then, don't you see, I changed them back again. And then I left the right one behind."

"Left it behind?" repeated Flambeau, and for the first time there was another note in his voice beside his triumph.

"Well, it was like this," said the little priest, speaking in the same unaffected way. "I went back to that sweet-shop and asked if I'd left a parcel, and gave them a particular address if it turned up. Well, I knew I hadn't; but when I went away again I did. So, instead of running after me with that valuable parcel, they have sent it flying to a friend of mine in Westminster." Then he added rather sadly: "I learnt that, too, from a poor fellow in Hartlepool. He used to do it with handbags he stole at railway stations, but he's in a monastery now. Oh, one gets to know, you know," he added, rubbing his head again with the same sort of desperate apology. "We can't help being priests. People come and tell us these things."

Flambeau tore a brown-paper parcel out of his inner pocket and rent it in pieces. There was nothing but paper and sticks of lead inside it. He sprang to his feet with a gigantic gesture, and cried:

"I don't believe you. I don't believe a bumpkin like you could manage all that. I believe you've still got the stuff on you, and if you don't give it up—why, we're all alone, and I'll take it by force!"

"No," said Father Brown simply, and stood up also, "you won't take it by force. First, because I really haven't still got it. And, second, because we are not alone."

Flambeau stopped in his stride forward.

"Behind that tree," said Father Brown, pointing, "are two strong policemen and the greatest detective alive. How did they come here, do you ask? Why, I brought them, of course! How did I do it? Why, I'll tell you if you like! Lord bless you, we have to know twenty such things when we work among the criminal classes! Well, I wasn't sure you were a thief, and it would never do to make a scandal against one of our own clergy. So I just tested you to see if anything would make you show yourself. A man generally makes a small scene if he finds salt in his coffee; if he doesn't, he has some reason for keeping quiet. I changed the salt and sugar, and you kept quiet. A man generally objects if his bill is three times too big. If he pays it, he has some motive for passing unnoticed. I altered your bill, and you paid it."

The world seemed waiting for Flambeau to leap like a tiger. But he was held back as by a spell; he was stunned with the utmost curiosity.

"Well," went on Father Brown, with lumbering lucidity, "as you wouldn't leave any tracks for the police, of course somebody had to. At every place we went to, I took care to do something that would get us talked about for the rest of the day. I didn't do much harm—a splashed wall, spilt apples, a broken window; but I saved the cross, as the cross will always be saved. It is at Westminster by now. I rather wonder you didn't stop it with the Donkey's Whistle."

"With the what?" asked Flambeau.

"I'm glad you've never heard of it," said the priest, making a face. "It's a foul thing. I'm sure you're too good a man for a Whistler. I couldn't have countered it even with the Spots myself; I'm not strong enough in the legs."

"What on earth are you talking about?" asked the other.

"Well, I did think you'd know the Spots," said Father Brown, agreeably surprised. "Oh, you can't have gone so very wrong yet!"

"How in blazes do you know all these horrors?" cried Flambeau.

The shadow of a smile crossed the round, simple face of his clerical opponent.

"Oh, by being a celibate simpleton, I suppose," he said. "Has it never struck you that a man who does next to nothing but hear men's real sins is not likely to be wholly unaware of human evil? But, as a matter of fact, another part of my trade, too, made me sure you weren't a priest."

"What?" asked the thief, almost gaping.

"You attacked reason," said Father Brown. "It's bad theology."

And even as he turned away to collect his property, the three policemen came out from under the twilight trees. Flambeau was an artist and a sportsman. He stepped back and swept Valentin a great bow.

"Do not bow to me, mon ami," said Valentin with silver clearness. "Let us both bow to our master."

And they both stood an instant uncovered while the little Essex priest blinked about for his umbrella.

# THE CASE OF THE POCKET
# DIARY FOUND IN THE SNOW
## BY AUGUSTA GRÖNER

ORIGINALLY PUBLISHED IN 1910

# THE CASE OF THE POCKET DIARY FOUND IN THE SNOW

## BY AUGUSTA GRÖNER

What makes Joe Muller of interest is that he works not in London or Paris, but in Vienna, the capital of the Austro-Hungarian Empire as a member of the Imperial police. At one time he had been falsely accused and convicted of a crime, and it was only after he had been exonerated that he became a member of the police. Because of this, he had an unusual perspective on the law and has a devotion to the truth.

As a detective, he has none of the flare or brilliance of most of his contemporaries. He is a slight, middle aged man who dresses shabbily and lives plainly. His methods rely more on dogged persistence than flashes of deductive logic. His success owes more to his understanding of human nature than anything else. He is sometimes at odds with his superiors who hold their positions more through birth than ability, but they value his ability to produce results on even the most difficult cases. Despite his natural reticence he has acquired a certain reputation in his field.

Not much information is available about the publishing history of The Joe Muller stories. They were originally written in German by Augusta Groner and translated into English for a 1910 collection, *Joe Muller, Detective: Being the Account of Some Adventures in the Professional Experience of a Member of the Imperial Austrian Police*, by the American, Grace Isabel Colbron.

Additional stories featuring Joe Muller may be found in the Resurrected Press release *Joe Muller, Imperial Detective*.

# The Case of The Pocket Diary
# Found in the Snow

## CHAPTER ONE. THE DISCOVERY IN THE SNOW

A quiet winter evening had sunk down upon the great city. The clock in the old clumsy church steeple of the factory district had not yet struck eight, when the side door of one of the large buildings opened and a man came out into the silent street.

It was Ludwig Amster, one of the working-men in the factory, starting on his homeward way. It was not a pleasant road, this street along the edge of the city. The town showed itself from its most disagreeable side here, with malodorous factories, rickety tenements, untidy open stretches and dumping grounds offensive both to eye and nostril.

Even by day the street that Amster took was empty; by night it was absolutely quiet and dark, as dark as were the thoughts of the solitary man. He walked along, brooding over his troubles. Scarcely an hour before he had been discharged from the factory because of his refusal to submit to the injustice of his foreman.

The yellow light of the few lanterns show nothing but high board walls and snow drifts, stone heaps, and now and then the remains of a neglected garden. Here and there a stunted tree or a wild shrub bent their twigs under the white burden which the winter had laid upon them. Ludwig Amster, who had walked this street for several years, knew his path so well that he could take it blindfolded. The darkness did not worry him, but he walked somewhat more slowly than usual, for he knew that under the thin covering of fresh-fallen snow there lay the ice of the night before. He walked carefully, watching for the slippery places.

He had been walking about half an hour, perhaps, when he came to a cross street. Here he noticed the tracks of a wagon, the trace still quite fresh, as the slowly falling flakes did not yet cover it. The tracks led out towards the north, out on to the hilly, open fields.

Amster was somewhat astonished. It was very seldom that a carriage came into this neighbourhood, and yet these narrow wheel-tracks could have been made only by an equipage of that character. The heavy trucks which passed these roads occasionally had much wider wheels. But Amster was to find still more to astonish him.

In one corner near the cross-roads stood a solitary lamp-post. The light of the lamp fell sharply on the snow, on the wagon tracks, and—on something else besides.

Amster halted, bent down to look at it, and shook his head as if in doubt.

A number of small pieces of glass gleamed up at him and between them, like tiny roses, red drops of blood shone on the white snow. All this was a few steps to one side of the wagon tracks.

"What can have happened here—here in this weird spot, where a cry for help would never be heard? where there would be no one to bring help?"

So Amster asked himself, but his discovery gave him no answer. His curiosity was aroused, however, and he wished to know more. He followed up the tracks and saw that the drops of blood led further on, although there was no more glass. The drops could still be seen for a yard further, reaching out almost to the board fence that edged the sidewalk. Through the broken planks of this fence the rough bare twigs of a thorn bush stretched their brown fingers. On the upper side of the few scattered leaves there was snow, and blood.

Amster's wide serious eyes soon found something else. Beside the bush there lay a tiny package. He lifted it up. It was a small, light, square package, wrapped in ordinary brown paper. Where the paper came together it was fastened by two little lumps of black bread, which were still moist. He turned the package over and shook his head again. On the other side was written, in pencil, the lettering uncertain, as if scribbled in great haste and in agitation, the sentence, "Please take this to the nearest police station."

The words were like a cry for help, frozen on to the ugly paper. Amster shivered; he had a feeling that this was a matter of life and death.

The wagon tracks in the lonely street, the broken pieces of glass and the drops of blood, showing that some occupant of the vehicle had broken the window, in the hope of escape, perhaps, or to throw out the package which should bring assistance—all these facts grouped themselves together in the brain of the intelligent working-man to form some terrible tragedy where his assistance, if given at once, might be of great use. He had a warm heart besides, a heart that reached out to this unknown who was in distress, and who threw out the call for help which had fallen into his hands.

He waited no longer to ponder over the matter, but started off at a full run for the nearest police station. He rushed into the room and told his story breathlessly.

They took him into the next room, the office of the commissioner for the day. The official in charge, who had been engaged in earnest conversation with a small, frail-looking, middle-aged man, turned to Amster with a question as to what brought him there.

"I found this package in the snow."

"Let me see it."

Amster laid it on the table. The older man looked at it, and as the commissioner was about to open it, he handed him a paper-knife with the words: "You had better cut it open, sir."

"Why?"

"It is best not to injure the seals that fasten a package."

"Just as you say, Muller," answered the young commissioner, smiling. He was still very young to hold such an office, but then he was the son of a Cabinet Minister, and family connections had obtained this responsible position for him so soon. Kurt von Mayringen was his name, and he was a very good-looking young man, apparently a very good-natured young man also, for he took this advice from a subordinate with a most charming smile. He knew, however, that this quiet, pale-faced little man in the shabby clothes was greater than he, and that it was mere accident of birth that put him, Kurt von Mayringen, instead of Joseph Muller, in the position of superior.

The young commissioner had had most careful advice from headquarters as to Muller, and he treated the secret service detective, who was one of the most expert and best known men in the profession, with the greatest deference, for he knew that anything Muller might say could be only of value to him with his very slight knowledge of his business. He took the knife, therefore, and carefully cut open the paper, taking out a tiny little notebook, on the outer side of which a handsome monogram gleamed up at him in golden letters.

"A woman made this package," said Muller, who had been looking at the covering very carefully; "a blond woman."

The other two looked at him in astonishment. He showed them a single blond hair which had been in one of the bread seals.

"How I was murdered." Those were the words that Commissioner von Mayringen read aloud after he had hastily turned the first few pages of the notebook, and had come to a place where the writing was heavily underscored.

The commissioner and Amster were much astonished at these words, but the detective still gazed quietly at the seals of the wrapping.

"This heading reads like insanity," said the commissioner. Muller shrugged his shoulders, then turned to Amster. "Where did you find the package?"

"In Garden street."

"When?"

"About twenty minutes ago."

Amster gave a short and lucid account of his discovery. His intelligent face and well-chosen words showed that he had observation and the power to describe correctly what he had observed. His honest eyes inspired confidence.

"Where could they have been taking the woman?" asked the detective, more of himself than of the others.

The commissioner searched hastily through the notebook for a signature, but without success. "Why do you think it is a woman? This writing looks more like a man's hand to me. The letters are so heavy and—"

"That is only because they are written with broad pen," interrupted Muller, showing him the writing on the package; "here is the same hand, but it is written with a fine hard pencil, and you can see distinctly that this is a woman's handwriting. And besides, the skin on a man's thumb does not show the fine markings that you can see here on these bits of bread that have been used for seals."

The commissioner rose from his seat. "You may be right, Muller. We will take for granted, then, that there is a woman in trouble. It remains to be seen whether she is insane or not."

"Yes, that remains to be seen," said Muller dryly, as he reached for his overcoat.

"You are going before you read what is in the notebook?" asked Commissioner von Mayringen.

Muller nodded. "I want to see the wagon tracks before they are lost; it may help me to discover something else. You can read the book and make any arrangements you find necessary after that."

Muller was already wrapped in his overcoat. "Is it snowing now?" He turned to Arnster.

"Some flakes were falling as I came here."

"All right. Come with me and show me the way." Muller nodded carelessly to his superior officer, his mind evidently already engrossed in thoughts of the interesting case, and hurried out with Amster. The commissioner was quite satisfied with the state of affairs. He knew the case was in safe hands. He seated himself at his desk again and began to read the little book which had come into his hands so strangely. His eyes ran more and more rapidly over the closely written pages, as his interest grew and grew.

When, half an hour later, he had finished the reading, he paced restlessly up and down the room, trying to bring order into the thoughts that rushed through his brain. And one thought came again and again, and would not be denied in spite of many improbabilities, and many strange things with which the book was full; in spite, also, of the varying, uncertain handwriting and style of the message. This one thought was, "This woman is not insane."

While the young official was pondering over the problem, Muller entered as quietly as ever, bowed, put his hat and cane in their places, and shook the snow off his clothing. He was evidently pleased about something. Kurt von Mayringen did not notice his entrance. He was again at the desk with the open book before him, staring at the mysterious words, "How I was murdered."

"It is a woman, a lady of position. And if she is mad, then her madness certainly has method." Muller said these words in his usual quiet way, almost indifferently. The young commissioner started up and snatched for the fine white handkerchief which the detective handed him. A strong sweet perfume filled the room. "It is hers?" he murmured.

"It is hers," said Muller. "At least we can take that much for granted, for the handkerchief bears the same monogram, A. L., which is on the notebook."

Commissioner von Mayringen rose from his chair in evident excitement. "Well?" he asked.

It was a short question, but full of meaning, and one could see that he was waiting in great excitement for the answer. Muller reported what he had discovered. The commissioner thought it little enough, and shrugged his shoulders impatiently when the other had finished.

Muller noticed his chief's dissatisfaction and smiled at it. He himself was quite content with what he had found.

"Is that all?" murmured the commissioner, as if disappointed.

"That is all," repeated the detective calmly, and added, "That is a good deal. We have here a closely written notebook, the contents of which, judging by your excitement, are evidently important. We have also a handkerchief with an unusual perfume on it. I repeat that this is quite considerable. Besides this, we have the seals, and we know several other things. I believe that we can save this lady, or if it be too late, we can avenge her at least."

The commissioner looked at Muller in surprise. "We are in a city of more than a million inhabitants," he said, almost timidly.

"I have hunted criminals in two hemispheres, and I have found them," said Muller simply. The young commissioner smiled and held out his hand. "Ah, yes, Muller—I keep forgetting the great things you have done. You are so quiet about it."

"What I have done is only what any one could do who has that particular faculty. I do only what is in human power to do, and the cleverest criminal can do no more. Besides which, we all know that every criminal commits some stupidity, and leaves some trace behind him. If it is really a crime which we have found the trace of here, we will soon discover it." Muller's editorial "we" was a matter of formality. He might with more truth have used the singular pronoun.

"Very well, then, do what you can," said the commissioner with a friendly smile.

The older man nodded, took the book and its wrappings from the desk, and went into a small adjoining room.

The commissioner sent for an attendant and gave him the order to fetch a pot of tea from a neighbouring saloon. When the tray arrived, he placed several good cigars upon it, and sent it in to Muller. Taking a cigar himself, the commissioner leaned back in his sofa corner to think over this first interesting case of his short professional experience. That it concerned a lady in distress made it all the more romantic.

In his little room the detective, put in good humour by the thoughtful attention of his chief, sat down to read the book carefully. While he studied its contents his mind went back over his search in the silent street outside.

He and Amster had hurried out into the raw chill of the night, reaching the spot of the first discovery in about ten or fifteen minutes. Muller found nothing new there. But he was able to discover in which direction the carriage had been going. The hoof marks of the single horse which had drawn it were still plainly to be seen in the snow.

"Will you follow these tracks in the direction from which they have come?" he asked of Amster. "Then meet me at the station and report what you have seen."

"Very well, sir," answered the workman. The two men parted with a hand shake.

Before Muller started on to follow up the tracks in the other direction, he took up one of the larger pieces' of glass. "Cheap glass," he said, looking at it carefully. "It was only a hired cab, therefore, and a one-horse cab at that."

He walked on slowly, following the marks of the wheels. His eyes searched the road from side to side, looking for any other signs that might have been left by the hand which had thrown the package out of the window. The snow, which had been falling softly thus far, began to come down in heavier flakes, and Muller quickened his pace. The tracks would soon be covered, but they could still be plainly seen. They led out into the open country, but when the first little hill had been climbed a drift heaped itself up, cutting off the trail completely.

Muller stood on the top of this knoll at a spot where the street divided. Towards the right it led down into a factory suburb; towards the left the road led on to a residence colony, and straight ahead the way was open, between fields, pastures and farms, over moors, to another town of considerable size lying beside a river. Muller knew all this, but his knowledge of the locality was of little avail, for all traces of the carriage wheels were lost.

He followed each one of the streets for a little distance, but to no purpose. The wind blew the snow up in such heaps that it was quite impossible to follow any trail under such conditions.

With an expression of impatience Muller gave up his search and turned to go back again. He was hoping that Amster might have had better luck. It was not possible to find the goal towards which the wagon had taken its prisoner—if prisoner she was—as soon as they had hoped. Perhaps the search must be made in the direction from which she had been brought.

Muller turned back towards the city again. He walked more quickly now, but his eyes took in everything to the right and to the left of his path. Near the place where the street divided a bush waved its bare twigs in the wind. The snow which had settled upon it early in the day had been blown away by the freshening wind, and just as Muller neared the bush he saw something white fluttering from one twig. It was a handkerchief, which had probably hung heavy and lifeless when he had passed that way before. Now when the wind held it out straight, he saw it at once. He loosened it carefully from the thorny twigs. A delicate and rather unusual perfume wafted up to his face. There was more of the odour on the little cloth than is commonly used by people of good taste. And yet this handkerchief was far too fine and delicate in texture to belong to the sort of people who habitually passed along this street. It must have something to do with the mysterious carriage. It was still quite dry, and in spite of the fact that the wind had been playing with it, it had been but slightly torn. It could therefore have been in that position for a short time only. At the nearest lantern Muller saw that the monogram on the handkerchief was the same in style and initials as that on the notebook. It was the letters A. L.

CHAPTER TWO. THE STORY OF THE NOTEBOOK

It was warm and comfortable in the little room where Muller sat. He closed the windows, lit the gas, took off his overcoat—Muller was a pedantically careful person—smoothed his hair and sat down comfortably at the table. Just as he took up the little book, the attendant brought the tea, which he proceeded at once to enjoy. He did not take up his little book again until he had lit himself a cigar. He looked at the cover of the dainty little notebook for many minutes before he opened it. It was a couple of inches long, of the usual form, and had a cover of brown leather. In the left upper corner were the letters A. L. in gold. The leaves of the book, about fifty in all, were of a fine quality of paper and covered with close writing. On the first leaves the writing was fine and delicate, calm and orderly, but later on it was irregular and uncertain, as if penned by a trembling hand under stress of terror. This change came in the leaves of the book which followed the strange and terrible title, "How I was murdered."

Before Muller began to read he felt the covers of the book carefully. In one of them there was a tiny pocket, in which he found a little piece of wall paper of a noticeable and distinctly ugly pattern. The paper had a dark blue ground with clumsy lines of gold on it. In the pocket he found also a tramway ticket, which had been crushed and then carefully smoothed out again. After looking at these papers, Muller replaced them in the cover of the notebook. The book itself was strongly perfumed with the same odour which had exhaled from the handkerchief.

The detective did not begin his reading in that part of the book which followed the mysterious title, as the commissioner had done. He began instead at the very first words.

"Ah! she is still young," he murmured, when he had read the first lines. "Young, in easy circumstances, happy and contented."

These first pages told of pleasure trips, of visits from and to good friends, of many little events of every-day life. Then came some accounts, written in pencil, of shopping expeditions to the city. Costly laces and jewels had been bought, and linen garments for children by the dozen. "She is rich, generous, and charitable," thought the detective, for the book showed that the considerable sums which had been spent here had not been for the writer herself. The laces bore the mark, "For our church";

behind the account for the linen stood the words, "For the charity school."

Muller began to feel a strong sympathy for the writer of these notices. She showed an orderly, almost pedantic, character, mingled with generosity of heart. He turned leaf after leaf until he finally came to the words, written in intentionally heavy letters, "How I was murdered."

Muller's head sank down lower over these mysterious words, and his eyes flew through the writing that followed. It was quite a different writing here. The hand that penned these words must have trembled in deadly terror. Was it terror of coming death, foreseen and not to be escaped? or was it the trembling and the terror of an overthrown brain? It was undoubtedly, in spite of the difference, the same hand that had penned the first pages of the book. A few characteristic turns of the writing were plainly to be seen in both parts of the story. But the ink was quite different also. The first pages had been written with a delicate violet ink, the later leaves were penned with a black ink of uneven quality, of the kind used by poor people who write very seldom. The words of this later portion of the book were blurred in many places, as if the writer had not been able to dry them properly before she turned the leaves. She therefore had had neither blotting paper nor sand at her disposal.

And then the weird title!

Was it written at the dictation of insanity? or did A. L. know, while she wrote it, that it was too late for any help to reach her? Did she see her doom approaching so clearly that she knew there was no escape?

Muller breathed a deep breath before he continued his reading. Later on his breath came more quickly still, and he clinched his fist several times, as if deeply moved. He was not a cold man, only thoroughly self-controlled. In his breast there lived an unquenchable hatred of all evil. It was this that awakened the talents which made him the celebrated detective he had become.

"I fear that it will be impossible for any one to save me now, but perhaps I may be avenged. Therefore I will write down here all that has happened to me since I set out on my journey." These were the first words that were written under the mysterious title. Muller had just read them when the commissioner entered.

"Will you speak to Amster; he has just returned?" he asked.

Muller rose at once. "Certainly. Did you telegraph to all the railway stations?"

"Yes," answered the commissioner, "and also to the other police stations."

"And to the hospitals?—asylums?"

"No, I did not do that." Commissioner von Mayringen blushed, a blush that was as becoming to him as was his frank acknowledgment of his mistake. He went out to remedy it at once, while Muller heard Amster's short and not particularly important report. The workingman was evidently shivering, and the detective handed him a glass of tea with a good portion of rum in it.

"Here, drink this; you are cold. Are you ill?" Amster smiled sadly. "No, I am not ill, but I was discharged to-day and am out of work now—that's almost as bad."

"Are you married?"

"No, but I have an old mother to support."

"Leave your address with the commissioner. He may be able to find work for you; we can always use good men here. But now drink your tea." Amster drank the glass in one gulp. "Well, now we have lost the trail in both directions," said Muller calmly. "But we will find it again. You can help, as you are free now anyway. If you have the talent for that sort of thing, you may find permanent work here."

A gesture and a look from the workingman showed the detective that the former did not think very highly of such occupation. Muller laid his hand on the other's shoulder and said gravely: "You wouldn't care to take service with us? This sort of thing doesn't rate very high, I know. But I tell you that if we have our hearts in the right place, and our brains are worth anything, we are of more good to humanity than many an honest citizen who wouldn't shake hands with us. There—and now I am busy. Goodnight."

With these words Muller pushed the astonished man out of the room, shut the door, and sat down again with his little book. This is what he read:

"Wednesday—is it Wednesday? They brought me a newspaper to-day which had the date of Wednesday, the 20th of November. The ink still smells fresh, but it is so damp here, the paper may have been older. I do not know surely on what day it is that I begin to write this narrative. I do not know either whether I may not have been ill for days and weeks; I do not know what may have been the matter with me—I know only that I was unconscious, and that when I came to myself again, I was here in this gloomy room. Did any physician see me? I have seen no one until to-day except the old woman, whose name I do not know and who has so little to say. She is kind to me otherwise, but I am afraid of her hard face and of the smile with which she answers all my questions and entreaties. 'You are ill.' These are the only words that she has ever said to me, and she pointed to her forehead as she spoke them. She thinks I am insane, therefore, or pretends to think so.

"What a hoarse voice she has. She must be ill herself, for she coughs all night long. I can hear it through the wall—she sleeps in the next room. But I am not ill, that is I am not ill in the way she says. I have no fever now, my pulse is calm and regular. I can remember everything, until I took that drink of tea in the railway station. What could there have been in that tea? I suppose I should have noticed how anxious my travelling companion was to have me drink it.

"Who could the man have been? He was so polite, so fatherly in his anxiety about me. I have not seen him since then. And yet I feel that it is he who has brought me into this trap, a trap from which I may never escape alive. I will describe him. He is very tall, stout and blond, and wears a long heavy beard, which is slightly mixed with grey. On his right cheek his beard only partly hides a long scar. His eyes are hidden by large smoked glasses. His voice is low and gentle, his manners most correct— except for his giving people poison or whatever else it was in that tea.

"I did not suffer any—at least I do not remember anything except becoming unconscious. And I seem to have felt a pain like an iron ring around my head. But I am not insane, and this fear that I feel does not spring from my imagination, but from the real danger by which I am surrounded. I am very hungry, but I do not dare to eat anything except eggs, which cannot be tampered with. I tasted some soup yesterday, and it seemed to me that it had a queer taste. I will eat nothing that is at all suspicious. I will be in my full senses when my murderers come; they shall not kill me by poison at least.

"When I came to my senses again—it was the evening of the day before yesterday—I found a letter on the little table beside my bed. It was written in French, in a handwriting that I had never seen before, and there was no signature.

"This strange letter demanded of me that I should write to my guardian, calmly and clearly, to say that for reasons which I did not intend to reveal, I had taken my own life. If I did this my present place of sojourn would be exchanged for a far more agreeable one, and I would soon be quite free. But if I did not do it, I would actually be put to death. A pen, ink and paper were ready there for the answer.

"'Never,' I wrote. And then despair came over me, and I may have indeed appeared insane. The old woman came in. I entreated and implored her to tell me why this dreadful fate should have overtaken me. She remained quite indifferent and I sank back, almost fainting, on the bed. She laid a moist cloth over my face, a cloth that had a peculiar odour. I soon fell asleep. It seemed to me that there was some one else besides the woman in the room with me. Or was she talking to herself? Next morning the letter and my answer had disappeared. It was as I thought; there was some one else in my room. Some one who had come on the tramway. I found the ticket on the carpet beside my bed. I took it and put it in my notebook!!!!!

"I believe that it is Sunday to-day. It is four days now since I have been conscious. The first sound that I remember hearing was the blast of a horn. It must come from a factory very near me. The old windows in my room rattle at the sound. I hear it mornings and evenings and at noon, on week days. I did not hear it to-day, so it must be Sunday. It was Monday, the 18th of November, that I set out on my trip, and reached here in the evening—(here? I do not know where I am), that is, I set out for Vienna, and I know that I reached the Northern Railway station there in safety.

"I was cold and felt a little faint—and then he offered me the tea—and what happened after that? Where am I? The paper that they gave me may have been a day or two old or more. And to-day is Sunday—is it the first Sunday since my departure from home? I do not know. I know only this, that I set out on the 18th of November to visit my kind old guardian, and to have a last consultation with him before my coming of age. And I know also that I have fallen into the hands of some one who has an interest in my disappearance.

"There is some one in the next room with the old woman. I hear a man's voice and they are quarrelling. They are talking of me. He wants her to do something which she will not do. He commands her to go away, but she refuses. What does he mean to do? I do not want her to leave me alone. I do not hate her any more; I know that she is not bad. When I listened I heard her speaking of me as of an insane person. She really believes that I am ill. When the man went away he must have been angry. He stamped down the stairs until the steps creaked under his tread: I know it is a wooden staircase therefore.

"I am safe from him to-day, but I am really ill of fright. Am I really insane? There is one thing that I have forgotten to write down. When I first came to myself I found a bit of paper beside me on which was written, 'Beware of calling in help from outside. One scream will mean death to you.' It was written in French like the letter. Why? Was it because the old woman could not read it? She knew of the piece of paper, for she took it away from me. It frightens me that I should have forgotten to write this down. Am I really ill? If I am not yet ill, this terrible solitude will make me so.

"What a gloomy room this is, this prison of mine. And such a strange ugly wall-paper. I tore off a tiny bit of it and hid it in this little book. Some one may find it some day and may discover from it this place where I am suffering, and where I shall die, perhaps. There cannot be many who would buy such a pattern, and it must be possible to find the factory where it was made. And I will also write down here what I can see from my barred window. Far down below me there is a rusty tin roof, it looks like as if it might belong to a sort of shed. In front and to the right there are windowless walls; to the left, at a little distance, I can see a slender church spire, greenish in colour, probably covered with copper, and before the church there are two poplar trees of different heights.

"Another day has passed, a day of torturing fear! Am I really insane? I know that I see queer things. This morning I looked towards the window and I saw a parrot sitting there! I saw it quite plainly. It ruffled up its red and green feathers and stared at me. I stared back at it and suddenly it was gone. I shivered. Finally I pulled myself together and went to the window. There was no bird outside nor was there a trace of any in the snow on the window sill. Could the wind have blown away the tracks so soon, or was it really my sick brain that appeared to see this tropical bird in the midst of the snow? It is Tuesday to-day; from now on I will carefully count the days—the days that still remain to me.

"This morning I asked the old woman about the parrot. She only smiled and her smile made me terribly afraid. The thought that this thing which is happening to me, this thing that I took to be a crime, may be only a necessity—the thought fills me with horror! Am I in a prison? or is this the cell of an insane asylum? Am I the victim of a villain? or am I really mad? My pulse is quickening, but my memory is quite clear; I can look back over every incident in my life.

"She has just taken away my food. I asked her to bring me only eggs as I was afraid of everything else. She promised that she would do it.

"Are they looking for me? My guardian is Theodore Fellner, Cathedral Lane, 14. My own name is Asta Langen.

"They took away my travelling bag, but they did not find this little book and the tiny bottle of perfume which I had in the pocket of my dress. And I found this old pen and a little ink in a drawer of the writing table in my room.

"Wednesday. The stranger was here again to-day. I recognised his soft voice. He spoke to the woman in the hall outside my room. I listened, but I could catch only a few words. 'To-morrow evening—I will come myself—no responsibility for you.' Were these words meant for me? Are they going to take me away? Where will they take me? Then they do not dare to kill me here? My head is burning hot. I have not dared to drink a drop of liquid for four days. I dare not take anything into which they might have put some drug or some poison.

"Who could have such an interest in my death? It cannot be because of the fortune which is to be mine when I come of age;

for if I die, my father has willed it to various charitable institutions. I have no relatives, at least none who could inherit my money. I had never harmed any one; who can wish for my death?

"There is somebody with her, somebody was listening at the door. I have a feeling as if I was being watched. And yet—I examined the door, but there is no crack anywhere and the key is in the lock. Still I seem to feel a burning glance resting on me. Ah! the parrot! is this another delusion? Oh God, let it end soon! I am not yet quite insane, but all these unknown dangers around me will drive me mad. I must fight against them.

"Thursday. They brought me back my travelling bag. My attendant is uneasy. She was longer in cleaning up the room than usual to-day. She seemed to want to say something to me, and yet she did not dare to speak. Is something to happen to-day then? I did not close my eyes all night. Can one be made insane from a distance? hypnotised into it, as it were? I will not allow fear alone to make me mad. My enemy shall not find it too easy. He may kill my body, but that is all—"

These were the last words which Asta Langen had written in her notebook, the little book which was the only confidant of her terrible need. When the detective had finished reading it, he closed his eyes for a few minutes to let the impression made by the story sink into his mind.

Then he rose and put on his overcoat. He entered the commissioner's room and took up his hat and cane.

"Where are you going, Muller?" asked Herr Von Mayringen.

"To Cathedral Lane, if you will permit it."

"At this hour? it is quarter past eleven! Is there any such hurry, do you think? There is no train from any of our stations until morning. And I have already sent a policeman to watch the house. Besides, I know that Fellner is a highly respected man.

"There is many a man who is highly respected until he is found out," remarked the detective.

"And you are going to find out about Fellner?" smiled the commissioner. "And this evening, too?"

"This very evening. If he is asleep I shall wake him up. That is the best time to get at the truth about a man."

The commissioner sat down at his desk and wrote out the necessary credentials for the detective. A few moments later

Muller was in the street. He left the notebook with the commissioner. It was snowing heavily, and an icy north wind was howling through the streets. Muller turned up the collar of his coat and walked on quickly. It was just striking a quarter to twelve when he reached Cathedral Lane. As he walked slowly along the moonlit side of the pavement, a man stepped out of the shadow to meet him. It was the policeman who had been sent to watch the house. Like Muller, he wore plain clothes.

"Well?" the latter asked.

"Nothing new. Mr. Fellner has been ill in bed several days, quite seriously ill, they tell me. The janitor seems very fond of him.

"Hm—we'll see what sort of a man he is. You can go back to the station now, you must be nearly frozen standing here."

Muller looked carefully at the house which bore the number 14. It was a handsome, old-fashioned building, a true patrician mansion which looked worthy of all confidence. But Muller knew that the outside of a house has very little to do with the honesty of the people who live in it. He rang the bell carefully, as he wished no one but the janitor to hear him.

The latter did not seem at all surprised to find a stranger asking for the owner of the house at so late an hour. "You come with a telegram, I suppose? Come right up stairs then, I have orders to let you in."

These were the words with which the old janitor greeted Muller. The detective could see from this that Mr. Theodore Fellner's conscience must be perfectly clear. The expected telegram probably had something to do with the non-appearance of Asta Langen, of whose terrible fate her guardian evidently as yet knew nothing. The janitor knocked on one of the doors, which was opened in a few moments by an old woman.

"Is it the telegram?" she asked sleepily.

"Yes," said the janitor.

"No," said Muller, "but I want to speak to Mr. Fellner."

The two old people stared at him in surprise.

"To speak to him?" said the woman, and shook her head as if in doubt. "Is it about Miss Langen?"

"Yes, please wake him."

"But he is ill, and the doctor—"

"Please wake him up. I will take the responsibility."

"But who are you?" asked the janitor.

Muller smiled a little at this belated caution on the part of the old man, and answered. "I will tell Mr. Fellner who I am. But please announce me at once. It concerns the young lady." His expression was so grave that the woman waited no longer, but let him in and then disappeared through another door. The janitor stood and looked at Muller with half distrustful, half anxious glances.

"It's no good news you bring," he said after a few minutes.

"You may be right."

"Has anything happened to our dear young lady?"

"Then you know Miss Asta Langen and her family?"

"Why, of course. I was in service on the estate when all the dreadful things happened."

"What things?"

"Why the divorce—and—but you are a stranger and I shouldn't talk about these family affairs to you. You had better tell me what has happened to our young lady."

"I must tell that to your master first."

The woman came back at this moment and said to Muller, "Come with me, please. Berner, you are to stay here until the gentleman goes out again."

Muller followed her through several rooms into a large bed-chamber where he found an elderly man, very evidently ill, lying in bed.

"Who are you?" asked the sick man, raising his head from the pillow. The woman had gone out and closed the door behind her.

"My name is Muller, police detective. Here are my credentials."

Fellner glanced hastily at the paper. "Why does the police send to me?"

"It concerns your ward."

Fellner sat upright in bed now. He leaned over towards his visitor as he said, pointing to a letter on the table beside his bed, "Asta's overseer writes me from her estate that she left home on the 18th of November to visit me. She should have reached here on the evening of the 18th, and she has not arrived yet. I did not receive this letter until to-day."

"Did you expect the young lady?"

"I knew only that she would arrive sometime before the third of December. That date is her twenty-fourth birthday and she was to celebrate it here."

"Did she not usually announce her coming to you?"

"No, she liked to surprise me. Three days ago I sent her a telegram asking her to bring certain necessary papers with her. This brought the answer from the overseer of her estate, an answer which has caused me great anxiety. Your coming makes it worse, for I fear—" The sick man broke off and turned his eyes on Muller; eyes so full of fear and grief that the detective's heart grew soft. He felt Fellner's icy hand on his as the sick man murmured: "Tell me the truth! Is Asta dead?"

The detective shrugged his shoulders. "We do not know yet. She was alive and able to send a message at half past eight this evening."

"A message? To whom?"

"To the nearest police station." Muller told the story as it had come to him.

The old man listened with an expression of such utter dazed terror that the detective dropped all suspicion of him at once.

"What a terrible riddle," stammered the sick man as the other finished the story.

"Would you answer me several questions?" asked Muller. The old gentleman answered quickly, "Any one, every one."

"Miss Langen is rich?"

"She has a fortune of over three hundred thousand guldens, and considerable land."

"Has she any relatives?"

"No," replied Fellner harshly. But a thought must have flashed through his brain for he started suddenly and murmured, "Yes, she has one relative, a step-brother."

The detective gave an exclamation of surprise.

"Why are you astonished at this?" asked Fellner.

"According to her notebook, the young lady does not seem to know of this step-brother."

"She does not know, sir. There was an ugly scandal in her family before her birth. Her father turned his first wife and their son out of his house on one and the same day. He had discovered that she was deceiving him, and also that her son, who was studying medicine at the time, had stolen money from his safe.

What he had discovered about his wife made Langen doubt whether the boy was his son at all. There was a terrible scene, and the two disappeared from their home forever. The woman died soon after. The young man went to Australia. He has never been heard of since and has probably come to no good."

"Might he not possibly be here in Europe again, watching for an opportunity to make a fortune?"

Fellner's hand grasped that of his visitor. The eyes of the two men gazed steadily at each other. The old man's glance was full of sudden helpless horror, the detective's eyes shone brilliantly. Muller spoke calmly: "This is one clue. Is there no one else who could have an interest in the young lady's death?"

"No one but Egon Langen, if he bear this name by right, and if he is still alive."

"How old would he be now?"

"He must be nearly forty. It was many years before Langen married again."

"Do you know him personally?"

"Have you a picture of Miss Langen?"

Fellner rang a bell and Berner appeared. "Give this gentleman Miss Asta's picture. Take the one in the silver frame on my desk;" the old gentleman's voice was friendly but faint with fatigue. His old servant looked at him in deep anxiety. Fellner smiled weakly and nodded to the man. "Sad news, Berner! Sad news and bad news. Our poor Asta is being held a prisoner by some unknown villain who threatens her with death."

"My God, is it possible? Can't we help the poor young lady?"

"We will try to help her, or if it is—too late, we will at least avenge her. My entire fortune shall be given up for it. But bring her picture now."

Berner brought the picture of a very pretty girl with a bright intelligent face. Muller took the picture out of the frame and put it in his pocket.

"You will come again? soon? And remember, I will give ten thousand guldens to the man who saves Asta, or avenges her. Tell the police to spare no expense—I will go to headquarters myself to-morrow."

Fellner was a little surprised that Muller, although he had already taken up his hat, did not go. The sick man had seen the light flash up in the eyes of the other as he named the sum. He thought he understood this excitement, but it touched him unpleasantly and he sank back, almost frightened, in his cushions as the detective bent over him with the words "Good. Do not forget your promise, for I will save Miss Langen or avenge her. But I do not want the money for myself. It is to go to those who have been unjustly convicted and thus ruined for life. It may give the one or the other of them a better chance for the future."

"And you? what good do you get from that?" asked the old gentleman, astonished. A soft smile illumined the detective's plain features and he answered gently, "I know then that there will be some poor fellow who will have an easier time of it than I have had."

He nodded to Fellner, who had already grasped his hand and pressed it hard. A tear ran down his grey beard, and long after Muller had gone the old gentleman lay pondering over his last words.

Berner led the visitor to the door. As he was opening it, Muller asked: "Has Egon Langen a bad scar on his right cheek?"

Berner's eyes looked his astonishment. How did the stranger know this? And how did he come to mention this forgotten name.

"Yes, he has, but how did you know it?" he murmured in surprise. He received no answer, for Muller was already walking quickly down the street. The old man stared after him for some few minutes, then suddenly his knees began to tremble. He closed the door with difficulty, and sank down on a bench beside it. The wind had blown out the light of his lantern; Berner was sitting in the dark without knowing it, for a sudden terrible light had burst upon his soul, burst upon it so sharply that he hid his eyes with his hands, and his old lips murmured, "Horrible! Horrible! The brother against the sister."

The next morning was clear and bright. Muller was up early, for he had taken but a few hours sleep in one of the rooms of the station, before he set out into the cold winter morning. At the next corner he found Amster waiting for him. "What are you doing here?" he asked in astonishment.

"I have been thinking over what you said to me yesterday. Your profession is as good and perhaps better than many another."

"And you come out here so early to tell me that?"

Amster smiled. "I have something else to say."

"Well?"

"The commissioner asked me yesterday if I knew of a church in the city that had a slender spire with a green top and two poplars in front of it."

Muller looked his interest.

"I thought it might possibly be the Convent Church of the Grey Sisters, but I wasn't quite sure, so I went there an hour ago. It's all right, just as I thought. And I suppose it has something to do with the case of last night, so I thought I had better report at once. I was on my way to the station."

"That will do very well. You have saved us much time and you have shown that you are eminently fitted for this business."

"If you really will try me, then—"

"We'll see. You can begin on this. Come to the church with me now." Muller was no talker, particularly not when, as now, his brain was busy on a problem.

The two men walked on quickly. In about half an hour they found themselves in a little square in the middle of which stood an old church. In front of the church, like giant sentinels, stood a pair of tall poplars. One of them looked sickly and was a good deal shorter than its neighbour. Muller nodded as if content.

"Is this the church the commissioner was talking about?" queried Amster.

"It is," was the answer. Muller walked on toward a little house built up against the church, which was evidently the dwelling of the sexton.

The detective introduced himself to this official, who did not look over-intelligent, as a stranger in the city who had been told that the view from the tower of the church was particularly interesting. A bright silver piece banished all distrust from the soul of the worthy man. With great friendliness he inquired when the gentlemen would like to ascend the tower. "At once," was the answer.

The sexton took a bunch of keys and told the strangers to follow him. A few moments later Muller and his companion stood in the tiny belfry room of the slender spire. The fat sexton, to his own great satisfaction, had yielded to their request not to undertake the steep ascent. The cloudless sky lay crystal clear over the still sleeping city and the wide spread snow-covered fields which lay close at hand, beyond the church. On the one side were gardens and the low rambling buildings of the convent, and on the other were huddled high-piled dwellings of poverty.

Muller looked out of each of the four windows in turn. He spent some time at each window, but evidently without discovering what he looked for, for he shook his head in discontent. But when he went once more to the opening in the East, into which the sun was just beginning to pour its light, something seemed to attract his attention. He called Amster and pointed from the window. "Your eyes are younger than mine, lend them to me. What do you see over there to the right, below the tall factory chimney?" Muller's voice was calm, but there was something in his manner that revealed excitement. Amster caught the infection without knowing why. He looked sharply in the direction towards which Muller pointed, and began: "There is a tall house near the chimney, to the right of it, one wall touching it. The house is crowded in between other newer buildings, and looks to be very old and of a much better sort than its neighbours. The other houses are plain stone, but this house has carvings and statues on it, which are white with snow. But the house is in bad condition, one can see cracks in the wall."

"And its windows?"

"I cannot see them. They must be on the other side of the house, towards the courtyard which seems to be hemmed in by the blank walls of the other houses."

"And at the front of the house?"

"There is a low wall in front which shuts off the courtyard from a narrow, ill-kept street."

"Yes, I see it myself now. The street is bordered mainly by gardens and vacant lots."

"Yes, sir, that is it." Muller nodded as if satisfied. Amster looked at him in surprise, still more surprised, however, at the excitement he felt himself. He did not understand it, but Muller understood it. He knew that he had found in Amster a talent akin to his own, one of those natures who once having taken up a trail cannot rest until they reach their goal. He looked for a few moments in satisfaction at the assistant he had found by such chance, then he turned and hastened down the stairs again.

"We're going to that house?" asked Amster when they were down in the street. Muller nodded.

Without hesitation the two men made their way through a tangle of dingy, uninteresting alleys, between modern tenements, until about ten minutes later they stood before an old three-storied building, which had a frontage of four windows on the street. "This is our place," said the detective, looking up at the tall, handsome gateway and the rococo carvings that ornamented the front of this decaying dwelling. It was very evidently of a different age and class from those about it.

Muller had already raised his hand to pull the bell, when he stopped and let it sink again. His eye caught sight of a placard pasted up on the wall of the next house, and already half torn off by the wind. The detective walked over, and raising the placard with his cane, read the words on it. "That's right," he said to himself. Amster gave a look on the paper. But he could not connect the contents of the notice with the case of the kidnapped lady, and he shook his head in surprise when Muller turned to him with the words: "The lady we are looking for is not insane." On the paper was announced in large letters that a reward would be offered to the finder of a red and green parrot which had escaped from a neighbouring house.

Muller rang the bell and they had to wait some few minutes before the door opened with great creakings, and the towsled head of an old woman peered out.

"What do you want?" she asked hoarsely, with distrustful looks.

"Let us in, and then give us the keys of the upstairs rooms." Muller's voice was friendly, but the woman grew perceptibly paler.

"Who are you?" she stammered. Muller threw back his overcoat and showed her his badge. "But there is nobody here, the house is quite empty."

"There were a lady and gentleman here last evening." The woman threw a frightened look at Muller, then she said hesitatingly: "The lady was insane and has been taken to an asylum."

"That is what the man told you. He is a criminal and the police are looking for him."

"Come with me," murmured the woman. She seemed to understand that further resistance was useless. She carefully locked the outside door. Amster remained down stairs in the corridor, while Muller followed the old woman up the stairs. The staircase to the third story was made of wood. The house was evidently very old, with low ceilings and many dark corners.

The woman led Muller into the room in which she had cared for the strange lady at the order of the latter's "husband." He had told her that it was only until he could take the lady to an asylum. One look at the wall paper, a glance out of the window, and Muller knew that this was where Asta Langen had been imprisoned. He sat down on a chair and looked at the woman, who stood frightened before him.

"Do you know where they have taken the lady?"

"No, sir.

"Do you know the gentleman's name?"

"No, sir.

"You did not send the lady's name to the authorities?" *

  * *Any stranger taking rooms in a hotel or lodging house must be registered with the police authorities by the proprietor of the house within forty-eight hours of arrival.*

"No, sir."

"Were you not afraid you would get into trouble?"

"The gentleman paid me well, and I did not think that he meant anything bad, and—and—"

"And you did not think that it would be found out?" said Muller sternly.

"I took good care of the lady."

"Yes, we know that."

"Did she escape from her husband?"

"He was not her husband. But now tell me all you know about these people; the more truthful you are the better it will be for you."

The old woman was so frightened that she could scarcely find strength to talk. When she finally got control of herself again she began: "He came here on the first of November and rented this room for himself. But he was here only twice before he brought the lady and left her alone here. She was very ill when he brought her here—so ill that he had to carry her upstairs. I wanted to go for a doctor, but he said he was a doctor himself, and that he could take care of his wife, who often had such attacks. He gave me some medicine for her after I had put her to bed. I gave her the drops, but it was a long while before she came to herself again.

"Then he told me that she had lost her mind, and that she believed everybody was trying to harm her. She was so bad that he was taking her to an asylum. But he hadn't found quite the right place yet, and wanted me to keep her here until he knew where he could take her. Once he left a revolver here by mistake. But I hid it so the lady wouldn't see it, and gave it to the gentleman the next time he came. He was angry at that, though I couldn't see why, and said I shouldn't have touched it."

The woman had told her story with much hesitation, and stopped altogether at this point. She had evidently suddenly realised that the lady was not insane, but only in great despair, and that people in such a state will often seek death, particularly if any weapon is left conveniently within their reach.

"What did this gentleman look like?" asked Muller, to start her talking again. She described her tenant as very tall and stout with a long beard slightly mixed with grey. She had never seen his eyes, for he wore smoked glasses.

"Did you notice anything peculiar about his face?"

"No, nothing except that his beard was very heavy and almost covered his face."

"Could you see his cheeks at all?"

"No, or else I didn't notice."

"Did he leave nothing that might enable us to find him?"

"No, sir, nothing. Or yes, perhaps, but I don't suppose that will be any good."

"What was it? What do you mean?"

"It gave him a good deal of trouble to get the lady into the wagon, because she had fainted again. He lost his glove in doing it. I have it down stairs in my room, for I sleep down stairs again since the lady has gone."

Muller had risen from his chair and walked over to the old writing desk which stood beside one window. There were several sheets of ordinary brown paper on it and sharp pointed pencil and also something not usually found on writing desks, a piece of bread from which some of the inside had been taken.

"Everything as I expected it," he said to himself. "The young lady made up the package in the last few moments that she was left alone here."

He turned again to the old woman and commanded her to lead him down stairs. "What sort of a carriage was it in which they took the lady away?" he asked as they went down.

"A closed coupe."

"Did you see the number?"

"No, sir. But the carriage was very shabby and so was the driver."

"Was he an old man?"

"He was about forty years old, but he looked like a man who drank. He had a light-coloured overcoat on."

"Good. Is this your room?"

"Yes, sir."

They were now in the lower corridor, where they found Amster walking up and down. The woman opened the door of the little room, and took a glove from a cupboard. Muller put it in his pocket and told the woman not to leave the house for anything, as she might be sent for to come to the police station at any moment. Then he went out into the street with Amster. When they were outside in the sunlight, he looked at the glove. It was a remarkably small size, made for a man with a slender, delicate hand, not at all in accordance with the large stout body of the man described by the landlady. Muller put his hand into the glove and found something pushed up into the middle finger. He took it out and found that it was a crumpled tramway ticket.

"Look out for a shabby old closed coupe, with a driver about forty years old who looks like a drunkard and wears a light overcoat. If you find such a cab, engage it and drive in it to the nearest police station. Tell them there to hold the man until further notice. If the cab is not free, at least take his number. And one thing more, but you will know that yourself,—the cab we are looking for will have new glass in the right-hand window." Thus Muller spoke to his companion as he put the glove into his pocket and unfolded the tramway ticket. Amster understood that they had found the starting point of the drive of the night before.

"I will go to all coupe stands," he said eagerly.

"Yes, but we may be able to find it quicker than that." Muller took the little notebook, which he was now carrying in his pocket, and took from it the tramway ticket which was in the cover. He compared it with the one he had just found. They were both marked for the same hour of the day and for the same ride.

"Did the man use them?" asked Amster. The detective nodded. "How can they help us?"

"Somewhere on this stretch of the street railroad you will probably find the stand of the cab we are looking for. The man who hired it evidently arrived on the 6:30 train at the West Station—I have reason to believe that he does not live here,—and then took the street car to this corner. The last ticket is marked for yesterday. In the car he probably made his plans to hire a cab. So you had better stay along the line of the car tracks. You will find me in room seven, Police Headquarters, at noon to-day. The authorities have already taken up the case. You may have something to tell us then. Good luck to you."

Muller hurried on, after he had taken a quick breakfast in a little cafe. He went at once to headquarters, made his report there and then drove to Fellner's house. The latter was awaiting him with great impatience. There the detective gathered much valuable information about the first marriage of Asta Langen's long-dead father. It was old Berner who could tell him the most about these long-vanished days.

When he reached his office at headquarters again, he found telegrams in great number awaiting him. They were from all the hospitals and insane asylums in the entire district. But in none of them had there been a patient fitting the description of the vanished girl. Neither the commissioner nor Muller was surprised at this negative result. They were also not surprised at all that the other branches of the police department had been able to discover so little about the disappearance of the young lady. They were aware that they had to deal with a criminal of great ability who would be careful not to fall into the usual slips made by his kind.

There was no news from the cab either, although several detectives were out looking for it. It was almost nightfall when Amster ran breathlessly into room number seven. "I have him! he's waiting outside across the way!" This was Amster's report.

Muller threw on his coat hastily. "You didn't pay him, did you? On a cold day like this the drivers don't like to wait long in any one place."

"No danger. I haven't money enough for that," replied Amster with a sad smile. Muller did not hear him as he was already outside. But the commissioner with whom he had been talking and to whom Muller had already spoken of his voluntary assistant, entered into a conversation with Amster, and said to him finally: "I will take it upon myself to guarantee your future, if you are ready to enter the secret service under Muller's orders. If you wish to do this you can stay right on now, for I think we will need you in this case."

Amster bowed in agreement. His life had been troubled, his reputation darkened by no fault of his own, and the work he was doing now had awakened, an interest and an ability that he did not know he possessed. He was more than glad to accept the offer made by the official.

Muller was already across the street and had laid his hand upon the door of the cab when the driver turned to him and said crossly, "Some one else has ordered me. But I am not going to wait in this cold, get in if you want to."

"All right. Now tell me first where you drove to last evening with the sick lady and her companion?" The man looked astonished but found his tongue again in a moment. "And who are you?" he asked calmly.

"We will tell you that upstairs in the police station," answered Muller equally calmly, and ordered the man to drive through the gateway into the inner courtyard. He himself got into the wagon, and in the course of the short drive he had made a discovery. He had found a tiny glass stopper, such as is used in perfume bottles. He could understand from this why the odour of perfume which had now become familiar to him was still so strong inside the old cab. Also why it was so strong on the delicate handkerchief. Asta Langen had taken the stopper from the bottle in her pocket, so as to leave a trail of odour behind her.

## CHAPTER THREE. THE LONELY COTTAGE

Fifteen minutes after the driver had made his report to Commissioner Von Mayringen, the latter with Amster entered another cab. A well-armed policeman mounted the box of this second vehicle. "Follow that cab ahead," the commissioner told his driver. The second cab followed the one-horse coupe in which Muller was seated. They drove first to No. 14 Cathedral Lane, where Muller told Berner to come with him. He found Mr. Fellner ready to go also, and it was with great difficulty that he could dissuade the invalid, who was greatly fatigued by his morning visit to the police station, from joining them.

The carriages then drove off more quickly than before. It was now quite dark, a gloomy stormy winter evening. Muller had taken his place on the box of his cab and sat peering out into the darkness. In spite of the sharp wind and the ice that blew against his face the detective could see that they were going out from the more closely built up portions of the city, and were now in new streets with half-finished houses. Soon they passed even these and were outside of the city. The way was lonely and dreary, bordered by wooden fences on both sides. Muller looked sharply to right and to left.

"You should have become alarmed here," he said to the driver, pointing to one part of the fence.

"Why?" asked the man.

"Because this is where the window was broken."

"I didn't know that—until I got home."

"H'm; you must have been nicely drunk."

The driver murmured something in his beard.

"Stop here, this is your turn, down that street," Muller said a few moments later, as the driver turned the other way.

"How do you know that?" asked the man, surprised.

"None of your business."

"This street will take us there just the same."

"Probably, but I prefer to go the way you went yesterday."

"Very well, it's all the same to me." They were silent again, only the wind roared around them, and somewhere in the distance a fog horn moaned.

It was now six o'clock. The snow threw out a mild light which could not brighten the deep darkness around them. About half an hour later the first cab halted. "There's the house up there. Shall I drive to the garden gate?"

"No, stop here." Muller was already on the ground. "Are there any dogs here?" he asked.

"I didn't hear any yesterday."

"That's of no value. You didn't seem to hear much of anything yesterday." Muller opened the door of the cab and helped Berner out. The old man was trembling. "That was a dreadful drive!" he stammered.

"I hope you will be happier on the drive back," said the detective and added, "You stay here with the commissioner now."

The latter had already left his cab with his companion. His sharp eyes glanced over the heavily shaded garden and the little house in its midst. A little light shone from two windows of the first story. The men's eyes looked toward them, then the detective and Amster walked toward a high picket fence which closed the garden on the side nearest its neighbours. They shook the various pickets without much caution, for the wind made noise enough to kill any other sound. Amster called to Muller, he had found a loose picket, and his strong young arms had torn it out easily. Muller motioned to the other three to join them. A moment later they were all in the garden, walking carefully toward the house.

The door was closed but there were no bars at the windows of the ground floor. Amster looked inquiringly at the commissioner and the latter nodded and said, "All right, go ahead."

The next minute Amster had broken in through one pane of the window and turned the latch. The inner window was broken already so that it was not difficult for him to open it without any further noise. He disappeared into the dark room within. In a few seconds they heard a key turn in the door and it opened gently. The men entered, all except the policeman, who remained outside. The blind of his lantern was slightly opened, and he had his revolver ready in his hand.

Muller had opened his lantern also, and they saw that they were in a prettily furnished corridor from which the staircase and one door led out.

The four men tiptoed up the stairway and the commissioner stepped to the first of the two doors which opened onto the upper corridor. He turned the key which was in the lock, and opened the door, but they found themselves in a room as dark as was the corridor. From somewhere, however, a ray of light fell into the blackness. The official stepped into the room, pulling Berner in after him. The poor old man was in a state of trembling excitement when he found himself in the house where his beloved young lady might already be a corpse. One step more and a smothered cry broke from his lips. The commissioner had opened the door of an adjoining room, which was lighted and handsomely furnished. Only the heavy iron bars across the closed windows showed that the young lady who sat leaning back wearily in an arm-chair was a prisoner.

She looked up as they entered. The expression of utter despair and deep weariness which had rested on her pale face changed to a look of terror; then she saw that it was not her would-be murderer who was entering, but those who came to rescue. A bright flush illumined her cheeks and her eyes gleamed. But the change was too sudden for her tortured soul. She rose from her chair, then sank fainting to the floor.

Berner threw himself on his knees beside her, sobbing out, "She is dying! She is dying!"

Muller turned on the instant, for he had heard the door on the other side of the hall open, and a tall slender man with a smooth face and a deep scar on his right cheek stood on the threshold looking at them in dazed surprise. For an instant only had he lost his control. The next second he was in his room again, slamming the door behind him. But it was too late. Amster's foot was already in the crack of the door and he pushed it open to let Muller enter. "Well done," cried the latter, and then he turned to the man in the room. "Here, stop that. I can fire twice before you get the window open."

The man turned and walked slowly to the centre of the room, sinking down into an arm-chair that stood beside the desk. Neither Amster nor Muller turned their eyes from him for a moment, ready for any attempt on his part to escape. But the detective had already seen something that told him that Langen was not thinking of flight. When he turned to the desk, Muller had seen his eyes glisten while a scornful smile parted his thin, lips. A second later he had let his handkerchief fall, apparently carelessly, upon the desk. But in this short space of time the detective's sharp eyes had seen a tiny bottle upon which was a black label with a grinning skull. Muller could not see whether the bottle was full or empty, but now he knew that it must hold sufficient poison to enable the captured criminal to escape open disgrace. Knowing this, Muller looked with admiration at the calmness of the villain, whose intelligent eyes were turned towards him in evident curiosity.

"Who are you and who else is here with you?" asked the man calmly.

"I am Muller of the Secret Service," replied his visitor and added, "You must put up with us for the time being, Mr. Egon Langen. The police commissioner is occupied with your step-sister, whom you were about to murder."

Langen put his hand to his cheek, looking at Muller between his lashes as he said, "To murder? Who can prove that?"

"We have all the proofs we need."

"I will acknowledge only that I wanted Asta to disappear."

Muller smiled. "What good would that have done you? You wanted her entire fortune, did you not? But that could have come to you only after thirty years, and you are not likely to have waited that long. Your plan was to murder your step-sister, even if you could not get a letter from her telling of her intention to commit suicide."

Langen rose suddenly, but controlled himself again and sank back easily in his chair. "Then the old woman has been talking?" he asked.

Muller shook his head. "We knew it through Miss Langen herself."

"She has spoken to no one for over ten days."

"But you let her throw her notebook out of the window of the cab."

"Ah—"

"There, you see, you should not have let that happen."

Drops of perspiration stood out on Langen's forehead. Until now, perhaps, he had had some possible hope of escape. It was useless now, he knew.

As calmly as he had spoken thus far Muller continued. "For twenty years I have been studying the hearts of criminals like yourself. But there are things I do not understand about this case and it interests me very much."

Langen had wiped the drops from his forehead and he now turned on Muller a face that seemed made of bronze. There was but one expression on it, that of cold scorn.

"I feel greatly flattered, sir, to think that I can offer a problem to one of your experience," Langen began. His voice, which had been slightly veiled before, was now quite clear. "Ask me all you like. I will answer you."

Muller began: "Why did you wait so long before committing the murder? and why did you drag your victim from place to place when you could have killed her easily in the compartment of the railway train?"

"The windows of the compartment were open, my honoured friend, and it was a fine warm evening for the season, because of which the windows in the other compartment were also open. There was nothing else I could do at that time then, except to offer Asta a cup of tea when she felt a little faint upon leaving the train. I am a physician and I know how to use the right drugs at the right time. When Asta had taken the tea, she knew nothing more until she woke up a day later in a room in the city."

"And the piece of paper with the threat on it? and the revolver you left so handy for her? oh, but I forgot, the old woman took the weapon away before the lady could use it in her despair," said Muller.

"Quite right. I see you know every detail."

"But why didn't you complete your crime in the room in the old house?" persisted Muller.

"Because I lost my false beard one day upon the staircase, and I feared the old woman might have seen my face enough to recognise me again. I thought it better to look for another place."

"And then you found this house."

"Yes, but several days later."

"And you hired it in the name of Miss Asta Langen? Who would then have been found dead here several days after you had entered the house?"

"Several days, several weeks perhaps. I preferred to wait until the woman who rented the house had read in the papers that Asta Langen had disappeared and was being sought for. Somebody would have found her here, and her identity would have easily been established, for I knew that she had some important family documents with her."

Muller was silent a moment, with an expression of deep pity on his face. Then he continued: "Yes, someone would have found her, and her suicide would have been a dark mystery, unless, of course, malicious tongues would have found ugly reasons enough why a beautiful young lady should hide herself in a lonely cottage to take her own life."

Muller had spoken as if to himself. Egon Langen's lips, parted in a smile so evil that Amster clenched his fists.

"And you would not have regretted this ruining the reputation as well as taking the life of an innocent girl?" asked the detective low and tense.

"No, for I hated her."

"You hated her because she was rich and innocent. She was very charitable and would gladly have helped you if you were in need. Beside this, you were entitled to a portion of your father's estate. It is almost thirty thousand guldens, as Mr. Fellner tells me. Why did you not take that?"

"Fellner did not know that I had already received twenty thousand of this when my father turned me out. He probably would have heard of it later, for Berner was the witness. I did not care for the remaining ten thousand because I would have the entire fortune after Asta's death. I would have seen the official notice and the call for heirs in Australia, and would have written from there, announcing that I was still alive. If you had come several days later I should have been a rich man within a year."

His clenched fist resting on his knee, the rascal stared out ahead of him when he ended his shameless confession. In his rage and disappointment he had not noticed that Muller's hand dropped gently to the desk and softly took a little bottle from under the handkerchief. Langen came out of his dark thoughts only when Muller's voice broke the silence. "But you miscalculated, if you expected to inherit from your sister. She is still a minor and your father's will would have given you only ten thousand guldens.

"But you forget that Asta will be twenty-four on the third of December."

"Ah, then you would have kept her alive until then."

"You understand quickly," said Langen with a mocking smile.

"But she disappeared on the eighteenth of November. How could you prove that she died after her birthday, therefore in full possession of her fortune and without leaving any will?"

"That is very simple. I buy several newspapers every day. I would have taken them up to the fourth and fifth of December and left them here with the body."

"You are more clever even than I thought," said the detective dryly as he heard the commissioner's steps behind him. Muller put a whistle to his lips and its shrill tone ran through the house, calling up the policeman who stood by the door.

Egon Langen's face was grey with pallor, his features were distorted, and yet there was the ghost of a smile on his lips as he saw his captors enter the door. He put his hand out, raised his handkerchief hastily and then a wild scream echoed through the room, a scream that ended in a ghastly groan.

"I have taken your bottle, you might as well give yourself up quietly," said Muller calmly, holding his revolver near Langen's face. The prisoner threw himself at the detective but was caught and overpowered by Amster and the policeman.

A quarter of an hour later the cabs drove back toward the city. Inside one cowered Egon Langen, watched by the policeman and Amster. Berner was on the box beside the driver, telling the now interested man the story of what had happened to his dear young lady. In the other cab sat Asta Langen with Kurt von Mayringen and Muller.

"Do you feel better now?" asked the young commissioner in sincere sympathy that was mingled with admiration for the delicate beauty of the girl beside him, an admiration heightened by her romantic story and marvelous escape.

Asta nodded and answered gently: "I feel as if some terrible weight were lifted from my heart and brain. But I doubt if I will ever forget these horrible days, when I had already come to accept it as a fact that—that I was to be murdered."

"This is the man to whom you owe your escape," said the commissioner, laying his hand on Muller's knee. Asta did not speak, but she reached out in the darkness of the cab, caught Muller's hand and would have raised it to her lips, had not the little man drawn it away hastily. "It was only my duty, dear young lady," he said. "A duty that is not onerous when it means the rescue of innocence and the preventing of crime. It is not always so, unfortunately—nor am I always so fortunate as in this case."

This indeed is what Muller calls a "case with a happy ending," for scarcely a year later, to his own great embarrassment, he found himself the most honoured guest, and a centre of attraction equally with the bridal couple, at the marriage of Kurt von Mayringen and Asta Langen. Muller asserts, however, that he is not a success in society, and that he would rather unravel fifty difficult cases than again be the "lion" at a fashionable function.

# THE NINESCORE MYSTERY
## BY BARONESS EMMUSKA ORCZY

Baronnes Emmuska Orczy

## ORIGINALLY PUBLISHED IN 1910

# The Ninescore Mystery

## By Baroness Emmuska Orczy

Lady Molly Robertson-Kirk is one of the earliest examples of a female detective. At a time when women were almost completely absent from any form of police work, Lady Molly has joined Scotland Yard in order to save her fiancee who has been wrongly accused of a crime. At first she meets resistence on the part of her superiors, but eventually, through persistence, is assigned to her first case which she solves through her ability to apply a feminine viewpoint. It is this knowledge of domestic life and her intuition which leads to success in subsequent cases until she is finally prove her fiancee innocent, at which point she leaves Scotland Yard and marries. Lady Molly is accompanied in her investigations by an assistant, another member of Scotland Yard's Female Department.

The twelve Lady Molly stories were first published in 1910 in *Lady Molly of Scotland Yard*. The book was extremely popular and went through three editions in the first year. As with much of the detective fiction of the period, the stories were written more for entertainment value than as an accurate presentation of police work at the time.

The author of the Lady Molly stories was the Baroness Emma Orczy, who, as has been noted elsewhere in this volume also wrote the stories featuring the "Old Man in the Corner," those stories also being narrated by a female character. More stories featuring Lady Molly may be found in the Resurrected Press edition *Lady Molly of Scotland Yard*.

# THE NINESCORE MYSTERY

## 1

WELL, you know, some say she is the daughter of a duke, others that she was born in the gutter, and that the handle has been soldered on to her name in order to give her style and influence.

I could say a lot, of course, but "my lips are sealed," as the poets say. All through her successful career at the Yard she honoured me with her friendship and confidence, but when she took me in partnership, as it were, she made me promise that I would never breathe a word of her private life, and this I swore on my Bible oath—"wish I may die," and all the rest of it.

Yes, we always called her "my lady," from the moment that she was put at the head of our section; and the chief called her "Lady Molly" in our presence. We of the Female Department are dreadfully snubbed by the men, though don't tell me that women have not ten times as much intuition as the blundering and sterner sex; my firm belief is that we shouldn't have half so many undetected crimes if some of the so-called mysteries were put to the test of feminine investigation.

Do you suppose for a moment, for instance, that the truth about that extraordinary case at Ninescore would ever have come to light if the men alone had had the handling of it? Would any man have taken so bold a risk as Lady Molly did when—But I am anticipating.

Let me go back to that memorable morning when she came into my room in a wild state of agitation.

"The chief says I may go down to Ninescore if I like, Mary," she said in a voice all a-quiver with excitement.

"You!" I ejaculated. "What for?"

"What for—what for?" she repeated eagerly. "Mary, don't you understand? It is the chance I have been waiting for—the chance of a lifetime? They are all desperate about the case up at the Yard; the public is furious, and columns of sarcastic letters appear in the daily press. None of our men know what to do;

they are at their wits' end, and so this morning I went to the chief—"

"Yes?" I queried eagerly, for she had suddenly ceased speaking.

"Well, never mind now how I did it—I will tell you all about it on the way, for we have just got time to catch the 11 a.m. down to Canterbury. The chief says I may go, and that I may take whom I like with me. He suggested one of the men, but somehow I feel that this is woman's work, and I'd rather have you, Mary, than anyone. We will go over the preliminaries of the case together in the train, as I don't suppose that you have got them at your fingers' ends yet, and you have only just got time to put a few things together and meet me at Charing Cross booking-office in time for that 11.0 sharp."

She was off before I could ask her any more questions, and anyhow I was too flabbergasted to say much. A murder case in the hands of the Female Department! Such a thing had been unheard of until now. But I was all excitement, too, and you may be sure I was at the station in good time.

Fortunately Lady Molly and I had a carriage to ourselves. It was a non-stop run to Canterbury, so we had plenty of time before us, and I was longing to know all about this case, you bet, since I was to have the honour of helping Lady Molly in it.

The murder of Mary Nicholls had actually been committed at Ash Court, a fine old mansion which stands in the village of Ninescore. The Court is surrounded by magnificently timbered grounds, the most fascinating portion of which is an island in the midst of a small pond, which is spanned by a tiny rustic bridge. The island is called "The Wilderness," and is at the furthermost end of the grounds, out of sight and earshot of the mansion itself. It was in this charming spot, on the edge of the pond, that the body of a girl was found on the 5th of February last.

I will spare you the horrible details of this gruesome discovery. Suffice it to say for the present that the unfortunate woman was lying on her face, with the lower portion of her body on the small grass- covered embankment, and her head, arms, and shoulders sunk in the slime of the stagnant water just below.

It was Timothy Coleman, one of the under-gardeners at Ash Court, who first made this appalling discovery. He had crossed the rustic bridge and traversed the little island in its entirety, when he noticed something blue lying half in and half out of the water beyond. Timothy is a stolid, unemotional kind of yokel, and, once having ascertained that the object was a woman's body in a blue dress with white facings, he quietly stooped and tried to lift it out of the mud.

But here even his stolidity gave way at the terrible sight which was revealed before him. That the woman—whoever she might be—had been brutally murdered was obvious, her dress in front being stained with blood; but what was so awful that it even turned old Timothy sick with horror, was that, owing to the head, arms and shoulders having apparently been in the slime for some time, they were in an advanced state of decomposition.

Well, whatever was necessary was immediately done, of course. Coleman went to get assistance from the lodge, and soon the police were on the scene and had removed the unfortunate victim's remains to the small local police-station.

Ninescore is a sleepy, out-of-the-way village, situated some seven miles from Canterbury and four from Sandwich. Soon everyone in the place had heard that a terrible murder had been committed in the village, and all the details were already freely discussed at the Green Man.

To begin with, everyone said that though the body itself might be practically unrecognisable, the bright blue serge dress with the white facings was unmistakable, as were the pearl and ruby ring and the red leather purse found by Inspector Meisures close to the murdered woman's hand.

Within two hours of Timothy Coleman's gruesome find the identity of the unfortunate victim was firmly established as that of Mary Nicholls, who lived with her sister Susan at 2, Elm Cottages, in Ninescore Lane, almost opposite Ash Court. It was also known that when the police called at that address they found the place locked and apparently uninhabited.

Mrs. Hooker, who lived at No. 1 next door, explained to Inspector Meisures that Susan and Mary Nicholls had left home about a fortnight ago, and that she had not seen them since.

"It'll be a fortnight to-morrow," she said. "I was just inside my own front door a-calling to the cat to come in. It was past seven o'clock, and as dark a night as ever you did see. You could hardly see your 'and afore your eyes, and there was a nasty damp drizzle comin' from everywhere. Susan and Mary come out of their cottage; I couldn't rightly see Susan, but I 'eard Mary's voice quite distinck. She says: 'We'll have to 'urry,' says she. I, thinkin' they might be goin' to do some shoppin' in the village, calls out to them that I'd just 'eard the church clock strike seven, and that bein' Thursday, and early closin', they'd find all the shops shut at Ninescore. But they took no notice, and walked off towards the village, and that's the last I ever seed o' them two."

Further questioning among the village folk brought forth many curious details. It seems that Mary Nicholls was a very flighty young woman, about whom there had already been quite a good deal of scandal, whilst Susan, on the other hand—who was very sober and steady in her conduct—had chafed considerably under her younger sister's questionable reputation, and, according to Mrs. Hooker, many were the bitter quarrels which occurred between the two girls. These quarrels, it seems, had been especially violent within the last year whenever Mr. Lionel Lydgate called at the cottage. He was a London gentleman, it appears—a young man about town, it afterwards transpired—but he frequently stayed at Canterbury, where he had some friends, and on those occasions he would come over to Ninescore in his smart dogcart and take Mary out for drives.

Mr. Lydgate is brother to Lord Edbrooke, the multimillionaire, who was the recipient of birthday honours last year. His lordship resides at Edbrooke Castle, but he and his brother Lionel had rented Ash Court once or twice, as both were keen golfers and Sandwich Links are very close by. Lord Edbrooke, I may add, is a married man. Mr. Lionel Lydgate, on the other hand, is just engaged to Miss Marbury, daughter of one of the canons of Canterbury.

No wonder, therefore, that Susan Nicholls strongly objected to her sister's name being still coupled with that of a young man far above her in station, who, moreover, was about to marry a young lady in his own rank of life.

But Mary seemed not to care. She was a young woman who only liked fun and pleasure, and she shrugged her shoulders at public opinion, even though there were ugly rumours anent the parentage of a little baby girl whom she herself had placed under the care of Mrs. Williams, a widow who lived in a somewhat isolated cottage on the Canterbury road. Mary had told Mrs. Williams that the father of the child, who was her own brother, had died very suddenly, leaving the little one on her and Susan's hands; and, as they couldn't look after it properly, they wished Mrs. Williams to have charge of it. To this the latter readily agreed.

The sum for the keep of the infant was decided upon, and thereafter Mary Nicholls had come every week to see the little girl, and always brought the money with her.

Inspector Meisures called on Mrs. Williams, and certainly the worthy widow had a very startling sequel to relate to the above story.

"A fortnight to-morrow," explained Mrs. Williams to the inspector, "a little after seven o'clock, Mary Nicholls come runnin' into my cottage. It was an awful night, pitch dark and a nasty drizzle. Mary says to me she's in a great hurry; she is goin' up to London by a train from Canterbury and wants to say good-bye to the child. She seemed terribly excited, and her clothes were very wet. I brings baby to her, and she kisses it rather wild-like and says to me: 'You'll take great care of her, Mrs. Williams,' she says; 'I may be gone some time.' Then she puts baby down and gives me £2, the child's keep for eight weeks."

After which, it appears, Mary once more said "good-bye" and ran out of the cottage, Mrs. Williams going as far as the front door with her. The night was very dark, and she couldn't see if Mary was alone or not, until presently she heard her voice saying tearfully: "I had to kiss baby—" then the voice died out in the distance "on the way to Canterbury," Mrs. Williams said most emphatically.

So far, you see, Inspector Meisures was able to fix the departure of the two sisters Nicholls from Ninescore on the night of January 23rd. Obviously they left their cottage about seven, went to Mrs. Williams, where Susan remained outside while Mary went in to say good-bye to the child.

After that all traces of them seem to have vanished. Whether they did go to Canterbury, and caught the last up train, at what station they alighted, or when poor Mary came back, could not at present be discovered.

According to the medical officer, the unfortunate girl must have been dead twelve or thirteen days at the very least, as, though the stagnant water may have accelerated decomposition, the head could not have got into such an advanced state much under a fortnight.

At Canterbury station neither the booking-clerk nor the porters could throw any light upon the subject. Canterbury West is a busy station, and scores of passengers buy tickets and go through the barriers every day. It was impossible, therefore, to give any positive information about two young women who may or may not have travelled by the last up train on Saturday, January 23rd—that is, a fortnight before.

One thing only was certain—whether Susan went to Canterbury and travelled by that up train or not, alone or with her sister—Mary had undoubtedly come back to Ninescore either the same night or the following day, since Timothy Coleman found her half-decomposed remains in the grounds of Ash Court a fortnight later.

Had she come back to meet her lover, or what? And where was Susan now?

From the first, therefore, you see, there was a great element of mystery about the whole case, and it was only natural that the local police should feel that, unless something more definite came out at the inquest, they would like to have the assistance of some of the fellows at the Yard.

So the preliminary notes were sent up to London, and some of them drifted into our hands. Lady Molly was deeply interested in it from the first, and my firm belief is that she simply worried the chief into allowing her to go down to Ninescore and see what she could do.

## 2

AT first it was understood that Lady Molly should only go down to Canterbury after the inquest, if the local police still felt that they were in want of assistance from London. But nothing was further from my lady's intentions than to wait until then.

"I was not going to miss the first act of a romantic drama," she said to me just as our train steamed into Canterbury station. "Pick up your bag, Mary. We're going to tramp it to Ninescore— two lady artists on a sketching tour, remember—and we'll find lodgings in the village, I dare say."

We had some lunch in Canterbury, and then we started to walk the six and a half miles to Ninescore, carrying our bags. We put up at one of the cottages, where the legend "Apartments for single respectable lady or gentleman" had hospitably invited us to enter, and at eight o'clock the next morning we found our way to the local police-station, where the inquest was to take place. Such a funny little place, you know— just a cottage converted for official use—and the small room packed to its utmost holding capacity. The entire able-bodied population of the neighbourhood had, I verily believe, congregated in these ten cubic yards of stuffy atmosphere.

Inspector Meisures, apprised by the chief of our arrival, had reserved two good places for us well in sight of witnesses, coroner and jury. The room was insupportably close, but I assure you that neither Lady Molly nor I thought much about our comfort then. We were terribly interested.

From the outset the case seemed, as it were, to wrap itself more and more in its mantle of impenetrable mystery. There was precious little in the way of clues, only that awful intuition, that dark unspoken suspicion with regard to one particular man's guilt, which one could feel hovering in the minds of all those present.

Neither the police nor Timothy Coleman had anything to add to what was already known. The ring and purse were produced, also the dress worn by the murdered woman. All were sworn to by several witnesses as having been the property of Mary Nicholls.

Timothy, on being closely questioned, said that, in his opinion, the girl's body had been pushed into the mud, as the head was absolutely embedded in it, and he didn't see how she could have fallen like that.

Medical evidence was repeated; it was as uncertain—as vague—as before. Owing to the state of the head and neck it was impossible to ascertain by what means the death blow had been dealt. The doctor repeated his statement that the unfortunate girl must have been dead quite a fortnight. The body was discovered on February 5th—a fortnight before that would have been on or about January 23rd.

The caretaker who lived at the lodge at Ash Court could also throw but little light on the mysterious event. Neither he nor any member of his family had seen or heard anything to arouse their suspicions. Against that he explained that "The Wilderness," where the murder was committed, is situated some 200 yards from the lodge, with the mansion and flower garden lying between. Replying to a question put to him by a juryman, he said that that portion of the grounds is only divided off from Ninescore Lane by a low, brick wall, which has a door in it, opening into the lane almost opposite Elm Cottages. He added that the mansion had been empty for over a year, and that he succeeded the last man, who died, about twelve months ago. Mr. Lydgate had not been down for golf since witness had been in charge.

It would be useless to recapitulate all that the various witnesses had already told the police, and were now prepared to swear to. The private life of the two sisters Nicholls was gone into at full length, as much, at least, as was publicly known. But you know what village folk are; except when there is a bit of scandal and gossip, they know precious little of one another's inner lives.

The two girls appeared to be very comfortably off. Mary was always smartly dressed; and the baby girl, whom she had placed in Mrs. Williams's charge, had plenty of good and expensive clothes, whilst her keep, 5s. a week, was paid with unfailing regularity. What seemed certain, however, was that they did not get on well together, that Susan violently objected to Mary's association with Mr. Lydgate, and that recently she had spoken to the vicar asking him to try to persuade her sister to go away from Ninescore altogether, so as to break entirely with the past. The Reverend Octavius Ludlow, Vicar of Ninescore, seems thereupon to have had a little talk with Mary on the subject, suggesting that she should accept a good situation in London.

"But," continued the reverend gentleman, "I didn't make much impression on her. All she replied to me was that she certainly need never go into service, as she had a good income of her own, and could obtain £5,000 or more quite easily at any time if she chose."

"Did you mention Mr. Lydgate's name to her at all?" asked the coroner.

"Yes, I did," said the vicar, after a slight hesitation.

"Well, what was her attitude then?"

"I am afraid she laughed," replied the Reverend Octavius, primly, "and said very picturesquely, if somewhat ungrammatically, that 'some folks didn't know what they was talkin' about.'"

All very indefinite, you see. Nothing to get hold of, no motive suggested—beyond a very vague suspicion, perhaps, of blackmail—to account for a brutal crime. I must not, however, forget to tell you the two other facts which came to light in the course of this extraordinary inquest. Though, at the time, these facts seemed of wonderful moment for the elucidation of the mystery, they only helped ultimately to plunge the whole case into darkness still more impenetrable than before.

I am alluding, firstly, to the deposition of James Franklin, a carter in the employ of one of the local farmers. He stated that about half-past six on that same Saturday night, January 23rd, he was walking along Ninescore Lane leading his horse and cart, as the night was indeed pitch dark. Just as he came somewhere near Elm Cottages he heard a man's voice saying in a kind of hoarse whisper:

"Open the door, can't you? It's as dark as blazes!"

Then a pause, after which the same voice added:

"Mary, where the dickens are you?" Whereupon a girl's voice replied: "All right, I'm coming."

James Franklin heard nothing more after that, nor did he see anyone in the gloom.

With the stolidity peculiar to the Kentish peasantry, he thought no more of this until the day when he heard that Mary Nicholls had been murdered; then he voluntarily came forward and told his story to the police. Now, when he was closely questioned, he was quite unable to say whether these voices proceeded from that side of the lane where stand Elm Cottages or from the other side, which is edged by the low, brick wall.

Finally, Inspector Meisures, who really showed an extraordinary sense of what was dramatic, here produced a document which he had reserved for the last. This was a piece of paper which he had found in the red leather purse already mentioned, and which at first had not been thought very important, as the writing was identified by several people as that of the deceased, and consisted merely of a series of dates and hours scribbled in pencil on a scrap of notepaper. But suddenly these dates had assumed a weird and terrible significance: two of them, at least—December 26th and January 1st followed by "10 a.m."—were days on which Mr. Lydgate came over to Ninescore and took Mary for drives. One or two witnesses swore to this positively. Both dates had been local meets of the harriers, to which other folk from the village had gone, and Mary had openly said afterwards how much she had enjoyed these.

The other dates (there were six altogether) were more or less vague. One Mrs. Hooker remembered as being coincident with a day Mary Nicholls had spent away from home; but the last date, scribbled in the same handwriting, was January 23rd, and below it the hour—6 p.m.

The coroner now adjourned the inquest. An explanation from Mr. Lionel Lydgate had become imperative.

3

PUBLIC excitement had by now reached a very high pitch; it was no longer a case of mere local interest. The country inns all round the immediate neighbourhood were packed with visitors from London, artists, journalists, dramatists, and actor-managers, whilst the hotels and fly-proprietors of Canterbury were doing a roaring trade.

Certain facts and one vivid picture stood out clearly before the thoughtful mind in the midst of a chaos of conflicting and irrelevant evidence: the picture was that of the two women tramping in the wet and pitch dark night towards Canterbury. Beyond that everything was a blur.

When did Mary Nicholls come back to Ninescore, and why?

To keep an appointment made with Lionel Lydgate, it was openly whispered; but that appointment—if the rough notes were interpreted rightly—was for the very day on which she and her sister went away from home. A man's voice called to her at half-past six certainly, and she replied to it. Franklin, the carter, heard her; but half an hour afterwards Mrs. Hooker heard her voice when she left home with her sister, and she visited Mrs. Williams after that.

The only theory compatible with all this was, of course, that Mary merely accompanied Susan part of the way to Canterbury, then went back to meet her lover, who enticed her into the deserted grounds of Ash Court, and there murdered her.

The motive was not far to seek. Mr. Lionel Lydgate, about to marry, wished to silence for ever a voice that threatened to be unpleasantly persistent in its demands for money and in its threats of scandal.

But there was one great argument against that theory—the disappearance of Susan Nicholls. She had been extensively advertised for. The murder of her sister was published broadcast in every newspaper in the United Kingdom—she could not be ignorant of it. And, above all, she hated Mr. Lydgate. Why did she not come and add the weight of her testimony against him if, indeed, he was guilty?

And if Mr. Lydgate was innocent, then where was the criminal? And why had Susan Nicholls disappeared?

Why? Why? Why?

Well, the next day would show. Mr. Lionel Lydgate had been cited by the police to give evidence at the adjourned inquest.

Good-looking, very athletic, and obviously frightfully upset and nervous, he entered the little courtroom, accompanied by his solicitor, just before the coroner and jury took their seats.

He looked keenly at Lady Molly as he sat down, and from the expression on his face I guessed that he was much puzzled to know who she was.

He was the first witness called. Manfully and clearly he gave a concise account of his association with the deceased.

"She was pretty and amusing," he said. "I liked to take her out when I was in the neighborhood; it was no trouble to me. There was no harm in her, whatever the village gossips might say. I know she had been in trouble, as they say, but that had nothing to do with me. It wasn't for me to be hard on a girl, and I fancy that she has been very badly treated by some scoundrel."

Here he was hard pressed by the coroner, who wished him to explain what he meant. But Mr. Lydgate turned obstinate, and to every leading question he replied stolidly and very emphatically:

"I don't know who it was. It had nothing to do with me, but I was sorry for the girl because of everyone turning against her, including her sister, and I tried to give her a little pleasure when I could."

That was all right. Very sympathetically told. The public quite liked this pleasing specimen of English cricket-, golf—and football-loving manhood. Subsequently Mr. Lydgate admitted meeting Mary on December 26th and January 1st, but he swore most emphatically that that was the last he ever saw of her.

"But the 23rd of January," here insinuated the coroner; "you made an appointment with the deceased then?"

"Certainly not," he replied.

"But you met her on that day?"

"Most emphatically no," he replied quietly. "I went down to Edbrooke Castle, my brother's place in Lincolnshire, on the 20th of last month, and only got back to town about three days ago."

"You swear to that, Mr. Lydgate?" asked the coroner.

"I do, indeed, and there are a score of witnesses to bear me out. The family, the house-party, the servants."

He tried to dominate his own excitement. I suppose, poor man, he had only just realised that certain horrible suspicions had been resting upon him. His solicitor pacified him, and presently he sat down, whilst I must say that everyone there present was relieved at the thought that the handsome young athlete was not a murderer, after all. To look at him it certainly seemed preposterous.

But then, of course, there was the deadlock, and as there were no more witnesses to be heard, no new facts to elucidate, the jury returned the usual verdict against some person or persons unknown; and we, the keenly interested spectators, were left to face the problem—Who murdered Mary Nicholls, and where was her sister Susan?

4

AFTER the verdict we found our way back to our lodgings. Lady Molly tramped along silently, with that deep furrow between her brows which I knew meant that she was deep in thought.

"Now we'll have some tea," I said, with a sigh of relief, as soon as we entered the cottage door.

"No, you won't," replied my lady, dryly. "I am going to write out a telegram, and we'll go straight on to Canterbury and send it from there."

"To Canterbury!" I gasped. "Two hours' walk at least, for I don't suppose we can get a trap, and it is past three o'clock. Why not send your telegram from Ninescore?"

"Mary, you are stupid," was all the reply I got.

She wrote out two telegrams—one of which was at least three dozen words long—and, once more calling to me to come along, we set out for Canterbury.

I was tea-less, cross, and puzzled. Lady Molly was alert, cheerful, and irritatingly active.

We reached the first telegraph office a little before five. My lady sent the telegram without condescending to tell me anything of its destination or contents; then she took me to the Castle Hotel and graciously offered me tea.

"May I be allowed to inquire whether you propose tramping back to Ninescore to-night?" I asked with a slight touch of sarcasm, as I really felt put out.

"No, Mary," she replied, quietly munching a bit of Sally Lunn; "I have engaged a couple of rooms at this hotel and wired the chief that any message will find us here to-morrow morning."

After that there was nothing for it but quietude, patience, and finally supper and bed.

The next morning my lady walked into my room before I had finished dressing. She had a newspaper in her hand, and threw it down on the bed as she said calmly:

"It was in the evening paper all right last night. I think we shall be in time."

No use asking her what "it" meant. It was easier to pick up the paper, which I did. It was a late edition of one of the leading London evening shockers, and at once the front page, with its startling headline, attracted my attention:

THE NINESCORE MYSTERY MARY NICHOLL'S BABY DYING

Then, below that, a short paragraph:—

"We regret to learn that the little baby daughter of the unfortunate girl who was murdered recently at Ash Court, Ninescore. Kent, under such terrible and mysterious circumstances, is very seriously ill at the cottage of Mrs. Williams, in whose charge she is. The local doctor who visited her to-day declares that she cannot last more than a few hours.

At the time of going to press the nature of the child's complaint was not known to our special representative at Ninescore."

"What does this mean?" I gasped.

But before she could reply there was a knock at the door.

"A telegram for Miss Granard," said the voice of the hall-porter.

"Quick, Mary," said Lady Molly, eagerly. "I told the chief and also Meisures to wire here and to you."

The telegram turned out to have come from Ninescore, and was signed "Meisures." Lady Molly read it aloud:

"Mary Nicholls arrived here this morning. Detained her at station. Come at once."

"Mary Nicholls! I don't understand," was all I could contrive to say.

But she only replied:

"I knew it! I knew it! Oh, Mary, what a wonderful thing is human nature, and how I thank Heaven that gave me a knowledge of it!"

She made me get dressed all in a hurry, and then we swallowed some breakfast hastily whilst a fly was being got for us. I had, perforce, to satisfy my curiosity from my own inner consciousness. Lady Molly was too absorbed to take any notice of me. Evidently the chief knew what she had done and approved of it: the telegram from Meisures pointed to that.

My lady had suddenly become a personality. Dressed very quietly, and in a smart close-fitting hat, she looked years older than her age, owing also to the seriousness of her mien.

The fly took us to Ninescore fairly quickly. At the little police- station we found Meisures awaiting us. He had Elliot and Pegram from the Yard with him. They had obviously got their orders, for all three of them were mighty deferential.

"The woman is Mary Nicholls, right enough," said Meisures, as Lady Molly brushed quickly past him, "the woman who was supposed to have been murdered. It's that silly bogus paragraph about the infant brought her out of her hiding-place. I wonder how it got in," he added blandly; "the child is well enough."

"I wonder," said Lady Molly, whilst a smile—the first I had seen that morning—lit up her pretty face.

"I suppose the other sister will turn up too, presently," rejoined Elliot. "Pretty lot of trouble we shall have now. If Mary

Nicholls is alive and kickin', who was murdered at Ash Court, say I?"

"I wonder," said Lady Molly, with the same charming smile.

Then she went in to see Mary Nicholls.

The Reverend Octavius Ludlow was sitting beside the girl, who seemed in great distress, for she was crying bitterly.

Lady Molly asked Elliott and the others to remain in the passage whilst she herself went into the room, I following behind her.

When the door was shut, she went up to Mary Nicholls, and assuming a hard and severe manner, she said:

"Well, you have at last made up your mind, have you, Nicholls? I suppose you know that we have applied for a warrant for your arrest?"

The woman gave a shriek which unmistakably was one of fear.

"My arrest?" she gasped. "What for?"

"The murder of your sister Susan."

"'Twasn't me!" she said quickly.

"Then Susan is dead?" retorted Lady Molly, quietly.

Mary saw that she had betrayed herself. She gave Lady Molly a look of agonised horror, then turned as white as a sheet and would have fallen had not the Reverend Octavius Ludlow gently led her to a chair.

"It wasn't me," she repeated, with a heart-broken sob.

"That will be for you to prove," said Lady Molly dryly. "The child cannot now, of course remain with Mrs. Williams; she will be removed to the workhouse, and—"

"No, that shan't be," said the mother excitedly. "She shan't be, I tell you. The workhouse, indeed," she added in a paroxysm of hysterical tears, "and her father a lord!"

The reverend gentleman and I gasped in astonishment; but Lady Molly had worked up to this climax so ingeniously that it was obvious she had guessed it all along, and had merely led Mary Nicholls on in order to get this admission from her.

How well she had known human nature in pitting the child against the sweetheart! Mary Nicholls was ready enough to hide herself, to part from her child even for a while, in order to save the man she had once loved from the consequences of his crime; but when she heard that her child was dying, she no longer could bear to leave it among strangers, and when Lady Molly taunted her with the workhouse, she exclaimed in her maternal pride:

"The workhouse! And her father a lord!"

Driven into a corner, she confessed the whole truth.

Lord Edbrooke, then Mr. Lydgate, was the father of her child. Knowing this, her sister Susan had, for over a year now, systematically blackmailed the unfortunate man—not altogether, it seems, without Mary's connivance. In January last she got him to come down to Ninescore under the distinct promise that Mary would meet him and hand over to him the letters she had received from him, as well as the ring he had given her, in exchange for the sum of £5,000.

The meeting-place was arranged, but at the last moment Mary was afraid to go in the dark. Susan, nothing daunted, but anxious about her own reputation in case she should be seen talking to a man so late at night, put on Mary's dress, took the ring and the letters, also her sister's purse, and went to meet Lord Edbrooke.

What happened at that interview no one will ever know. It ended with the murder of the blackmailer. I suppose the fact that Susan had, in measure, begun by impersonating her sister, gave the murderer the first thought of confusing the identity of his victim by the horrible device of burying the body in the slimy mud. Anyway, he almost did succeed in hoodwinking the police, and would have done so entirely but for Lady Molly's strange intuition in the matter.

After his crime he ran instinctively to Mary's cottage. He had to make a clean breast of it to her, as, without her help, he was a doomed man.

So he persuaded her to go away from home and to leave no clue or trace of herself or her sister in Ninescore. With the help of money which he would give her, she could begin life anew somewhere else, and no doubt he deluded the unfortunate girl with promises that her child would be restored to her very soon.

Thus he enticed Mary Nicholls away, who would have been the great and all-important witness against him the moment his crime was discovered. A girl of Mary's type and class instinctively obeys the man she has once loved, the man who is the father of her child. She consented to disappear and to allow all the world to believe that she had been murdered by some unknown miscreant.

Then the murderer quietly returned to his luxurious home at Edbrooke Castle, unsuspected. No one had thought of mentioning his name in connection with that of Mary Nicholls. In the days when he used to come down to Ash Court he was Mr. Lydgate, and, when he became a peer, sleepy, out-of-the-way Ninescore ceased to think of him.

Perhaps Mr. Lionel Lydgate knew all about his brother's association with the village girl. From his attitude at the inquest I should say he did, but of course he would not betray his own brother unless forced to do so.

Now, of course, the whole aspect of the case was changed: the veil of mystery had been torn asunder owing to the insight, the marvelous intuition, of a woman who, in my opinion, is the most wonderful psychologist of her time.

You know the sequel. Our fellows at the Yard, aided by the local police, took their lead from Lady Molly, and began their investigations of Lord Edbrooke's movements on or about the 23rd of January.

Even their preliminary inquiries revealed the fact that his lordship had left Edbrooke Castle on the 21st. He went up to town, saying to his wife and household that he was called away on business, and not even taking his valet with him. He put up at the Langham Hotel.

But here police investigations came to an abrupt ending. Lord Edbrooke evidently got wind of them. Anyway, the day after Lady Molly so cleverly enticed Mary Nicholls out of her hiding-place, and surprised her into an admission of the truth, the unfortunate man threw himself in front of the express train at Grantham railway station, and was instantly killed. Human justice cannot reach him now!

But don't tell me that a man would have thought of that bogus paragraph, or of the taunt which stung the motherly pride of the village girl to the quick, and thus wrung from her an admission which no amount of male ingenuity would ever have obtained.

# THE RIDDLE OF THE
# NINTH FINGER
## BY THOMAS W. HANSHEW

ORIGINALLY PUBLISHED IN 1910

# THE RIDDLE OF THE
# NINTH FINGER

### By Thomas W. Hanshew

In a period when eccentric detectives were the rule, Hamilton Cleek certainly fit the mold. A former criminal with an almost pathological predilection for crime, he renounces crime after meeting a young woman and offers his services to Scotland Yard. His greatest asset as a detective is his mastery of disguise which has earned him the nickname of "the man of the forty faces." He is assisted in his endeavors by a young cockney street urchin named Dollop, whom he has befriended, and reports to Inspector Narkom of Scotland Yard. Often his nemesis is a French woman, Margot "Queen of the Apaches" and her partner Merode.

The Cleek stories tend to the melodramatic and are rife with the manners and morality of the day. Cleek's former experience as a master criminal has given him familiarity with the haunts and habits of the underworlds of London, Paris, and other cities around the world.

The first Cleek stories appeared in 1910 and were collected in several books including *Cleek: The Man of Forty Faces* and *Cleek of Scotland Yard*. In addition, there were a number of novels featuring the character, continuing into the 20's.

The author of the Cleek stories was the American actor, Thomas W. Hanshew. Residing in London later in life, he authored over 150 books. In later years he shared authorship with his wife, Mary E. Hanshew.

# THE RIDDLE OF THE NINTH FINGER

The inn of "The Three Jolly Fishermen," which, as you may know, lies on the left bank of the Thames, within a gunshot of Richmond, was all but empty when Cleek, answering the superintendent's note, strolled into it, and discovered Narkom enjoying his tea in solitary state at a little round table in the embrasure of a bay window at the far end of the little private parlour which lies immediately behind the bar-room.

"My dear fellow, do pardon me for not waiting," said the superintendent, as his famous ally entered, looking like a college-bred athlete in his boating flannels and his brim-tilted panama, "but the fact is, you're a little behind time for once, and besides, I was absolutely famishing."

"Share the blame of my lateness with me, Mr. Narkom," said Cleek, as he tossed aside his hat and threw the fag-end of the cigarette he was smoking out through the open window. "You said in your note that there was no immediate necessity for haste, so I improved the shining hour by another spin down the river. It isn't often that duty-calls bring me to a little Eden like this. The air is like balm to-day, and as for the river—oh, the river is a sheer delight!"

Narkom rang for a fresh pot of tea and a further supply of buttered toast, and, when these were served, Cleek sat down and joined him.

"I dare say," said the superintendent, opening fire at once, "that you wonder what in the world induced me to bring you out here to meet me, my dear fellow, instead of following the usual course and calling at Clarges Street? Well, the fact is, Cleek, that the gentleman with whom I am now about to put you in touch lives in this vicinity, and is so placed that he cannot get away without running the risk of having the step he is taking discovered."

"Humph! He is closely spied upon, then?" commented Cleek. "The trouble arises from some one or something in his own household?"

"No, in his father's. The 'trouble,' so far as I can gather, seems to emanate from his stepmother, a young and very beautiful woman, who was born on the island of Java, where the father of our client met and married her some two years ago. He had gone there to probe into the truth of the amazing statement that a runic stone had been unearthed in that part of the globe."

"Ah, then you need not tell me the gentleman's name, Mr. Narkom," interposed Cleek. "I remember perfectly well the stir which that ridiculous and unfounded statement created at the time. Despite the fact that scholars of all nations scoffed at the thing and pointed out that the very term 'rune' is of Teutonic origin, one enthusiastic old gentleman—Mr. Michael Bawdrey, a retired brewer, thirsting for something more enduring than malt to carry his name down the ages—became fired with enthusiasm upon the subject, and set forth for Java 'hot foot,' as one might say. I remember that the papers made great game of him; but I heard, I fancy, that, in spite of all, he was a dear, lovable old chap, and not at all like the creature the cartoonists portrayed him."

"What a memory you have, my dear Cleek. Yes, that is the party; and he is a dear, lovable old chap at bottom. Collects old china, old weapons, old armour, curiosities of all sorts—lots of 'em bogus, no doubt, catch the charlatans among the dealers letting a chance like that slip them—and is never so happy as when showing his 'collection' to his friends and being mistaken by the ignorant for a man of deep learning."

"A very human trait, Mr. Narkom. We all are anxious that the world should set the highest possible valuation upon us. It is only when we are underrated that we object. So this dear, deluded old gentleman, having failed to secure a 'rune' in Java brought back something equally cryptic—a woman? Was the lady of his choice a native or merely an inhabitant of the island?"

"Merely an inhabitant, my dear fellow. As a matter of fact, she is English. Her father, a doctor, long since deceased, took her out there in her childhood. She was none too well off, I believe: but that did not prevent her having many suitors, among whom was Mr. Bawdrey's own son, the gentleman who is anxious to have you take up this case."

"Oho!" said Cleek, with a strong rising inflection. "So the lady was of the careful and calculating kind? She didn't care for youth and all the rest of it when she could have papa and the money-chest without waiting. A common enough occurrence. Still, this does not make up an 'affair,' and especially an 'affair' which requires the assistance of a detective, and you spoke of 'a case.' What is the case, Mr. Narkom?"

"I will leave Mr. Philip Bawdrey himself to tell you that," said Narkom, as the door opened to admit a young man of about eight and twenty, clothed in tennis flannels, and looking very much perturbed. He was a handsome, fair-haired, fair-moustached young fellow, with frank, boyish eyes and that unmistakable something which stamps the products of the 'Varsities. "Come in, Mr. Bawdrey. You said we were not to wait tea, and you see that we haven't. Let me have the pleasure of introducing Mr.——"

"Headland," put in Cleek adroitly, and with a look at Narkom as much as to say, "Don't give me away. I may not care to take the case when I hear it, so what's the use of letting everybody know who I am?" Then he switched round in his chair, rose, and held out his hand. "Mr. George Headland, of the Yard, Mr. Bawdrey. I don't trust Mr. Narkom's proverbially tricky memory for names. He introduced me as Jones once, and I lost the opportunity of handling the case because the party in question couldn't believe that anybody named Jones would be likely to ferret it out."

"Funny idea that!" commented young Bawdrey, smiling and accepting the proffered hand. "Rum lot of people you must run across in your line, Mr. Headland. Shouldn't take you for a detective myself, shouldn't even in a room full of them. College man, aren't you? Thought so. Oxon or Cantab?"

"Cantab—Emmanuel."

"Oh, Lord! Never thought I'd ever live to appeal to an Emmanuel man to do anything brilliant. I'm an Oxon chap; Brasenose is my alma mater. I say, Mr. Narkom, do give me a cup of tea, will you? I had to slip off while the others were at theirs, and I've run all the way. Thanks very much. Don't mind if I sit in that corner and draw the curtain a little, do you?" his frank, boyish face suddenly clouding. "I don't want to be seen by anybody passing. It's a horrible thing to feel that you are being spied upon at every turn, Mr. Headland, and that want of caution may mean the death of the person you love best in all the world."

"Oh, it's that kind of case, is it?" queried Cleek, making room for him to pass round the table and sit in the corner, with his back to the window and the loosened folds of the chintz curtain keeping him in the shadow.

"Yes," answered young Bawdrey, with a half-repressed shudder and a deeper clouding of his rather pale face. "Sometimes I try to make myself believe that it isn't, that it's all fancy, that she never could be so inhuman, and yet how else is it to be explained? You can't go behind the evidence; you can't make things different simply by saying that you will not believe." He stirred his tea nervously, gulped down a couple of mouthfuls of it, and then set the cup aside. "I can't enjoy anything; it takes the savour out of everything when I think of it," he added, with a note of pathos in his voice. "My dad, my dear, bully old dad, the best and dearest old boy in all the world! I suppose, Mr. Headland, that Mr. Narkom has told you something about the case?"

"A little—a very little indeed. I know that your father went to Java, and married a second wife there; and I know, too, that you yourself were rather taken with the lady at one time, and that she threw you over as soon as Mr. Bawdrey senior became a possibility."

"That's a mistake," he replied. "She never threw me over, Mr. Headland; she never had the chance. I found her out long before my father became anything like what you might call a rival, found her out as a mercenary, designing woman, and broke from her voluntarily. I only wish that I had known that he had one serious thought regarding her. I could have warned him; I could have spoken then. But I never did find out until it was too late. Trust her for that. She waited until I had gone up-country to look after some fine old porcelains and enamels that the governor had heard about; then she hurried him off and tricked him into a hasty marriage. Of course, after that I couldn't speak, I wouldn't speak. She was my father's wife, and he was so proud of her, so happy, dear old boy, that I'd have been little better than a brute to say anything against her."

"What could you have said if you had spoken?"

"Oh, lots of things; the things that made me break away from her in the beginning. She'd had other love affairs for one thing; her late father's masquerading as a doctor for another. They had only used that as a cloak. They had run a gambling-house on the sly—he as the card-sharper, she as the decoy. They had drained one poor fellow dry, and she had thrown him over after leading him on to think that she cared for him and was going to marry him. He blew out his brains in front of her, poor wretch. They say she never turned a hair. You wouldn't believe it possible, if you saw her; she is so sweet and caressing, and so young and beautiful, you'd almost believe her an angel. But there's Travers in the background—always Travers!"

"Travers! Who is he?"

"Oh, one of her old flames, the only one she ever really cared for, they say. She was supposed to have broken with him out there in Java, because they were too poor to marry; and now he's come over to England, and he's there, in the house with the dear old dad and me, and they are as thick as thieves together. I've caught them whispering and prowling about together, in the grounds and along the lanes, after she has said 'Good-night' and gone to her room and is supposed to be in bed. There's a houseful of her old friends three parts of the time. They come and they go, but Travers never goes. I know why"—waxing suddenly excited, suddenly vehement—"Yes! I know why. He's in the game with her!"

"Game! What game, Mr. Bawdrey? What is it that she is doing?"

"She's killing my old dad!" he answered, with a sort of sob in his excited voice. "She's murdering him by inches, that's what she's doing, and I want you to help me bring it home to her. God knows what it is she's using or how she uses it; but you know what demons they are for secret poisons, those Javanese, what means they have of killing people without a trace. And she was out there for years and years. So, too, was Travers, the brute! They know all the secrets of those beastly barbarians, and between them they're doing something to my old dad."

"How do you know that?"

"I don't know it, that's the worst of it. But I couldn't be surer of it if they took me into their secrets. But there's the evidence of his condition; there's the fact that it didn't begin until after

Travers came. Look here, Mr. Headland, you don't know my dad.
He's got the queerest notions sometimes. One of his fads is that
it's unlucky to make a will. Well, if he dies without one, who will
inherit his money, as I am an only child?"

"Undoubtedly you and his widow."

"Exactly. And if I die at pretty nearly the same time—and
they'll see to that, never fear; it will be my turn the moment they
are sure of him—she will inherit everything. Now, let me tell you
what's happening. From being a strong, healthy man, my father
has, since Travers's arrival, begun to be attacked by a
mysterious malady. He has periodical fainting fits, sometimes
convulsions. He'll be feeling better for a day or so; then, without
a word of warning, whilst you're talking to him, he'll drop like a
shot bird and go into the most horrible convulsions. The doctors
can't stop it; they don't even know what it is. They only know
that he's fading away—turning from a strong, virile old man into
a thin, nervous, shivering wreck. But I know! I know! They're
dosing him somehow with some diabolical Javanese thing, those
two. And yesterday—God help me!—yesterday I, too, dropped
like a shot bird; I, too, had the convulsions and the weakness
and the fainting fit. My time has begun also!"

"Bless my soul! what a diabolical thing!" put in Narkom
agitatedly. "No wonder you appealed to me!"

"No wonder!" Bawdrey replied. "I felt that it had gone as far
as I dared let it; that it was time to call in the police and to have
help before it was too late. That's the case, Mr. Headland. I want
you to find some way of getting at the truth, of looking into
Travers's luggage, into my stepmother's effects, and unearthing
the horrible stuff with which they are doing this thing; and
perhaps, when that is known, some antidote may be found to
save the dear old dad and restore him to what he was. Can't you
do this? For God's sake, say that you can."

"At all events, I can try, Mr. Bawdrey," responded Cleek.

"Oh, thank you, thank you!" said Bawdrey gratefully. "I don't
care a hang what it costs, what your fees are, Mr. Headland. So
long as you run those two to earth, and get hold of the horrible
stuff, whatever it is, that they are using, I'll pay any price in the
world, and count it cheap as compared with the life of my dear
old dad. When can you take hold of the case? Now?"

"I'm afraid not. Mysterious things like this require a little thinking over. Suppose we say to-morrow noon? Will that do?"

"I suppose it must, although I should have liked to take you back with me. Every moment's precious at a time like this. But if it must be delayed until to-morrow—well, it must, I suppose. But I'll take jolly good care that nobody gets a chance to come within touching distance of the pater, bless him! until you do come, if I have to sit on the mat before his door until morning. Here's the address on this card, Mr. Headland. When and how shall I expect to see you again? You'll use an alias, of course?"

"Oh, certainly! Had you any old friend in your college days whom your father knew only by name and who is now too far off for the imposture to be discovered?"

"Yes. Jim Rickaby. We were as inseparable as the Siamese twins in our undergrad. days. He's in Borneo now. Haven't heard from him in a dog's age."

"Couldn't be better," said Cleek. "Then 'Jim Rickaby' let it be. You'll get a letter from him first thing in the morning saying that he's back in England, and about to run down and spend the week-end with you. At noon he will arrive, accompanied by his Borneo servant named—er—Dollops. You can put the 'blackie' up in some quarter of the house where he can move about at will without disturbing any of your own servants and can get in and out at all hours; he will be useful, you know, in prowling about the grounds at night and ascertaining if the lady really does go to bed when she retires to her room. As for 'Jim Rickaby' himself—well, you can pave the way for his operations by informing your father, when you get the letter, that he has gone daft on the subject of old china and curios and things of that sort, don't you know."

"What a ripping idea!" commented young Bawdrey. "I twig. He'll get chummy with you of course, and you can lead him on and adroitly 'pump' him regarding her, and where she keeps her keys and things like that. That's the idea, isn't it?"

"Something of that sort. I'll find out all about her, never fear," said Cleek in reply. Then they shook hands and parted, and it was not until after young Bawdrey had gone that either he or Narkom recollected that Cleek had overlooked telling the young man that Headland was not his name.

"Oh, well, it doesn't matter. Time enough to tell him that when it comes to making out the cheque," said Cleek, as the superintendent remarked upon the circumstance. Then he pushed back his chair and walked over to the window, and stood looking silently out upon the flowing river. Narkom did not disturb his reflections. He knew from past experience, as well as from the manner in which he took his lower lip between his teeth and drummed with his finger-tips upon the window ledge, that some idea relative to the working out of the case had taken shape within his mind, and so, with the utmost discretion, went on with his tea and refrained from speaking. Suddenly Cleek turned. "Mr. Narkom, do me a favour, will you? Look me up a copy of Holman's 'Diseases of the Kidneys' when you go back to town. I'll send Dollops round to the Yard to-night to get it."

"Right you are," said Narkom, taking out his pocket-book and making a note of it. "But I say, look here, my dear fellow, you can't possibly believe that it's anything of that sort, anything natural, I mean, in the face of what we've heard?"

"No, I don't. I think it's something confoundedly unnatural, and that that poor old chap is being secretly and barbarously murdered. I think that—and—I think, too——" His voice trailed off. He stood silent and preoccupied for a moment, and then, putting his thoughts into words, without addressing them to anybody: "Ayupee!" he said reflectively; "Pohon-Upas, Antjar, Galanga root, Ginger and Black Pepper—that's the Javanese method of procedure, I believe. Ayupee!—yes, assuredly, Ayupee!"

"What the dickens are you talking about, Cleek? And what does all that gibberish and that word 'Ayupee' mean?"

"Nothing—nothing. At least, just yet. I say, put on your hat and let's go for a pull on the river, Mr. Narkom. I've had enough of mysteries for to-day and am spoiling for another hour in a boat."

Then he screwed round on his heel and walked out into the brilliant summer sunshine.

II

Promptly at the hour appointed "Mr. Jim Rickaby" and his black servant arrived at Laburnam Villa and certainly the former had no cause to complain of the welcome he received at the hands of his beautiful young hostess.

He found her not only an extremely lovely woman to the eye, but one whose gentle, caressing ways, whose soft voice and simple girlish charm were altogether fascinating, and, judging from outward appearances, from the tender solicitude for her elderly husband's comfort and well-being, from the look in her eyes when she spoke to him, the gentleness of her hand when she touched him, one would have said that she really and truly loved him, and that it needed no lure of gold to draw this particular May to the arms of this one December.

He found Captain Travers a laughing, rollicking, fun-loving type of man—at least, to all outward appearances—who seemed to delight in sports and games and to have an almost childish love of card tricks and that species of entertainment which is known as parlour magic. He found the three other members of the little house-party—to wit: Mrs. Somerby-Miles, Lieutenant Forshay, and Mr. Robert Murdock—respectively, a silly, flirtatious, little gadfly of a widow; a callow, love-struck, lap-dog, young naval officer, with a budding moustache and a full-blown idea of his own importance; a dour Scotchman of middle age, with a passion for chess, a glowering scorn of frivolities, a deep abiding conviction that Scotland was the only country in the world for a self-respecting human being to dwell in, and that everything outside of the Established Church was foredoomed to flames and sulphur and the perpetual prodding of red-hot pitchforks. And last, but not least by any means, he found Mr. Michael Bawdrey just what he had been told he would find him, namely, a dear, lovable, sunny-tempered old man, who fairly idolized his young wife and absolutely adored his frank-faced, affectionate, big boy of a son, and who ought not, in the common course of things, to have an enemy or an evil wisher in all the world.

The news, which, of course, had preceded Cleek's arrival, that this whilom college chum of his son's was as great an enthusiast as he himself on the subject of old china, old porcelain, bric-a-brac, and curios of every sort, filled him with the utmost delight, and he could scarcely refrain from rushing him off at once to view his famous collection.

"Michael, dear, you mustn't overdo yourself just because you happen to have been a little stronger these past two days," said his wife, laying a gentle hand upon his arm. "Besides, we must give Mr. Rickaby time to breathe. He has had a long journey, and I am sure he will want to rest. You can take him in to see that wonderful collection after dinner, dear."

"Humph! Full of fakes, as I supposed—and she knows it," was Cleek's mental comment upon this. And he was not surprised when, finding herself alone with him a few minutes later, she said, in her pretty, pleading way:

"Mr. Rickaby, if you are an expert, don't undeceive him. I could not let you go to see the collection without first telling you. It is full of bogus things, full of frauds and shams that unscrupulous dealers have palmed off on him. But don't let him know. He takes such pride in them, and—and he's breaking down. God pity me, his health is breaking down every day, Mr. Rickaby, and I want to spare him every pang, if I can, even so little a pang as the discovery that the things he prizes are not real."

"Set your mind at rest, Mrs. Bawdrey," promised Cleek. "He will not find it out from me. He will not find anything out from me. He is just the kind of man to break his heart, to crumple up like a burnt glove, and come to the end of all things, even life, if he were to discover that any of his treasures, anything that he loved and trusted in, is a sham and a fraud."

His eyes looked straight into hers as he spoke, his hand rested lightly on her sleeve. She sucked in her breath suddenly, a brief pallor chased the roses from her cheeks, a brief confusion sat momentarily upon her. She appeared to hesitate, then looked away and laughed uneasily.

"I don't think I quite grasp what you mean, Mr. Rickaby," she said.

"Don't you?" he made answer. "Then I will tell you some time—tomorrow, perhaps. But if I were you, Mrs. Bawdrey— well, no matter. This I promise you: that dear old man shall have no ideal shattered by me."

And, living up to that promise, he enthused over everything the old man had in his collection when, after dinner that night, they went, in company with Philip, to view it. But bogus things were on every hand. Spurious porcelains, fraudulent armour, faked china were everywhere. The loaded cabinets and the glazed cases were one long procession of faked Dresden and bogus faience, of Egyptian enamels that had been manufactured in Birmingham, and of sixth-century "treasures" whose makers were still plying the trade and battening upon the ignorance of collectors.

"Now, here's a thing I am particularly proud of," said the gulled old man, reaching into one of the cases and holding out for Cleek's admiration an irregular disc of dull, hammered gold that had an iridescent beetle embedded in the flat face of it. "This scarab, Mr. Rickaby, has helped to make history, as one might say. It was once the property of Cleopatra. I was obliged to make two trips to Egypt before I could persuade the owner to part with it. I am always conscious of a certain sense of awe, Mr. Rickaby, when I touch this wonderful thing. To think, sir, to think! that this bauble once rested on the bosom of that marvellous woman; that Mark Antony must have seen it, may have touched it; that Ptolemy Auletse knew all about it, and that it is older, sir, than the Christian religion itself!"

He held it out upon the flat of his palm, the better for Cleek to see and to admire it, and signed to his son to hand the visitor a magnifying glass.

"Wonderful, most wonderful!" observed Cleek, bending over the spurious gem and focussing the glass upon it; not, however, for the purpose of studying the fraud, but to examine something he had just noticed—something round and red and angry-looking—which marked the palm itself, at the base of the middle finger. "No wonder you are proud of such a prize. I think I should go off my head with rapture if I owned an antique like that. But, pardon me, have you met with an accident, Mr. Bawdrey? That's an ugly place you have on your palm."

"That? Oh, that's nothing," he answered gaily. "It itches a great deal at times, but otherwise it isn't troublesome. I can't think how in the world I got it, to tell the truth. It came out as a sort of red blister in the beginning, and since it broke it has been spreading a great deal. But, really, it doesn't amount to anything at all."

"Oh, that's just like you, dad," put in Philip, "always making light of the wretched thing. I notice one thing, however, Rickaby, it seems to grow worse instead of better. And dad knows as well as I do when it began. It came out suddenly about a fortnight ago, after he had been holding some green worsted for my stepmother to wind into balls. Just look at it, will you, old chap?"

"Nonsense, nonsense!" chimed in the old man laughingly. "Don't mind the silly boy, Mr. Rickaby. He will have it that that green worsted is to blame, just because he happened to spy the thing the morning after."

"Let's have a look at it," said Cleek, moving nearer the light. Then, after a close examination, "I don't think it amounts to anything, after all," he added, as he laid aside the glass. "I shouldn't worry myself about it if I were you, Phil. It's just an ordinary blister, nothing more. Let's go on with the collection, Mr. Bawdrey; I'm deeply interested in it, I assure you. Never saw such a marvellous lot. Got any more amazing things, gems, I mean, like that wonderful scarab? I say!"—halting suddenly before a long, narrow case with a glass front, which stood on end in a far corner, and, being lined with black velvet, brought into ghastly prominence the suspended shape of a human skeleton contained within—"I say! What the dickens is this? Looks like a doctor's specimen, b'gad. You haven't let anybody—I mean, you haven't been buying any prehistoric bones, have you, Mr. Bawdrey?"

"Oh, that?" laughed the old man, turning round and seeing to what he was alluding. "Oh, that's a curiosity of quite a different sort, Mr. Rickaby. You are saying it looks like a doctor's specimen. It is—or, rather, it was. Mrs. Bawdrey's father was a doctor, and it once belonged to him. Properly, it ought to have no place in a collection of this sort, but—well, it's such an amazing thing I couldn't quite refuse it a place, sir. It's a freak of nature. The skeleton of a nine-fingered man."

"Of a what?"

"A nine-fingered man."

"Well, I can't say that I see anything remarkable in that. I've got nine fingers myself, nine and one over, when it comes to that."

"No, you haven't, you duffer!" put in young Bawdrey, with a laugh. "You've got eight fingers—eight fingers and two thumbs. This bony Johnny has nine fingers and two thumbs. That's what makes him a freak. I say, dad, open the beggar's box, and let Rickaby see."

His father obeyed the request. Lifting the tiny brass latch which alone secured it, he swung open the glazed door of the case, and, reaching in, drew forward the flexible left arm of the skeleton.

"There you are," he said, supporting the bony hand upon his palm, so that all its fingers were spread out and Cleek might get a clear view of the monstrosity. "What a trial he must have been to the glove trade, mustn't he?" laughing gaily. "Fancy the confusion and dismay, Mr. Rickaby, if a fellow like this walked into a Bond Street shop and asked for a pair of gloves in a hurry."

Cleek bent over and examined the thing with interest. At first glance the hand was no different from any other skeleton hand one might see any day in any place where they sold anatomical specimens for the use of members of the medical profession; but as Mr. Bawdrey, holding it on the palm of his right hand, flattened it out with the fingers of his left, the abnormality at once became apparent. Springing from the base of the fourth finger, a perfectly developed fifth appeared, curling inward toward what had once been the palm of the hand, as though, in life, it had been the owner's habit of screening it from observation by holding it in that position. It was, however, perfectly flexible, and Mr. Bawdrey had no difficulty in making it lie out flat after the manner of its mates.

The sight was not inspiring—the freaks of Mother Nature rarely are. No one but a doctor would have cared to accept the thing as a gift, and no one but a man as mad on the subject of curiosities and with as little sense of discrimination as Mr. Bawdrey would have dreamt for a moment of adding it to a collection.

"It's rather uncanny," said Cleek, who had no palate for the abnormal in Nature. "For myself, I may frankly admit that I don't like things of that sort about me."

"You are very much like my wife in that," responded the old man. "She was of the opinion that the skeleton ought to have been destroyed or else handed over to some anatomical museum. But—well, it is a curiosity, you know, Mr. Rickaby. Besides, as I have said, it was once the property of her late father, a most learned man, sir, most learned, and as it was of sufficient interest for him to retain it—oh, well, we collectors are faddists, you know, so I easily persuaded Mrs. Bawdrey to allow me to bring it over to England with me when we took our leave of Java.

And now that you have seen it, suppose we have a look at more artistic things. I have some very fine specimens of neolithic implements and weapons which I am most anxious to show you. Just step this way, please."

He let the skeleton's hand slip from his own, swing back into the case, and forthwith closed the glass door upon it; then, leading the way to the cabinet containing the specimens referred to, he unlocked it, and invited Cleek's opinion of the flint arrowheads, stone hatchets, and granite utensils within.

For a minute they lingered thus, the old man talking, laughing, exulting in his possessions, the detective examining and pretending to be deeply impressed. Then, of a sudden, without hint or warning to lessen the shock of it, the uplifted lid of the cabinet fell with a crash from the hand that upheld it, shivering the glass into fifty pieces, and Cleek, screwing round on his heel with a "jump" of all his nerves, was in time to see the figure of his host crumple up, collapse, drop like a thing shot dead, and lie writhing on the polished floor.

"Dad! Oh, heavens! Dad!" The cry was young Bawdrey's. He seemed fairly to throw himself across the intervening space and to reach his father in the instant he fell. "Now you know! Now you know!" he went on wildly, as Cleek dropped down beside him and began to loosen the old man's collar. "It's like this always; not a hint, not a sign, but just this utter collapse. My God, what are they doing it with? How are they managing it, those two? They're coming, Headland. Listen! Don't you hear them?"

The crash of the broken glass and the jar of the old man's fall had swept through all the house, and a moment later, headed by Mrs. Bawdrey herself, all the members of the little house-party came piling excitedly into the room.

The fright and suffering of the young wife seemed very real as she threw herself down beside her husband and caught him to her with a little shuddering cry. Then her voice, uplifting in a panic, shrilled out a wild appeal for doctor, servants—help of any kind. And, almost as she spoke, Travers was beside her, Travers and Forshay and Robert Murdock—yes, and silly little Mrs. Somerby-Miles, too, forgetting in the face of such a time as this to be anything but helpful and womanly—and all of these gave such assistance as was in their power.

"Help me get him up to his own room, somebody, and send a servant post-haste for the doctor," said Captain Travers, taking the lead after the fashion of a man who is used to command. "Calm yourself as much as possible, Mrs. Bawdrey. Here, Murdock, lend a hand and help him."

"Eh, mon, there is nae help but Heaven's in sic a case as this," dolefully responded Murdock, as he came forward and solemnly stooped to obey. "The puir auld laddie! The Laird giveth and the Laird taketh awa', and the weel o' mon is as naething."

"Oh, stow your croaking, you blundering old fool!" snapped Travers, as Mrs. Bawdrey gave a heart-wrung cry and hid her face in her hands. "You and your eternal doldrums! Here, Bawdrey, lend a hand, old chap. We can get him upstairs without the assistance of this human trombone, I know."

But "this human trombone" was not minded that they should; and so it fell out that, when Lieutenant Forshay led Mrs. Somerby-Miles from the room, and young Bawdrey and Captain Travers carried the stricken man up the stairs to his own bedchamber, his wife flying in advance to see that everything was prepared for him, Cleek, standing all alone beside the shattered cabinet, could hear Mr. Robert Murdock's dismal croakings rumbling steadily out as he mounted the staircase with the others.

For a moment after the closing door of a room overhead had shut them from his ears, he stood there, with puckered brows and pursed-up lips, drumming with his finger-tips a faint tattoo upon the framework of the shattered lid; then he walked over to the skeleton case, and silently regarded the gruesome thing within.

"Nine fingers," he muttered sententiously, "and the ninth curves inward to the palm!" He stepped round and viewed the case from all points; both sides, the front, and even the narrow space made at the back by the angle of the corner where it stood. And after this he walked to the other end of the room, took the key from the lock, slipped it in his pocket, and went out, closing the door behind him, that none might remember it had not been locked when the master of the place was carried above.

It was, perhaps, twenty minutes later that young Bawdrey came down and found him all alone in the smoking-room, bending over the table whereon the butler had set the salver containing the whisky decanter, the soda siphon, and the glasses that were always laid out there that the gentlemen might help themselves to the regulation "night-cap" before going to bed.

"I've slipped away to have a word in private with you, Headland," he said in an agitated voice, as he came in. "Oh, what consummate actors they are, those two. You'd think her heart was breaking, wouldn't you? You'd think—— Hallo! I say! What on earth are you doing?" For as he came nearer he could see that Cleek had removed the glass stopper of the decanter, and was tapping with his finger-tips a little funnel of white paper, the narrow end of which he had thrust into the neck of the bottle.

"Just adding a harmless little sleeping-draught to the nightly beverage," said Cleek, in reply, as he screwed up the paper funnel and put it in his pocket. "A good sound sleep is an excellent thing, my dear fellow, and I mean to make sure that the gentlemen of this house-party have it—one gentleman in particular: Captain Travers."

"Yes; but—I say! What about me, old chap? I don't want to be drugged, and you know I have to show them the courtesy of taking a 'night-cap' with them."

"Precisely. That's where you can help me out. If any of them remark anything about the whisky having a peculiar taste, you must stoutly assert that you don't notice; and, as they've seen you drinking from the same decanter—why, there you are. Don't worry over it. It's a very, very harmless draught; you won't even have a headache from it. Listen here, Bawdrey. Somebody is poisoning your father."

"I know it. I told you so from the beginning, Headland," he answered, with a sort of wail. "But what's that got to do with drugging the whisky?"

"Everything. I'm going to find out to-night whether Captain Travers is that somebody or not. Sh-h-h! Don't get excited. Yes, that's my game. I want to get into his room whilst he is sleeping, and be free to search his effects. I want to get into every man's room here, and wherever I find poison—well, you understand?"

"Yes," he replied, brightening as he grasped the import of the matter. "What a ripping idea! And so simple."

"I think so. Once let me find the poison, and I'll know my man. Now, one other thing: the housekeeper must have a master-key that opens all the bedrooms in the place. Get it for me. It will be easier and swifter than picking the locks."

"Right you are, old chap. I'll slip up to Mrs. Jarret's room and fetch it to you at once."

"No; tuck it under the mat just outside my door. As it won't do for me to be drugged as well as the rest of you, I shan't put in an appearance when the rest come down. Say I've got a headache, and have gone to bed. As for my own 'night-cap'—well, I can send Dollops down to get the butler to pour me one out of another decanter, so that will be all right. Now, toddle off and get the key, there's a good chap. And, I say, Bawdrey, as I shan't see you again until morning—good-night."

"Good-night, old chap!" he answered in his impulsive, boyish way. "You are a friend, Headland. And you'll save my dad, God bless you! A true, true friend that's what you are. Thank God I ran across you."

Cleek smiled and nodded to him as he passed out and hurried away; then, hearing the other gentlemen coming down the stairs, he, too, made haste to get out of the room and to creep up to his own after they had assembled, and the cigar cabinet and the whisky were being passed round, and the doctor was busy above with the man who was somebody's victim.

\*    \*    \*    \*    \*

The big old grandfather clock at the top of the stairs pointed ten minutes past two, and the house was hushed of every sound save that which is the evidence of deep sleep, when the door of Cleek's room swung quietly open, and Cleek himself, in dressing-gown and wadded bedroom slippers, stepped out into the dark hall, and, leaving Dollops on guard, passed like a shadow over the thick, unsounding carpet.

The rooms of all the male occupants of the house, including that of Philip Bawdrey himself, opened upon this passage. He went to each in turn, unlocked it, stepped in, closed it after him, and lit the bedroom candle.

The sleeping-draught had accomplished all that was required of it; and in each and every room he entered—Captain Travers's,

Lieutenant Forshay's, Mr. Robert Murdock's—there lay the occupant thereof stretched out at full length in the grip of that deep and heavy sleep which comes of drugs.

Cleek made the round of the rooms as quietly as any shadow, even stopping as he passed young Bawdrey's on his way back to his own to peep in there. Yes; he, too, had got his share of the effective draught, for there he lay snarled up in the bedclothes, with his arms over his head and his knees drawn up until they were on a level with his waist, and his handsome boyish face a little paler than usual.

Cleek didn't go into the room, simply looked at him from the threshold, then shut the door, and went back to Dollops.

"All serene, guv'ner?" questioned that young man in an eager whisper.

"Yes, quite," his master replied, as he turned to a writing-table whereon there lay a sealed note, and, pulling out the chair, sat down before it and took up a pen. "Wait a bit, and then you can go to bed. I'll give you still another note to deliver. While I'm writing it you may lay out my clothes."

"Slipping off, sir?"

"Yes. You will stop here, however. Now, then, hold your tongue; I'm busy."

Then he pulled a sheet of paper to him and wrote rapidly:

*DEAR MR. BAWDREY—I've got my man, and am off to consult with Mr. Narkom and to have what I've found analysed. I don't know when I shall be back—probably not until the day after to-morrow. You are right. It is murder, and Java is at the bottom of it. Dollops will hand you this. Say nothing—just wait till I get back.*

This he slipped, unsigned in his haste, into an envelope, handed it to Dollops, and then fairly jumped into his clothes. Ten minutes later he was out of the house, and—the end of the riddle was in sight.

### III

On the morrow Mrs. Bawdrey made known the rather surprising piece of news that Mr. Rickaby had written her a note to say that he had received a communication of such vital importance that he had been obliged to leave the house that morning before anybody was up, and might not be able to return to it for several days.

"No very great hardship in that, my dear," commented Mrs. Somerby-Miles, "for a more stupid and uninteresting person I never encountered. Fancy! he never even offered to assist the gentlemen to get poor Mr. Bawdrey upstairs last night. How is the poor old dear this morning, darling? Better?"

"Yes—much," said Mrs. Bawdrey in reply. "Doctor Phillipson came to the house before four o'clock, and brought some wonderful new medicine that has simply worked wonders. Of course, he will have to stop in bed and be perfectly quiet for three or four days; but, although the attack was by far the worst he has ever had, the doctor feels quite confident that he will pull him safely through."

Now although, in the light of her apparent affection for her aged husband, she ought, one would have thought, to be exceedingly happy over this, it was distinctly noticeable that she was nervous and ill at ease, that there was a hunted look in her eyes, and that, as the day wore on, these things seemed to be accentuated. More than that, there seemed added proof of the truth of young Bawdrey's assertion that she and Captain Travers were in league with each other, for that day they were constantly together, constantly getting off into out-of-the-way places, and constantly talking in an undertone of something that seemed to worry them.

Even when dinner was over, and the whole party adjourned to the drawing-room for coffee, and the lady ought, in all conscience, to have given herself wholly up to the entertainment of her guests, it was observable that she devoted most of her time to whispered conferences with Captain Travers. They kept going to the window and looking up at the sky, as if worried and annoyed that the twilight should be so long in fading and the night in coming on. But worse than this, at ten o'clock Captain Travers made an excuse of having letters to write, and left the room, and it was scarcely six minutes later that she followed suit.

But the captain had not gone to write letters, as it had happened. Instead, he had gone straight to the morning-room, an apartment immediately behind that in which the elder Mr. Bawdrey's collection was housed, and from which a broad French window opened out upon the grounds, and it might have caused a scandal had it been known that Mrs. Bawdrey joined him there one minute after leaving the drawing-room.

"It is the time, Walter, it is the time!" she said in a breathless sort of way, as she closed the door and moved across the room to where he stood, a dimly-seen figure in the dim light. "God help and pity me! but I am so nervous I hardly know how to contain myself. The note said at ten to-night in the morning-room, and it is ten now. The hour is here, Walter, the hour is here!"

"So is the man, Mrs. Bawdrey," answered a low voice from the outer darkness; then a figure lifted itself above the screening shrubs just beyond the ledge of the open window, and Cleek stepped into the room.

She gave a little hysterical cry and reached out her hands to him.

"Oh, I am so glad to see you, even though you hint at such awful things, I am so glad, so glad!" she said. "I almost died when I read your note. To think that it is murder—murder! And but for you he might be dead even now. You will like to know that the doctor brought the stuff you sent by him and my darling is better—better."

Before Cleek could venture any reply to this, Captain Travers stalked across the room and gripped his hand.

"And so you are that great man Cleek, are you?" he said. "Bully boy! Bully boy! And to think that all the time it wasn't some mysterious natural affliction; to think that it was crime, murder, poison. What poison, man, what poison?"

"Ayupee, or, as it is variously called in the several islands of the Eastern Archipelago, Pohon-Upas, Antjar, and Ipo," said Cleek in reply. "The deadly venom which the Malays use in poisoning the heads of their arrows."

"What! that awful stuff!" said Mrs. Bawdrey, with a little shuddering cry. "And some one in this house——" Her voice broke. She plucked at Cleek's sleeve and looked up at him in an agony of entreaty. "Who?" she implored. "Who in this house could? You said you would tell to-night—you said you would. Oh, who could have the heart? Ah! who? It is true, if you have not heard it, that once upon a time there was bad blood between Mr. Murdock and him; that Mr. Murdock is a family connection; but even he, oh, even he—— Tell me—tell me, Mr. Cleek?"

"Mrs. Bawdrey, I can't just yet," he made reply. "In my heart I am as certain of it as though the criminal had confessed; but I am waiting for a sign, and, until that comes, absolute proof is not possible. That it will come, and may, indeed, come at any moment now that it is quite dark, I am very certain. When it does——"

He stopped and threw up a warning hand. As he spoke a queer thudding sound struck one dull note through the stillness of the house. He stood, bent forward, listening, absolutely breathless; then, on the other side of the wall, there rippled and rolled a something that was like the sound of a struggle between two voiceless animals, and—the sign that he awaited had come!

"Follow me quickly, as noiselessly as you can. Let no one hear, let no one see!" he said in a breath of excitement. Then he sprang cat-like to the door, whirled it open, scudded round the angle of the passage to the entrance of the room where the fraudulent collection was kept, and went in with the silent fleetness of a panther. And a moment later, when Captain Travers and Mrs. Bawdrey swung in through the door and joined him, they came upon a horrifying sight.

For there, leaning against the open door of the case where the skeleton of the nine-fingered man hung, was Dollops, bleeding and faint, and with a score of toothmarks on his neck and throat. On the floor at his feet Cleek was kneeling on the writhing figure of a man who bit and tore and snarled like a cornered wolf and fought with teeth and feet and hands alike in the wild effort to get free from the grip of destiny. A locked handcuff clamped one wrist, and from it swung, at the end of the connecting chain, its unlocked mate; the marks of Dollops's fists were on his lips and cheeks, and at the foot of the case, where the hanging skeleton doddered and shook to the vibration of the floor, lay a shattered phial of deep-blue glass.

"Got you, you hound!" said Cleek through his teeth as he wrenched the man's two wrists together and snapped the other handcuff into place. "You beast of ingratitude—you Judas! Kissing and betraying like any other Iscariot! And a dear old man like that! Look here, Mrs. Bawdrey; look here, Captain Travers; what do you think of a little rat like this?"

They came forward at his word, and, looking down, saw that the figure he was bending over was the figure of Philip Bawdrey.

"Oh!" gulped Mrs. Bawdrey, and then shut her two hands over her eyes and fell away weak and shivering. "Oh, Mr. Cleek, it can't be—it can't! To do a thing like that?"

"Oh, he'd have done worse, the little reptile, if he hadn't been pulled up short," said Cleek in reply. "He'd have hanged you for it, if it had gone the way he planned. You look in your boxes; you, too, Captain Travers. I'll wager each of you finds a phial of Ayupee hidden among them somewhere. Came in to put more of the cursed stuff on the ninth finger of the skeleton, so that it would be ready for the next time, didn't he, Dollops?"

"Yes, guv'ner. I waited for him behind the case just as you told me to, sir, and when he ups and slips the finger of the skilligan into the neck of the bottle, I nips out and whacks the bracelet on him. But he was too quick for me, sir, so I only got one on; and then, the hound, he turns on me like a blessed hyena, sir, and begins a-chawin' of me windpipe. I say, guv'ner, take off his silver wristlets, will you, sir, and lemme have jist ten minutes with him on my own? Five for me, sir, and five for his poor old dad!"

"Not I," said Cleek. "I wouldn't let you soil those honest hands of yours on his vile little body, Dollops. Thought you had a noodle to deal with, didn't you, Mr. Philip Bawdrey? Thought you could lead me by the nose, and push me into finding those phials just where you wanted them found, didn't you? Well, you've got a few more thoughts coming. Look here, Captain Travers; what do you think of this fellow's little game? Tried to take me in about you and Mrs. Bawdrey being lovers, and trying to do away with him and his father to get the old man's money."

"Why, the contemptible little hound! Bless my soul, man, I'm engaged to Mrs. Bawdrey's cousin. And as for his stepmother, why, she threw the little worm over as soon as he began making love to her, and tried to make her take up with him by telling her how much he'd be worth when his father died."

"I guessed as much. I didn't fancy him from the first moment; and he was so blessed eager to have me begin by suspecting you two, that I smelt a rat at once. Oh, but he's been crafty enough in other things. Putting that devilish stuff on the ninth finger of the skeleton, and never losing an opportunity to get his poor old father to handle it and to show it to people. It's a strong, irritant poison—sap of the upas tree is the base of it—producing first an irritation of the skin, then a blister, and, when that broke, communicating the poison directly to the blood every time the skeleton hand touched it. A weak solution at first, so that the decline would be natural, the growth of the malady gradual. But if I'd found that phial in your room last night, as he hoped and believed I had done—well, look for yourself. The finger of the skeleton is thick with the beastly, gummy stuff to-night. Double strength, of course. The next time his father touched it he'd have died before morning. And the old chap fairly worshipping him. I suspected him, and suspected what the stuff that was being used really was from the beginning. Last night I drugged him, and then I knew."

"Knew, Mr. Cleek? Why, how could you?"

"The most virulent poisons have their remedial uses, Captain," he made reply. "You can kill a man with strychnine; you can put him in his grave with arsenic; you can also use both these powerful agents to cure and to save, in their proper proportions and in the proper way. The same rule applies to ayupee. Properly diluted and properly used, it is one of the most powerful agents for the relief, and, in some cases, the cure, of Bright's disease of the kidneys. But the Government guards this unholy drug most carefully. You can't get a drop of it in Java for love nor money, unless on the order of a recognized physician; and you can't bring it into the ports of England unless backed by that physician's sworn statement and the official stamp of the Javanese authorities. A man undeniably afflicted with Bright's disease could get these things—no other could. Well, I wanted to know who had succeeded in getting ayupee into this country and into this house. Last night I drugged every man in it, and I found out."

"But how?"

"By finding the one who could not sleep stretched out at full length. One of the strongest symptoms of Bright's disease is a tendency to draw the knees up close to the body in sleep, Captain, and to twist the arms above the head. Of all the men under this roof, this man here was the only one who slept like that last night!" He paused and looked down at the scowling, sullen creature on the floor. "You wretched little cur!" he said with a gesture of unspeakable contempt. "And all for the sake of an old man's money! If I did my duty, I'd gaol you. But if I did, it would be punishing the innocent for the crimes of the guilty. It would kill that dear old man to learn this; and so he's not going to learn it, and the law's not going to get its own." He twitched out his hand, and something tinkled on the floor. "Get up!" he said sharply. "There's the key of the handcuffs; take it and set yourself free. Do you know what's going to happen to you? To-morrow morning Dr. Phillipson is going to examine you, and to report that you'll be a dead man in a year's time if you stop another week in this country. You are going out of it, and you are going to stop out of it. Do you understand? *Stop* out of it to the end of your days. For if ever you put foot in it again I'll handle you as a terrier handles a rat! Dollops?"

"Yes, guv'ner?"

"My things packed and ready?"

"Yes, sir. And all waitin' in the arbour, sir, as you told me to have 'em."

"Good lad! Get them, and we'll catch the first train back. Mrs. Bawdrey, my best respects. Captain, all good luck to you. The riddle is solved. Good-night."

# The Knight's Cross Signal Problem
## By Ernest Bramah

Ernest Bramah

## Originally Published in 1914

# THE KNIGHT'S CROSS SIGNAL PROBLEM

### BY ERNEST BRAMAH

While the Edwardian period produced more than its share of distinctive detectives, the most unusual of them all may have been Max Carrados. Blinded in a riding accident, he heightened His other senses, his memory, and his deductive skills to compensate. These skills allowed him to tell that a person is wearing a disguise by the smell of the wig, to read newspaper headlines by touch, and recognize people by the sounds of the footsteps.

Max Carrados is a gentleman of independent means living in a comfortable London house along with his manservant, Parkinson. He only takes cases of interest, often at the request of his friend Louis Carlyle, a professional "inquiry agent." His primary goal is justice, not fame or money. He is an expert in numismatics, the study of coins, and several of the stories revolve around this interest.

While most of the stories deal with murder and tragedy, or at least serious crime such as fraud or robbery, they occasionally branch off into the comic. The tone, even in the more serious stories is light and entertaining. The impression of Carrados is that he is a genial man, enjoys his pleasures and is generous to his friends.

The first Max Carrados stories appeared in 1914 in The Strand magazine at the same time as some of the Sherlock Holmes stories of Arthur Conan Doyle. At times they received top billing and were even more popular than his contemporary. They were collected in several volumes, *Max Carrados* (1914), *The Eyes of Max Carrados* (1923), and *Max Carrados Mysteries* (1927).

*The Knight's Cross Signal Problem*, which appeared in the first book, is interesting in that it demonstrates the period's fascination with puzzles involving things such as train schedules which feature in much of the detective fiction of the time.

The author, Ernest Bramah Smith (usually referred to as just Ernest Bramah) was a prolific author in a number of genres. He is perhaps best known for his humorous stories featuring the Chinese story-teller Kai Lung. In addition to these stories and the detective stories featuring Max Carrados, he wrote stories with a supernatural theme and a politico-science fiction novel *What Might Have Been* that George Orwell acknowledged as influencing *1984.*

Further stories featuring Max Carrados can be found in the Resurrected Press books *Max Carrados Resurrected* and *Max Carrados Resurrected, Volume II: More Stories of Max Carrados.*

# THE KNIGHT'S CROSS SIGNAL PROBLEM

"Louis," exclaimed Mr. Carrados, with the air of genial gaiety that Carlyle had found so incongruous to his conception of a blind man, "you have a mystery somewhere about you! I know it by your step."

Nearly a month had passed since the incident of the false Dionysius had led to the two men meeting. It was now December. Whatever Mr. Carlyle's step might indicate to the inner eye it betokened to the casual observer the manner of a crisp, alert, self-possessed man of business. Carlyle, in truth, betrayed nothing of the pessimism and despondency that had marked him on the earlier occasion.

"You have only yourself to thank that it is a very poor one," he retorted. "If you hadn't held me to a hasty promise——"

"To give me an option on the next case that baffled you, no matter what it was——"

"Just so. The consequence is that you get a very unsatisfactory affair that has no special interest to an amateur and is only baffling because it is—well——"

"Well, baffling?"

"Exactly, Max. Your would-be jest has discovered the proverbial truth. I need hardly tell you that it is only the insoluble that is finally baffling and this is very probably insoluble. You remember the awful smash on the Central and Suburban at Knight's Cross Station a few weeks ago?"

"Yes," replied Carrados, with interest. "I read the whole ghastly details at the time."

"You read?" exclaimed his friend suspiciously.

"I still use the familiar phrases," explained Carrados, with a smile. "As a matter of fact, my secretary reads to me. I mark what I want to hear and when he comes at ten o'clock we clear off the morning papers in no time."

"And how do you know what to mark?" demanded Mr. Carlyle cunningly.

Carrados's right hand, lying idly on the table, moved to a newspaper near. He ran his finger along a column heading, his eyes still turned towards his visitor.

"'The Money Market. Continued from page 2. British Railways,'" he announced.

"Extraordinary," murmured Carlyle.

"Not very," said Carrados. "If someone dipped a stick in treacle and wrote 'Rats' across a marble slab you would probably be able to distinguish what was there, blindfold."

"Probably," admitted Mr. Carlyle. "At all events we will not test the experiment."

"The difference to you of treacle on a marble background is scarcely greater than that of printers' ink on newspaper to me. But anything smaller than pica I do not read with comfort, and below long primer I cannot read at all. Hence the secretary. Now the accident, Louis."

"The accident: well, you remember all about that. An ordinary Central and Suburban passenger train, non-stop at Knight's Cross, ran past the signal and crashed into a crowded electric train that was just beginning to move out. It was like sending a garden roller down a row of handlights. Two carriages of the electric train were flattened out of existence; the next two were broken up. For the first time on an English railway there was a good stand-up smash between a heavy steam-engine and a train of light cars, and it was 'bad for the coo.'"

"Twenty-seven killed, forty something injured, eight died since," commented Carrados.

"That was bad for the Co.," said Carlyle. "Well, the main fact was plain enough. The heavy train was in the wrong. But was the engine-driver responsible? He claimed, and he claimed vehemently from the first, and he never varied one iota, that he had a 'clear' signal—that is to say, the green light, it being dark. The signalman concerned was equally dogged that he never pulled off the signal—that it was at 'danger' when the accident happened and that it had been for five minutes before. Obviously, they could not both be right."

"Why, Louis?" asked Mr. Carrados smoothly.

"The signal must either have been up or down—red or green."

"Did you ever notice the signals on the Great Northern Railway, Louis?"

"Not particularly, Why?"

"One winterly day, about the year when you and I were concerned in being born, the engine-driver of a Scotch express received the 'clear' from a signal near a little Huntingdon station called Abbots Ripton. He went on and crashed into a goods train and into the thick of the smash a down express mowed its way. Thirteen killed and the usual tale of injured. He was positive that the signal gave him a 'clear'; the signalman was equally confident that he had never pulled it off the 'danger.' Both were right, and yet the signal was in working order. As I said, it was a winterly day; it had been snowing hard and the snow froze and accumulated on the upper edge of the signal arm until its weight bore it down. That is a fact that no fiction writer dare have invented, but to this day every signal on the Great Northern pivots from the centre of the arm instead of from the end, in memory of that snowstorm."

"That came out at the inquest, I presume?" said Mr. Carlyle. "We have had the Board of Trade inquiry and the inquest here and no explanation is forthcoming. Everything was in perfect order. It rests between the word of the signalman and the word of the engine-driver—not a jot of direct evidence either way. Which is right?"

"That is what you are going to find out, Louis?" suggested Carrados.

"It is what I am being paid for finding out," admitted Mr. Carlyle frankly. "But so far we are just where the inquest left it, and, between ourselves, I candidly can't see an inch in front of my face in the matter."

"Nor can I," said the blind man, with a rather wry smile. "Never mind. The engine-driver is your client, of course?"

"Yes," admitted Carlyle. "But how the deuce did you know?"

"Let us say that your sympathies are enlisted on his behalf. The jury were inclined to exonerate the signalman, weren't they? What has the company done with your man?"

"Both are suspended. Hutchins, the driver, hears that he may probably be given charge of a lavatory at one of the stations. He is a decent, bluff, short-spoken old chap, with his heart in his work. Just now you'll find him at his worst—bitter and suspicious. The thought of swabbing down a lavatory and taking pennies all day is poisoning him."

"Naturally. Well, there we have honest Hutchins: taciturn, a little touchy perhaps, grown grey in the service of the company, and manifesting quite a bulldog-like devotion to his favourite 538."

"Why, that actually was the number of his engine—how do you know it?" demanded Carlyle sharply.

"It was mentioned two or three times at the inquest, Louis," replied Carrados mildly.

"And you remembered—with no reason to?"

"You can generally trust a blind man's memory, especially if he has taken the trouble to develop it."

"Then you will remember that Hutchins did not make a very good impression at the time. He was surly and irritable under the ordeal. I want you to see the case from all sides."

"He called the signalman—Mead—a 'lying young dog,' across the room, I believe. Now, Mead, what is he like? You have seen him, of course?"

"Yes. He does not impress me favourably. He is glib, ingratiating, and distinctly 'greasy.' He has a ready answer for everything almost before the question is out of your mouth. He has thought of everything."

"And now you are going to tell me something, Louis," said Carrados encouragingly.

Mr. Carlyle laughed a little to cover an involuntary movement of surprise.

"There is a suggestive line that was not touched at the inquiries," he admitted. "Hutchins has been a saving man all his life, and he has received good wages. Among his class he is regarded as wealthy. I daresay that he has five hundred pounds in the bank. He is a widower with one daughter, a very nice-mannered girl of about twenty. Mead is a young man, and he and the girl are sweethearts—have been informally engaged for some time. But old Hutchins would not hear of it; he seems to have taken a dislike to the signalman from the first, and latterly he had forbidden him to come to his house or his daughter to speak to him."

"Excellent, Louis," cried Carrados in great delight. "We shall clear your man in a blaze of red and green lights yet and hang the glib, 'greasy' signalman from his own signal-post."

"It is a significant fact, seriously?"

"It is absolutely convincing."

"It may have been a slip, a mental lapse on Mead's part which he discovered the moment it was too late, and then, being too cowardly to admit his fault, and having so much at stake, he took care to make detection impossible. It may have been that, but my idea is rather that probably it was neither quite pure accident nor pure design. I can imagine Mead meanly pluming himself over the fact that the life of this man who stands in his way, and whom he must cordially dislike, lies in his power. I can imagine the idea becoming an obsession as he dwells on it. A dozen times with his hand on the lever he lets his mind explore the possibilities of a moment's defection. Then one day he pulls the signal off in sheer bravado—and hastily puts it at danger again. He may have done it once or he may have done it oftener before he was caught in a fatal moment of irresolution. The chances are about even that the engine-driver would be killed. In any case he would be disgraced, for it is easier on the face of it to believe that a man might run past a danger signal in absentmindedness, without noticing it, than that a man should pull off a signal and replace it without being conscious of his actions."

"The fireman was killed. Does your theory involve the certainty of the fireman being killed, Louis?"

"No," said Carlyle. "The fireman is a difficulty, but looking at it from Mead's point of view—whether he has been guilty of an error or a crime—it resolves itself into this: First, the fireman may be killed. Second, he may not notice the signal at all. Third, in any case he will loyally corroborate his driver and the good old jury will discount that."

Carrados smoked thoughtfully, his open, sightless eyes merely appearing to be set in a tranquil gaze across the room.

"It would not be an improbable explanation," he said presently. "Ninety-nine men out of a hundred would say: 'People do not do these things.' But you and I, who have in our different ways studied criminology, know that they sometimes do, or else there would be no curious crimes. What have you done on that line?"

To anyone who could see, Mr. Carlyle's expression conveyed an answer.

"You are behind the scenes, Max. What was there for me to do? Still I must do something for my money. Well, I have had a very close inquiry made confidentially among the men. There might be a whisper of one of them knowing more than had come out—a man restrained by friendship, or enmity, or even grade jealousy. Nothing came of that. Then there was the remote chance that some private person had noticed the signal without attaching any importance to it then, one who would be able to identify it still by something associated with the time. I went over the line myself. Opposite the signal the line on one side is shut in by a high blank wall; on the other side are houses, but coming below the butt-end of a scullery the signal does not happen to be visible from any road or from any window."

"My poor Louis!" said Carrados, in friendly ridicule. "You were at the end of your tether?"

"I was," admitted Carlyle. "And now that you know the sort of job it is I don't suppose that you are keen on wasting your time over it."

"That would hardly be fair, would it?" said Carrados reasonably. "No, Louis, I will take over your honest old driver and your greasy young signalman and your fatal signal that cannot be seen from anywhere."

"But it is an important point for you to remember, Max, that although the signal cannot be seen from the box, if the mechanism had gone wrong, or anyone tampered with the arm, the automatic indicator would at once have told Mead that the green light was showing. Oh, I have gone very thoroughly into the technical points, I assure you."

"I must do so too," commented Mr. Carrados gravely.

"For that matter, if there is anything you want to know, I dare say that I can tell you," suggested his visitor. "It might save your time."

"True," acquiesced Carrados. "I should like to know whether anyone belonging to the houses that bound the line there came of age or got married on the twenty-sixth of November."

Mr. Carlyle looked across curiously at his host.

"I really do not know, Max," he replied, in his crisp, precise way. "What on earth has that got to do with it, may I inquire?"

"The only explanation of the Pont St. Lin swing-bridge disaster of '75 was the reflection of a green bengal light on a cottage window."

Mr. Carlyle smiled his indulgence privately.

"My dear chap, you mustn't let your retentive memory of obscure happenings run away with you," he remarked wisely. "In nine cases out of ten the obvious explanation is the true one. The difficulty, as here, lies in proving it. Now, you would like to see these men?"

"I expect so; in any case, I will see Hutchins first."

"Both live in Holloway. Shall I ask Hutchins to come here to see you—say to-morrow? He is doing nothing."

"No," replied Carrados. "To-morrow I must call on my brokers and my time may be filled up."

"Quite right; you mustn't neglect your own affairs for this— experiment," assented Carlyle.

"Besides, I should prefer to drop in on Hutchins at his own home. Now, Louis, enough of the honest old man for one night. I have a lovely thing by Eumenes that I want to show you. To-day is—Tuesday. Come to dinner on Sunday and pour the vials of your ridicule on my want of success."

"That's an amiable way of putting it," replied Carlyle. "All right, I will."

Two hours later Carrados was again in his study, apparently, for a wonder, sitting idle. Sometimes he smiled to himself, and once or twice he laughed a little, but for the most part his pleasant, impassive face reflected no emotion and he sat with his useless eyes tranquilly fixed on an unseen distance. It was a fantastic caprice of the man to mock his sightlessness by a parade of light, and under the soft brilliance of a dozen electric brackets the room was as bright as day. At length he stood up and rang the bell.

"I suppose Mr. Greatorex isn't still here by any chance, Parkinson?" he asked, referring to his secretary.

"I think not, sir, but I will ascertain," replied the man.

"Never mind. Go to his room and bring me the last two files of *The Times*. Now"—when he returned—"turn to the earliest you have there. The date?"

"November the second."

"That will do. Find the Money Market; it will be in the Supplement. Now look down the columns until you come to British Railways."

"I have it, sir."

"Central and Suburban. Read the closing price and the change."

"Central and Suburban Ordinary, 66-1/2-67-1/2, fall 1/8. Preferred Ordinary, 81-81-1/2, no change. Deferred Ordinary, 27-1/2-27-3/4, fall 1/4. That is all, sir."

"Now take a paper about a week on. Read the Deferred only."

"27-27-1/4, no change."

"Another week."

"29-1/2-30, rise 5/8."

"Another."

"31-1/2-32-1/2, rise 1."

"Very good. Now on Tuesday the twenty-seventh November."

"31-7/8-32-3/4, rise 1/2."

"Yes. The next day."

"24-1/2-23-1/2, fall 9."

"Quite so, Parkinson. There had been an accident, you see."

"Yes, sir. Very unpleasant accident. Jane knows a person whose sister's young man has a cousin who had his arm torn off in it—torn off at the socket, she says, sir. It seems to bring it home to one, sir."

"That is all. Stay—in the paper you have, look down the first money column and see if there is any reference to the Central and Suburban."

"Yes, sir. 'City and Suburbans, which after their late depression on the projected extension of the motor bus service, had been steadily creeping up on the abandonment of the scheme, and as a result of their own excellent traffic returns, suffered a heavy slump through the lamentable accident of Thursday night. The Deferred in particular at one time fell eleven points as it was felt that the possible dividend, with which rumour has of late been busy, was now out of the question.'"

"Yes; that is all. Now you can take the papers back. And let it be a warning to you, Parkinson, not to invest your savings in speculative railway deferreds."

"Yes, sir. Thank you, sir, I will endeavour to remember." He lingered for a moment as he shook the file of papers level. "I may say, sir, that I have my eye on a small block of cottage property at Acton. But even cottage property scarcely seems safe from legislative depredation now, sir."

The next day Mr. Carrados called on his brokers in the city. It is to be presumed that he got through his private business quicker than he expected, for after leaving Austin Friars he continued his journey to Holloway, where he found Hutchins at home and sitting morosely before his kitchen fire. Rightly assuming that his luxuriant car would involve him in a certain amount of public attention in Klondyke Street, the blind man dismissed it some distance from the house, and walked the rest of the way, guided by the almost imperceptible touch of Parkinson's arm.

"Here is a gentleman to see you, father," explained Miss Hutchins, who had come to the door. She divined the relative positions of the two visitors at a glance.

"Then why don't you take him into the parlour?" grumbled the ex-driver. His face was a testimonial of hard work and general sobriety but at the moment one might hazard from his voice and manner that he had been drinking earlier in the day.

"I don't think that the gentleman would be impressed by the difference between our parlour and our kitchen," replied the girl quaintly, "and it is warmer here."

"What's the matter with the parlour now?" demanded her father sourly. "It was good enough for your mother and me. It used to be good enough for you."

"There is nothing the matter with it, nor with the kitchen either." She turned impassively to the two who had followed her along the narrow passage. "Will you go in, sir?"

"I don't want to see no gentleman," cried Hutchins noisily. "Unless"—his manner suddenly changed to one of pitiable anxiety—"unless you're from the Company sir, to—to—"

"No; I have come on Mr. Carlyle's behalf," replied Carrados, walking to a chair as though he moved by a kind of instinct.

Hutchins laughed his wry contempt.

"Mr. Carlyle!" he reiterated; "Mr. Carlyle! Fat lot of good he's been. Why don't he *do* something for his money?"

"He has," replied Carrados, with imperturbable good-humour; "he has sent me. Now, I want to ask you a few questions."

"A few questions!" roared the irate man. "Why, blast it, I have done nothing else but answer questions for a month. I didn't pay Mr. Carlyle to ask me questions; I can get enough of that for nixes. Why don't you go and ask Mr. Herbert Ananias Mead your few questions—then you might find out something."

There was a slight movement by the door and Carrados knew that the girl had quietly left the room.

"You saw that, sir?" demanded the father, diverted to a new line of bitterness. "You saw that girl—my own daughter, that I've worked for all her life?"

"No," replied Carrados.

"The girl that's just gone out—she's my daughter," explained Hutchins.

"I know, but I did not see her. I see nothing. I am blind."

"Blind!" exclaimed the old fellow, sitting up in startled wonderment. "You mean it, sir? You walk all right and you look at me as if you saw me. You're kidding surely."

"No," smiled Carrados. "It's quite right."

"Then it's a funny business, sir—you what are blind expecting to find something that those with their eyes couldn't," ruminated Hutchins sagely.

"There are things that you can't see with your eyes, Hutchins."

"Perhaps you are right, sir. Well, what is it you want to know?"

"Light a cigar first," said the blind man, holding out his case and waiting until the various sounds told him that his host was smoking contentedly. "The train you were driving at the time of the accident was the six-twenty-seven from Notcliff. It stopped everywhere until it reached Lambeth Bridge, the chief London station on your line. There it became something of an express, and leaving Lambeth Bridge at seven-eleven, should not stop again until it fetched Swanstead on Thames, eleven miles out, at seven-thirty-four. Then it stopped on and off from Swanstead to Ingerfield, the terminus of that branch, which it reached at eight-five."

Hutchins nodded, and then, remembering, said: "That's right, sir."

"That was your business all day—running between Notcliff and Ingerfield?"

"Yes, sir. Three journeys up and three down mostly."

"With the same stops on all the down journeys?"

"No. The seven-eleven is the only one that does a run from the Bridge to Swanstead. You see, it is just on the close of the evening rush, as they call it. A good many late business gentlemen living at Swanstead use the seven-eleven regular. The other journeys we stop at every station to Lambeth Bridge, and then here and there beyond."

"There are, of course, other trains doing exactly the same journey—a service, in fact?"

"Yes, sir. About six."

"And do any of those—say, during the rush—do any of those run non-stop from Lambeth to Swanstead?"

Hutchins reflected a moment. All the choler and restlessness had melted out of the man's face. He was again the excellent artisan, slow but capable and self-reliant.

"That I couldn't definitely say, sir. Very few short-distance trains pass the junction, but some of those may. A guide would show us in a minute but I haven't got one."

"Never mind. You said at the inquest that it was no uncommon thing for you to be pulled up at the 'stop' signal east of Knight's Cross Station. How often would that happen—only with the seven-eleven, mind."

"Perhaps three times a week; perhaps twice."

"The accident was on a Thursday. Have you noticed that you were pulled up oftener on a Thursday than on any other day?"

A smile crossed the driver's face at the question.

"You don't happen to live at Swanstead yourself, sir?" he asked in reply.

"No," admitted Carrados. "Why?"

"Well, sir, we were *always* pulled up on Thursday; practically always, you may say. It got to be quite a saying among those who used the train regular; they used to look out for it."

Carrados's sightless eyes had the one quality of concealing emotion supremely. "Oh," he commented softly, "always; and it was quite a saying, was it? And *why* was it always so on Thursday?"

"It had to do with the early closing, I'm told. The suburban traffic was a bit different. By rights we ought to have been set back two minutes for that day, but I suppose it wasn't thought worth while to alter us in the time-table so we most always had to wait outside Three Deep tunnel for a west-bound electric to make good."

"You were prepared for it then?"

"Yes, sir, I was," said Hutchins, reddening at some recollection, "and very down about it was one of the jury over that. But, mayhap once in three months, I did get through even on a Thursday, and it's not for me to question whether things are right or wrong just because they are not what I may expect. The signals are my orders, sir—stop! go on! and it's for me to obey, as you would a general on the field of battle. What would happen otherwise! It was nonsense what they said about going cautious; and the man who stated it was a barber who didn't know the difference between a 'distance' and a 'stop' signal down to the minute they gave their verdict. My orders, sir, given me by that signal, was 'Go right ahead and keep to your running time!'"

Carrados nodded a soothing assent. "That is all, I think," he remarked.

"All!" exclaimed Hutchins in surprise. "Why, sir, you can't have got much idea of it yet."

"Quite enough. And I know it isn't pleasant for you to be taken along the same ground over and over again."

The man moved awkwardly in his chair and pulled nervously at his grizzled beard.

"You mustn't take any notice of what I said just now, sir," he apologized. "You somehow make me feel that something may come of it; but I've been badgered about and accused and cross-examined from one to another of them these weeks till it's fairly made me bitter against everything. And now they talk of putting me in a lavatory—me that has been with the company for five and forty years and on the foot-plate thirty-two—a man suspected of running past a danger signal."

"You have had a rough time, Hutchins; you will have to exercise your patience a little longer yet," said Carrados sympathetically.

"You think something may come of it, sir? You think you will be able to clear me? Believe me, sir, if you could give me something to look forward to it might save me from—" He pulled himself up and shook his head sorrowfully. "I've been near it," he added simply.

Carrados reflected and took his resolution.

"To-day is Wednesday. I think you may hope to hear something from your general manager towards the middle of next week."

"Good God, sir! You really mean that?"

"In the interval show your good sense by behaving reasonably. Keep civilly to yourself and don't talk. Above all"—he nodded towards a quart jug that stood on the table between them, an incident that filled the simple-minded engineer with boundless wonder when he recalled it afterwards—"above all, leave that alone."

Hutchins snatched up the vessel and brought it crashing down on the hearthstone, his face shining with a set resolution.

"I've done with it, sir. It was the bitterness and despair that drove me to that. Now I can do without it."

The door was hastily opened and Miss Hutchins looked anxiously from her father to the visitors and back again.

"Oh, whatever is the matter?" she exclaimed. "I heard a great crash."

"This gentleman is going to clear me, Meg, my dear," blurted out the old man irrepressibly. "And I've done with the drink for ever."

"Hutchins! Hutchins!" said Carrados warningly.

"My daughter, sir; you wouldn't have her not know?" pleaded Hutchins, rather crest-fallen. "It won't go any further."

Carrados laughed quietly to himself as he felt Margaret Hutchins's startled and questioning eyes attempting to read his mind. He shook hands with the engine-driver without further comment, however, and walked out into the commonplace little street under Parkinson's unobtrusive guidance.

"Very nice of Miss Hutchins to go into half-mourning, Parkinson," he remarked as they went along. "Thoughtful, and yet not ostentatious."

"Yes, sir," agreed Parkinson, who had long ceased to wonder at his master's perceptions.

"The Romans, Parkinson, had a saying to the effect that gold carries no smell. That is a pity sometimes. What jewellery did Miss Hutchins wear?"

"Very little, sir. A plain gold brooch representing a merry-thought—the merry-thought of a sparrow, I should say, sir. The only other article was a smooth-backed gun-metal watch, suspended from a gun-metal bow."

"Nothing showy or expensive, eh?"

"Oh dear no, sir. Quite appropriate for a young person of her position."

"Just what I should have expected." He slackened his pace. "We are passing a hoarding, are we not?"

"Yes, sir."

"We will stand here a moment. Read me the letterpress of the poster before us."

"This 'Oxo' one, sir?"

"Yes."

"'Oxo,' sir."

Carrados was convulsed with silent laughter. Parkinson had infinitely more dignity and conceded merely a tolerant recognition of the ludicrous.

"That was a bad shot, Parkinson," remarked his master when he could speak. "We will try another."

For three minutes, with scrupulous conscientiousness on the part of the reader and every appearance of keen interest on the part of the hearer, there were set forth the particulars of a sale by auction of superfluous timber and builders' material.

"That will do," said Carrados, when the last detail had been reached. "We can be seen from the door of No. 107 still?"

"Yes, sir."

"No indication of anyone coming to us from there?"

"No, sir."

Carrados walked thoughtfully on again. In the Holloway Road they rejoined the waiting motor-car.

"Lambeth Bridge Station" was the order the driver received.

From the station the car was sent on home and Parkinson was instructed to take two first-class singles for Richmond, which could be reached by changing at Stafford Road. The "evening rush" had not yet commenced and they had no difficulty in finding an empty carriage when the train came in.

Parkinson was kept busy that journey describing what he saw at various points between Lambeth Bridge and Knight's Cross. For a quarter of a mile Carrados's demands on the eyes and the memory of his remarkable servant were wide and incessant. Then his questions ceased. They had passed the "stop" signal, east of Knight's Cross Station.

The following afternoon they made the return journey as far as Knight's Cross. This time, however, the surroundings failed to interest Carrados. "We are going to look at some rooms," was the information he offered on the subject, and an imperturbable "Yes, sir" had been the extent of Parkinson's comment on the unusual proceeding. After leaving the station they turned sharply along a road that ran parallel with the line, a dull thoroughfare of substantial, elderly houses that were beginning to sink into decrepitude. Here and there a corner residence displayed the brass plate of a professional occupant, but for the most part they were given up to the various branches of second-rate apartment letting.

"The third house after the one with the flagstaff," said Carrados.

Parkinson rang the bell, which was answered by a young servant, who took an early opportunity of assuring them that she was not tidy as it was rather early in the afternoon. She informed Carrados, in reply to his inquiry, that Miss Chubb was at home, and showed them into a melancholy little sitting-room to await her appearance.

"I shall be 'almost' blind here, Parkinson," remarked Carrados, walking about the room. "It saves explanation."

"Very good, sir," replied Parkinson.

Five minutes later, an interval suggesting that Miss Chubb also found it rather early in the afternoon, Carrados was arranging to take rooms for his attendant and himself for the short time that he would be in London, seeing an oculist.

"One bedroom, mine, must face north," he stipulated. "It has to do with the light."

Miss Chubb replied that she quite understood. Some gentlemen, she added, had their requirements, others their fancies. She endeavoured to suit all. The bedroom she had in view from the first *did* face north. She would not have known, only the last gentleman, curiously enough, had made the same request.

"A sufferer like myself?" inquired Carrados affably.

Miss Chubb did not think so. In his case she regarded it merely as a fancy. He had said that he could not sleep on any other side. She had had to turn out of her own room to accommodate him, but if one kept an apartment-house one had to be adaptable; and Mr. Ghoosh was certainly very liberal in his ideas.

"Ghoosh? An Indian gentleman, I presume?" hazarded Carrados.

It appeared that Mr. Ghoosh was an Indian. Miss Chubb confided that at first she had been rather perturbed at the idea of taking in "a black man," as she confessed to regarding him. She reiterated, however, that Mr. Ghoosh proved to be "quite the gentleman." Five minutes of affability put Carrados in full possession of Mr. Ghoosh's manner of life and movements—the dates of his arrival and departure, his solitariness and his daily habits.

"This would be the best bedroom," said Miss Chubb.

It was a fair-sized room on the first floor. The window looked out on to the roof of an outbuilding; beyond, the deep cutting of the railway line. Opposite stood the dead wall that Mr. Carlyle had spoken of.

Carrados "looked" round the room with the discriminating glance that sometimes proved so embarrassing to those who knew him.

"I have to take a little daily exercise," he remarked, walking to the window and running his hand up the woodwork. "You will not mind my fixing a 'developer' here, Miss Chubb—a few small screws?"

Miss Chubb thought not. Then she was sure not. Finally she ridiculed the idea of minding with scorn.

"If there is width enough," mused Carrados, spanning the upright critically. "Do you happen to have a wooden foot-rule convenient?"

"Well, to be sure!" exclaimed Miss Chubb, opening a rapid succession of drawers until she produced the required article. "When we did out this room after Mr. Ghoosh, there was this very ruler among the things that he hadn't thought worth taking. This is what you require, sir?"

"Yes," replied Carrados, accepting it, "I think this is exactly what I require." It was a common new white-wood rule, such as one might buy at any small stationer's for a penny. He carelessly took off the width of the upright, reading the figures with a touch; and then continued to run a finger-tip delicately up and down the edges of the instrument.

"Four and seven-eighths," was his unspoken conclusion.

"I hope it will do sir."

"Admirably," replied Carrados. "But I haven't reached the end of my requirements yet, Miss Chubb."

"No, sir?" said the landlady, feeling that it would be a pleasure to oblige so agreeable a gentleman, "what else might there be?"

"Although I can see very little I like to have a light, but not any kind of light. Gas I cannot do with. Do you think that you would be able to find me an oil lamp?"

"Certainly, sir. I got out a very nice brass lamp that I have specially for Mr. Ghoosh. He read a good deal of an evening and he preferred a lamp."

"That is very convenient. I suppose it is large enough to burn for a whole evening?"

"Yes, indeed. And very particular he was always to have it filled every day."

"A lamp without oil is not very useful," smiled Carrados, following her towards another room, and absent-mindedly slipping the foot-rule into his pocket.

Whatever Parkinson thought of the arrangement of going into second-rate apartments in an obscure street it is to be inferred that his devotion to his master was sufficient to overcome his private emotions as a self-respecting "man." At all events, as they were approaching the station he asked, and without a trace of feeling, whether there were any orders for him with reference to the proposed migration.

"None, Parkinson," replied his master. "We must be satisfied with our present quarters."

"I beg your pardon, sir," said Parkinson, with some constraint. "I understand that you had taken the rooms for a week certain."

"I am afraid that Miss Chubb will be under the same impression. Unforeseen circumstances will prevent our going, however. Mr. Greatorex must write to-morrow, enclosing a cheque, with my regrets, and adding a penny for this ruler which I seem to have brought away with me. It, at least, is something for the money."

Parkinson may be excused for not attempting to understand the course of events.

"Here is your train coming in, sir," he merely said.

"We will let it go and wait for another. Is there a signal at either end of the platform?"

"Yes, sir; at the further end."

"Let us walk towards it. Are there any of the porters or officials about here?"

"No, sir; none."

"Take this ruler. I want you to go up the steps—there are steps up the signal, by the way?"

"Yes, sir."

"I want you to measure the glass of the lamp. Do not go up any higher than is necessary, but if you have to stretch be careful not to mark off the measurement with your nail, although the impulse is a natural one. That has been done already."

Parkinson looked apprehensively round and about. Fortunately the part was a dark and unfrequented spot and everyone else was moving towards the exit at the other end of the platform. Fortunately, also, the signal was not a high one.

"As near as I can judge on the rounded surface, the glass is four and seven-eighths across," reported Parkinson.

"Thank you," replied Carrados, returning the measure to his pocket, "four and seven-eighths is quite near enough. Now we will take the next train back."

Sunday evening came, and with it Mr. Carlyle to The Turrets at the appointed hour. He brought to the situation a mind poised for any eventuality and a trenchant eye. As the time went on and the impenetrable Carrados made no illusion to the case, Carlyle's manner inclined to a waggish commiseration of his host's position. Actually, he said little, but the crisp precision of his voice when the path lay open to a remark of any significance left little to be said.

It was not until they had finished dinner and returned to the library that Carrados gave the slightest hint of anything unusual being in the air. His first indication of coming events was to remove the key from the outside to the inside of the door.

"What are you doing, Max?" demanded Mr. Carlyle, his curiosity overcoming the indirect attitude.

"You have been very entertaining, Louis," replied his friend, "but Parkinson should be back very soon now and it is as well to be prepared. Do you happen to carry a revolver?"

"Not when I come to dine with you, Max," replied Carlyle, with all the aplomb he could muster. "Is it usual?"

Carrados smiled affectionately at his guest's agile recovery and touched the secret spring of a drawer in an antique bureau by his side. The little hidden receptacle shot smoothly out, disclosing a pair of dull-blued pistols.

"To-night, at all events, it might be prudent," he replied, handing one to Carlyle and putting the other into his own pocket. "Our man may be here at any minute, and we do not know in what temper he will come."

"Our man!" exclaimed Carlyle, craning forward in excitement. "Max! you don't mean to say that you have got Mead to admit it?"

"No one has admitted it," said Carrados. "And it is not Mead."

"Not Mead.... Do you mean that Hutchins—?"

"Neither Mead nor Hutchins. The man who tampered with the signal—for Hutchins was right and a green light *was* exhibited—is a young Indian from Bengal. His name is Drishna and he lives at Swanstead."

Mr. Carlyle stared at his friend between sheer surprise and blank incredulity.

"You really mean this, Carrados?" he said.

"My fatal reputation for humour!" smiled Carrados. "If I am wrong, Louis, the next hour will expose it."

"But why—why—why? The colossal villainy, the unparalleled audacity!" Mr. Carlyle lost himself among incredulous superlatives and could only stare.

"Chiefly to get himself out of a disastrous speculation," replied Carrados, answering the question. "If there was another motive—or at least an incentive—which I suspect, doubtless we shall hear of it."

"All the same, Max, I don't think that you have treated me quite fairly," protested Carlyle, getting over his first surprise and passing to a sense of injury. "Here we are and I know nothing, absolutely nothing, of the whole affair."

"We both have our ideas of pleasantry, Louis," replied Carrados genially. "But I dare say you are right and perhaps there is still time to atone." In the fewest possible words he outlined the course of his investigations. "And now you know all that is to be known until Drishna arrives."

"But will he come?" questioned Carlyle doubtfully. "He may be suspicious."

"Yes, he will be suspicious."

"Then he will not come."

"On the contrary, Louis, he will come because my letter will make him suspicious. He *is* coming; otherwise Parkinson would have telephoned me at once and we should have had to take other measures."

"What did you say, Max?" asked Carlyle curiously.

"I wrote that I was anxious to discuss an Indo-Scythian inscription with him, and sent my car in the hope that he would be able to oblige me."

"But is he interested in Indo-Scythian inscriptions?"

"I haven't the faintest idea," admitted Carrados, and Mr. Carlyle was throwing up his hands in despair when the sound of a motor-car wheels softly kissing the gravel surface of the drive outside brought him to his feet.

"By Gad, you are right, Max!" he exclaimed, peeping through the curtains. "There is a man inside."

"Mr. Drishna," announced Parkinson a minute later.

The visitor came into the room with leisurely self-possession that might have been real or a desperate assumption. He was a slightly built young man of about twenty-five, with black hair and eyes, a small, carefully trained moustache, and a dark olive skin. His physiognomy was not displeasing, but his expression had a harsh and supercilious tinge. In attire he erred towards the immaculately spruce.

"Mr. Carrados?" he said inquiringly.

Carrados, who had risen, bowed slightly without offering his hand.

"This gentleman," he said, indicating his friend, "is Mr. Carlyle, the celebrated private detective."

The Indian shot a very sharp glance at the object of this description. Then he sat down.

"You wrote me a letter, Mr. Carrados," he remarked, in English that scarcely betrayed any foreign origin, "a rather curious letter, I may say. You asked me about an ancient inscription. I know nothing of antiquities; but I thought, as you had sent, that it would be more courteous if I came and explained this to you."

"That was the object of my letter," replied Carrados.

"You wished to see me?" said Drishna, unable to stand the ordeal of the silence that Carrados imposed after his remark.

"When you left Miss Chubb's house you left a ruler behind." One lay on the desk by Carrados and he took it up as he spoke.

"I don't understand what you are talking about," said Drishna guardedly. "You are making some mistake."

"The ruler was marked at four and seven-eighths inches—the measure of the glass of the signal lamp outside."

The unfortunate young man was unable to repress a start. His face lost its healthy tone. Then, with a sudden impulse, he made a step forward and snatched the object from Carrados's hand.

"If it is mine I have a right to it," he exclaimed, snapping the ruler in two and throwing it on to the back of the blazing fire. "It is nothing."

"Pardon me, I did not say that the one you have so impetuously disposed of was yours. As a matter of fact, it was mine. Yours is—elsewhere."

"Wherever it is you have no right to it if it is mine," panted Drishna, with rising excitement. "You are a thief, Mr. Carrados. I will not stay any longer here."

He jumped up and turned towards the door. Carlyle made a step forward, but the precaution was unnecessary.

"One moment, Mr. Drishna," interposed Carrados, in his smoothest tones. "It is a pity, after you have come so far, to leave without hearing of my investigations in the neighbourhood of Shaftesbury Avenue."

Drishna sat down again.

"As you like," he muttered. "It does not interest me."

"I wanted to obtain a lamp of a certain pattern," continued Carrados. "It seemed to me that the simplest explanation would be to say that I wanted it for a motor-car. Naturally I went to Long Acre. At the first shop I said: 'Wasn't it here that a friend of mine, an Indian gentleman, recently had a lamp made with a green glass that was nearly five inches across?' No, it was not there but they could make me one. At the next shop the same; at the third, and fourth, and so on. Finally my persistence was rewarded. I found the place where the lamp had been made, and at the cost of ordering another I obtained all the details I wanted. It was news to them, the shopman informed me, that in some parts of India green was the danger colour and therefore tail lamps had to show a green light. The incident made some impression on him and he would be able to identify their customer—who paid in advance and gave no address—among a thousand of his countrymen. Do I succeed in interesting you, Mr. Drishna?"

"Do you?" replied Drishna, with a languid yawn. "Do I look interested?"

"You must make allowance for my unfortunate blindness," apologized Carrados, with grim irony.

"Blindness!" exclaimed Drishna, dropping his affectation of unconcern as though electrified by the word, "do you mean—really blind—that you do not see me?"

"Alas, no," admitted Carrados.

The Indian withdrew his right hand from his coat pocket and with a tragic gesture flung a heavy revolver down on the table between them.

"I have had you covered all the time, Mr. Carrados, and if I had wished to go and you or your friend had raised a hand to stop me, it would have been at the peril of your lives," he said, in a voice of melancholy triumph. "But what is the use of defying fate, and who successfully evades his destiny? A month ago I went to see one of our people who reads the future and sought to know the course of certain events. 'You need fear no human eye,' was the message given to me. Then she added: 'But when the sightless sees the unseen, make your peace with Yama.' And I thought she spoke of the Great Hereafter!"

"This amounts to an admission of your guilt," exclaimed Mr. Carlyle practically.

"I bow to the decree of fate," replied Drishna. "And it is fitting to the universal irony of existence that a blind man should be the instrument. I don't imagine, Mr. Carlyle," he added maliciously, "that you, with your eyes, would ever have brought that result about."

"You are a very cold-blooded young scoundrel, sir!" retorted Mr. Carlyle. "Good heavens! do you realize that you are responsible for the death of scores of innocent men and women?"

"Do *you* realize, Mr. Carlyle, that you and your Government and your soldiers are responsible for the death of thousands of innocent men and women in my country every day? If England was occupied by the Germans who quartered an army and an administration with their wives and their families and all their expensive paraphernalia on the unfortunate country until the whole nation was reduced to the verge of famine, and the appointment of every new official meant the callous death sentence on a thousand men and women to pay his salary, then if you went to Berlin and wrecked a train you would be hailed a patriot. What Boadicea did and—and Samson, so have I. If they were heroes, so am I."

"Well, upon my word!" cried the highly scandalized Carlyle, "what next! Boadicea was a—er—semi-legendary person, whom we may possibly admire at a distance. Personally, I do not profess to express an opinion. But Samson, I would remind you, is a Biblical character. Samson was mocked as an enemy. You, I do not doubt, have been entertained as a friend."

"And haven't I been mocked and despised and sneered at every day of my life here by your supercilious, superior, empty-headed men?" flashed back Drishna, his eyes leaping into malignity and his voice trembling with sudden passion. "Oh! how I hated them as I passed them in the street and recognized by a thousand petty insults their lordly English contempt for me as an inferior being—a nigger. How I longed with Caligula that a nation had a single neck that I might destroy it at one blow. I loathe you in your complacent hypocrisy, Mr. Carlyle, despise and utterly abominate you from an eminence of superiority that you can never even understand."

"I think we are getting rather away from the point, Mr. Drishna," interposed Carrados, with the impartiality of a judge. "Unless I am misinformed, you are not so ungallant as to include everyone you have met here in your execration?"

"Ah, no," admitted Drishna, descending into a quite ingenuous frankness. "Much as I hate your men I love your women. How is it possible that a nation should be so divided—its men so dull-witted and offensive, its women so quick, sympathetic and capable of appreciating?"

"But a little expensive, too, at times?" suggested Carrados.

Drishna sighed heavily.

"Yes; it is incredible. It is the generosity of their large nature. My allowance, though what most of you would call noble, has proved quite inadequate. I was compelled to borrow money and the interest became overwhelming. Bankruptcy was impracticable because I should have then been recalled by my people, and much as I detest England a certain reason made the thought of leaving it unbearable."

"Connected with the Arcady Theatre?"

"You know? Well, do not let us introduce the lady's name. In order to restore myself I speculated on the Stock Exchange. My credit was good through my father's position and the standing of the firm to which I am attached. I heard on reliable authority, and very early, that the Central and Suburban, and the Deferred especially, was safe to fall heavily, through a motor bus amalgamation that was then a secret. I opened a bear account and sold largely. The shares fell, but only fractionally, and I waited. Then, unfortunately, they began to go up. Adverse forces were at work and rumours were put about. I could not stand the settlement, and in order to carry over an account I was literally compelled to deal temporarily with some securities that were not technically my own property."

"Embezzlement, sir," commented Mr. Carlyle icily. "But what is embezzlement on the top of wholesale murder!"

"That is what it is called. In my case, however, it was only to be temporary. Unfortunately, the rise continued. Then, at the height of my despair, I chanced to be returning to Swanstead rather earlier than usual one evening, and the train was stopped at a certain signal to let another pass. There was conversation in the carriage and I learned certain details. One said that there would be an accident some day, and so forth. In a flash—as by an inspiration—I saw how the circumstance might be turned to account. A bad accident and the shares would certainly fall and my position would be retrieved. I think Mr. Carrados has somehow learned the rest."

"Max," said Mr. Carlyle, with emotion, "is there any reason why you should not send your man for a police officer and have this monster arrested on his own confession without further delay?"

"Pray do so, Mr. Carrados," acquiesced Drishna. "I shall certainly be hanged, but the speech I shall prepare will ring from one end of India to the other; my memory will be venerated as that of a martyr; and the emancipation of my motherland will be hastened by my sacrifice."

"In other words," commented Carrados, "there will be disturbances at half-a-dozen disaffected places, a few unfortunate police will be clubbed to death, and possibly worse things may happen. That does not suit us, Mr. Drishna."

"And how do you propose to prevent it?" asked Drishna, with cool assurance.

"It is very unpleasant being hanged on a dark winter morning; very cold, very friendless, very inhuman. The long trial, the solitude and the confinement, the thoughts of the long sleepless night before, the hangman and the pinioning and the noosing of the rope, are apt to prey on the imagination. Only a very stupid man can take hanging easily."

"What do you want me to do instead, Mr. Carrados?" asked Drishna shrewdly.

Carrados's hand closed on the weapon that still lay on the table between them. Without a word he pushed it across.

"I see," commented Drishna, with a short laugh and a gleaming eye. "Shoot myself and hush it up to suit your purpose. Withhold my message to save the exposures of a trial, and keep the flame from the torch of insurrectionary freedom."

"Also," interposed Carrados mildly, "to save your worthy people a good deal of shame, and to save the lady who is nameless the unpleasant necessity of relinquishing the house and the income which you have just settled on her. She certainly would not then venerate your memory."

"What is that?"

"The transaction which you carried through was based on a felony and could not be upheld. The firm you dealt with will go to the courts, and the money, being directly traceable, will be held forfeit as no good consideration passed."

"Max!" cried Mr. Carlyle hotly, "you are not going to let this scoundrel cheat the gallows after all?"

"The best use you can make of the gallows is to cheat it, Louis," replied Carrados. "Have you ever reflected what human beings will think of us a hundred years hence?"

"Oh, of course I'm not really in favour of hanging," admitted Mr. Carlyle.

"Nobody really is. But we go on hanging. Mr. Drishna is a dangerous animal who for the sake of pacific animals must cease to exist. Let his barbarous exploit pass into oblivion with him. The disadvantages of spreading it broadcast immeasurably outweigh the benefits."

"I have considered," announced Drishna. "I will do as you wish."

"Very well," said Carrados. "Here is some plain notepaper. You had better write a letter to someone saying that the financial difficulties in which you are involved make life unbearable."

"But there are no financial difficulties—now."

"That does not matter in the least. It will be put down to an hallucination and taken as showing the state of your mind."

"But what guarantee have we that he will not escape?" whispered Mr. Carlyle.

"He cannot escape," replied Carrados tranquilly. "His identity is too clear."

"I have no intention of trying to escape," put in Drishna, as he wrote. "You hardly imagine that I have not considered this eventuality, do you?"

"All the same," murmured the ex-lawyer, "I should like to have a jury behind me. It is one thing to execute a man morally; it is another to do it almost literally."

"Is that all right?" asked Drishna, passing across the letter he had written.

Carrados smiled at this tribute to his perception.

"Quite excellent," he replied courteously. "There is a train at nine-forty. Will that suit you?"

Drishna nodded and stood up. Mr. Carlyle had a very uneasy feeling that he ought to do something but could not suggest to himself what.

The next moment he heard his friend heartily thanking the visitor for the assistance he had been in the matter of the Indo-Scythian inscription, as they walked across the hall together. Then a door closed.

"I believe that there is something positively uncanny about Max at times," murmured the perturbed gentleman to himself.

# THE PROBLEM OF CELL 13
## BY JACQUES FUTRELLE

Jacques Futrelle

# ORIGINALLY PUBLISHED IN 1905

# THE PROBLEM OF CELL 13
## BY JACQUES FUTRELLE

"The Thinking Machine".

Long before the invention of computers, this term was used to refer to the extraordinary detective created by the American author Jacques Futrelle. Professor Augustus S. F. X. Van Dusen, Ph. D., LL. D., F. R. S., M.D., etc., etc, used his enormous intellect to solve cases using only logic.

Described as having "a head out of all proportion to his body, domelike, enormous, with a wilderness of straw-yellow hair, Van Dusen was almost the caricature of a scientist. He claimed to be knowledgeable on just about everything and once defeated a chess grandmaster by merely studying the rules. He was often assisted, or at least observed, on his various cases by the news reporter Hutchinson Hatch.

His methods were extremely simple. He would hear about a case, make a few observations, establish a few facts and then apply logic to deduce the answer.

Prof. Van Dusen first appeared in a serialized version of the story "The Problem of Cell 13" in *The Boston American* in 1905. Further stories appeared in that newspaper and in *The Saturday Evening Post*. He appeared in fifty some stories. Some of these were collected in *The Thinking Machine* (1907) *and The Thinking Machine on the Case*. A novel was also produced, *The Chase of the Golden Plate* (1906). The professors career was unfortunately cut short when the author perished on the *Titanic* in 1912 having insisted that his wife board one of the life boats while he remained behind.

# THE PROBLEM OF CELL 13

Practically all those letters remaining in the alphabet after Augustus S. F. X. Van Dusen was named were afterward acquired by that gentleman in the course of a brilliant scientific career, and, being honorably acquired, were tacked on to the other end. His name, therefore, taken with all that belonged it, was a wonderfully imposing structure. He was a Ph.D., an LL.D., an F.R.S., an M.D., and an M.D.S. He was also some other things—just what he himself couldn't say— through recognition of his ability by various foreign educational and scientific institutions.

In appearance he was no less striking than in nomenclature. He was slender with the droop of the student in his thin shoulders and the pallor of a close, sedentary life on his clean-shaven face. His eyes wore a perceptual, forbidding squint—the squint of a man who studies little things—and when they could be seen at all through his thick spectacles, were mere slits of watery blue. But above his eyes was his most striking feature. This was a tall, broad brow, almost abnormal in height and width, crowned by a heavy shock of bushy, yellow hair. All these things conspired to give him a peculiar, almost grotesque, personality.

Professor Van Dusen was remotely German. For generations his ancestors had been noted in the sciences; he was the logical result, the mastermind. First and above all he was a logician. At least thirty-five years of the half century or so of his existence had been devoted exclusively to providing that two and two always equal four, except in unusual cases, where they equaled three or five, as the case may be. He stood broadly on the general propositions that all things that start must go somewhere, and was able to bring the concentrated mental force of his forefathers to bear on a given problem. Incidentally it may be remarked that Professor Van Dusen wore a No. 8 hat.

The world at large had heard vaguely of Professor Van Dusen as The Thinking Machine. It was a newspaper catchphrase applied to him at the time of a remarkable exhibition at chess; he had demonstrated then that a stranger to the game might, by the force of inevitable logic, defeat a champion who had devoted a lifetime to its study. The Thinking Machine! Perhaps that more nearly described him than all his honorary initials, for he had spent week after week, month after month, in the seclusion of his small laboratory from which had gone forth thoughts that staggered scientific associates and deeply stirred the world at large.

It was only occasionally that The Thinking Machine had visitors, and these were usually men who, themselves high in the sciences, dropped in to argue a point and perhaps convince themselves. Two of these men, Dr. Charles Ransome and Alfred Fielding, called one evening to discuss some theory which is not of consequence here.

"Such a thing is impossible," declared Dr. Ransome emphatically, in the course of the conversation.

"Nothing is impossible," declared The Thinking Machine with equal emphasis. He always spoke petulantly. "The mind is master of all things. When science fully recognizes that fact a great advance will have been made."

"How about the airship?" asked Dr. Ransome.

"That's not impossible at all," asserted The Thinking Machine "it will be invented some time. I'd do it myself, but I'm busy."

Dr. Ransome laughed tolerantly.

"I've heard you say such things before," he said. "But they mean nothing. Mind may be master of matter, but it hasn't yet found a way to apply itself. There are some things that can't be thought out of existence, or rather which would not yield to any amount of thinking."

"What, for instance?" demanded The Thinking Machine.

Dr. Ransome was thoughtful for a moment as he smoked.

"Well, say prison walls," he replied. "No man can think himself out of a cell. If he could, there would be no prisoners."

"A man can so apply his brain and ingenuity that he can leave a cell, which is the same thing," snapped The Thinking Machine.

Dr. Ransome was slightly amused.

"Let's suppose a case," he said, after a moment. "Take a cell where prisoners under sentence of death are confined—men who are desperate and, maddened by fear, would take any chance to escape—suppose you were locked in such a cell. Could you escape?"

"Certainly," declared The Thinking Machine.

"Of course," said Mr. Fielding, who entered the conversation for the first time, "you might wreck the cell with an explosive—but inside, a prisoner, you couldn't have that."

"There would be nothing of that kind," said The Thinking Machine. "You might treat me precisely as you treated prisoners under sentence of death, and I would leave the cell."

"Not unless you entered it with tools prepared to get out," said Dr. Ransome.

The Thinking Machine was visibly annoyed and his blue eyes snapped.

"Lock me in any cell in any prison anywhere at any time, wearing only what is necessary, and I'll escape in a week," he declared, sharply. Dr. Ransome sat up straight in his chair, interested. Mr. Fielding lighted a new cigar.

"You mean you could actually think yourself out?" asked Dr. Ransome.

"I would get out," was the response.

"Are you serious?"

"Certainly I am serious."

Dr. Ransome and Mr. Fielding were silent for a long time.

"Would you be willing to try it?" asked Mr. Fielding, finally.

"Certainly," said Professor Van Dusen, and there was a trace of irony in his voice. "I have done more asinine things than that to convince other men of less important truths."

The tone was offensive and there was an undercurrent strongly resembling anger on both sides. Of course it was an absurd thing, but Professor Van Dusen reiterated his willingness to undertake the escape and it was decided on.

"To begin now," added Dr. Ransome.

"I'd prefer that it begin to-morrow," said The Thinking Machine, "because—"

"No, now," said Mr. Fielding, flatly. "You are arrested, figuratively speaking, of course, without any warning locked in a cell with no chance to communicate with friends, and left there with identically the same care and attention that would be given to a man under sentence of death. Are you willing?"

"All right, now, then," said The Thinking Machine, and he arose.

"Say, the death cell in Chisholm Prison."

"The death cell in Chisholm Prison."

"And what will you wear?"

"As little as possible," said The Thinking Machine. "Shoes, stockings, trousers and a shirt."

"You will permit yourself to be searched, of course?"

"I am to be treated precisely as all prisoners are treated," said The Thinking Machine. "No more attention and no less."

There were some preliminaries to be arranged in the matter of obtaining permission for the test, but all these were influential men and everything was done satisfactorily by telephone, albeit the prison commissioners, to whom the experiment was explained on purely scientific grounds, were sadly bewildered. Professor Van Dusen would be the most distinguished prisoner they had ever entertained.

When The Thinking Machine had donned those things which he was to wear during his incarceration, he called the little old woman who was his housekeeper, cook and maidservant all in one.

"Martha," he said, "it is now twenty-seven minutes past nine o'clock. I am going away. One week from to-night, at half past nine, these gentlemen and one, possibly two, others will take supper with me here. Remember Dr. Ransome is very fond of artichokes."

The three men were driven to Chisholm Prison, where the warden was awaiting them, having been informed of the matter by telephone. He understood merely that the eminent Professor Van Dusen was to be his prisoner, if he could keep him, for one week; that he had committed no crime, but that he was to be treated as all other prisoners were treated.

"Search him," instructed Dr. Ransome.

The Thinking Machine was searched. Nothing was found on him; the pockets of the trousers were empty; the white, stiff-bosomed shirt had no pocket. The shoes and stockings were removed, examined, then replaced. As he watched all these preliminaries, and noted the pitiful, childlike physical weakness of the man—the colorless face, and the thin, white hands—Dr. Ransome almost regretted his part in the affair.

"Are you sure you want to do this?" he asked

"Would you be convinced if I did not?" inquired The Thinking Machine in turn.

"No."

"All right. I'll do it."

What sympathy Dr. Ransome had was dissipated by the tone. It nettled him, and he resolved to see the experiment to the end; it would be a stinging reproof to egotism.

"It will be impossible for him to communicate with anyone outside?" he asked.

"Absolutely impossible," replied the warden. "He will not be permitted writing materials of any sort."

"And your jailers, would they deliver a message from him?"

"Not one word, directly or indirectly," said the warden. "You may rest assured of that. They will report anything he might say or turn over to me, anything he might give them."

"That seems entirely satisfactory," said Mr. Fielding, who was frankly interested in the problem.

"Of course, in the event he fails," said Dr. Ransome, "and asks for his liberty, you understand you are to set him free?"

"I understand," replied the warden.

The Thinking Machine stood listening, but had nothing to say until all this was ended, then:

"I should like to make three small requests. You may grant them or not, as you wish."

"No special favors, now," warned Mr. Fielding.

"I am asking none," was the stiff response. "I should like to have some tooth powder—buy it yourself to see that it is tooth powder—and I should like to have one five-dollar and two ten-dollar bills."

Dr. Ransome, Mr. Fielding and the warden exchanged astonished glances. They were not surprised at the request for tooth powder, but were at the request for money.

"Is there any man with whom our friend would come in contact that he could bribe with twenty-five dollars?"

"Not for twenty-five hundred dollars," was the positive reply.

"And what is the third request?" asked Dr. Ransome.

"I should like to have my shoes polished."

Again the astonished glances were exchanged. This last request was the height of absurdity, so they agreed to it. These things all being attended to, The Thinking Machine was led back into the prison from which he had undertaken to escape.

"Here is Cell 13," said the warden, stopping three doors down the steel corridor. "This is where we keep condemned murderers. No one can leave it without my permission; and no one in it can communicate with the outside. I'll stake my reputation on that. It's only three doors back of my office and I can readily hear any unusual noise."

"Will this cell do, gentleman?" asked The Thinking Machine. There was a touch of irony in his voice.

"Admirably," was the reply.

The heavy steel door was thrown open, there was a great scurrying and scampering of tiny feet, and The Thinking Machine passed into the gloom of the cell. Then the door was closed and double locked by the warden.

"What is that noise in there?" asked Dr. Ransome, through the bars.

"Rats—dozens of them," replied The Thinking Machine, tersely.

The three men, with final good nights, were turning away when The Thinking Machine called:

"What time is it exactly, Warden?"

"Eleven-seventeen," replied the warden.

"Thanks. I will join you gentlemen in your office at half past eight o'clock one week from tonight," said The Thinking Machine.

"And if you do not?"

"There is no "if" about it."

Chisolm Prison was a great, spreading structure of granite, four stories in all, which stood in the center of acres of open space. It was surrounded by a wall of solid masonry eighteen feet high, and so smoothly finished inside and out as to offer no foothold to a climber, no matter how expert. Atop of this fence, as a further precaution, was a five-foot fence of steel rods, each terminating in a keen point. This fence in itself marked an absolute deadline between freedom and imprisonment, for, even if a man escaped from his cell, it would seem impossible for him to pass the wall.

The yard, which on all sides of the prison building was twenty-five feet wide, that being the distance from the building to the wall, was by day an exercises ground for those prisoners to whom was granted the boon of occasional semi-liberty. But that was not for those in Cell 13. At all times of the day there were armed guards in the yard, four of them, one patrolling each side of the prison building.

By night the yard was almost as brilliantly lighted as by day. On each of the four sides was a great arc light which rose above the prison wall and gave to the guards a clear sight. The lights, too, brightly illuminated the spiked top of the wall. The wires which fed the arc lights ran up the side of the prison building on insulators and from the top story led out to the poles supporting the arc lights. All these things were seen and comprehended by The Thinking Machine, who was only enabled to see out his closely barred cell window by standing on his bed. This was on the morning following his incarceration. He gathered, too, that the river lay over there beyond the wall somewhere, because he heard faintly the pulsation of a motor boat and high up in the air he saw a river bird. From that same direction came the shouts of boys at play and the occasional crack of a batted ball. He knew then that between the prison wall and the river was an open space, a playground.

Chisolm Prison was regarded as absolutely safe. No man had ever escaped from it. The Thinking Machine, from his perch on the bed, seeing what he saw, could readily understand why. The wall of the cell, though built he judged twenty years before, were perfectly solid, and the window bars of new iron had not a shadow of rust on them. The window itself, even with the bars out, would be a difficult mode of egress because it was small.

Yet, seeing these things, The Thinking Machine was not discouraged. Instead, he thoughtfully squinted at the great arc light—there was bright sunlight now—and traced with his eyes the wire which led from it to the building. That electric wire, he reasoned, must come down the side of the building not a great distance from his cell. That might be worth knowing.

Cell 13 was on the same floor with the offices of the prison— that is, not in the basement, nor yet upstairs. There were only four steps up to the office floor, therefore the level of the floor must be only three or four feet above the ground. He couldn't see the ground directly beneath his window, but he could see it further out toward the wall. It would be an easy drop from the window. Well and good.

Then The Thinking Machine fell to remembering how he had come to the cell. First, there was the outside guards booth, a part of the wall. There were two heavily barred gates there, both of steel. At this gate was one man always on guard. He admitted persons to the prison after much clanking of keys and locks, and let them out when ordered to do so. The warden's office was in the prison building, and in order to reach that official from the prison yard one had to pass a gate of solid steel with only a peephole in it. Then coming from that inner office to Cell 13, where he was now, one must pass a heavy wooden door and two steel doors into the corridors of the prison; and always there was the double-locked door of Cell 13 to reckon with.

There were then, The Thinking Machine recalled, seven doors to be overcome before one could pass from Cell 13 into the outer world, a free man. But against this was the fact that he was rarely interrupted. A jailer appeared at his cell door at six in the morning with a breakfast of prison fare; he would come again at noon, and again at six in the afternoon. At nine o'clock at night would come the inspection tour. That would be all.

"It's admirably arranged, this prison system," was the mental tribute paid by The Thinking Machine. "I'll have to study it a little when I get out. I had no idea there was such great care exercised in the prisons."

There was nothing, positively nothing, in his cell, except his iron bed, so firmly put together that no man could tear it to pieces save with sledges or a file. He had neither of these. There was not even a chair, or a small table, or a bit of crockery. Nothing! The jailer stood by when he ate, then took away the wooden spoon and bowl which he had used.

One by one these things sank into the brain of The Thinking Machine. When the last possibility had been considered he began an examination of his cell. From the roof, down the walls on all sides, he examined the stones and the cement between them. He stamped over the floor carefully time after time, but it was cement, perfectly solid. After the examination he sat on the edge of the iron bed and was lost in thought for a long time. For Professor Augustus S. F. X. Van Dusen, The Thinking Machine, had something to think about.

He was disturbed by a rat, which ran across his foot, then scampered away into a dark corner of the cell, frightened at its own daring. After a while The Thinking Machine, squinting steadily into the darkness of the corner where the rat had gone, was able to make out in the gloom many little beady eyes staring at him. He counted six pair, and there were perhaps others; he didn't see very well.

Then The Thinking Machine, from his seat on the bed, noticed for the first time the bottom of his cell door. There was an opening there of two inches between the steel bar and the floor. Still looking steadily at the opening, The Thinking Machine backed suddenly into the corner where he had seen the beady eyes. There was a great scampering of tiny feet, several squeaks of frightened rodents, and then silence.

None of the rats had gone out the door, yet there were none in the cell. Therefore there must be another way out of the cell, however small. The Thinking Machine, on hands and knees, started a search for the spot, feeling in the darkness with his long, slender fingers.

At last his search was rewarded. He came upon a small opening in the floor, level with the cement. It was perfectly round and somewhat larger than a silver dollar. This was the way the rats had gone. He put his fingers deep into the opening; it seemed to be a disused drainage pipe and was dry and dusty.

Having satisfied himself on this point, he sat on the bed again for an hour, then made another inspection of his surroundings through the small cell window. One of the outside guards stood directly opposite, beside the wall, and happened to be looking at the window of Cell 13 when the head of The Thinking Machine appeared. But the scientist didn't notice the guard.

Noon came and the jailer appeared with the prison dinner of repulsively plain food. At home The Thinking Machine merely ate to live; here he took what was offered without comment. Occasionally he spoke to the jailer who stood outside the door watching him.

"Any improvements made here in the last few years?" he asked.

"Nothing particularly," replied the jailer. "New wall was built four years ago."

"Anything done to the prison proper?"

"Painted the woodwork outside, and I believe about seven years ago a new system of plumbing was put in."

"Ah!" said the prisoner. "How far is the river over there?"

"About three hundred feet. The boys have a baseball ground between the wall and the river."

The Thinking Machine had nothing further to say just then, but when the jailer was ready to go he asked for some water.

"I get very thirsty here," he explained. "Would it be possible for you to leave a little water in a bowl for me?"

"I'll ask the warden," replied the jailer, and he went away.

Half an hour later he returned with water in a small earthen bowl.

"The warden says you may keep this bowl," he informed the prisoner. "But you must show it to me when I ask for it. If it is broken, it will be the last."

"Thank you," said The Thinking Machine. "I shan't break it."

The jailer went on about his duties. For just the fraction of a second it seemed that The Thinking Machine wanted to ask a question, but he didn't.

Two hours later this same jailer, in passing the door of Cell No. 13, heard a noise inside and stopped. The Thinking Machine was down on his hands and knees in a corner of the cell, and from that same corner came several frightened squeaks. The jailer looked on interestedly.

"Ah, I've got you," he heard the prisoner say.

"Got what?" he asked, sharply.

"One of these rats," was the reply. "See?" And between the scientist's long fingers the jailer saw a small gray rat struggling. The prisoner brought it over to the light and looked at it closely.

"It's a water rat," he said.

"Ain't you got anything better to do than catch rats?" asked the jailer.

"It's disgraceful that they should be here at all," was the irritated reply. "Take this one away and kill it. There are dozens more where it came from."

The jailer took the wriggling, squirmy rodent and flung it down on the floor violently. It gave one squeak and lay still. Later he reported the incident to the warden, who only smiled.

Still later that afternoon the outside armed guard on the Cell 13 side of the prison looked up again at the window and saw the prisoner looking out. He saw a hand raised to the barred window and then something white fluttered to the ground, directly under the window of Cell 13. It was a little roll of linen, evidently of white shirting material, and tied around it was a five-dollar bill. The guard looked up at the window again, but the face had disappeared.

With a grim smile he took the little linen roll and the five-dollar bill to the warden's office. There together they deciphered something which was written on it in a queer sort of ink, frequently blurred. On the outside was this:

"Finder of this please deliver to Dr. Charles Ransome."

"Ah," said the warden, with a chuckle, "plan of escape number one has gone wrong." Then, as an afterthought: "But why did he address it to Dr. Ransome?"

"And where did he get the pen and ink to write with?" asked the guard.

The warden looked at the guard and the guard looked at the warden. There was no apparent solution of that mystery. The warden studied the writing carefully, then shook his head.

"Well, let's see what he was going to say to Dr. Ransome," he said at length, still puzzled, and he unrolled the inner piece of linen.

"Well, if that—what—what do you think of that?" he asked dazed.

The guard took the bit of linen and read this:—

"Epa cseot d'net niiy awe htto n'si sih. T."

The warden spent an hour wondering what sort of cipher it was, and half an hour wondering why his prisoner should attempt to communicate with Dr. Ransome, who was the cause of his being there. After this the warden devoted some thought to the question of where the prisoner got writing materials, and what sort of writing materials he had. With the idea of illuminating this point, he examined the linen again. It was a torn part of a white shirt and had ragged edges.

Now it was possible to account for the linen, but what the prisoner had used to write with was another matter. The warden knew it would have been impossible for him to have either pen or pencil, and, besides, neither pen nor pencil had been used in this writing. What then? The warden decided to investigate personally. The Thinking Machine was his prisoner; he had orders to hold his prisoners; if this one sought to escape by sending cipher messages to persons outside, he would stop it, as he would have stopped it in the case of any other prisoner.

The warden went back to Cell 13 and found The Thinking Machine on his hands and knees on the floor, engaged in nothing more alarming than catching rats. The prisoner heard the warden's step and turned to him quickly.

"It's disgraceful," he snapped, "these rats. There are scores of them."

"Other men have been able to stand them," said the warden. "Here is another shirt for you—let me have the one you have on."

"Why?" demanded The Thinking Machine, quickly. His tone was hardly natural, his manner suggested actual perturbation.

"You have attempted to communicate with Dr. Ransome," said the warden severely. "As my prisoner, it is my duty to put a stop to it."

The Thinking Machine was silent for a moment.

"All right," he said, finally. "Do your duty."

The warden smiled grimly. The prisoner arose from the floor and removed the white shirt, putting on instead a striped convict shirt the warden had bought. The warden took the white shirt eagerly, and then and there compared the pieces of linen on which was written the cipher with certain torn places in the shirt. The Thinking Machine looked on curiously.

"The guard brought you those, then?" he asked.

"He certainly did," relied the warden triumphantly. "And that ends your first attempt to escape."

The Thinking Machine watched the warden as he, by comparison, established to his own satisfaction that only two pieces of linen had been torn from the white shirt.

"What did you write this with?' demanded the warden.

"I should think it part of your duty to find out," said The Thinking Machine, irritably.

The warden started to say some harsh things, then restrained himself and made a minute search of the cell and of the prisoner instead. He found absolutely nothing; not even a match or toothpick which might have been used for a pen. The same mystery surrounded the fluid with which the cipher had been written. Although the warden left Cell 13 visibly annoyed, he took the torn shirt in triumph.

"Well, writing notes on a shirt won't get him out, that's certain," he told himself with some complacency. He put the linen scraps into his desk to await developments. "If that man escapes from that cell I'll—hang it—I'll resign."

On the third day of his incarceration The Thinking Machine openly attempted to bribe his way out. The jailer had brought his dinner and was leaning against the barred door, waiting, when The Thinking Machine began the conversation.

"The drainage pipes of the prison lead to the river, don't they?" he asked.

"Yes," said the jailer.

"I suppose they are very small."

"Too small to crawl through, if that's what your thinking about," was the grinning response.

There was a silence until The Thinking Machine finished his meal. Then:

"You know I'm not a criminal, don't you?"

"Yes."

"And that I've a perfect right to be freed if I demand it?"

"Yes."

"Well, I came here believing I could make my escape," said the prisoner, and his squint eyes studied the face of the jailer. "Would you consider a financial reward for aiding me to escape?"

The jailer, who happened to be an honest man, looked at the slender, weak figure of the prisoner, at the large head with its mass of yellow hair, and was almost sorry.

"I guess prisons like these were not built for the likes of you to get out of," he said at last.

"But would you consider a proposition to help me get out?" the prisoner insisted, almost beseechingly.

"No," said the jailer, shortly.

"Five hundred dollars," urged The Thinking Machine. "I am not a criminal."

"No," said the jailer.

"A thousand?"

"No," again said the jailer, and he started away hurriedly to escape further temptation. Then he turned back. "If you should give me ten thousand dollars I couldn't get you out. You'd have to pass through seven doors, and I only have the keys to two."

Then he told the warden all about it.

"Plan number two fails," said the warden, smiling grimly. "First a cipher, then bribery."

When the jailer was on his way to Cell 13 at six o'clock, again bearing food to The Thinking Machine, he paused, startled by the unmistakable scrape, scrape of steel versus steel. It stopped at the sound of his steps, then craftily the jailer, who was beyond the prisoners range of vision, resumed his trampling, the sound being apparently that of a man going away from Cell 13. As a matter of fact he was in the same spot.

After a moment there came again the steady scrape, scrape, and the jailer crept cautiously on tiptoes to the door and peered between the bars. The Thinking Machine was standing in the iron bed working at the bars of the little window. He was using a file, judging from the backward and forward swing of his arms.

Cautiously the jailer crept back to the office, summoned the warden in person, and they returned to Cell 13 on tiptoes. The steady scrape was still audible. The warden listened to satisfy himself and then suddenly appeared at the door.

"Well?" he demanded, and there was a smile on his face.

The Thinking Machine glanced back from his perch on the bed and leaped suddenly to the floor, making frantic efforts to hide something. The warden went in, with hand extended.

"Give it up," he said.

"No," said the prisoner, sharply.

"Come, give it up," urged the warden. "I don't want to have to search you again."

"No," repeated the prisoner.

"What was it—a file?" asked the warden.

The Thinking Machine was silent and stood squinting at the warden with something very nearly approaching disappointment on his face— nearly, but not quite. The warden was almost sympathetic.

"Plan number three fails, eh?" he asked, good-naturedly. "Too bad, isn't it?"

The prisoner didn't say.

"Search him." instructed the warden.

The jailer searched the prisoner carefully. At last, artfully concealed in the waistband of the trousers, he found a piece of steel about two inches long, with one side curved like a half moon.

"Ah," said the warden, as he received it from the jailer. "From your shoe heel," and he smiled pleasantly.

The jailer continued his search and on the other side of the trousers waistband found another piece of steel identical with the first. The edges showed where they had been worn against the bars of the window.

"You couldn't saw through those bars with these," said the warden.

"I could have," said The Thinking Machine firmly.

"In six months, perhaps," said the warden, good-naturedly.

The warden shook his head slowly as he gazed into the slightly flushed face of his prisoner.

"Ready to give up?" he asked.

"I haven't started yet," was the prompt reply.

Then came another exhaustive search of the cell. Carefully the two men went over it, finally turning out the bed and searching that. Nothing. The warden in person climbed upon the bed and examined the bars of the window where the prisoner had been sawing. When he looked he was amused.

"Just made it a little bright by hard rubbing," he said to the prisoner, who stood looking on with a somewhat crestfallen air. The warden grasped the iron bars in his strong hands and tried to shake them. They were immovable, set firmly in the solid granite. He examined each in turn and found them all satisfactory. Finally he climbed down from the bed.

"Give it up, Professor," he advised.

The Thinking Machine shook his head and the warden and jailer passed on again. As they disappeared down the corridor The Thinking Machine sat on the edge of the bed with his head in his hands.

"He's crazy to try and get out of that cell," commented the jailer.

"Of course he can't get out," said the warden. "But he's clever. I would like to know what he wrote that cipher with."

It was four o'clock next morning when an awful, heartracking shriek of terror resounded through the great prison. It came from a cell, somewhere about the center, and its tone told a tale of horror, agony, terrible fear. The warden heard and with three of his men rushed into the long corridor leading to Cell 13.

As they ran there came again that awful cry. It died away in a sort of a wail. The white faces of prisoners appeared at cell doors upstairs and down, staring out wonderingly, frightened.

"It's that fool in Cell 13," grumbled the warden.

He stopped and stared in as one of the jailers flashed a lantern. "That fool in Cell 13" lay comfortably on his cot, flat on his back with his mouth open, snoring. Even as they looked there came again the piercing cry, from somewhere above. The wardens face blanched a little as he started up the stairs. There on the top floor he found a man in Cell 43, directly above Cell 13, but two floors higher, cowering in the corner of his cell.

"What's the matter?" demanded the warden.

"Thank God you've come," exclaimed the prisoner, and he cast himself against the bars of his cell.

"What is it?" demanded the warden again.

He threw open the door and went in. The prisoner dropped on his knees and clasped the warden about the body. His face was white with terror, his eyes were widely distended, and he was shuddering. His hands, icy cold, clutched at the warden's.

"Take me out of this cell, please take me out," he pleaded.

"What's the matter with you, anyhow?" insisted the warden, impatiently.

"I've heard something—something," said the prisoner, and his eyes roved nervously around the cell.

"What did you hear?"

"I—I can't tell you," stammered the prisoner. Then in a sudden burst of terror: "Take me out of this cell—put me anywhere—but take me out of here."

The warden and the three jailers exchanged glances.

"Who is this fellow? What's he accused of?" asked the warden.

"Joseph Ballard," said one of the jailers. "He's accused of throwing acid in a woman's face. She died from it."

"But they can't prove it," gasped the prisoner. "They can't prove it. Please put me in some other cell."

He was still clinging to the warden, and that official threw his arms off roughly. Then for a time he stood looking at the cowering wretch, who seemed possessed of all the wild, unreasoning terror of a child.

"Look here, Ballard," said the warden, finally, "if you heard anything, I want to know what it was. Now tell me."

"I can't, I can't," was the reply. He was sobbing.

"Where did it come from?"

"I don't know. Everywhere—nowhere. I just heard it."

"What was it—a voice?"

"Please don't make me answer," pleaded the prisoner.

"You must answer," said the warden, sharply.

"It was a voice—but—but it wasn't human," was the sobbing reply.

"Voice, but not human?" repeated the warden, puzzled.

"It sounded muffled and—and far away—and ghostly," explained the man.

"Did it come from inside or outside the prison?"

"It didn't seem to come from anywhere—it was just here, here, everywhere. I heard it. I heard it."

For an hour the warden tried to get the story, but Ballard had become suddenly obstinate and would say nothing—only pleaded to be placed in another cell, or to have one of the jailers remain near him until daylight. These requests were gruffly refused.

"And see here," said the warden, in conclusion, "if there's any more of this screaming I'll put you in a padded cell."

Then the warden went his way, a sadly puzzled man. Ballard sat at his cell door until daylight, his face, drawn and white with terror, pressed against the bars, and looked out into the prison with wide, staring eyes.

That day, the fourth since the incarceration of The Thinking Machine, was enlivened considerably by the volunteer prisoner, who spent most of his time at the little window of his cell. He began proceedings by throwing another piece of linen down to the guard, who picked it up dutifully and took it to the warden. On it was written:

"Only three days more."

The warden was in no way surprised at what he read; he understood that The Thinking Machine meant only three days more of his imprisonment, and he regarded the note as a boast. But how was the thing written? Where had The Thinking

Machine found the new piece of linen? Where? How? He carefully examined the linen. It was white, of fine texture, shirting material. He took the shirt which he had taken and carefully fitted the two original pieces of the linen to the torn places. The third pieces was entirely superfluous; it didn't fit anywhere, and yet it was unmistakably the same goods.

"And where—where does he get anything to write with?" demanded the warden of the world at large.

Still later on the fourth day The Thinking Machine, through the window of his cell, spoke to the armed guard outside.

"What day of the month is it?" he asked.

"The fifteenth," was the answer.

The Thinking Machine made a mental astronomical calculation and satisfied himself that the moon would not rise until after nine o'clock that night. Then he asked another question:

"Who attends to those arc lights?"

"Man from the company."

"You have no electricians in the building?"

"No."

"I should think you could save money if you had your own man."

"None of my business," relied the guard.

The guard noticed The Thinking Machine at the cell window frequently during that day, but always the face seemed listless and there was a certain wistfulness in the squint eyes behind the glasses. After a while he accepted the presence of the leonine head as a matter of course. He had seen other prisoners do the same thing; it was the longing for the outside world.

That afternoon, just before the day guard was relieved, the head appeared at the window again, and The Thinking Machine's hand held something out between the bars. It fluttered to the ground and the guard picked it up. It was five-dollar bill.

"That's for you," called the prisoner.

As usual, the guard took it to the warden. The gentleman looked at it suspiciously; he looked at everything that came from Cell 13 with suspicion.

"He said it was for me," explained the guard.

"It's a sort of tip, I suppose," said the warden. "I see no particular reason why you shouldn't accept—"

Suddenly he stopped. He had remembered that The Thinking Machine had gone into Cell 13 with one five-dollar bill and two ten-dollar bills; twenty-five dollars in all. Now a five-dollar bill had been tied around the first pieces of linen that came from the cell. The warden still had it, and to convince himself he took it out and looked at it. It was five dollars; yet here was another five dollars, and The Thinking Machine had only had ten-dollar bills.

"Perhaps somebody changed one of the bills for him," he thought at last, with a sigh of relief.

But then and there he made up his mind. He would search Cell 13 as a cell was never searched in this world. When a man could write at will, and change money, and do other wholly inexplicable things, there was something radically wrong with his prison. He planned to enter the cell at night—three o'clock would be an excellent time. The Thinking Machine must do all the weird things he did sometime. Night seemed the most reasonable.

Thus it happened that the warden stealthily descended upon Cell 13 that night at three o'clock. He paused at the door and listened. There was no sound save the steady, regular breathing of the prisoner. The keys unfastened the double locks with scarcely a clank, and the warden entered, locking the door behind him. Suddenly he flashed his dark lantern in the face of the recumbent figure.

If the warden had planned to startle The Thinking Machine he was mistaken, for that individual merely opened his eyes quietly, reached for his glasses and inquired, in a most matter-of-fact tone: "Who is it?"

It would be useless to describe the search that the warden made. It was minute. Not one inch of the cell or the bed was overlooked. He found the round hole in the floor, and with a flash of inspiration thrust his fingers into it. After a moment of fumbling there he drew up something and looked at it in the light of his lantern.

"Ugh!" he exclaimed.

The thing he had taken out was a rat—a dead rat. His inspiration fled as a mist before the sun. But he continued the search. The Thinking Machine, without a word, arose and kicked the rat out of the cell into the corridor.

The warden climbed on the bed and tried the steel bars in the tiny window. They were perfectly rigid; every bar of the door was the same.

Then the warden searched the prisoners clothing, beginning at the shoes. Nothing hidden in them! Then the trousers waistband. Still nothing! Then the pockets of the trousers. From one side he drew out some paper money and examined it.

"Five one-dollar bills," he gasped.

"That's right," said the prisoner.

"But the—you had two tens and a five—what the—how do you do it?"

"That's my business," said The Thinking Machine.

"Did any of my men change this money for you—on your word of honor?"

The Thinking Machine paused just a fraction of a second.

"No," he said.

"Well, do you make it?" asked the warden. He was prepared to believe anything.

"That's my business," again said the prisoner.

The warden glared at the eminent scientist fiercely. He felt— he knew—that this man was making a fool out of him, yet he didn't know how. If he were a real prisoner he would get the truth—but, then, perhaps, these inexplicable things which had happened would nit have been brought before him so sharply. Neither of the men spoke for a long time, then suddenly the warden turned fiercely and left the cell, slamming the door behind him. He didn't dare speak then.

He glanced at the clock. It was ten minutes to four. He had hardly settled himself in bed when again came the heartbreaking shriek through the prison. With a few muttered words, which, while not elegant, were highly expressive, he relighted his lantern and rushed through the prison again to the cell on the upper floor.

Again Ballard was crushing himself against the steel door, shrieking, shrieking at the top of his voice. He stopped only when the warden flashed his lamp in the cell.

"Take me out, take me out," he screamed. "I did it, I did it, I killed her. Take it away."

"Take what away?" asked the warden.

"I threw the acid in her face—I did it—I confess. Take me out of here."

Ballard's condition was pitiable; it was only an act of mercy to let him out into the corridor. There he crouched in a corner, like an animal at bay, and clasped his hands to his ears. It took half an hour to calm him sufficiently to speak. Then he told incoherently what had happened. On the night before at four o'clock he had heard a voice—a sepulchral voice, muffled and wailing in tone.

"What did it say?" asked the warden, curiously.

"Acid—acid—acid!" gasped the prisoner. "It accused me. Acid! I threw the acid, and the woman died. Oh!" It was a long, shuddering wail of terror.

"Acid?" echoed the warden, puzzled. The case was beyond him.

"Acid. That's all I heard—that one word, repeated several times. There were other things too, but I didn't hear them."

"That was last night, eh?" asked the warden. "What happened tonight— what frightened you just now?"

"It was the same thing," gasped the prisoner. "Acid—acid—acid!" He covered his face with his hands and sat shivering. "It was acid I used on her, but I didn't mean to kill her. I just heard the words. It was something accusing me—accusing me." He mumbled, and was silent.

"Did you hear anything else?"

"Yes—but I could understand—only a little bit—just a word or two."

"Well, what was it?"

"I heard 'acid' three times, then I heard a long, moaning sound, then—then—I heard 'No. 8 hat.' I heard that twice."

"No. 8 hat," repeated the warden. "What the devil—No. 8 hat? Accusing voices of conscience have never talked about No. 8 hats, so far as I ever heard."

"He's insane," said one of the jailers, with an air of finality.

"I believe you," said the warden. "He must be. He probably heard something and got frightened. He's trembling now. No. 8 hat! What the—"

When the fifth day of The Thinking Machine's imprisonment rolled around the warden was wearing a hunted look. He was anxious for the end of the thing. He could not help but feel that his distinguished prisoner had been amusing himself. And if this were so, The Thinking Machine had lost none of his sense of humor. For on this fifth day he flung down another linen note to the outside guard, bearing the words: "Only two days more." Also he flung down half a dollar.

Now the warden knew—he knew—that the man in Cell 13 didn't have any half dollars—he couldn't have any half dollars, no more than he could have pen and ink and linen, and yet he did have them. It was a condition, not a theory; that is one reason why the warden was wearing a hunted look.

That ghastly, uncanny thing, too, about "Acid" and "No. 8 hat" clung to him tenaciously. They didn't mean anything, of course, merely the ravings of an insane murderer who had been driven by fear to confess his crime, still there were so many things that "didn't mean anything" happening in the prison now since The Thinking Machine was there.

On the sixth day the warden received a card stating that Dr. Ransome and Mr. Fielding would be at Chisholm Prison on the following evening, Thursday, and in the event of Professor Van Dusen had not yet escaped—and they presumed he had not because they had not heard from him—they would meet him there.

"In the event he had not yet escaped!" The warden smiled grimly. Escaped!

The Thinking Machine enlivened this day for the warden with three notes. They were on the usual linen and bore generally on the appointment at half past eight o'clock Thursday night, which appointment the scientist had made at the time of his imprisonment.

On the afternoon of the seventh day the warden passed Cell 13 and glanced in. The Thinking Machine was lying on the iron bed, apparently sleeping lightly. The cell appeared precisely as it always did from a casual glance. The warden would swear that no man was going to leave it between that hour—it was then four o'clock—and half past eight o'clock that evening.

On his way back past the cell the warden heard the steady breathing again, and coming close to the door looked in. He wouldn't have done so if The Thinking Machine had been looking, but now—well, it was different.

A ray of light came through the high window and fell on the face of the sleeping man. It occurred to the warden for the first time that his prisoner appeared haggard and weary. Just then The Thinking Machine stirred slightly and the warden hurried on up the corridor guiltily. That evening after six o'clock he saw the jailer.

"Everything all right in Cell 13?" he asked.

"Yes sir," replied the jailer. "He didn't eat much, though."

It was with a feeling of having done his duty that the warden received Dr. Ransome and Mr. Fielding shortly after seven o'clock. He intended to show them the linen notes and lay before them the full story of his woes, which was a long one. But before this came to pass the guard from the river side of the prison yard entered the office.

"The arc light in my side of the yard won't light," he informed the warden.

"Confound it, that man's a hoodoo," thundered the official. "everything has happened since he's been here."

The guard went back to his post in the darkness, and the warden phoned to the electric light company.

"This is Chisholm Prison," he said through the phone. "Send three or four men down here quick, to fix an arc light."

The reply was evidently satisfactory, for the warden hung up the receiver and passed out into the yard. While Dr. Ransome and Mr. Fielding sat waiting, the guard at the outer gate came in with a special-delivery letter. Dr. Ransome happened to notice the address, and, when the guard went out, looked at the letter more closely.

"By George!" he exclaimed.

"What is it?" asked Mr. Fielding.

Silently the doctor offered the letter. Mr. Fielding examined it closely.

"Coincidence," he said. "It must be."

It was nearly eight o'clock when the warden returned to his office. The electricians had arrived in a wagon, and were now at work. The warden pressed the buzz-button communicating with the man at the outer gate in the wall.

"How many electricians came in?" he asked, over the short phone. "Four? Three workmen in jumpers and overalls and the manager? Frock coat and silk hat? All right. Be certain that only four go out. That's all."

He turned to Dr. Ransome and Mr. Fielding.

"We have to be careful here—particularly," and there was broad sarcasm in his tone, "since we have scientists locked up."

The warden picked up the special delivery letter carelessly, and then began to open it.

"When I read this I want to tell you gentlemen something about how— Great Caesar!" he ended, suddenly, as he glanced at the letter. He sat with mouth open, motionless, from astonishment.

"What is it?" asked Mr. Fielding.

"A special delivery letter from Cell 13," gasped the warden. "An invitation to supper."

"What?" and the two others arose, unanimously.

The warden sat dazed, staring at the letter for a moment, then called sharply to a guard outside the corridor.

"Run down to Cell 13 and see if that man's in there."

The guard went as directed, while Dr. Ransome and Mr. Fielding examined the letter.

"It's Van Dusen's handwriting; there's no question of that," said Dr. Ransome. "I've seen too much of it."

Just then the buzz on the telephone from the outer gate sounded, and the warden, in a semi-trance, picked up the receiver.

"Hello! Two reporters, eh? Let 'em come in." He turned suddenly to the doctor and Mr. Fielding. "Why; the man can't be out. He must be in his cell."

Just at that moment the guard returned.

"He's still in his cell, sir," he reported, "I saw him. He's lying down."

"There, I told you so," said the warden, and he breathed freely again. "But how did he mail that letter?"

There was a rap on the steel door which led from the jail yard into the warden's office.

"It's the reporters," said the warden. "Let them in," he instructed the guard; then to the other two gentlemen: "Don't say anything about this before them, because I'd never hear the last of it."

The door opened, and the two men from the front gate entered.

"Good-evening, gentlemen," said one. That was Hutchinson Hatch; the warden knew him well.

"Well?" demanded the other, irritably. "I'm here."

That was The Thinking Machine.

He squinted belligerently at the warden, who sat with mouth agape. For the moment that official had nothing to say. Dr. Ransome and Mr. Fielding were amazed, but they didn't know what the warden knew. They were only amazed; he was paralyzed. Hutchinson Hatch, the reporter, took in the scene with greedy eyes.

"How—how—how did you do it?" gasped the warden, finally.

"Come back to the cell," said The Thinking Machine, in the irritated voice which his scientific associates knew so well.

The warden, still in a condition bordering on trance, led the way.

"Flash your light in there," directed The Thinking Machine.

The warden did so. There was nothing unusual in the appearance of the cell, and there—there on the bed lay the figure of The Thinking Machine. Certainly! There was the yellow hair! Again the warden looked at the man beside him and wondered at the strangeness of his own dreams.

With trembling hands he unlocked the cell door and The Thinking Machine passed inside.

"See here," he said.

He kicked at the steel bars in the bottom of the cell door and three of them were pushed out of place. A fourth broke off and rolled away in the corridor.

"And here, too," directed the erstwhile prisoner as he stood on the bed to reach the small window. He swept his hand across the opening and every bar came out.

"What's this in bed?" demanded the warden, who was slowly recovering.

"A wig," was the reply. "Turn down the cover."

The warden did so. Beneath it lay a large coil of strong rope, thirty feet or more, a dagger, three files, ten feet of electric wire, a thin, powerful pair of steel pliers, a small track hammer with its handle, and—a derringer pistol.

"How did you do it?" demanded the warden.

"You gentlemen have an engagement to supper with me at half past nine o'clock," said The Thinking Machine. "Come on, or we shall be late."

"But how did you do it?" insisted the warden.

"Don't ever think you can hold any man who can use his brain," said The Thinking Machine. "Come on; we shall be late."

It was an impatient supper party in the rooms of Professor Van Dusen and a somewhat silent one. The guests were Dr. Ransome, Alfred Fielding, the warden, and Hutchinson Hatch, reporter, The meal was served to the minute, in accordance with Professor Van Dusen's instructions of one week before; Dr. Ransome found the artichokes delicious. At last supper was finished and The Thinking Machine turned on Dr. Ransome and squinted at him fiercely.

"Do you believe it now?" he demanded.

"I do," replied Dr. Ransome.

"Do you admit that it was a fair test?"

"I do."

With the others, particularly the warden, he was waiting anxiously for the explanation.

"Suppose you tell us how—" began Mr. Fielding.

"Yes, tell us how," said the warden.

The Thinking Machine readjusted his glasses, took a couple of preparatory squints at his audience, and began his story. He told it from the beginning logically; and no man ever talked to more interested listeners.

"My agreement was," he began, "to go into a cell, carrying nothing except what was necessary to wear, and to leave that cell within a week. I had never seen Chisholm Prison. When I went into the cell I asked for tooth powder, two ten—and one five-dollar bills, and also to have my shoes blacked. Even if these requests had been refused it would not have mattered seriously. But you agreed to them.

"I knew there would be nothing in the cell which you thought I might use to advantage. So when the warden locked the door on me I was apparently helpless, unless I could turn three seemingly innocent things to use. They were things which would have been permitted any prisoner under sentence of death, were they not, warden?"

"Tooth powder and polished shoes, yes, but not money," replied the warden.

"Anything is dangerous in the hands of a man who knows how to use it," went on The Thinking Machine. "I did nothing that first night but sleep and chase rats." he glared at the warden. "When the subject was broached I knew I could do nothing that night, so suggested the next day. You gentleman thought I wanted time to arrange an escape with outside assistance, but this was not true. I knew I could communicate with whom I pleased, when I pleased."

The warden stared at him a moment, then went on smoking solemnly.

"I was aroused next morning at six o'clock by the jailer with my breakfast," continued the scientist. "He told me dinner was at twelve and supper at six. Between these times, I gathered, I would be pretty much to myself. So immediately after breakfast I examined my outside surroundings from my cell window. One look told me it would be useless to try to scale the wall, even should I decide to leave my cell by the window, for my purpose was to leave not only the cell, but the prison. Of course, I could have gone over the wall, but it would have taken me longer to lay my plans that way. Therefore, for the moment, I dismissed all idea of that.

"From this first observation I knew the river was on that side of the prison, and that there was also a playground there. Subsequently these surmises were verified by a keeper. I knew then one important thing— that anyone might approach the prison wall from that side if necessary without attracting any particular attention. That was well to remember. I remembered it.

"But the outside thing which most attracted my attention was the feed wire to the arc light which ran within a few feet— probably three or four—of my cell window. I knew that would be valuable in the event I found it necessary to cut off that arc light."

"Oh, you shut it off to-night, then?" asked the warden.

"Having learned all I could from the window," resumes The Thinking Machine, without heeding the interruption, "I considered the idea of escaping through the prison proper. I recalled just how I had come into the cell, which I knew would be the only way. Seven doors lay between me and the outside. So, also for the time being, I gave up the idea of escaping that way. And I couldn't go through the solid granite walls of the cell."

The Thinking Machine paused for a moment and Dr. Ransome lighted a new cigar. For several minutes there was silence, then the scientific jailbreaker went on:

"While I was thinking about these things a rat ran across my foot. It suggested a new line of thought. There were at least half a dozen rats in the cell—I could see their beady eyes. Yet I had noticed none come under the cell door. I frightened them purposely and watched the cell door to see if they went out that way. They did not, but they were gone. Obviously they went another way. Another way meant another opening.

"I searched for this opening and found it. It was an old drain pipe, long unused and partly choked with dirt and dust. But this was the way the rats had come. They came from somewhere. Where? Drain pipes usually lead outside prison grounds. This one probably led to the river, or near it. The rats must therefore come from that direction. If they came a part of the way, I reasoned they came all the way, because it was extremely unlikely that a solid iron or lead pipe would have any hole in it except at the exit.

"When the jailer came with my luncheon he told me two important things, although he didn't know it. One was that a new system of plumbing had been put in the prison seven years before; another that the river was only three hundred feet away. Then I knew positively that the pipe was a part of the old system; I knew, too, that it slanted generally toward the river. But did the pipe end on the water or on land?

"This was the next question to be decided. I decided it by catching several of the rats in the cell. My jailer was surprised to see me engaged in this work. I examined at least a dozen of them. They were perfectly dry; they had come through the pipe, and, most important of all, they were not house rats, but field rats. The other end of the pipe was on land, then, outside the prison walls. So far, so good.

"Then, I knew that if I worked freely from this point I must attract the warden's attention in another direction. You see, by telling the warden that I had come to escape you made the test more severe, because I had to trick him by false scents."

The warden looked up with a sad expression in his eyes.

"The first thing was to make him think I was trying to communicate with you, Dr. Ransome. So I wrote a note on a piece of linen I tore from my shirt, addressed it to Dr. Ransome, tied a five-dollar bill around it and threw it out the window. I knew the guard would take it to the warden, but I rather hoped the warden would send it as addressed. Have you the first linen note, warden?"

The warden produced the cipher.

"What does it mean, anyhow?" he asked.

"Read it backward, beginning with the 'T' signature and disregard the division into words," instructed The Thinking Machine.

The warden did so. "T-h-i-s, this," he spelled, studied it for a moment, then read it off, grinning:

"This is not the way I intend to escape.

"Well, now what do you think o' that? he demanded, still grinning.

"I knew that would attract your attention, just as it did," said The Thinking Machine, "and if you really found out what it was it would be a sort of gentle rebuke."

"What did you write it with?" asked Dr. Ransome, after he had examined the linen and passed it to Mr. Fielding.

"This," said the erstwhile prisoner, and he extended his foot. On it was the shoe he had worn in prison, though the polish was gone— scraped off clean. "The shoe blacking, moistened with water, was my ink; the metal tip of the shoe lace made a fairly good pen."

The warden looked up and suddenly burst into a laugh, half of relief, half of amusement.

"You're a wonder," he said, admiringly. "Go on."

"That precipitated a search of my cell by the warden, as I had intended," continued The Thinking Machine. "I was anxious to get the warden in the habit of searching my cell, so that finally, constantly finding nothing, he would get disgusted and quit. This at last happened, practically."

The warden blushed.

"He then took my white shirt away and gave me a prison shirt. He was satisfied that those two pieces of the shirt were all that was missing. But while he was searching my cell I had another pieces of that same shirt, about nine inches square, rolled up into a small ball in my mouth."

"Nine inches of that shirt?" demanded the warden. "Where did it come from?"

"The bosoms of all stiff white shirts are of triple thickness," was the explanation. "I tore out the inside thickness, leaving the bosom only two thicknesses. I knew you wouldn't see it. So much for that."

There was a little pause, and the warden looked from one to another of the men with a sheepish grin.

"Having disposed of the warden for the time being by giving him something else to think about, I took my first serious step toward freedom," said Professor Van Dusen. "I knew, within reason, that the pipe led somewhere to the playground outside; I knew a great many boys played there; I knew the rats came into my cell from out there. Could I communicate with some one outside with these things at hand?

"First was necessary, I saw, a long and fairly reliable thread, so— but here," he pulled up his trousers legs and showed that the tops of both stockings, of fine, strong lisle, were gone. "I unraveled those— after I got them started it wasn't difficult— and I had easily a quarter of a mile of thread that I could depend on.

"Then on half of my remaining linen I wrote, laboriously enough I assure you, a letter explaining my situation to this gentleman here," and he indicated Hutchinson Hatch. "I knew he would assist me—for the value of the newspaper story. I tied firmly to this linen letter a ten-dollar bill—there is no surer way of attracting the eye of anyone—and wrote on the linen: 'finder of this deliver to Hutchinson Hatch, Daily American, who will give another ten dollars for the information'".

The next thing was to get this note outside on that playground where a boy might find it. There were two ways, but I chose the best. I took one of the rats—I became adept at catching them—tied the linen and money firmly to one leg, fastened my lisle thread to another, and turned him loose in the drain pipe. I reasoned that the natural fright of the rodent would make him run until he was outside the pipe and then out on earth he would probably stop to gnaw off the linen and money.

"From the moment the rat disappeared into that dusty pipe I became anxious. I was taking so many chances. The rat might gnaw the string, of which I held one end; other rats might gnaw at it; the rat might run out of the pipe and leave the linen and money where they would never be found; a thousand other things might have happened. So began some nervous hours, but the fact that the rat ran on until only a few feet of the string remained in my cell made me think he was outside the pipe. I had carefully instructed Mr. Hatch what to do in case the note reached him. The question was: Would it reach him?

"This done, I could only wait and make other plans in case this one failed. I openly attempted to bribe my jailer, and I learned from him that he held the keys to only two of seven doors between me and freedom. Then I did something else to make the warden nervous. I took the steel supports out of the heels of my shoes and made a pretense of sawing the bars of my cell window. The warden raised a pretty row about that. He developed, too, the habit of shaking the bars of my cell window to see if they were solid. They were—then"

Again the warden grinned. He had ceased being astonished.

"With this one plan I had done all I could and could only wait to see what happened," the scientist went on. "I couldn't know whether my note had been delivered or even found, or whether the mouse had gnawed it up. And I didn't dare to draw back through the pipe the one slender thread which connected me with the outside.

"When I went to bed that night I didn't sleep, for fear there would come the slight signal twitch at the thread which was to tell me that Mr. Hatch had received the note. At half past three o'clock, I judge, I felt this twitch, and no prisoner actually under sentence of death ever welcomed a thing more heartily."

The Thinking Machine stopped and turned to the reporter.

"You'd better explain just what you did," he said.

"The linen note was brought to me by a small boy who had been playing baseball," said Mr. Hatch. "I immediately saw a big story in it, so I gave the boy another ten dollars, and got several spools of silk, some twine, and a roll of light, pliable wire. The Professor's note suggested that I have the finder of the note show me just where it was picked up, and told me to make my search from there, beginning at two o'clock in the morning. If I found the other end of the thread, I was to twitch it gently three times, then a fourth.

"I began the search with a small-bulb electric light. It was an hour and twenty minutes before I found the end of the drain pipe, half hidden in the weeds. The pipe was very large there, say twelve inches across. Then I found the end of the lisle thread, twitched it as directed and immediately I got an answering twitch.

"Then I fastened the silk to this and Professor Van Dusen began to pull it into his cell. I nearly had heart disease for fear the string would break. To the end of the silk I fastened the twine, and when that had been pulled in I tied on the wire. Then that was drawn into the pipe and we had a substantial line, which rats couldn't gnaw, from the mouth of the drain into the cell."

The Thinking Machine raised his hand and Hatch stopped.

"All this was done in absolute silence," said the scientist, "but when the wire reached my hand I could have shouted. Then we tried another experiment, which Mr. Hatch was prepared for. I tested the pipe as a speaking tube. Neither of us could hear very clearly, but I dared not speak loud for fear of attracting attention in the prison. At last I made him understand what I wanted immediately. He seemed to have great difficulty in understanding when I asked for nitric acid, and I repeated the word 'acid' several times.

"Then I heard a shriek from a cell above me. I knew instantly that someone had overheard, and when I heard you coming, Mr. Warden, I feigned sleep. If you had entered my cell at that moment the whole plan of escape would have ended there. But you passed on. That was the nearest I ever came to being caught.

"Having established this improvised trolley it is easy to see how I got things into the cell and made them disappear at will. I merely dropped them back into the pipe. You, Mr. Warden, could not have reached the connecting wire with your fingers; they are too large. My fingers, you see, are longer and more slender. In addition I guarded the top of that pipe with a rat—you remember how."

"I remember," said the warden, with a grimace.

"I thought that if anyone were tempted to investigate that hole the rat would dampen his ardor. Mr. Hatch could not send me anything useful through the pipe until next night, although he did send me change for ten dollars as a test, so I proceeded with other parts of my plan. Then I evolved the method of escape I finally employed.

"In order to carry this out successfully it was necessary for the guard in the yard to get accustomed to seeing me at the cell window. I arranged this by dropping linen notes to him, boastful in tone, to make the warden believe, if possible, one of his assistants was communicating with the outside for me. I would stand at my window for hours gazing out, so the guard could see me, and occasionally I spoke to him. In that way I learned the prison had no electricians of its own, but was dependent upon the lighting company should anything go wrong.

"That cleared the way to freedom perfectly. Early in the evening of the last day of my imprisonment, when it was dark, I planned to cut the feed wire which was only a few feet from my window, reaching it with an acid tipped wire I had. That would make that side of the prison perfectly dark while the electricians were searching for the break. That would also bring Mr. Hatch into the prison yard."

"There was only one more thing to do before I actually began the work of setting myself free. This was to arrange final details with Mr. Hatch through our speaking tube. I did this within half an hour after the warden left my cell on the fourth night of my imprisonment. Mr. Hatch again had serious difficulty in understanding me, and I repeated the word 'acid' to him several time, and later on the words: 'No. 8 hat'—that's my size—and these were the things which made the prisoner upstairs confess to murder, so one of the jailers told me the next day. The prisoner had heard our voices, confused of course, through the pipe, which also went to his cell. The cell directly over me was not occupied, hence no one else heard.

"Of course the actual work of cutting the steel bars out of the window and door was comparatively easy with nitric acid, which I got through the pipe in tin bottles, but it took time. Hour after hour on the fifth and sixth and seventh days the guard below was looking at me as I worked on the bars of the window with the acid on a piece of wire. I used the tooth powder to prevent the acid spreading. I looked away abstractly as I worked and each minute the acid cut deeper into the metal. I noticed that the jailers always tried the door by shaking the upper part, never the lower bars, therefore I cut the lower bars, leaving them hanging in place by thin strips of metal. But that was a bit of daredeviltry. I could not have gone away so easily."

The Thinking Machine sat silent for several minutes.

"I think that makes everything clear," he went on. "Whatever points I have not explained were merely to confuse the warden and jailers. These things in my bed I brought in to please Mr. Hatch, who wanted to improve the story. Of course, the wig was necessary in my plan. The special delivery letter I wrote and directed in my cell with Mr. Hatch's fountain pen, then sent it out to him and he mailed it. That's all, I think."

"But your actually leaving the prison grounds and then coming in through the outer gate to my office?" asked the warden.

"Perfectly simple," said the scientist. "I cut the electric light wire with acid, as I said, when the current was off. Therefore when the current was turned on the arc didn't light. I knew it would take some time to find out what was the matter and make repairs. When the guard went to report to you the yard was dark, I crept out the window—it was a tight fit, too—replaced the bars by standing on a narrow ledge and remained in shadow until the force of electricians arrived. Mr. Hatch was one of them.

"When I saw him I spoke and he handed me a cap, a jumper and overalls, which I put on within ten feet of you, Mr. Warden, while you were in the yard. Later Mr. Hatch called me, presumably as a workman, and together we went out the gate to get something out of the wagon. The gate guard let us pass out readily as two workmen who had just passed in. We changed our clothing and reappeared, asking to see you. We saw you. That's all."

There was a silence for several minutes. Dr. Ransome was first to speak.

"Wonderful!" he exclaimed. "Perfectly amazing."

"How did Mr. Hatch happen to come in with the electricians?" asked Mr. Fielding.

"His father is manager of the company," relied The Thinking Machine.

"But what if there had been no Mr. Hatch outside to help?"

"Every prisoner has one friend outside who would help him escape if he could."

"Suppose—just suppose—there had been no old plumbing system there?" asked the warden, curiously.

"There were two other ways out," said The Thinking Machine, enigmatically.

Ten minutes later the telephone bell rang, it was a request for the warden.

"Light all right, eh?" the warden asked, through the phone. "Good. Wire cut beside Cell 13? Yes, I know. One electrician too many? What's that? Two came out?"

The warden turned to the others with a puzzled expression.

"He only let in four electricians, he has let out two and says there are three left."

"I was the odd one," said The Thinking Machine.

"Oh," said the warden. "I see." Then through the phone: "Let the fifth man go. He's all right."

# THE GATEWAY OF
# THE MONSTER

## BY WILLIAM HOPE HODGSON

William Hope Hodgson

## ORIGINALLY PUBLISHED IN 1913

# THE GATEWAY OF THE MONSTER

## BY WILLIAM HOPE HODGSON

William Hope Hodgson's Carnacki was certainly one of the most singular of the Edwardian detectives. His specialty was cases involving the alleged supernatural, hence the title Ghost-Finder.

Carnacki approach to the supernatural was very scientific and modern. His investigations involved some of the latest technologies including various electronic devices to both detect and ward off ghosts. He was also quite open minded on the subject. In a number of his cases he was able to prove them as hoaxes, but there were also instances of what appeared to be real supernatural manifestations.

The Carnacki stories first appeared in 1910 in the magazine *The Idler*. Seven of the stories appeared in the 1913 collection *Carnacki the Ghost-Finder*. Three additional stories were published after the author's death in various other magazines, with the last appearing in *WeirdTales* in 1947.

William Hope Hodgson (1877-1918) wrote in a number of genre's including horror and science fiction. Many of these stories involve the sea, the result of his early experiences as a sailor.

# THE GATEWAY OF THE MONSTER

(Thomas Carnacki, the famous Investigator of "real" ghost stories, tells here his incredibly weird experience in the Electric Pentacle)

In response to Carnacki's usual card of invitation to have dinner and listen to a story, I arrived promptly at 427, Cheyne Walk, to find the three others who were always invited to these happy little times, there before me. Five minutes later, Carnacki, Arkright, Jessop, Taylor and I were all engaged in the "pleasant occupation" of dining.

"You've not been long away, this time," I remarked as I finished my soup; forgetting momentarily, Carnacki's dislike of being asked even to skirt the borders of his story until such time as he was ready. Then he would not stint words.

"That's all," he replied with brevity; and I changed the subject, remarking that I had been buying a new gun, to which piece of news he gave an intelligent nod, and a smile which I think showed a genuinely good-humoured appreciation of my intentional changing of the conversation.

Later, when dinner was finished, Carnacki snugged himself comfortably down in his big chair, along with his pipe, and began his story, with very little circumlocution:

"As Dodgson was remarking just now, I've only been away a short time, and for a very good reason too—I've only been away a short distance. The exact locality I am afraid I must not tell you; but it is less than twenty miles from here; though, except for changing a name, that won't spoil the story. And it is a story too! One of the most extraordinary things I have ever run against.

"I received a letter a fortnight ago from a man I must call Anderson, asking for an appointment. I arranged a time, and when he came, I found that he wished me to investigate, and see whether I could not clear up a long-standing and well—too well—authenticated case of what he termed 'haunting.' He gave me very full particulars, and finally, as the thing seemed to present something unique, I decided to take it up.

"Two days later, I drove to the house, late in the afternoon. I found it a very old place, standing quite alone in its own grounds. Anderson had left a letter with the butler, I found, pleading excuses for his absence, and leaving the whole house at my disposal for my investigations. The butler evidently knew the object of my visit, and I questioned him pretty thoroughly during dinner, which I had in rather lonely state. He is an old and privileged servant, and had the history of the Grey Room exact in detail. From him I learned more particulars regarding two things that Anderson had mentioned in but a casual manner. The first was that the door of the Grey Room would be heard in the dead of night to open, and slam heavily, and this even though the butler knew it was locked, and the key on the bunch in his pantry. The second was that the bedclothes would always be found torn off the bed, and hurled in a heap into a corner.

"But it was the door slamming that chiefly bothered the old butler. Many and many a time, he told me, had he lain awake and just got shivering with fright, listening; for sometimes the door would be slammed time after time—thud! thud! thud!—so that sleep was impossible.

"From Anderson, I knew already that the room had a history extending back over a hundred and fifty years. Three people had been strangled in it—an ancestor of his and his wife and child. This is authentic, as I had taken very great pains to discover, so that you can imagine it was with a feeling that I had a striking case to investigate, that I went upstairs after dinner to have a look at the Grey Room.

"Peter, the old butler, was in rather a state about my going, and assured me with much solemnity that in all the twenty years of his service, no one had ever entered that room after nightfall. He begged me, in quite a fatherly way, to wait till the morning, when there would be no danger, and then he could accompany me himself.

"Of course, I smiled a little at him, and told me not to bother. I explained that I should do no more than look around a bit, and perhaps affix a few seals. He need not fear; I was used to that sort of thing. But he shook his head, when I said that.

"'There isn't many ghosts like ours, sir,' he assured me, with mournful pride. And, by Jove! he was right, as you will see.

"I took a couple of candles, and Peter followed, with his bunch of keys. He unlocked the door; but would not come inside with me. He was evidently in a fright, and renewed his request, that I would put off my examination, until daylight. Of course, I laughed at him again, and told him he could stand sentry at the door, and catch anything that came out.

"'It never comes outside, sir,' he said, in his funny, old, solemn manner. Somehow he managed to make me feel as if I were going to have the 'creeps' right away. Anyway, it was one to him, you know.

"I left him there, and examined the room. It is a big apartment, and well furnished in the grand style, with a huge four-poster, which stands with its head to the end wall. There were two candles on the mantelpiece and two on each of the three tables that were in the room. I lit the lot, and after that the room felt a little less inhumanly dreary; though, mind you, it was quite fresh, and well kept in every way.

"After I had taken a good look round I sealed lengths of baby ribbon across the windows, along the walls, over the pictures, and over the fireplace and the wall-closets. All the time, as I worked, the butler stood just without the door, and I could not persuade him to enter; though I jested with him a little, as I stretched the ribbons, and went here and there about my work. Every now and again, he would say:—'You'll excuse me, I'm sure, sir; but I do wish you would come out, sir. I'm fair in a quake for you.'

"I told him he need not wait; but he was loyal enough in his way to what he considered his duty. He said he could not go away and leave me all alone there. He apologised; but made it very clear that I did not realise the danger of the room; and I could see, generally, that he was in a pretty frightened state. All the same, I had to make the room so that I should know if anything material entered it; so I asked him not to bother me, unless he really heard something. He was beginning to get on my nerves, and the 'feel' of the room was bad enough, without making it any nastier.

"For a time further, I worked, stretching ribbons across the floor, and sealing them, so that the merest touch would have broken them, were anyone to venture into the room in the dark with the intention of playing the fool. All this had taken me far longer than I had anticipated; and, suddenly, I heard a clock strike eleven. I had taken off my coat soon after commencing work; now, however, as I had practically made an end of all that I intended to do, I walked across to the settee, and picked it up. I was in the act of getting into it when the old butler's voice (he had not said a word for the last hour) came sharp and frightened:—'Come out, sir, quick! There's something going to happen!' Jove! but I jumped, and then, in the same moment, one of the candles on the table to the left of the bed went out. Now whether it was the wind, or what, I do not know; but just for a moment, I was enough startled to make a run for the door; though I am glad to say that I pulled up before I reached it. I simply could not bunk out, with the butler standing there, after having, as it were, read him a sort of lesson on 'bein' brave, y'know.' So I just turned right round, picked up the two candles off the mantelpiece, and walked across to the table near the bed. Well, I saw nothing. I blew out the candle that was still alight; then I went to those on the two other tables, and blew them out. Then, outside of the door, the old man called again:—'Oh! sir, do be told! Do be told!'

"'All right, Peter,' I said, and, by Jove, my voice was not as steady as I should have liked! I made for the door, and had a bit of work, not to start running. I took some thundering long strides, as you can imagine. Near the door, I had a sudden feeling that there was a cold wind in the room. It was almost as if the window had been suddenly opened a little. I got to the door and the old butler gave back a step, in a sort of instinctive way. 'Collar the candles, Peter!' I said, pretty sharply, and shoved them into his hands. I turned, and caught the handle, and slammed the door shut, with a crash. Somehow, do you know, as I did so, I thought I felt something pull back on it; but it must have been only fancy. I turned the key in the lock, and then again, double-locking the door. I felt easier then, and set-to and sealed the door. In addition, I put my card over the keyhole, and sealed it there; after which I pocketed the key, and went downstairs—with Peter; who was nervous and silent, leading the way. Poor old beggar! It had not struck me until that moment that he had been enduring a considerable strain during the last two or three hours.

"About midnight, I went to bed. My room lay at the end of the corridor upon which opens the door of the Grey Room. I counted the doors between it and mine, and found that five rooms lay between. And I am sure you can understand that I was not sorry. Then, just as I was beginning to undress, an idea came to me, and I took my candle and sealing-wax, and sealed the doors of all the five rooms. If any door slammed in the night, I should know just which one.

"I returned to my room, locked the door, and went to bed. I was waked suddenly from a deep sleep by a loud crash somewhere out in the passage. I sat up in bed and listened, but heard nothing. Then I lit my candle. I was in the very act of lighting it when there came the bang of a door being violently slammed, along the corridor. I jumped out of bed, and got my revolver. I unlocked my door, and went out into the passage, holding my candle high, and keeping the pistol ready. Then a queer thing happened. I could not go a step towards the Grey Room. You all know I am not really a cowardly chap. I've gone into too many cases connected with ghostly things, to be accused of that; but I tell you I funked it; simply funked it, just like any blessed kid. There was something precious unholy in the air that night. I backed into my bedroom, and shut and locked the door. Then I sat on the bed all night, and listened to the dismal thudding of a door up the corridor. The sound seemed to echo through all the house.

"Daylight came at last, and I washed and dressed. The door had not slammed for about an hour, and I was getting back my nerve again. I felt ashamed of myself; though in some ways it was silly, for when you're meddling with that sort of thing, your nerve is bound to go, sometimes. And you just have to sit quiet and call yourself a coward until daylight. Sometimes it is more than just cowardice, I fancy. I believe at times it is something warning you, and fighting for you. But, all the same, I always feel mean and miserable, after a time like that.

"When the day came properly, I opened my door, and, keeping my revolver handy, went quietly along the passage. I had to pass the head of the stairs, on the way, and who should I see coming up, but the old butler, carrying a cup of coffee. He had merely tucked his nightshirt into his trousers, and he had an old pair of carpet slippers on.

"'Hello, Peter!' I said, feeling suddenly cheerful; for I was as glad as any lost child to have a live human being close to me. 'Where are you off to with the refreshments?'

"The old man gave a start, and slopped some of the coffee. He stared up at me and I could see that he looked white and done-up. He came on up the stairs and held out the little tray to me. 'I'm very thankful indeed, sir, to see you safe and well,' he said. 'I feared, one time, you might risk going into the Grey Room, sir. I've lain awake all night, with the sound of the door. And when it came light, I thought I'd make you a cup of coffee. I knew you would want to look at the seals, and somehow it seems safer if there's two, sir.'

"'Peter,' I said, 'you're a brick. This is very thoughtful of you.' And I drank the coffee. 'Come along,' I told him, and handed him back the tray. 'I'm going to have a look at what the brutes have been up to. I simply hadn't the pluck to in the night.'

"'I'm very thankful, sir,' he replied. 'Flesh and blood can do nothing, sir, against devils; and that's what's in the Grey Room after dark.'

"I examined the seals on all the doors, as I went along, and found them right; but when I got to the Grey Room, the seal was broken; though the card, over the keyhole, was untouched. I ripped it off, and unlocked the door, and went in, rather cautiously, as you can imagine; but the whole room was empty of anything to frighten one, and there was heaps of light. I examined all my seals, and not a single one was disturbed. The old butler had followed me in, and, suddenly, he called out:— 'The bedclothes, sir!'

"I ran up to the bed, and looked over; and, surely, they were lying in the corner to the left of the bed. Jove! you can imagine how queer I felt. Something had been in the room. I stared for a while, from the bed, to the clothes on the floor. I had a feeling that I did not want to touch either. Old Peter, though, did not seem to be affected that way. He went over to the bed-coverings, and was going to pick them up, as, doubtless, he had done every day these twenty years back; but I stopped him. I wanted nothing touched, until I had finished my examination. This, I must have spent a full hour over, and then I let Peter straighten up the bed; after which we went out and I locked the door; for the room was getting on my nerves.

"I had a short walk, and then breakfast; after which I felt more my own man, and so returned to the Grey Room, and, with Peter's help, and one of the maids, I had everything taken out except the bed, even the very pictures. I examined the walls, floor and ceiling then, with probe, hammer and magnifying glass; but found nothing suspicious. And I can assure you, I began to realise, in very truth, that some incredible thing had been loose in the room during the past night. I sealed up everything again, and went out, locking and sealing the door, as before.

"After dinner that night, Peter and I unpacked some of my stuff, and I fixed up my camera and flashlight opposite to the door of the Grey Room, with a string from the trigger of the flashlight to the door. Then, you see, if the door were really opened, the flashlight would blare out, and there would be, possibly, a very queer picture to examine in the morning. The last thing I did, before leaving, was to uncap the lens; and after that I went off to my bedroom, and to bed; for I intended to be up at midnight; and to ensure this, I set my little alarm to call me; also I left my candle burning.

"The clock woke me at twelve, and I got up and into my dressing-gown and slippers. I shoved my revolver into my right side-pocket, and opened my door. Then, I lit my dark-room lamp, and withdrew the slide, so that it would give a clear light. I carried it up the corridor, about thirty feet, and put it down on the floor, with the open side away from me, so that it would show me anything that might approach along the dark passage. Then I went back, and sat in the doorway of my room, with my revolver handy, staring up the passage towards the place where I knew my camera stood outside the door of the Grey Room.

"I should think I had watched for about an hour and a half, when, suddenly, I heard a faint noise, away up the corridor. I was immediately conscious of a queer prickling sensation about the back of my head, and my hands began to sweat a little. The following instant, the whole end of the passage flicked into sight in the abrupt glare of the flashlight. Then came the succeeding darkness, and I peered nervously up the corridor, listening tensely, and trying to find what lay beyond the faint glow of my dark-lamp, which now seemed ridiculously dim by contrast with the tremendous blaze of the flash-powder.... And then, as I stooped forward, staring and listening, there came the crashing thud of the door of the Grey Room. The sound seemed to fill the whole of the large corridor, and go echoing hollowly through the house. I tell you, I felt horrible—as if my bones were water. Simply beastly. Jove! how I did stare, and how I listened. And then it came again—thud, thud, thud, and then a silence that was almost worse than the noise of the door; for I kept fancying that some brutal thing was stealing upon me along the corridor. And then, suddenly, my lamp was put out, and I could not see a yard before me. I realised all at once that I was doing a very silly thing, sitting there, and I jumped up. Even as I did so, I thought I heard a sound in the passage, and quite near me. I made one backward spring into my room, and slammed and locked the door. I sat on my bed, and stared at the door. I had my revolver in my hand; but it seemed an abominably useless thing. I felt that there was something the other side of that door. For some unknown reason I knew it was pressed up against the door, and it was soft. That was just what I thought. Most extraordinary thing to think.

"Presently I got hold of myself a bit, and marked out a pentacle hurriedly with chalk on the polished floor; and there I sat in it almost until dawn. And all the time, away up the corridor, the door of the Grey Room thudded at solemn and horrid intervals. It was a miserable, brutal night.

"When the day began to break, the thudding of the door came gradually to an end, and, at last, I got hold of my courage, and went along the corridor, in the half light, to cap the lens of my camera. I can tell you, it took some doing; but if I had not done so my photograph would have been spoilt, and I was tremendously keen to save it. I got back to my room, and then set-to and rubbed out the five-pointed star in which I had been sitting.

"Half an hour later there was a tap at my door. It was Peter with my coffee. When I had drunk it, we both went along to the Grey Room. As we went, I had a look at the seals on the other doors, but they were untouched. The seal on the door of the Grey Room was broken, as also was the string from the trigger of the flashlight; but the card over the keyhole was still there. I ripped it off and opened the door. Nothing unusual was to be seen until we came to the bed; then I saw that, as on the previous day, the bedclothes had been torn off, and hurled into the left-hand corner, exactly where I had seen them before. I felt very queer; but I did not forget to look at all the seals, only to find that not one had been broken.

"Then I turned and looked at old Peter, and he looked at me, nodding his head.

"'Let's get out of here!' I said. 'It's no place for any living human to enter, without proper protection.'

"We went out then, and I locked and sealed the door, again.

"After breakfast, I developed the negative; but it showed only the door of the Grey Room, half opened. Then I left the house, as I wanted to get certain matters and implements that might be necessary to life; perhaps to the spirit; for I intended to spend the coming night in the Grey Room.

"I got back in a cab, about half-past-five, with my apparatus, and this, Peter and I carried up to the Grey Room, where I piled it carefully in the centre of the floor. When everything was in the room, including a cat which I had brought, I locked and sealed the door, and went towards my bedroom, telling Peter I should not be down to dinner. He said, 'Yes, sir, and went downstairs, thinking that I was going to turn in, which was what I wanted him to believe, as I knew he would have worried both me and himself, if he had known what I intended.

"But I merely got my camera and flashlight from my bedroom, and hurried back to the Grey Room. I locked and sealed myself in, and set to work, for I had a lot to do before it got dark.

"First I cleared away all the ribbons across the floor; then I carried the cat—still fastened in its basket—over towards the far wall, and left it. I returned then to the centre of the room, and measured out a space twenty-one feet in diameter, which I swept with a 'broom of hyssop.' About this I drew a circle of chalk, taking care never to step over the circle. Beyond this I smudged, with a bunch of garlic, a broad belt right around the chalked circle, and when this was complete, I took from among my stores in the centre a small jar of a certain water. I broke away the parchment and withdrew the stopper. Then, dipping my left forefinger in the little jar, I went round the circle again, making upon the floor, just within the line of chalk, the Second Sign of the Saaamaaa Ritual, and joining each Sign most carefully with the left-handed crescent. I can tell you, I felt easier when this was done and the 'water circle' complete. Then, I unpacked some more of the stuff that I had brought, and placed a lighted candle in the "valley" of each crescent. After that, I drew a pentacle, so that each of the five points of the defensive star touched the chalk circle. In the five points of the star I placed five portions of bread, each wrapped in linen, and in the five "vales," five opened jars of the water I had used to make the water circle. And now I had my first protective barrier complete.

"Now, anyone, except you who know something of my methods of investigation, might consider all this a piece of useless and foolish superstition; but you all remember the Black Veil case, in which I believe my life was saved by a very similar form of protection, whilst Aster, who sneered at it, and would not come inside, died. I got the idea from the Sigsand MS., written, so far as I can make out, in the Fourteenth Century. At first, naturally, I imagined it was just an expression of the superstition of his time; and it was not until a year later that it occurred to me to test his 'Defense,' which I did, as I've just said, in that horrible Black Veil business. You know how that turned out. Later, I used it several times, and always I came through safe, until that Moving Fur case. It was only a partial "Defense" there and I nearly died in the pentacle. After that I came across Professor Garder's 'Experiments with a Medium.' When they surrounded the medium with a current, in vacuum, he lost his power—almost as if it cut him off from the Immaterial. That made me think a lot; and that is how I came to make the Electric Pentacle, which is a most marvellous 'Defense' against certain manifestations. I used the shape of the defensive star for this protection, because I have, personally, no doubt at all but that there is some extraordinary virtue in the old magic figure. Curious thing for a Twentieth-Century man to admit, is it not? But then, as you all know, I never did, and never will, allow myself to be blinded by a little cheap laughter. I ask questions, and keep my eyes open!

"In this last case I had little doubt that I had run up against a supernatural monster, and I meant to take every possible care; for the danger is abominable.

"I turned—to now to fit the Electric Pentacle, setting it so that each of its 'points' and 'vales' coincided exactly with the 'points' and 'vales' of the drawn pentagram upon the floor. Then I connected up the battery, and the next instant the pale blue glare from the intertwining vacuum tubes shone out.

"I glanced about me then, with something of a sigh of relief, and realised suddenly that the dusk was upon me, for the window was grey and unfriendly. Then round at the big, empty room, over the double barrier of electric and candle light. I had an abrupt, extraordinary sense of weirdness thrust upon me—in the air, you know; as it were, a sense of something inhuman impending. The room was full of the stench of bruised garlic, a smell I hate.

"I turned now to my camera, and saw that it and the flashlight were in order. Then I tested my revolver, carefully; though I had little thought that it would be needed. Yet, to what extent materialisation of an ab-natural creature is possible, given favourable conditions, no one can say, and I had no idea what horrible thing I was going to see, or feel the presence of. I might, in the end, have to fight with a materialised monster. I did not know, and could only be prepared. You see, I never forgot that in the bed close to me three people had been strangled, and the fierce slamming of the door I had heard myself. I had no doubt that I was investigating a dangerous and ugly case.

"By this time the night had come; though the room was very light with the burning candles; and I found myself glancing behind me, constantly, and then all round the room. It was nervy work waiting for that thing to come. Then, suddenly, I was aware of a little, cold wind sweeping over me, coming from behind. I gave one great nerve-thrill, and a prickly feeling went all over the back of my head. Then I hove myself round with a sort of stiff jerk, and stared straight against that queer wind. It seemed to come from the corner of the room to the left of the bed—the place where both times I had found the heap of tossed bedclothes. Yet, I could see nothing unusual; no opening— nothing!...

"Abruptly I was aware that the candles were all a-flicker in that unnatural wind.... I believe I just squatted there and stared in a horribly frightened, wooden way for some minutes. I shall never be able to let you know how disgustingly horrible it was sitting in that vile, cold wind! And then, flick! flick! all the candles round the outer barrier went out; and there was I, locked and sealed in that room, and with no light beyond the weakish blue glare of the Electric Pentacle.

"A time of abominable tenseness passed, and still that wind blew upon me; and then, suddenly, I knew that something stirred in the corner to the left of the bed. I was made conscious of it, rather by some inward, unused sense, than by either sight or sound; for the pale, short-radius glare of the pentacle gave but a very poor light for seeing by. Yet, as I stared, something began slowly to grow upon my sight—a moving shadow, a little darker than the surrounding shadows. I lost the thing amid the vagueness, and for a moment or two I glanced swiftly from side to side, with a fresh, new sense of impending danger. Then my attention was directed to the bed. All the coverings were being drawn steadily off, with a hateful, stealthy sort of motion. I heard the slow, dragging slither of the clothes; but I could see nothing of the thing that pulled. I was aware in a funny, subconscious, introspective fashion that the 'creep' had come upon me; yet I was cooler mentally than I had been for some minutes; sufficiently so to feel that my hands were sweating coldly, and to shift my revolver, half-consciously, whilst I rubbed my right hand dry upon my knee; though never, for an instant, taking my gaze or my attention from those moving clothes.

"The faint noises from the bed ceased once, and there was a most intense silence, with only the sound of the blood beating in my head. Yet, immediately afterwards, I heard again the slurring of the bedclothes being dragged off the bed. In the midst of my nervous tension I remembered the camera, and reached round for it; but without looking away from the bed. And then, you know, all in a moment, the whole of the bed-coverings were torn off with extraordinary violence, and I heard the flump they made as they were hurled into the corner.

"There was a time of absolute quietness then for perhaps a couple of minutes; and you can imagine how horrible I felt. The bedclothes had been thrown with such savageness! And then again, the brutal unnaturalness of the thing that had just been done before me!

"Abruptly, over by the door, I heard a faint noise—a sort of crickling sound and then a pitter or two upon the floor. A great nervous thrill swept over me, seeming to run up my spine and over the back of my head; for the seal that secured the door had just been broken. Something was there. I could not see the door; at least, I mean to say that it was impossible to say how much I actually saw, and how much my imagination supplied. I made it out only as a continuation of the grey walls.... And then it seemed to me that something dark and indistinct moved and wavered there among the shadows.

"Abruptly, I was aware that the door was opening, and with an effort I reached again for my camera; but before I could aim it the door was slammed with a terrific crash that filled the whole room with a sort of hollow thunder. I jumped, like a frightened child. There seemed such a power behind the noise; as though a vast, wanton Force were 'out.' Can you understand?

"The door was not touched again; but, directly afterwards, I heard the basket, in which the cat lay, creak. I tell you, I fairly pringled all along my back. I knew that I was going to learn definitely whether what was abroad was dangerous to Life. From the cat there rose suddenly a hideous caterwaul, that ceased abruptly, and then—too late—I snapped on the flashlight. In the great glare, I saw that the basket had been overturned, and the lid was wrenched open, with the cat lying half in, and half out upon the floor. I saw nothing else, but I was full of the knowledge that I was in the presence of some Being or Thing that had power to destroy.

"During the next two or three minutes, there was an odd, noticeable quietness in the room, and you must remember I was half-blinded, for the time, because of the flashlight; so that the whole place seemed to be pitchy dark just beyond the shine of the pentacle. I tell you it was most horrible. I just knelt there in the star, and whirled round, trying to see whether anything was coming at me.

"My power of sight came gradually, and I got a little hold of myself; and abruptly I saw the thing I was looking for, close to the 'water circle.' It was big and indistinct, and wavered curiously, as though the shadow of a vast spider hung suspended in the air, just beyond the barrier. It passed swiftly round the circle, and seemed to probe ever towards me; but only to draw back with extraordinary jerky movements, as might a living person if he touched the hot bar of a grate.

"Round and round it moved, and round and round I turned. Then, just opposite to one of the 'vales' in the pentacles, it seemed to pause, as though preliminary to a tremendous effort. It retired almost beyond the glow of the vacuum light, and then came straight towards me, appearing to gather form and solidity as it came. There seemed a vast, malign determination behind the movement, that must succeed. I was on my knees, and I jerked back, falling on to my left hand and hip, in a wild endeavour to get back from the advancing thing. With my right hand I was grabbing madly for my revolver, which I had let slip. The brutal thing came with one great sweep straight over the garlic and the 'water circle,' almost to the vale of the pentacle. I believe I yelled. Then, just as suddenly as it had swept over, it seemed to be hurled back by some mighty, invisible force.

"It must have been some moments before I realised that I was safe; and then I got myself together in the middle of the pentacles, feeling horribly gone and shaken, and glancing round and round the barrier; but the thing had vanished. Yet I had learnt something, for I knew now that the Grey Room was haunted by a monstrous hand.

"Suddenly, as I crouched there, I saw what had so nearly given the monster an opening through the barrier. In my movements within the pentacle I must have touched one of the jars of water; for just where the thing had made its attack the jar that guarded the 'deep' of the 'vale' had been moved to one side, and this had left one of the 'five doorways' unguarded. I put it back, quickly, and felt almost safe again, for I had found the cause and the 'defense' was still good. And I began to hope again that I should see the morning come in. When I saw that thing so nearly succeed, I'd had an awful, weak, overwhelming feeling that the 'barriers' could never bring me safe through the night against such a Force. You can understand?

"For a long time I could not see the hand; but, presently, I thought I saw, once or twice, an odd wavering, over among the shadows near the door. A little later, as though in a sudden fit of malignant rage, the dead body of the cat was picked up, and beaten with dull, sickening blows against the solid floor. That made me feel rather queer.

"A minute afterwards, the door was opened and slammed twice with tremendous force. The next instant the thing made one swift, vicious dart at me, from out of the shadows. Instinctively I started sideways from it, and so plucked my hand from upon the Electric Pentacle, where—for a wickedly careless moment—I had placed it. The monster was hurled off from the neighbourhood of the pentacles; though—owing to my inconceivable foolishness—it had been enabled for a second time to pass the outer barriers. I can tell you, I shook for a time, with sheer funk. I moved right to the centre of the pentacles again, and knelt there, making myself as small and compact as possible.

"As I knelt, there came to me presently, a vague wonder at the two 'accidents' which had so nearly allowed the brute to get at me. Was I being influenced to unconscious voluntary actions that endangered me? The thought took hold of me, and I watched my every movement. Abruptly, I stretched a tired leg, and knocked over one of the jars of water. Some was spilled; but because of my suspicious watchfulness, I had it upright and back within the vale while yet some of the water remained. Even as I did so, the vast, black, half-materialised hand beat up at me out of the shadows, and seemed to leap almost into my face; so nearly did it approach; but for the third time it was thrown back by some altogether enormous, over-mastering force. Yet, apart from the dazed fright in which it left me, I had for a moment that feeling of spiritual sickness, as if some delicate, beautiful, inward grace had suffered, which is felt only upon the too near approach of the ab-human, and is more dreadful, in a strange way, than any physical pain that can be suffered. I knew by this, more of the extent and closeness of the danger; and for a long time I was simply cowed by the butt-headed brutality of that Force upon my spirit. I can put it no other way.

"I knelt again in the centre of the pentacles, watching myself with more fear, almost, than the monster; for I knew now that, unless I guarded myself from every sudden impulse that came to me, I might simply work my own destruction. Do you see how horrible it all was?

"I spent the rest of the night in a haze of sick fright, and so tense that I could not make a single movement naturally. I was in such fear that any desire for action that came to me might be prompted by the Influence that I knew was at work on me. And outside of the barrier that ghastly thing went round and round, grabbing and grabbing in the air at me. Twice more was the body of the dead cat molested. The second time, I heard every bone in its body scrunch and crack. And all the time the horrible wind was blowing upon me from the corner of the room to the left of the bed.

"Then, just as the first touch of dawn came into the sky, that unnatural wind ceased, in a single moment; and I could see no sign of the hand. The dawn came slowly, and presently the wan light filled all the room, and made the pale glare of the Electric Pentacle look more unearthly. Yet, it was not until the day had fully come, that I made any attempt to leave the barrier, for I did not know but that there was some method abroad, in the sudden stopping of that wind, to entice me from the pentacles.

"At last, when the dawn was strong and bright, I took one last look round, and ran for the door. I got it unlocked, in a nervous, clumsy fashion; then locked it hurriedly, and went to my bedroom, where I lay on the bed, and tried to steady my nerves. Peter came, presently, with the coffee, and when I had drunk it, I told him I meant to have a sleep, as I had been up all night. He took the tray, and went out quietly; and after I had locked my door I turned in properly, and at last got to sleep.

"I woke about midday, and after some lunch, went up to the Grey Room. I switched off the current from the pentacle, which I had left on in my hurry; also, I removed the body of the cat. You can understand I did not want anyone to see the poor brute. After that, I made a very careful search of the corner where the bedclothes had been thrown. I made several holes, and probed, but found nothing. Then it occurred to me to try with my instrument under the skirting. I did so, and heard my wire ring on metal. I turned the hook-end that way, and fished for the thing. At the second go, I got it. It was a small object, and I took it to the window. I found it to be a curious ring, made of some greyish metal. The curious thing about it was that it was made in the form of a pentagon; that is, the same shape as the inside of the magic pentacle, but without the "mounts" which form the points of the defensive star. It was free from all chasing or engraving.

"You will understand that I was excited, when I tell you that I felt sure I held in my hand the famous Luck Ring of the Anderson family; which, indeed, was of all things the one most intimately connected with the history of the haunting. This ring was handed on from father to son through generations, and always—in obedience to some ancient family tradition—each son had to promise never to wear the ring. The ring, I may say, was brought home by one of the Crusaders, under very peculiar circumstances; but the story is too long to go into here.

"It appears that young Sir Hulbert, an ancestor of Anderson's, made a bet, in drink, you know, that he would wear the ring that night. He did so, and in the morning his wife and child were found strangled in the bed, in the very room in which I stood. Many people, it would seem, thought young Sir Hulbert was guilty of having done the thing in drunken anger; and he, in an attempt to prove his innocence, slept a second night in the room. He also was strangled. Since, as you may imagine, no one has spent a night in the Grey Room, until I did so. The ring had been lost so long, that it had become almost a myth; and it was most extraordinary to stand there, with the actual thing in my hand, as you can understand.

"It was whilst I stood there, looking at the ring, that I got an idea. Supposing that it were, in a way, a doorway—You see what I mean? A sort of gap in the world-hedge. It was a queer idea, I know, and probably was not my own, but came to me from the Outside. You see, the wind had come from that part of the room where the ring lay. I thought a lot about it. Then the shape—the inside of a pentacle. It had no 'mounts,' and without mounts, as the Sigsand MS. has it:—'Thee mownts wych are thee Five Hills of safetie. To lack is to gyve pow'r to thee daemon; and surlie to fayvor thee Evill Thynge.' You see, the very shape of the ring was significant; and I determined to test it.

"I unmade my pentacle, for it must be made afresh and around the one to be protected. Then I went out and locked the door; after which I left the house, to get certain matters, for neither 'yarbs nor fyre nor water' must be used a second time. I returned about seven-thirty, and as soon as the things I had brought had been carried up to the Grey Room, I dismissed Peter for the night, just as I had done the evening before. When he had gone downstairs, I let myself into the room and locked and sealed the door. I went to the place in the centre of the room where all the stuff had been packed, and set to work with all my speed to construct a barrier about me and the ring.

"I do not remember whether I explained to you. But I had reasoned that if the ring were in any way a 'medium of admission,' and it were enclosed with me in the Electric Pentacle it would be, to express it loosely, insulated. Do you see? The Force, which had visible expression as a hand, would have to stay beyond the barrier which separates the Ab from the Normal; for the 'gateway' would be removed from accessibility.

"As I was saying, I worked with all my speed to get the barrier completed about me and the ring, for it was already later than I cared to be in that room 'unprotected.' Also, I had a feeling that there would be a vast effort made that night to regain the use of the ring. For I had the strongest conviction that the ring was a necessity to materialisation. You will see whether I was right.

"I completed the barriers in about an hour, and you can imagine something of the relief I felt when I saw the pale glare of the Electric Pentacle once more all about me. From then, onwards, for about two hours, I sat quietly, facing the corner from which the wind came. About eleven o'clock a queer knowledge came that something was near to me; yet nothing happened for a whole hour after that. Then, suddenly, I felt the cold, queer wind begin to blow upon me. To my astonishment, it seemed now to come from behind me, and I whipped round, with a hideous quake of fear. The wind met me in the face. It was blowing up from the floor close to me. I stared down, in a sickening maze of new frights. What on earth had I done now! The ring was there, close beside me, where I had put it. Suddenly, as I stared, bewildered, I was aware that there was something queer about the ring—funny shadowy movements and convolutions. I looked at them, stupidly. And then, abruptly, I knew that the wind was blowing up at me from the ring. A queer indistinct smoke became visible to me, seeming to pour upwards through the ring, and mix with the moving shadows. Suddenly, I realised that I was in more than any mortal danger; for the convoluting shadows about the ring were taking shape, and the death-hand was forming within the pentacle. My goodness! do you realise it! I had brought the 'gateway' into the pentacles, and the brute was coming through—pouring into the material world, as gas might pour out from the mouth of a pipe.

"I should think that I knelt for a moment in a sort of stunned fright. Then, with a mad, awkward movement, I snatched at the ring, intending to hurl it out of the pentacle. Yet it eluded me, as though some invisible, living thing jerked it hither and thither. At last, I gripped it; yet, in the same instant, it was torn from my grasp with incredible and brutal force. A great, black shadow covered it, and rose into the air, and came at me. I saw that it was the hand, vast and nearly perfect in form. I gave one crazy yell, and jumped over the pentacle and the ring of burning candles, and ran despairingly for the door. I fumbled idiotically and ineffectually with the key, and all the time I stared, with a fear that was like insanity, toward the barriers. The hand was plunging towards me; yet, even as it had been unable to pass into the pentacle when the ring was without, so, now that the ring was within, it had no power to pass out. The monster was chained, as surely as any beast would be, were chains rivetted upon it.

"Even then, I got a flash of this knowledge; but I was too utterly shaken with fright, to reason; and the instant I managed to get the key turned, I sprang into the passage, and slammed the door with a crash. I locked it, and got to my room, somehow; for I was trembling so that I could hardly stand, as you can imagine. I locked myself in, and managed to get the candle lit; then I lay down on the bed, and kept quiet for an hour or two, and so I got steadied.

"I got a little sleep, later; but woke when Peter brought my coffee. When I had drunk it I felt altogether better, and took the old man along with me whilst I had a look into the Grey Room. I opened the door, and peeped in. The candles were still burning, wan against the daylight; and behind them was the pale, glowing star of the Electric Pentacle. And there in the middle was the ring... the gateway of the monster, lying demure and ordinary.

"Nothing in the room was touched, and I knew that the brute had never managed to cross the pentacles. Then I went out, and locked the door.

"After a sleep of some hours, I left the house. I returned in the afternoon in a cab. I had with me an oxy-hydrogen jet, and two cylinders, containing the gases. I carried the things to the Grey Room, and there, in the centre of the Electric Pentacle, I erected the little furnace. Five minutes later the Luck Ring, once the 'luck,' but now the 'bane,' of the Anderson family, was no more than a little solid splash of hot metal."

Carnacki felt in his pocket, and pulled out something wrapped in tissue paper. He passed it to me. I opened it and found a small circle of greyish metal, something like lead, only harder and rather brighter.

"Well?" I asked, at length, after examining it and handing it round to the others. "Did that stop the haunting?"

Carnacki nodded. "Yes," he said. "I slept three nights in the Grey Room, before I left. Old Peter nearly fainted when he knew that I meant to; but by the third night he seemed to realise that the house was just safe and ordinary. And, you know, I believe, in his heart, he hardly approved."

Carnacki stood up and began to shake hands. "Out you go!" he said, genially. And, presently, we went, pondering to our various homes.

# THE AFFAIR OF THE AVALANCHE BICYCLE & TYRE CO., LTD

## BY ARTHUR MORRISON

Arthur Morrison

ORIGINALLY PUBLISHED IN 1897

EDITOR'S NOTES:

# THE AFFAIR OF THE AVALANCHE BICYCLE & TYRE CO., LTD

## BY ARTHUR MORRISON

In the person of Horace Dorrington, Arthur Morrison has provided the complete antithesis to his more famous creation, the detective Martin Hewitt and almost every other Edwardian detective. Whereas Hewitt is a man of honesty and integrity, Dorrington is almost completely amoral and cynical.

Horace Dorrington, a partner in the detective agency of Dorrington & Hicks, is a man with only his own best interests at heart. He certainly can not be said to have those of his clients in mind. Indeed, his clients are his principle victims, whom he fleeces at every opportunity. The only thing that can be said in Dorrington's favor are that his clients are even bigger crooks and con men than he is, only just not as competent.

Dorrington's methods were simple, he would discover what game his clients were actually up to and then devise a plan to foil them, walking away with any profits left behind.

The exploits of Horace Dorrington were chronicled in the 1897 *book The Dorrington Deed Box.*

# THE AFFAIR OF THE AVALANCHE
# BICYCLE & TYRE CO., LTD

Cycle companies were in the market everywhere. Immense fortunes were being made in a few days and sometimes little fortunes were being lost to build them up.

Mining shares were dull for a season, and any company with the word "cycle" or "tyre" in its title was certain to attract capital, no matter what its prospects were like in the eyes of the expert. All the old private cycle companies suddenly were offered to the public, and their proprietors, already rich men, built themselves houses on the Riviera, bought yachts, ran racehorses, and left business for ever. Sometimes the shareholders got their money's-worth, sometimes more, sometimes less—sometimes they got nothing but total loss; but still the game went on. One could never open a newspaper without finding, displayed at large, the prospectus of yet another cycle company with capital expressed in six figures at least, often in seven. Solemn old dailies, into whose editorial heads no new thing ever found its way till years after it had been forgotten elsewhere, suddenly exhibited the scandalous phenomenon of "broken columns" in their advertising sections, and the universal prospectuses stretched outrageously across half or even all the page—a thing to cause apoplexy in the bodily system of any self-respecting manager of the old school.

In the midst of this excitement it chanced that the firm of Dorrington & Hicks were engaged upon an investigation for the famous and long-established "Indestructible Bicycle & Tricycle Manufacturing Company," of London and Coventry. The matter was not one of sufficient intricacy or difficulty to engage Dorrington's personal attention, and it was given to an assistant. There was some doubt as to the validity of a certain patent having reference to a particular method of tightening the spokes and truing the wheels of a tricycle, and Dorrington's assistant had to make inquiries (without attracting attention to the matter) as to whether or not there existed any evidence, either documentary or in the memory of veterans, of the use of this method, or anything like it, before the year 1885. The assistant completed his inquiries and made his report to Dorrington. Now I think I have said that, from every evidence I have seen, the chief matter of Dorrington's solicitude was his own interest, and just at this time he had heard, as had others, much of the money being made in cycle companies. Also, like others, he had conceived a great desire to get the confidential advice of somebody "in the know"—advice which might lead him into the "good thing" desired by all the greedy who flutter about at the outside edge of the stock and share market. For this reason Dorrington determined to make this small matter of the wheel patent an affair of personal report. He was a man of infinite resource, plausibility and good-companionship, and there was money going in the cycle trade. Why then should he lose an opportunity of making himself pleasant, in the inner groves of that trade, and catch whatever might come his way— information, syndicate shares, directorships, anything? So that Dorrington made himself master of his assistant's information, and proceeded to the head office of the "Indestructible" company on Holborn Viaduct, resolved to become the entertaining acquaintance of the managing director.

On his way his attention was attracted by a very elaborately fitted cycle shop which his recollection told him was new. "The Avalanche Bicycle & Tyre Company" was the legend gilt above the great plate-glass window, and in the window itself stood many brilliantly enamelled and plated bicycles, each labelled on the frame with the flaming red and gold transfer of the firm; and in the midst of all was another bicycle covered with dried mud, of which, however, sufficient had been carefully cleared away to expose a similar glaring transfer to those that decorated the rest—with a placard announcing that on this particular machine somebody had ridden some incredible distance on bad roads in very little more than no time at all. A crowd stood about the window; and gaped respectfully at the placard, the bicycles, the transfers and the mud, though they paid little attention to certain piles of folded white papers, endorsed in bold letters with the name of the company, with the suffix "limited" and the word "prospectus" in bloated black letter below. These, however, Dorrington observed at once, for he had himself that morning, in common with several thousand other people, received one by post. Also half a page of his morning paper had been filled with a copy of that same prospectus, and the afternoon had brought another copy in the evening paper. In the list of directors there was a titled name or two, together with a few unknown names— doubtless the "practical men." And below this list there were such positive promises of tremendous dividends, backed up and proved beyond dispute by such ingenious piles of business-like figures, every line of figures referring to some other line for testimonials to its perfect genuineness and accuracy, that any reasonable man, it would seem, must instantly sell the hat off his head and the boots off his feet to buy one share at least, and so make his fortune for ever. True, the business was but lately established, but that was just it. It had rushed ahead with such amazing rapidity (as was natural with an avalanche) that it had got altogether out of hand, and orders couldn't be executed at all; wherefore the proprietors were reluctantly compelled to let the public have some of the luck. This was Thursday. The share list was to be opened on Monday morning and closed inexorably at four o'clock on Tuesday afternoon, with a merciful extension to Wednesday morning for the candidates for wealth who were so unfortunate as to live in the country. So that it behoved everybody to waste no time lest he be numbered among the unlucky whose subscription-money should be returned in full, failing allotment. The prospectus did not absolutely say it in so many words, but no rational person could fail to feel that the directors were fervently hoping that nobody would get injured in the rush.

Dorrington passed on and reached the well-known establishment of the "Indestructible Bicycle Company." This was already a limited company of a private sort, and had been so for ten years or more. And before that the concern had had eight or nine years of prosperous experience. The founder of the firm, Sir Paul Mallows, was now the managing director, and a great pillar of the cycling industry. Dorrington gave a clerk his card, and asked to see Mr. Mallows.

Mr. Mallows was out, it seemed, but Mr. Stedman, the secretary, was in, and him Dorrington saw. Mr. Stedman was a pleasant, youngish man, who had been a famous amateur bicyclist in his time, and was still an enthusiast. In ten minutes business was settled and dismissed, and Dorrington's tact had brought the secretary into a pleasant discursive chat, with much exchange of anecdote.

Dorrington expressed much interest in the subject of bicycling, and, seeing that Stedman had been a racing man, particularly as to bicycling races.

"There'll be a rare good race on Saturday, I expect," Stedman said. "Or rather," he went on, "I expect the fifty miles record will go. I fancy our man Gillett is pretty safe to win, but he'll have to move, and I quite expect to see a good set of new records on our advertisements next week. The next best man is Lant—the new fellow, you know—who rides for the 'Avalanche' people."

"Let's see, they're going to the public as a limited company, aren't they?" Dorrington asked, casually.

Stedman nodded, with a little grimace.

"You don't think it's a good thing, perhaps," Dorrington said, noticing the grimace. "Is that so?"

"Well," Stedman answered, "of course I can't say. I don't know much about the firm—nobody does, as far as I can tell—but they seem to have got a business together in almost no time; that is, if the business is as genuine as it looks at first sight. But they want a rare lot of capital, and then the prospectus—well I've seen more satisfactory ones, you know. I don't say it isn't all right, of course, but still I shan't go out of my way to recommend any friends of mine to plunge on it."

"You won't?"

"No, I won't. Though no doubt they'll get their capital, or most of it. Almost any cycle or tyre company can get subscribed just now. And this 'Avalanche' affair is both, and it is so well advertised, you know. Lant has been winning on their mounts just lately, and they've been booming it for all they're worth. By Jove, if they could only screw him up to win the fifty miles on Saturday, and beat our man Gillett, that would give them a push! Just at the correct moment too. Gillett's never been beaten yet at the distance, you know. But Lant can't do it—though, as I have said, he'll make some fast riding—it'd be a race, I tell you!"

"I should like to see it."

"Why not come? See about it, will you? And perhaps you'd like to run down to the track after dinner this evening and see our man training—awfully interesting, I can tell you, with all the pacing machinery and that. Will you come?" Dorrington expressed himself delighted, and suggested that Stedman should dine with him before going to the track. Stedman, for his part, charmed with his new acquaintance—as everybody was at a first meeting with Dorrington—assented gladly.

At that moment the door of Stedman's room was pushed open and a well-dressed, middle-aged man, with a shaven, flabby face, appeared. "I beg pardon," he said, "I thought you were alone. I've just ripped my finger against the handle of my brougham door as I came in—the screw sticks out. Have you a piece of sticking plaster?" He extended a bleeding finger as he spoke. Stedman looked doubtfully at his desk.

"Here is some court plaster," Dorrington exclaimed, producing his pocket-book. "I always carry it—it's handier than ordinary sticking plaster. How much do you want?"

"Thanks—an inch or so."

"This is Mr. Dorrington, of Messrs. Dorrington & Hicks, Mr. Mallows," Stedman said. "Our managing director, Mr. Paul Mallows, Mr. Dorrington." Dorrington was delighted to make Mr. Mallows's acquaintance, and he busied himself with a careful strapping of the damaged finger. Mr. Mallows had the large frame of a man of strong build who has had much hard bodily work, but there hung about it the heavier, softer flesh that told of a later period of ease and sloth. "Ah, Mr. Mallows," Stedman said, "the bicycle's the safest thing, after all! Dangerous things these broughams!"

"Ah, you younger men," Mr. Mallows replied, with a slow and rounded enunciation, "you younger men can afford to be active! We elders —"

"Can afford a brougham," Dorrington added, before the managing director began the next word. "Just so—and the bicycle does it all; wonderful thing the bicycle!" Dorrington had not misjudged his man, and the oblique reference to his wealth flattered Mr. Hallows. Dorrington went once more through his report as to the spoke patent and then Mr. Mallows bade him good-bye.

"Good day, Mr. Dorrington, good day," he said. "I am extremely obliged by your careful personal attention to this matter of the patent. We may leave it with Mr. Stedman now, I think. Good day. I hope soon to have the pleasure of meeting you again." And with clumsy stateliness Mr. Mallow's vanished.

## II.

"So you don't think the 'Avalanche' good business as an investment?" Dorrington said once more as he and Stedman, after an excellent dinner, were cabbing it to the track.

"No, no," Stedman answered, "don't touch it! There's better things than that coming along presently. Perhaps I shall be able to put you in for something you know a bit later; but don't be in a hurry. As to the 'Avalanche,' even if everything else were satisfactory, there's too much 'booming' being done just now to please me. All sorts of rumours, you know, of their having something 'up their sleeve,' and so on; mysterious hints in the papers, and all that; as to something revolutionary being in hand with the 'Avalanche' people. Perhaps there is. But why they don't fetch it out in view of the public subscription for shares is more than I can understand, unless they don't want too much of a rush. And as to that well they don't look like modestly shrinking from anything of that sort up to the present."

They were at the track soon after seven but Gillett was not yet riding. Dorrington remarked that Gillett appeared to begin late.

"Well," Stedman explained, "he's one of those fellows that afternoon training doesn't seem to suit, unless it is a bit of walking exercise. He just does a few miles in the morning and a spurt or two, and then he comes on just before sunset for a fast ten or fifteen miles—that is when he is getting fit for such a race as Saturday's. To-night will be his last spin of that length before Saturday, because to-morrow will be the day before the race. To-morrow he'll only go a spurt or two, and rest most of the day." They strolled about inside the track, the two highly "banked" ends whereof seemed to a near-sighted person in the centre to be solid erect walls, along the face of which the training riders skimmed, fly-fashion. Only three or four persons beside themselves were in the enclosure when they first came, but in ten minutes' time Mr. Paul Mallows came across the track.

"Why," said Stedman to Dorrington, "here's the governor! It isn't often he comes down here. But I expect he's anxious to see how Gillett's going, in view of Saturday."

"Good evening Mr. Mallows," said Dorrington. "I hope the finger's all right? Want any more plaster?"

"Good evening, good evening," responded Mr. Mallows heavily. "Thank you, the finger's not troubling me a bit." He held it up, still decorated by the black plaster. "Your plaster remains, you see—I was a little careful not to fray it too much in washing, that was all." And Mr. Mallows sat down on a light iron garden-chair (of which several stood here and there in the enclosure) and began to watch the riding.

The track was clear, and dusk was approaching when at last the great Gillett made his appearance on the track. He answered a friendly question or two put to him by Mallows and Stedman, and then, giving his coat to his trainer, swung off along the track on his bicycle, led in front by a tandem and closely attended by a triplet. In fifty yards his pace quickened, and he settled down into a swift even pace, regular as clockwork. Sometimes the tandem and sometimes the triplet went to the front, but Gillett neither checked nor heeded as, nursed by his pacers, who were directed by the trainer from the centre, he swept along mile after mile, each mile in but a few seconds over the two minutes.

"Look at the action!" exclaimed Stedman with enthusiasm. "Just watch him. Not an ounce of power wasted there! Did you ever see more regular ankle work? And did anybody ever sit a machine quite so well as that? Show me a movement anywhere above the hips!"

"Ah," said Mr. Hallows, "Gillett has a wonderful style—a wonderful style, really!" The men in the enclosure wandered about here and there on the grass, watching Gillett's riding as one watches the performance of a great piece of art—which, indeed, was what Gillett's riding was. There were, besides Mallows, Stedman, Dorrington and the trainer, two officials of the Cyclists' Union, an amateur racing man named Sparks, the track superintendent and another man. The sky grew darker, and gloom fell about the track. The machines became invisible, and little could be seen of the riders across the ground but the row of rhythmically working, legs and the white cap that Gillett wore. The trainer had just told Stedman that there would be three fast laps and then his man would come off the track.

"Well, Mr. Stedman," said Mr. Mallows, "I think we shall be all right for Saturday."

"Rather!" answered Stedman confidently. "Gillett's going great guns, and steady as a watch!" The pace now suddenly increased. The tandem shot once more to the front, the triplet hung on the rider's flank, and the group of swishing wheels flew round the track at a "one-fifty" gait. The spectators turned about, following the riders round the track with their eyes. And then swinging into the straight from the top bend, the tandem checked suddenly and gave a little jump. Gillett crashed into it from behind, and the triplet, failing to clear, wavered and swung, and crashed over and along the track too. All three machines and six men were involved in one complicated smash.

Everybody rushed across the grass, the trainer first. Then the cause of the disaster was seen. Lying on its side on the track, with men and bicycles piled over and against it, was one of the green painted light iron garden-chairs that had been standing in the enclosure. The triplet men were struggling to their feet, and though much cut and shaken, seemed the least hurt of the lot. One of the men of the tandem was insensible, and Gillett, who from his position had got all the worst of it, lay senseless too, badly cut and bruised, and his left arm was broken.

The trainer was cursing and tearing his hair. "If I knew; who'd done this," Stedman cried, "I'd pulp him with that chair!"

"Oh, that betting, that betting!" wailed Mr. Mallows, hopping about distractedly; "see what it leads people into doing! It can't have been an accident, can it?"

"Accident? Skittles! A man doesn't put a chair on a track in the dark and leave it there by accident. Is anybody getting away there from the outside of the track?"

"No, there's nobody. He wouldn't wait till this, he's clear off a minute ago and more. Here, Fielders! Shut the outer gate, and we'll see who's about." But there seemed to be no suspicious character. Indeed, except for the ground-man, his boy, Gillett's trainer, and a racing man, who had just finished dressing in the pavilion, there seemed to be nobody about beyond those whom everybody had seen standing in the enclosure. But there had been ample time for anybody, standing unnoticed at the outer rails, to get across the track in the dark, just after the riders had passed, place the obstruction, and escape before the completion of the lap.

The damaged men were helped or carried into the pavilion, and the damaged machines were dragged after them. "I will give fifty pounds gladly—more, a hundred," said Mr. Mallows, excitedly, "to anybody who will find out who put that chair on the track. It might have ended in murder. Some wretched bookmaker, I suppose, who has taken too many bets on Gillett. As I've said a thousand times, betting is the curse of all sport nowadays."

"The governor excites himself a great deal about betting and bookmakers," Stedman said to Dorrington, as they walked toward the pavilion, "but, between you and me, I believe some of the 'Avalanche' people are in this. The betting bee is always in Mallows's bonnet, but as a matter of fact there's very little betting at all on cycle races, and what there is is little more than a matter of half-crowns or at most half-sovereigns on the day of the race. No bookmaker ever makes a heavy book first. Still there may be something in it this time, of course. But look at the 'Avalanche' people. With Gillett away their man can certainly win on Saturday, and if only the weather keeps fair he can almost as certainly beat the record; just at present the fifty miles is fairly easy, and it's bound to go soon. Indeed our intention was that Gillett should pull it down on Saturday. He was a safe winner, bar accidents, and it was good odds on his altering the record, if the weather were and good at all.

"With Gillett out of it Lant is just about as certain a winner as our man would be if all were well. And there would be a boom for the 'Avalanche' company, on the very eve of the share subscription! Lant, you must know, was very second-rate till this season, but he has improved wonderfully in the last month or two, since he has been with the 'Avalanche' people. Let him win, and they can point to the machine as responsible for it all. 'Here,' they will say in effect, 'is a man who could rarely get in front, even in second-class company, till he rode an 'Avalanche.' Now he beats the world's record for fifty miles on it, and makes rings round the topmost professionals!' Why, it will be worth thousands of capital to them. Of course the subscription of capital won't hurt us, but the loss of the record may, and to have

Gillett knocked out like this in the middle of the season is serious."

"Yes, I suppose with you it is more than a matter of this one race."

"Of course. And so it mill be with the 'Avalanche' company. Don't you see, with Gillett probably useless for the rest of the season, Lant will have it all his own way at anything over ten miles. That'll help to boom up the shares and there'll be big profit made on trading in them. Oh, I tell you this thing seems pretty suspicious to me."

"Look here," said Dorrington, "can you borrow a light for me, and let me run over with it to the spot where the smash took place? The people have cleared into the pavilion, and I could go alone."

"Certainly. Will you have a try for the governor's hundred?"

"Well, perhaps. But any way there's no harm in doing you a good turn if I can, while I'm here. Some day perhaps you'll do me one."

"Right you are—I'll ask Fielders, the ground-man." A lantern was brought, and Dorrington betook himself to the spot where the iron chair still lay, while Stedman joined the rest of the crowd in the pavilion.

Dorrington minutely examined the grass within two yards of the place where the chair lay, and then, crossing the track and getting over the rails, did the same with the damp gravel that paved the outer ring. The track itself was of cement, and unimpressionable by footmarks, but nevertheless he scrutinized that with equal care, as well as the rails. Then he turned his attention to the chair. It was, as I have said, a light chair made of flat iron strip, bent to shape and riveted. It had seen good service, and its present coat of green paint was evidently far from being its original one. Also it was rusty in places, and parts had been repaired and strengthened with cross pieces secured by bolts and square nuts, some rusty and loose. It was from one of these square nuts, holding a cross-piece that stayed the back at the top, that Dorrington secured some object—it might have been a hair—which he carefully transferred to his pocket-book. This done, with one more glance round, he betook himself to the pavilion.

A surgeon had arrived, and he reported well of the chief patient. It was a simple fracture, and a healthy patient. When Dorrington entered, preparations were beginning for setting the limb. There was a sofa in the pavilion and the surgeon saw no reason for removing the patient till all was made secure.

"Found anything?" asked Stedman in a low tone of Dorrington.

Dorrington shook his head. "Not much," he answered at a whisper. "I'll think over it later." Dorrington asked one of the Cyclists' Union officials for the loan of a pencil, and, having made a note with it, immediately, in another part of the room, asked Sparks, the amateur, to lend him another.

Stedman had told Mr. Mallows of Dorrington's late employment with the lantern, and the managing director now said quietly, "You remember what I said about rewarding anybody who discovered the perpetrator of this outrage, Mr. Dorrington? Well, I was excited at the time, but I quite hold to it. It is a shameful thing. You have been looking about the grounds, I hear. I hope you have come across something that will enable you to find something out! Nothing will please me more than to have to pay you, I'm sure."

"Well," Dorrington confessed, "I'm afraid I haven't seen anything very big in the way of a clue, Mr. Mallows; but I'll think a bit. The worst of it is, you never know who these betting men are, do you, once they get away? There are so many, and it may be anybody. Not only that, but they may bribe anybody."

"Yes, of course—there's no end to their wickedness, I'm afraid. Stedman suggests that trade rivalry may have had something to do with it. But that seems an uncharitable view, don't you think? Of course we stand very high, and there are jealousies and all that, but this is a thing I'm sure no firm would think of stooping to, for a moment. No, it's betting that is at the bottom of this, I fear. And I hope, Mr. Dorrington that you will make some attempt to find the guilty parties." Presently Stedman spoke to Dorrington again. "Here's something that may help you," he said. "To begin with, it must have been done by someone from the outside of the track."

"Why?"

"Well, at least every probability's that way. Everybody inside was directly interested in Gillett's success, excepting the Union

Officials and Sparks, who's a gentleman and quite above suspicion, as much so, indeed, as the Union officials. Of course, there was the ground-man, but he's all right, I'm sure."

"And the trainer?"

"Oh, that's altogether improbable—altogether. I was going to say —"

"And there's that other man who was standing about; I haven't heard who he was."

"Right you are. I don't know him, either. Where is he now?" But the man had gone.

"Look here, I'll make some quiet inquiries about that man," Stedman pursued. "I forgot all about him in the excitement of the moment. I was going to say that although whoever did it could easily have got away by the gate before the smash came, he might not have liked to go that way in case of observation in passing the pavilion. In that case he could have got away (and indeed he could have got into the grounds to begin with) by way of one of those garden walls that bound the ground just by where the smash occurred. If that were so he must either live in one of the houses, or he must know somebody that does. Perhaps you might put a man to smell about along that road—it's only a short one; Chisnall Road's the name."

"Yes, yes," Dorrington responded patiently. "There might be something in that." By this time Gillett's arm was in a starched bandage and secured by splints, and a cab was ready to take him home. Mr. Mallows took Stedman away with him, expressing a desire to talk business, and Dorrington went home by himself. He did not turn down Chisnall Road. But he walked jauntily along toward the nearest cab-stand, and once or twice he chuckled, for he saw his way to a delightfully lucrative financial operation in cycle companies, without risk of capital.

The cab gained, he called at the lodgings of two of his men assistants and gave them instant instructions. Then he packed a small bag at his rooms in Conduit Street, and at midnight was in the late fast train for Birmingham.

## III.

THE prospectus of the "Avalanche Bicycle & Tyre Company" stated that the works were at Exeter and Birmingham. Exeter is a delightful old town, but it can scarcely be regarded as the centre of the cycle trade; neither is it in especially easy and short communication with Birmingham. It was the sort of thing that any critic anxious to pick holes in the prospectus might wonder at, and so one of Dorrington's assistants had gone by the night mail to inspect the works. It was from this man that Dorrington, in Birmingham, about noon on the day after Gillett's disaster, received this telegram—Works here old disused cloth-mills just out of town. Closed and empty but with big new signboard and notice that works now running are at Birmingham. Agent says only deposit paid—tenancy agreement not signed.—Farrish.

The telegram increased Dorrington's satisfaction, for he had just taken a look at the Birmingham works. They were not empty, though nearly so, nor were they large; and a man there had told him that the chief premises, where most of the work was done, were at Exeter. And the hollower the business the better prize he saw in store for himself. He had already, early in the morning, indulged in a telegram on his own account, though he had not signed it. This was how it ran—Mallows, 58 Upper Sandown Place, London, W.

Fear all not safe here. Run down by 10.10 train without fail.

Thus it happened that at a little later than half-past eight Dorrington's other assistant, watching the door of No. 58 Upper Sandown Place, saw a telegram delivered, and immediately afterward Mr. Paul Mallows in much haste dashed away in a cab which was called from the end of the street. The assistant followed in another. Mr. Mallows dismissed his cab at a theatrical wig-makers in Bow Street and entered. When he emerged in little more than forty minutes' time, none but a practiced watcher, who had guessed the reason of the visit, would have recognized him. He had not assumed the clumsy disguise of a false beard. He was "made up" deftly. His colour was heightened, and his face seemed thinner. There was no heavy accession of false hair, but a slight crepe-hair whisker at each side made a better and less pronounced disguise. He seemed a younger, healthier man. The watcher saw him safely off to Birmingham by the ten minutes past ten train, and then gave Dorrington note by telegraph of the guise in which Mr. Mallows was travelling.

Now this train was timed to arrive at Birmingham at one, which was the reason that Dorrington had named it in the anonymous telegram. The entrance to the "Avalanche" works was by a large gate, which was closed, but which was provided with a small door to pass a man. Within was a yard, and at a little before one o'clock Dorrington pushed open the small door, peeped and entered. Nobody was about in the yard, and what little noise could be heard came from a particular part of the building on the right. A pile of solid "export" crates stood to the left, and these Dorrington had noted at his previous visit that morning as making a suitable hiding-place for temporary use. Now he slipped behind them and awaited the stroke of one. Prompt at the hour a door on the opposite side of the yard swung open, and two men and a boy emerged and climbed one after another through the little door in the big gate. Then presently another man, not a workman, but apparently a sort of overseer, came from the opposite door, which he carelessly let fall-to behind him, and he also disappeared through the little door, which he then locked.

Dorrington was now alone in the sole active works of the "Avalanche Bicycle & Tyre Company, Limited." He tried the door opposite and found it was free to open. Within he saw in a dark corner a candle which had been left burning, and opposite him a large iron enamelling oven, like an immense safe, and round about, on benches, were strewn heaps of the glaring red and gold transfer which Dorrington had observed the day before on the machines exhibited in the Holborn Viaduct window. Some of the frames had the label newly applied, and others were still plain. It would seem that the chief business of the "Avalanche Bicycle & Tyre Company, Limited," was the attaching of labels to previously nondescript machines. But there was little time to examine further, and indeed Dorrington presently heard the noise of a key in the outer gate. So he stood and waited by the enamelling oven to welcome Mr. Mallows. As the door was pushed open Dorrington advanced and bowed politely.

Mallows started guiltily, but, remembering his disguise, steadied himself and asked gruffly, "Well sir, and who are you?"

"I," answered Dorrington with perfect composure, 'I am Mr. Paul Mallows—you may have heard of me in connection with the 'Indestructible Bicycle Company.'"

Mallows was altogether taken aback. But then it struck him that perhaps the detective, anxious to win the reward he had offered in the matter of the Gillett outrage, was here making inquiries in the assumed character of the man who stood, impenetrably disguised, before him. So after a pause he asked again, a little less gruffly, "And what may be your business?"

"Well," said Dorrington, "I did think of taking shares in this company. I suppose there would be no objection to the managing director of another company taking shares in this?"

"No," answered Mallows, wondering what all this was to lead to.

"Of course not; I'm sure you don't think so, eh?" Dorrington, as he spoke, looked in the other's face with a sly leer, and Mallows began to feel altogether uncomfortable. "But there's one other thing," Dorrington pursued, taking out his pocket-book, though still maintaining his leer in Mallows's face—"one other thing. And by the way, will you have another piece of court plaster now I've got it out? Don't say no. It's a pleasure to oblige you, really." And Dorrington, his leer growing positively fiendish, tapped the side of his nose with the case of court plaster.

" TAPPED THE SIDE OF HIS NOSE WITH THE CASE."

Mallows paled under the paint, gasped, and felt for support. Dorrington laughed pleasantly. "Come, come," he said, encouragingly, "don't be frightened. I admire your cleverness, Mr. Mallows, and I shall arrange everything pleasantly, as you will see. And as to the court plaster, if you'd rather not have it you needn't. You have another piece on now, I see. Why didn't you get them to paint it over at Clarkson's? They really did the face very well, though! And there again you were quite right. Such a man as yourself was likely to be recognized in such a place as Birmingham, and that would have been unfortunate for both of us—both of us, I assure you.... Man alive, don't look as though I was going to cut your throat! I'm not, I assure you. You're a smart man of business, and I happen to have spotted a little operation of yours, that's all. I shall arrange easy terms for you.... Pull yourself together and talk business before the men come back. Here, sit on this bench." Mallows, staring amazedly in Dorrington's face, suffered himself to be led to a bench, and sat on it.

"Now," said Dorrington, "the first thing is a little matter of a hundred pounds. That was the reward you promised if I should discover who broke Gillett's arm last night. Well I have. Do you happen to have any notes with you? If not, make it a cheque."

"But—but—how—I mean who—who —"

"Tut, tut! Don't waste time, Mr. Mallows. Who? Why, yourself, of course. I knew all about it before I left you last night, though it wasn't quite convenient to claim the reward then, for reasons you'll understand presently. Come, that little hundred."

"But what—what proof have you? I'm not to be bounced like this, you know," Mr. Mallows was gathering his faculties again.

"Proof? Why, man alive, be reasonable! Suppose I have none—none at all? What difference does that make? Am I to walk out and tell your fellow directors where I have met you—here—or am I to have that hundred? More, am I to publish abroad that Mr. Paul Mallows is the moving spirit in the rotten 'Avalanche Bicycle Company'?"

"Well," Mallows answered reluctantly, "if you put it like that —"

"But I only put it like that to make you see things reasonably. As a matter of fact your connection with this new company is enough to bring your little performance with the iron chair pretty near proof. But I got at it from the other side. See here—you're much too clumsy with your fingers, Mr. Mallows. First you go and tear the tip of your middle finger opening your brougham door, and have to get court plaster from me. Then you let that court plaster get frayed at the edge, and you still keep it on. After that you execute your very successful chair operation. When the eyes of the others are following the bicycles you take the chair in the hand with the plaster on it, catching hold of it at the place where a rough, loose, square nut protrudes, and you pitch it on to the track so clumsily and nervously that the nut carries away the frayed thread of the court plaster with it. Here it is, you see, still in my pocket-book, where I put it last night by the light of the lantern; just a sticky black silk thread, that's all. I've only brought it to show you I'm playing a fair game with you. Of course, I might easily have got a witness before I took the thread off the nut, if I had thought you were likely to fight the matter. But I knew you were not. You can't fight, you know, with this bogus company business known to me. So that I am only showing you this thread as an act of grace, to prove that I have stumped you with perfect fairness. And now the hundred. Here's a fountain pen, if you want one."

"Well," said Mallows glumly, "I suppose I must, then." He took the pen and wrote the cheque. Dorrington blotted it on the pad of his pocket-book and folded it away.

"So much for that!" he said. "That's just a little preliminary, you understand. We've done these little things just as a guarantee of good faith—not necessarily for publication, though you must remember that as yet there's nothing to prevent it. I've done you a turn by finding out who upset those bicycles, as you so ardently wished me to do last night, and you've loyally fulfilled your part of the contract by paying the promised reward—though I must say that you haven't paid with all the delight and pleasure you spoke of at the time. But I'll forgive you that, and now that the little hors d'œuvre is disposed of, we'll proceed to serious business." Mallows looked uncomfortably glum.

"But you mustn't look so ashamed of yourself, you know," Dorrington said, purposely misinterpreting his glumness. "It's all business. You were disposed for a little side flutter, so to speak—a little speculation outside your regular business. Well, you mustn't be ashamed of that."

"No," Mallows observed, assuming something of his ordinarily ponderous manner; "no, of course not. It's a little speculative deal. Everybody does it, and there's a deal of money going."

"Precisely. And since everybody does it, and there is so much money going, you are only making your share."

"Of course." Mr. Mallows was almost pompous by now.

"Of course." Dorrington coughed slightly. "Well now, do you know, I am exactly the same sort of man as yourself—if you don't mind the comparison. I am disposed for a little side butter, so to speak—a little speculation outside my regular business. I also am not ashamed of it. And since everybody does it, and there is so much money going—why, I am thinking of making my share. So that we are evidently a pair, and naturally intended for each other!" Mr. Paul Mallows here looked a little doubtful.

"See here, now," Dorrington proceeded. "I have lately taken it into my head to operate a little on the cycle share market. That was why I came round myself about that little spoke affair, instead of sending an assistant. I wanted to know somebody who understood the cycle trade, from whom I might get tips. Yon see I'm perfectly frank with you. Well, I have succeeded uncommonly well. And I want you to understand that I have gone every step of the way by fair work. I took nothing for granted, and I played the game fairly. When you asked me (as you had anxious reason to ask) if I had found anything, I told you there was nothing very big—and see what a little thing the thread was! Before I came away from the pavilion I made sure that you were really the only man there with black court plaster on his fingers. I had noticed the hands of every man but two, and I made all excuse of borrowing something, to see those. I saw your thin pretence of suspecting the betting men, and I played up to it. I have had a telegraphic report on your Exeter works this morning—a deserted cloth mills with nothing on it of yours but a sign-board, and only a deposit of rent paid.

There they referred to the works here. Here they referred to the works there. It was very clever, really! Also I have had a telegraphic report of your make-up adventure this morning.

Clarkson does it marvellously, doesn't he? And, by the way, that telegram bringing you down to Birmingham was not from your confederate here, as perhaps you fancied. It was from me. Thanks for coming so promptly. I managed to get a quiet look round here just before you arrived, and on the whole the conclusion I come to as to the 'Avalanche Bicycle & Tyre Company, Limited,' is this: A clever man, whom it gives me great pleasure to know," with a bow to Mallows, "conceives the notion of offering the public the very rottenest cycle company ever planned, and all without appearing in it himself. He finds what little capital is required, his two or three confederates help to make up a board of directors, with one or two titled guinea-pigs, who know nothing of the company and care nothing, and the rest's easy. A professional racing man is employed to win races and make records, on machines which have been specially made by another firm (perhaps it was the 'Indestructible,' who knows?) to a private order and afterwards decorated with the name and style of the bogus company on a transfer. For ordinary sale, bicycles of the 'trade' description are bought—so much a hundred from the factors, and put your own name on 'em. They come cheap, and they sell at a good price—the profit pays all expenses and perhaps a bit over; and by the time they all break down the company will be successfully floated, the money—the capital—will be divided, the moving spirit and his confederates will have disappeared, and the guinea-pigs will be left to stand the racket—if there is a racket. And the moving spirit will remain unsuspected, a man of account in the trade all the time! Admirable! All the work to be done at the 'works' is the sticking on of labels and a bit of enamelling. Excellent, all round! Isn't that about the size of your operations?"

"Well, yes," Mallows answered, a little reluctantly, but with something of modest pride in his manner, "that was the notion since you speak so plainly."

"And it shall be the notion. All—everything—shall be as you have planned it, with one exception, which is this. The moving spirit shall divide his plunder with me."

"You? But—but—why, I gave you a hundred just now!"

"Dear, dear! Why will you harp so much on that vulgar little hundred? That's settled and done with. That's our little personal bargain in the matter of the lamentable accident with the chair.

We are now talking of bigger business—not hundreds but thousands, and not one of them, but a lot. Come now, a mind like yours should be wide enough to admit of a broad and large view of things. If I refrain from exposing this charming scheme of yours I shall be promoting a piece of scandalous robbery. Very well then, I want my promotion money, in the regular way. Can I shut my eyes and allow a piece of iniquity like this to go on unchecked, without getting anything by way of damages for myself? Perish the thought! When all expenses are paid, and the confederates are sent off with as little as they will take, you and I will divide fairly, Mr. Mallows, respectable brothers in rascality. Mind, I might say we'd divide to begin with; and leave you to pay expenses, but I am always fair to a partner in anything of this sort. I shall just want a little guarantee, you know—it's safest in such matters as these; say a bill at six months for ten thousand pounds—which is very low. When a satisfactory division is made you shall have the bill back. Come—I have a bill-stamp ready, being so much convinced of your reasonableness as to buy it this morning, though it cost five pounds."

"But that's nonsense—you're trying to impose. I'll give you anything reasonable—half is out of the question. What, after all the trouble and worry and risk that I've had —"

"Which would suffice for no more than to put you in gaol if I held up my finger!"

"But, hang it, be reasonable! You're a mighty clever man, and you've got me on the hip, as I admit. Say ten per cent."

"You're wasting time, and presently the men will be back. Your choice is between making half, or making none, and going to gaol into the bargain. Choose!"

"But just consider —"

"Choose!"

Mallows looked despairingly about him. "But really," he said, "I want the money more than you think. I —"

"For the last time—choose!"

Mallows's despairing gaze stopped at the enamelling oven. "Well, well," he said, "if I must, I must, I suppose. But I warn you, you may regret it."

"Oh dear no, I'm not so pessimistic. Come, you wrote a cheque—now I'll write the bill. 'Six months after date, pay to me on my order the sum of ten thousand pounds for value received'—excellent value too, I think. There you are!" When the bill was written and signed Mallows scribbled his acceptance with more readiness than might have been expected. Then he rose, and said with something of brisk cheerfulness in his tone, "Well, that's done, and the least said the soonest mended. You've won it, and I won't grumble any more. I think I've done this thing pretty neatly, eh? Come and see the 'works.'"

Every other part of the place was empty of machinery. There were a good many finished frames and wheels, bought separately, and now in course of being fitted together for sale, and there were many more complete bicycles of cheap but showy make to which nothing needed to be done but to fix the red and gold "transfer" of the "Avalanche" company. Then Mallows opened the tall iron door of the enamelling oven.

"See this," he said, "this is the enamelling oven. Get in and look round. The frames and other different parts hang on the racks after the enamel is laid on, and all those gas jets are lighted to harden it by heat. Do you see that deeper part there by the back?—go closer." Dorrington felt a push at his back and the door was swung to with a bang, and the latch dropped. He was in the dark, trapped in a great icon chamber. And instantly Dorrington's nostrils were filled with the smell of escaping gas. He realized his peril on the instant. Mallows had given him the bill with the idea of silencing him by murder and recovering it. He had pushed him into the oven and had turned on the gas. It was dark, but to light a match would mean death instantly, and without the match it must be death by suffocation and poison of gas in a very few minutes. To appeal to Mallow was useless—Dorrington knew too much. It would seem that at last a horribly-fitting retribution had overtaken Dorrington in death by a mode parallel to that which he and his creatures had prepared for others. Dorrington's victims had drowned in water—or at least Crofton's had, for I never ascertained definitely whether anybody had met his death by the tank after the Croftons had taken service with Dorrington—and now Dorrington himself was to drown in gas.

The oven was of sheet iron, fastened by a latch in the centre. Dorrington flung himself desperately against the door, and it gave outwardly at the extreme bottom. He snatched a loose angle-iron with which his hand came in contact, dashed against the door once more, and thrust the iron through where it strained open. Then, with another tremendous plunge, he drove the door a little more outward and raised the angle-iron in the crack; then once more, and raised it again. He was near to losing his senses, when, with one more plunge the catch of the latch, not designed for such treatment, suddenly gave way, the door flew open, and Dorrington, blue in the face, staring, stumbling and gasping, came staggering out into the fresher air, followed by a gush of gas.

Mallows had retreated to the rooms behind, and thither Dorrington followed him, gaining vigour and fury at every step. At sight of him the wretched Mallows sank in a corner, sighing and shivering with terror. Dorrington hauled the struggling wretch across the room, tearing off the crepe whiskers as he came, while Mallows supplicated and whined, fearing that it might be the other's design to imprison him in the enamelling oven. But at the door of the room against that containing the oven their progress came to an end, for the escaped gas had reached the lighted candle, and with one loud report the partition wall fell in, half burying Mallows where he lay, and knocking Dorrington over.

Windows fell out of the balding, and men broke through the front gate, climbed into the ruined rooms and stopped the still escaping gas. When the two men and the boy returned, with the conspirator who had been in charge of the works, they found a crowd from the hardware and cycle factories thereabout, surveying with great interest the spectacle of the extrication of Mr. Paul Mallows, managing director of the "Indestructible Bicycle Company," from the broken bricks, mortar, bicycles and transfers of the "Avalanche Bicycle & Tyre Company, Limited," and the preparations for carrying him to a surgeon's where his broken leg might be set. And in a couple of hours it was all over Birmingham, and spreading to other places, that the business of the "Avalanche Bicycle & Tyre Company" consisted of sticking brilliant labels on factors' bicycles, bought in batches. So that when, next day, Lant won the fifty miles race in London, he was greeted with ironical shouts of "Gum on yer transfer!"

"Hi! mind yer label!"

"Where did you steal that bicycle?"

"Sold yer shares?" and so forth.

Somehow the "Avalanche Bicycle & Tyre Company, Limited," never went to allotment. It was found politic, also, that Mr. Paul Mallows should retire from the directorate of the "Indestructible Bicycle Company." As for Dorrington, he had his hundred pounds reward. But the bill for £10,000 he never presented. Why, I do not altogether know, unless he found that Mr. Mallows's financial position, as he had hinted, was not altogether so good as was supposed.

# THE CONUNDRUM OF THE GOLF LINKS

## BY PERCY JAMES BREBNER

ORIGINALLY PUBLISHED IN 1914

# THE CONUNDRUM OF
# THE GOLF LINKS
## BY PERCY JAMES BREBNER

With the success of Sir Arthur Conan Doyles Sherlock Holmes, it is not surprising that there followed a host of imitators trying to cash in on the public's hunger for detective fiction. One of the lesser known of these detectives is Professor Christopher Quarles, the creation of Percy James Brebner, who was primarily an author of historical romances.

The stories are told from the viewpoint of a Scotland Yard detective, Inspector Murray Wigam, who, having consulted the professor on one case, finds himself maintaining contact with the professor. At first, his interest is mainly in the professors granddaughter Zena, but he finds himself calling on the professor's intellect whenever he is involved with a particularly baffling crime.

The professor's method of operation is to retire to a sparsely furnished room at the rear of his house to ponder on the facts of the case before reaching a solution though a combination of intellect and intuition. Often, his meditation is spurred on by some apparently random question of Zena, which nevertheless manages to get to the heart of the problem.

Professor Quarles and Inspector Wigam were to figure in more than thirty stories. While covering no particularly original ground, these stories, with their mix of clever puzzles and action, odd criminals and secret societies, are nonetheless entertaining and still worth reading.

Percy James Brebner (1864-1922) was an English author of historical romances such as "The Princess Maritza" "The Brown Mask" and "A Royal Ward." His short stories featuring the detective Professor Christopher Quarles were collected in two volumes entitles "Christopher Quarles - College Professor and Master Detective" and "The Master Detective - Being Some Further Investigations of Christopher Quarles."

More stories featuring Christopher Quarles may be found in the Resurrected Press volume *Christopher Quarles Ressurected* which contains the stories from both of the above mentioned volumes.

# THE CONUNDRUM OF THE GOLF LINKS

I have wondered sometimes whether I have ever really liked Christopher Quarles; at times I have certainly resented his treatment, and had he been requested to make out a list of his friends, quite possibly my name would not have figured in the list unless Zena had written it out for him. Some remark of the professor's had annoyed me at this time, and I had studiously kept away from Chelsea for some days, when one morning I received a telegram:

"If nothing better to do, join us here for a few days.—Quarles, Marine Hotel, Lingham."

I did not even know they were out of town, for Zena and I never wrote to each other, and I had a strong suspicion the invitation meant that the professor wanted my help in some case in which he was interested. Still, there would be leisure hours, and I had visions of pleasant rambles with Zena. If I could manage it, some of them should be when the moon traced a pale gold path across the sleeping waters. I may say at once that some moonlight walks were accomplished, though fewer than I could have wished, and that, although there was no business behind the professor's invitation, my visit to Lingham resulted in the solution of a mystery which had begun some months before and had baffled all inquiry ever since.

Lingham, as everybody knows, is a great yachting center, and as I journeyed down to the East Coast I wondered if yachting interested Quarles, and, if not, why he had chosen Lingham for a holiday.

The professor was a man of surprises. I have seen him looking so old that a walk to the end of the short street in Chelsea might reasonably be expected to try his capacity for exercise; and, again, I have seen him look almost young; indeed, in these reminiscences I have shown that at times he did not seem to know what fatigue meant. When he met me in the vestibule of the Marine Hotel he looked no more than middle-aged, and as physically fit as a man could be. He was dressed in loose tweeds, and wore a pair of heavy boots which, even to look at, almost made one feel tired.

"Welcome, my dear fellow!" he said. "But why bring such infernal weather with you? It began to blow at the very time you must have been leaving town, and has been increasing ever since. It has put a stop to all racing."

"I didn't know you took an interest in yachting."

"I don't. Golf, Wigan! At golf I am an enthusiast. There's a good sporting course here, that's why I came to Lingham. You've brought your clubs, I see."

"Chance. You did not say anything about golf in your wire."

"Why should I? Useless waste of money. I remembered your telling me once that you never went for your holiday without taking your clubs. We shall have grand sport."

He laughed quite boisterously, and a man who was passing through the hall looked at me and smiled. I recollected that smile afterward, but took little notice of it just then, because Zena was coming down the stairs.

Before dinner that evening it blew a gale, and from windows overlooking the deserted parade we watched a sullen, angry sea pounding the sandy shore and hissing into long lines of foam, which the wind caught up and carried viciously inland.

"Isn't that a sail—a yacht?" said Zena suddenly, pointing out to sea, over which darkness was gathering like a pall.

It was, and those on board of her must be having a bad time, not to say a perilous one. She was certainly not built for such weather as this, but she must be a stout little craft to stand it as she did, and they were no fools who had the handling of her.

"Blown right out of her course, I should think," said Quarles. "The yachts shelter in the creek to the south yonder. I should not wonder if that boat hopes to make the creek which lies on the other side of the golf course."

"She's more likely to come ashore," said a man standing behind us, and he spoke with the air of an expert in such matters. "There's no anchorage in that creek, and, besides, a bar of mud lies right across the mouth of it."

As the curved line of the sea front presently hid the yacht from our view the gong sounded for dinner—a very welcome sound, and I, for one, thought no more about the yacht that night.

Before morning the gale had subsided, but the day was sullen and cloudy, threatening rain, and we did not attempt golf until after lunch.

It was an eighteen-hole course, and might be reckoned sporting, but it was not ideal. There was too much loose sand, and a great quantity of that rank grass which flourishes on sand dunes. It said much for the management that the greens were as good as they were.

I had just played two holes with the professor before I remembered the man who had smiled in the hall of the hotel yesterday. Certainly Quarles was an enthusiast. In all the etiquette of the game he was perfect, but as a player he was the very last word. He persisted in driving with a full swing, usually with comic effect; he was provided with a very full complement of clubs, and was precise in always using the right one; but he seemed physically incapable of keeping his eye on the ball, and constantly hit out, as if he were playing cricket; yet the bigger ass he made of himself the greater seemed his enjoyment. He never lost his temper. Other men would have emptied themselves of the dregs of their vocabulary; Quarles only smiled, cheerfully explaining how he had come to top a ball, or why he had taken half a dozen shots to get out of a bunker. No wonder the man in the hotel had laughed.

There was one particularly difficult hole. The bogey was six. It required a good drive to get over a ridge of high ground; beyond was a brassey shot, then an iron, and a mashie on to the green. To the left lay a creek, a narrow water course between mud. My drive did not reach the ridge, on the top of which was a direction post; and the professor pulled his ball, which landed perilously near the mud. It took him three shots to come up with me, and when at last we mounted the ridge we saw there was a man on the distant green, which lay in a hollow surrounded by bunkers, behind which was the bank of the curving creek.

"Fore!" shouted Quarles.

I almost laughed. It was certain the man would have ample time to get off the green before the professor arrived there.

Quarles waited for a moment, but the man ahead took no notice, possibly had not heard him.

The professor took a full swing with his brassey, and, for a wonder, the ball went as straight and true as any golfer could desire.

"Ah! I am getting into form, Wigan," he exclaimed. "What is that fool doing yonder? Fore!"

This time the man looked round and waved to us to come on, which we did slowly, for Quarles's form was speedily out again.

The man on the green was a curiosity. Thirty-five or thereabouts, I judged him to be; a thin man, but wiry, with a stiff figure and an immobile face, which looked as if he had never been guilty of showing an emotion. His eyes were beady, and fixed you; his mouth gave the impression of being so seldom used for speech that it had become partially atrophied. His costume, perhaps meant to be sporting, missed the mark—looked as if he had borrowed the various articles from different friends; and he was practicing putting with a thin-faced mashie, very rusty in the head, and dilapidated in the shaft.

He stood aside and watched Quarles miss two short puts.

"Difficult," he remarked. "I'm practicing it."

Quarles looked at the speaker, then at the mashie.

"With that?"

"Why not?" asked the man.

"Why?" asked Quarles.

"If I can do it with this I can do it with anything," was the answer.

"That's true," said the professor, making for the next tee. There was no arguing with a man of this type.

The tee was on the top of the creek bank.

"I was right," said Quarles. "Look, Wigan, they did make for this haven last night."

It was almost low water. The bank on the golf course side was steep, varying in height, but comparatively low near the tee, and an irregular line of piles stuck up out of the mud below, the tops of half a dozen of them rising higher than the bank. On the other side of the creek the shore sloped up gradually from a wide stretch of mud.

In the narrow waterway was a yacht, about eighteen tons, I judged. That she was the same we had seen laboring in the gale last night I could not say, but certainly she was much weather-marked and looked forlorn. She had not had a coat of paint recently, the brasswork on her was green with neglect, and her ropes and sails looked old and badly cared for. Yet her lines were dainty, and, straining at her hawser, she reminded me of a disappointed woman fretting to free herself from an undesirable position.

A yacht is always so sentient a thing, and seems so full of conscious life.

Quarles appeared to understand my momentary preoccupation.

"Don't take any notice of her," he said. "We're out for golf. I always manage a good drive from this tee."

This time was an exception, at any rate, and, in fact, for the remainder of the round he played worse than before, if that were possible. But he was perfectly satisfied with himself, and talked nothing but golf as we walked back, until we were close to the hotel, when he stopped suddenly.

"Queer chap, that, on the green."

"Very."

"Do you think he came from the yacht?"

"I was wondering whether he hadn't escaped from an asylum," I answered.

"I wonder what he was doing on the green," Quarles went on. "I saw no one else playing this afternoon, so he had the green to himself, except for the little time we disturbed him. When I first saw him it didn't seem to me that he was practicing putting, and I thought he watched us rather curiously."

"A theory, professor?" I asked with a smile.

"No, no; just wonder. By the way, don't say anything to that expert who was so certain that the yacht couldn't get into the creek. He mightn't like to know he was mistaken."

After dinner that evening Zena and I went out. There was no moon; indeed, it was not very pleasant weather, but it was a pleasant walk, and entirely to my satisfaction.

When we returned I found Quarles in a corner of the smoking room leaning back in an armchair with his eyes closed. He looked up suddenly as I approached him.

"Cold out?" he asked.

"Nothing to speak of."

"Feel inclined to go a little way with me now?"

"Certainly."

"Good! Say in a quarter of an hour's time. I shall get out of this dress and put on some warmer clothes. I should advise you to do the same."

I took his advice, and I was not surprised when he turned to me as soon as we had left the hotel and said:

"That yacht, Wigan; we'll go and have a look at her."

"It's too dark to see her."

"She may show a light," he chuckled. "Anyway, we will go and have a look."

We started along the front in the direction of the golf course, but at the end of the parade, instead of turning inland as I expected, to cross the course to the creek, Quarles led the way on to the sands. Here was a favorite bathing place, and there were many small tents nestling under the sandhills, looking a little the worse for last night's gale. At this hour the spot was quite deserted.

"Getting toward high water," said the professor, "and a smooth sea to-night. Can you row, Wigan?"

"An oarsman would probably say I couldn't," I answered.

"There's a stout little boat hereabouts—takes swimmers out for a dive into deep water. We'll borrow it, and see what you can do."

Always there was something in Quarles's way of going to work which had the effect of giving one a thrill, of stringing up the nerves, and making one eager to know all that was in his mind. You were satisfied there was something more to learn, and felt it would be worth learning. I asked no questions now as I helped to push a good-sized dinghy into the water. Oars were in it, and a coil of rope.

"Anyone might go off with it," said Quarles. "I noticed the other day that the boatman did not trouble to take the oars out. I suppose he believes in the honesty of Lingham."

If I am no great stylist, I am not deficient in muscle, and, with the set of the tide to help me, we were not long in making the mouth of the creek.

"The yacht is some way up, Wigan, and maybe there are sharp ears on her. Tie your handkerchief round that rowlock, and I'll tie mine round this. You must pull gently and make no noise. The tide is still running in, and will carry us up. By the way, when you're on holiday do you still keep your hip pocket filled?"

"Yes, when I go on expeditions of this sort."

"Good! Keep under the bank as much as possible, and don't stick on the mud."

I did little more than keep the boat straight, was careful not to make any noise, and in the shadow of the bank we were not very likely to be seen. A heavy, leaden sky made the night dark, and there was a sullen rush in the water.

"Steady!" whispered Quarles.

We were abreast of the first of the piles which I had noticed in the morning. Now it was standing out of water instead of mud.

"She shows no light," said Quarles. "We'll get alongside."

With the incoming tide the yacht had swung around, and was straining at the hawser which held her, the water slapping at her bows with fretful insistency. Quarles held on to her, bringing us with a slight bump against her side. Keen ears would have heard the contact, but no voice challenged.

We had come up on the side of the yacht which was nearest the golf course.

"There's no boat fastened to her, Wigan," said Quarles. "Probably there is no one on board. Let's go round to the other side."

There we found the steps used for boarding her.

"If there's anyone here, Wigan, we're two landlubbers who've got benighted and have a bad attack of nerves," whispered Quarles. "Hitch one end of that coil of rope to the painter, so that when we fasten our boat to the stays on the other side of the yacht she'll float far astern. When they return they are almost certain to come up on this side to the steps, so will not be likely either to see the rope or our boat in the dark."

I fastened the rope to the painter as Quarles suggested, and climbed on to the yacht after him. Then I let the tide carry our boat astern, and, crossing the deck, tied the other end of the rope securely to the stays on the other side.

The sky seemed to have become heavier and more leaden; it was too dark to see anything clearly. There was little wind, yet a subdued and ghostly note sounded in the yacht's rigging, and the water swirling at her bows seemed to emphasize her loneliness. So far as I could see, she was in exactly the same condition as when I had seen her from the golf course. No one was on deck, and no sound came from below.

"Queer feeling about her, don't you think?" said Quarles. "We're just deadly afraid of the night and spooks, that's what we are if there is anyone to question us."

I followed him down into the cabin. At the foot of the companion Quarles flashed a pocket electric torch. It was only a momentary flash, then darkness again as he gave a warning little hiss.

Three glasses on the table was all I had seen. I supposed the professor had seen something more, but I was wrong.

After standing perfectly motionless for a minute or so, he flashed the light again, and sent the ray round the cabin. The appointments were faded, the covering of the long, fixed seats on either side of the table was torn in places. One of these seats had evidently served as a bunk, for a pillow and folded blanket were lying upon it. All the paint work was dirty and scratched. Forward, there was a door into the galley; aft, another door to another cabin.

"A crew of three," said Quarles. "Three glasses, plenty of liquor left in the bottle in the rack yonder, a pipe and a pouch, and a conundrum."

He let the light rest on a sheet of paper lying beside the glasses. On it was written: "S. B. Piles—one with chain—9th link. N. B. Direct. Mud—high water—90 and 4 feet."

"A conundrum, Wigan. What do you make of it?"

He held out the paper to me, a useless thing to do, since he allowed the ray from the torch to wander slowly round the cabin again.

"We must look at the pile with the chain," he muttered in a disconnected way, as though he were thinking of something quite different.

"And at the ninth link of the chain," I said.

"Yes, at the ninth link. A conundrum, Wigan. A——"

He stopped. His eyes had suddenly become fixed upon some object behind me. The electric ray fell slanting close by me, and when I turned I saw that the end of it was under the cushioned seat on one side of the table. The light fell upon a golf club—a rusty mashie.

"That man on the green was one of the crew, Wigan," said Quarles; and then when I picked up the club we looked into each other's eyes.

"Did I not say the yacht had a queer feeling about her?" he said in a whisper.

I knew what he meant. The mashie had something besides rust on it now, something wet, moist and sticky.

Quarles glanced at the door of the galley as he put the paper on the table, careful to place it in the exact position in which he had found it; then he went quickly to the cabin aft.

On either side of a fixed washing cabinet there was a bunk, and in one of them lay the man we had seen on the green. The wound upon his head told to what a terrible use the club had been put since he had played with it that afternoon. He had been fiercely struck from behind, and then strong fingers had strangled out whatever life remained in him. He was fully dressed, and there had been little or no struggle. His would-be sportsmanlike attire was barely disarranged, and even in death his pose was stiff, and his set face exhibited no emotion. Quarles lifted up one of his hands and looked at the palm and at the nails. He let the light rest upon the hand that I might see it. Then he pointed to a straight mark across the forehead, just below the hair, and nodded.

We were back in the saloon-cabin again when I touched the professor's arm, and in an instant the torch was out. I had caught the sound of splashing oars.

"Put the club back under the seat," said Quarles, and then, with movements stealthy as a cat's, he led the way to the galley door. We were in our hiding place not a moment too soon.

Two men came hurriedly down the companion. A match was struck, but there was not a chink in the boarding through which we could see into the cabin. It seemed certain they had not discovered our dinghy, and had no suspicion that they were not alone upon the yacht.

"It's plain enough. There's no other meaning to it." The speaker had a heavy voice, a gurgle in it, and I judged the heavier tread of the two was his. "Ninety feet, it says, captain; and we measured that string to exactly ninety feet."

"Feet might only refer to the four, and not to both figures," was the answer in a sharp, incisive voice.

"He said it was both."

"And I'm not sure he lied," returned the man addressed as captain. "The distance was originally paced out no doubt, and pacing out ninety feet ain't the same as an exact measurement."

"We made allowances," growled the other.

"We'd been wiser to go on looking instead of coming back. You're too previous, mate."

"You didn't trust him any more'n I did."

"No; but he had the name right enough," answered the captain, "and the time—a year last February. I always put that job down to Glider. Let's get back while the dark lasts."

"Come to think of it, it's strange Glider should have made a confidant of him," said the other.

"Sized him up, and took his chance for the sake of the missus," returned the captain.

"I'm not going back until I've seen whether he's got other papers about him."

"He chucked his clothes overboard," said the captain.

"He'd keep papers tied round him, maybe. I'll soon find out."

There was a heavy tread, and the opening of the door of the cabin aft. There was the rending of cloth, and the man swore the whole time, perhaps to keep up his courage for the horrible task.

"Nothing!" he said, coming back into the saloon-cabin. "Say, captain, supposing it's all a plant—a trap!"

There was a pause and my hand went to my revolver. If the suggestion should take root, would they not at once search the galley?

"He'd a mind to get the lot, that was his game," said the captain.

They went on deck, we could hear them stamping about overhead. Then came an oath, and a quick movement. I thought they were coming down again, but a moment later there was the soft swish of oars, followed by silence.

"Carefully!" said Quarles, as I fumbled at the galley door. "One of them may have remained to shoot us from the top of the companion."

He was wrong, but it was more than probable that such an idea had occurred to them. They had discovered our dinghy! It had been cut adrift, and the scoundrels had escaped, leaving us isolated on the yacht. I snapped out a good round oath.

"Can you swim, Wigan?" asked the professor.

At full tide the creek was wide, and the sullen, rushing water had a hungry and cruel sound.

"Not well enough to venture here, and in the dark," I said.

"And I cannot swim at all," said Quarles. "We are caught until morning and low-water. It's cold, and beginning to rain. With all its defects I prefer the cabin."

He went below and declared that he must get a little sleep. Whether he did or not, I cannot say; I know that I never felt less inclined to close my eyes. We had been trapped, that made me mad; and I could not forget our gruesome companion behind the door of the aft cabin.

There was a glimmer of daylight when Quarles moved.

"This is nearly as good a place to think in as my empty room at Chelsea, Wigan. What do you make of the mystery?"

"A trio of villains after buried treasure."

"Which they could not find; and two of them are scuttling away to save their necks."

"So you think the dead man yonder fooled them?"

"No. I think there is some flaw in the conundrum. By the way, why is a golf course called links?"

"It's a Scotch word for a sandy tract near the sea, isn't it?"

"But to an untutored mind, Wigan, especially if it were not Scotch, there might be another meaning, one based on number, for instance. As a chain consists of links, so a golf course, which has eighteen links. It is a possible view, eh?"

"Perhaps."

"I see they have taken the paper," said Quarles; "but I dare say you remember the wording. S. B., that means south bank; N. B., north bank. I have no doubt there is a pile with a chain on it, whether with nine or ninety links does not matter. It was on the green of the ninth hole that the man was practicing. For the word "link" substitute "hole," and you get a particular pile connected with the ninth hole, which, of course, has a flag, and so we get a particular direction indicated. From the high-water line of mud on the north bank we continue this ascertained direction for ninety feet, and then we dig down four feet."

"And find nothing," I said.

"Exactly! There is a flaw somewhere, but the treasure is there," said Quarles. "The rascals who have given us an uncomfortable night evidently believed that the man they called Glider had told the truth; more, they had already put the job down to him, you will remember. Now, how was it Glider gave his secret away to the man in yonder cabin? Obviously he couldn't come and get the treasure himself."

"A convict," I said, "who gave information to a fellow convict about to be released."

"I don't think so," said Quarles. "As a convict, these men, who have been convicts themselves, or will be, would have had sympathy with him. They hadn't any. They were afraid of him. They felt it was strange that Glider should have confided in him, and could only find an explanation by supposing that Glider had sized him up and taken his chance for the sake of the missus. We may assume, therefore, that Glider had trusted a man no one would expect him to trust. This suggests urgency, and I fancy a man, nicknamed Glider, has recently died in one of His Majesty's prisons—Portland I should guess. Probably our adventurers sailed from Weymouth. Now, Glider could not have been in Portland long. A year last February he was free to do the job with which this expedition is connected, and of which I should imagine he is not suspected by the police. Probably he was taken for some other crime soon after he had committed this one. He had no opportunity to dig up the treasure he had buried, which he certainly would have done as soon as possible. Yet Glider must have been long enough in prison to size up the dead man yonder—a work of some time, I fancy. You noticed his hands. Did they show any evidence of his having worked as a convict? You saw the mark across the forehead. That was made by a stiff cap worn constantly until a day or two ago. I think we shall find there is a warder missing from Portland."

"A warder!"

The idea was startling, yet I could pick no hole in the professor's argument.

"Even a warder is not free from temptation, and I take it this man was tempted, and fell. Glider, no doubt, told him of the captain and his mate. He had worked with them before, probably, and trusted them; also, he might think they would be a check upon the warder. I shouldn't be surprised if the warder

were the only one of the three who insisted that the widow
should have her share, and so came by his death. The flaw in the
riddle keeps the treasure safe. Perhaps I shall solve it during the
day. By the way, Wigan, it must be getting near low-water."

It was a beastly morning, persistent rain from a leaden sky.
The tide was out, only a thin strip of water separating the yacht
from the mud.

"I fear there will be no golfers on the links to-day to whom we
might signal," said Quarles; "and I could not even swim that."

"I can," I answered.

"It would be better than spending another night here," said
the professor. "Send a boat round for me, and inform the police. I
am afraid the captain and his mate have got too long a start; but
don't leave Lingham until we have had another talk. While I am
alone I may read the riddle."

The ducking I did not mind, and the swim was no more than
a few vigorous strokes, but I had forgotten the mud. As I
struggled through it, squelching, knee-deep, Quarles called to
me:

"They must have landed him at high-water yesterday,
Wigan, and then crossed over and taken the direction from him.
I thought he was feeling about with the flag when we first saw
him on the green. No doubt he made some sign to the others
across the creek to lie low when he saw us coming. They marked
the place in daylight and went at night to dig."

I sank at least ten inches deeper into the mud while he was
speaking. He got no answer out of me. I felt like hating my best
friend just then.

After changing my clothes at the hotel, where I accounted for
my condition by a story, original but not true, I told Zena shortly
what had happened, then sent a boat for the professor. I then
told the Lingham police, who wired to the police at Colchester,
and I also telegraphed to Scotland Yard and to Portland Prison.

I did not see Quarles again until the afternoon.

"Have you solved the riddle?" I asked.

"I think so. We'll go to that ninth hole at once. The police are
continuing the excavations begun by our friends. I've had a talk
to the professional at the golf club. They move the position of the
holes on a green from time to time, you know, Wigan; and with
the professional's help I think we shall be able to find out where

it was a year last February. He is a methodical fellow. That will give us a different direction on the north bank of the creek. It was a natural oversight on the convict's part. Were I not a golfer I might not have thought of the solution."

We found the treasure a long way from where the other digging had been done. It consisted of jewels which, in the early part of the previous year, had been stolen from Fenton Hall, some two miles inland. The theft, which had taken place when the house was full of week-end visitors, had been quickly discovered, and the thief, finding it impossible to get clear away with his spoil, had buried it on the desolate bank of the creek, marking the spot by a mental line drawn through the chained pile and the flag on the golf course. He must have known the neighborhood, and knew this was the ninth hole, or link as he called it, or as the warder had written it down. For Quarles was right, a warder was missing from Portland, and was found dead in that aft cabin.

The yacht was known at Weymouth, and belonged to a retired seaman, a Captain Wells, who lived at a little hotel when he was in the town. He was often away—sometimes in his yacht, sometimes in London—and there was little doubt that his boat had often been used to take stolen property across to the Continent. Neither the captain nor his mate could be traced now, but it was some satisfaction that they had not secured the jewels.

As I have said, I did manage to get some moonlight walks with Zena, but not many, for a week after we had recovered the Fenton Hall jewels I was called back to town to interview Lord Leconbridge.

# THE SILKWORMS
# OF FLORENCE
## BY CLIFFORD ASHDOWN

## ORIGINALLY PUBLISHED IN 1902

# THE SILKWORMS
# OF FLORENCE

### BY CLIFFORD ASHDOWN

Romney Pringle wasn't so much a detective as a con man who always seems to prosper from the schemes of other con men. He was the product of a collaboration between John Pitcairn, the medical officer at Holloway Prison, and R. Austin Freeman who went on later to write the Dr. John Thorndyke series of stories and novels.

Much like Arthur Morrison's Horace Dorrington, Pringle's *modus operandi* was to discover some con man in the middle of a swindle, scare them off, and then walk away with the loot. The stories are amusing for the manner in which Pringle outsmarts his adversaries at their own game rather than serious examples of detection. Their chief interest lies in their being the first works of Freeman who was to become one of the best writers of detective fiction over the next four decades.

Romney Pringle first made his appearance in the 1902 collection *The Adventures of Romney Pringle*. Additional stories appeared the following year in *The Further Adventures of Romney Pringle*. Pitcairn and Freeman collaborated on a number of other projects for the next few years before Freeman published his first Thorndyke novel *The Red Thumbmark* in 1907.

# THE SILKWORMS OF FLORENCE

"AND this is all that's left of Brede now." The old beadle withdrew his hand, and the skull, with a rattle as of an empty wooden box, fell in its iron cage again.

"How old do you say it is?" asked Mr. Pringle.

"Let me see," reflected the beadle, stroking his long grey beard. "He killed Mr. Grebble in 1742, I think it was—the date's on the tombstone over yonder in the church—and he hung in these irons a matter of sixty or seventy year. I don't rightly know the spot where the gibbet stood, but it was in a field they used to call in my young days 'Gibbet Marsh.' You'll find it round by the Tillingham, back of the windmill."

"And is this the gibbet? How dreadful!" chorused the two daughters of a clergyman, very summery, very gushing, and very inquisitive, who with their father completed the party.

"Lor, no, miss! Why, that's the Rye pillory. It's stood up here nigh a hundred year! And now I'll show you the town charters." And the beadle, with some senile hesitation of gait, led the way into a small attic.

Mr. Pringle's mythical literary agency being able to take care of itself, his chambers in Furnival's Inn had not seen him for a month past. To a man of his cultured and fastidious bent the Bank Holiday resort was especially odious; he affected regions unknown to the tripper, and his presence at Rye had been determined by Jeakes' quaint "Perambulation of the Cinque Ports," which he had lately picked up in Booksellers' Row. Wandering with his camera from one decayed city to another, he had left Rye only to hasten back when disgusted with the modernity of the other ports, and for the last fortnight his tall slim figure had haunted the town, his fair complexion swarthy and his port-wine mark almost lost in the tanning begotten of the marsh winds and the sun.

"The town's had a rare lot of charters and privileges granted to it," boasted the beadle, turning to a chest on which for all its cobwebs and mildew the lines of elaborate carving showed distinctly. Opening it, he began to dredge up parchments from the huddled mass inside, giving very free translations of the old Norman-French or Latin the while.

"Musty, dirty old things!" was the comment of the two ladies.

Pringle turned to a smaller chest standing neglected in a dark corner, whose lid, when he tried it, he found also unlocked, and which was nearly as full of papers as the larger one.

"Are these town records also?" inquired Pringle, as the beadle gathered up his robes preparatory to moving on.

"Not they," was the contemptuous reply. "That there chest was found in the attic of an old house that's just been pulled down to build the noo bank, and it's offered to the Corporation; but I don't think they'll spend money on rubbish like that!"

"Here's something with a big seal!" exclaimed the clergyman, pouncing on a discoloured parchment with the avid interest of an antiquary. The folds were glued with damp, and endeavouring to smooth them out the parchment slipped through his fingers; it dropped plumb by the weight of its heavy seal, and as he sprang to save it his glasses fell off and buried themselves among the papers. While he hunted for them Pringle picked up the document, and began to read.

"Not much account, I should say," commented the beadle, with a supercilious snort. "Ah! you should have seen our Jubilee Address, with the town seal to it, all in blue and red and gold— cost every penny of fifty pound! That's the noo bank what you're looking at from this window. How the town is improving, to be sure!" He indicated a nightmare in red brick and stucco which had displaced a Jacobean mansion.

And while the beadle prosed Pringle read:

"CINQUE PORTS TO WIT:

"TO ALL and every the Barons Bailiffs Jurats and Commonalty of the Cinque Port of Rye and to Anthony Shipperbolt to Mayor thereof:

"WHEREAS it hath been adjudged by the Commission appointed under His Majesty's sign-manual of date March the twenty-third one thousand eight hundred and five that Anthony Shipperbolt Mayor of Rye hath been guilty of conduct unbefitting his office as a magistrate of the Cinque Ports and hath acted traitorously enviously and contrary to the love and affection his duty towards His Most Sacred Majesty and the good order of this Realm TO WIT that the said Anthony Shipperbolt hath accepted bribes from the enemies of His Majesty hath consorted with the same and did plot compass and go about to assist a certain prisoner of war the same being his proper ward and charge to escape from lawful custody. NOW I William Pitt Lord Warden of the Cinque Ports do order and command you the said Anthony Shipperbolt and you are hereby required to forfeit and pay the sum of ten thousand pounds sterling into His Majesty's Treasury AND as immediate officer of His Majesty and by virtue and authority of each and every the ancient charters of the Cinque Ports I order and command you the said Anthony Shipperbolt to forthwith determine and refrain and you are hereby inhibited from exercising the office and dignity of Mayor of the said Cinque Port of Rye Speaker of the Cinque Ports Summoner of Brotherhood and Guestling and all and singular the liberties freedoms licences exemptions and jurisdictions of Stallage Pontage Panage Keyage Murage Piccage Passage Groundage Scutage and all other powers franchises and authorities appertaining thereunto AND I further order and command you the said Anthony Shipperbolt to render to me within seven days of the date hereof a full and true account of all monies fines amercements redemptions issues forfeitures tallies seals records lands messuages and hereditaments whatsoever and wheresoever that you hold have present custody of or have at any time received in trust for the said Cinque Port of Rye wherein fail not at your peril. AND I further order and command you the said Barons Bailiffs Jurats and Commonalty of the said Cinque Port of Rye that you straightway meet and choose some true and loyal subject of His Majesty the same being of your number as fitting to hold the said office of Mayor of the said Cinque Port whose name you shall submit to my pleasure as soon as may be FOR ALL which this shall be your sufficient authority. Given at Downing Street this sixteenth day of May in the year of our Lord one thousand eight hundred and five.

"GOD SAVE THE KING."

The last two or three inches of the parchment were folded down, and seemed to have firmly adhered to the back—probably through the accidental running of the seal in hot weather. But the fall had broken the wax, and Pringle was now able to open the sheet to the full, disclosing some lines of script, faded and tremulously scrawled, it is true, but yet easy to be read: "To my son.—Seek for the silkworms of Florence in Gibbet Marsh Church Spire SE x S, Winchelsea Mill SW 1/2 W. A.S."

Pringle read this curious endorsement more than once, but could make no sense of it. Concluding it was of the nature of a cypher, he made a note of it in his pocket-book with the idea of attempting a solution in the evening—a time which he found it difficult to get through, Rye chiefly depending for its attractions on its natural advantages.

By this time the clergyman had recovered his glasses, and, handing the document back to him, Pringle joined the party by the window. The banalities of the bank and other municipal improvements being exhausted, and the ladies openly yawning, the beadle proposed to show them what he evidently regarded as the chief glory of the Town Hall of Rye. The inquisitive clergyman was left studying the parchment, while the rest of the party adjourned to the council chamber. Here the guide proudly indicated the list of mayors, whose names were emblazoned on the chocolate-coloured walls to a length rivalling that of the dynasties of Egypt.

"What does this mean?" inquired Pringle. He pointed to the year 1805, where the name "Anthony Shipperbolt" appeared bracketed with another.

"That means he died during his year of office," promptly asserted the old man. He seemed never at a loss for an answer, although Pringle began to suspect that the prompter the reply the more inaccurate was it likely to be.

"Oh, what a smell of burning!" interrupted one of the ladies.

"And where's papa?" screamed the other. "He'll be burnt to death."

There was certainly a smell of burning, which, being of a strong and pungent nature, perhaps suggested to the excited imagination of the ladies the idea of a clergyman on fire. Pringle gallantly raced up the stairs. The fumes issued from a smouldering mass upon the floor, and beside it lay something which burnt with pyrotechnic sputtering; but neither bore any relation to the divine. He, though well representing what Gibbon has styled "the fat slumbers of the Church," was hopping about the miniature bonfire, now sucking his fingers and anon shaking them in the air as one in great agony. Intuitively Pringle understood what had happened, and with a bound he stamped the smouldering parchment into unrecognisable tinder, and smothering the more viciously burning seal with his handkerchief he pocketed it as the beadle wheezed into the room behind the ladies, who were too concerned for their father's safety to notice the action.

"What's all this?" demanded the beadle, and glared through his spectacles.

"I've dr-r-r-r-opped some wa-wa-wa-wax—oh!—upon my hand!"

"Waxo?" echoed the beadle, sniffing suspiciously.

"He means a wax match, I think," Pringle interposed chivalrously. The parchment was completely done for, and he saw no wisdom in advertising the fact.

"I'll trouble you for your name and address," insisted the beadle in all the pride of office.

"What for?" the incendiary objected.

"To report the matter to the Fire Committee."

"Very well, then—Cornelius Hardgiblet, rector of Logdown," was the impressive reply; and tenderly escorted by his daughters the rector departed with such dignity as an occasional hop, when his fingers smarted a little more acutely, would allow him to assume.

It still wanted an hour or two to dinner-time as Pringle unlocked the little; studio he rented on the Winchelsea road. Originally an office, he had made it convertible into a very fair dark-room, and here he was accustomed to spend his afternoons in developing the morning's photographs. But photography had little interest for him to-day. Ever since Mr. Hardgiblet's destruction of the document—which, he felt certain, was no accident—Pringle had cast about for some motive for the act. What could it be but that the parchment contained a secret, which the rector, guessing, had wanted to keep to himself? He must look up the incident of the mayor's degradation. So sensational an event, even for such stirring days as those, would scarcely go unrecorded by local historians. Pringle had several guide-books at hand in the studio, but a careful search only disclosed that they were unanimously silent as to Mr. Shipperbolt and his affairs. Later on, when returning, he had reason to bless his choice of an hotel. The books in the smoking-room were not limited, as usual, to a few timetables and an ancient copy of Ruff's "Guide." On the contrary, Murray and Black were prominent, and above all Hillpath's monumental "History of Rye," and in this last he found the information he sought. Said Hillpath: -

"In 1805 Anthony Shipperbolt, then Mayor of Rye, was degraded from office, his property confiscated, and himself condemned to stand in the pillory with his face to the French coast, for having assisted Jules Florentin, a French prisoner of war, to escape from the Ypres Tower Prison. He was suspected of having connived at the escape of several other prisoners of distinction, presumably for reward. He had been a shipowner trading with France, and his legitimate trade suffering as a result of the war he had undoubtedly resorted to smuggling, a form of trading which, to the principals engaged in it at least, carried little disgrace with it, being winked at by even the most law-abiding persons. Shipperbolt did not long survive his degradation, and, his only son being killed soon after while resisting a revenue cutter when in charge of his father's vessel, the family became extinct."

Here, thought Pringle, was sufficient corroboration of the parchment. The details of the story were clear, and the only mysterious thing about it was the endorsement. His original idea of its being a cypher hardly squared with the simple address, "To my son," and the "A. S." with which it concluded could only stand for the initials of the deposed mayor. There was no mystery either about "Gibbet Marsh," which, according to the beadle's testimony, must have been a well-known spot a century ago, while the string of capitals he easily recognised as compass-bearings. There only remained the curious expression, "The silkworms of Florence," and that was certainly a puzzle. Silkworms are a product of Florence, he knew; but they were unlikely to be exported in such troublous times. And why were they deposited in such a place as Gibbet Marsh? He turned for enlightenment to Hillpath, and pored over the passage again and again before he saw a glimmer of sense. Then suddenly he laughed, as the cypher resolved itself into a pun, and a feeble one at that. While Hillpath named the prisoner as Florentin and more than hinted at payment for services rendered, the cypher indicated where Florentine products were to be found. Shipperbolt ruined, his property confiscated, what more likely than that he should conceal the price of his treason in Gibbet Marsh—a spot almost as shunned in daylight as in darkness? Curious as the choice of the parchment for such a purpose might be, the endorsement was practically a will. He had nothing else to leave.

Pringle was early afoot the next day. Gibbet Marsh has long been drained and its very name forgotten, but the useful Murray indicated its site clearly enough for him to identify it; and it was in the middle of a wide and lonely field, embanked against the winter inundations, that Pringle commenced to work out the bearings approximately with a pocket-compass. He soon fixed his starting-point, the church tower dominating Rye from every point of view; but of Winchelsea there was nothing to be seen for the trees. Suddenly, just where the green mass thinned away to the northward, something rose and caught the sunbeams for a moment, again and still again, and with a steady gaze he made out the revolving sails of a windmill. This was as far as he cared to go for the moment; without a good compass and a sounding-spud it would be a mere waste of time to attempt to fix the spot. He walked across the field, and was in the very act of mounting the stile when he noticed a dark object, which seemed to skim in jerky progression along the top of the embankment. While he looked the thing enlarged, and as the path behind the bank rose uplifted itself into the head, shoulders, and finally the entire person of the rector of Logdown. He had managed to locate Gibbet Marsh, it appeared; but as he stepped into the field and wandered aimlessly about, Pringle judged that he was still a long way from penetrating the retreat of the silkworms.

Among the passengers by the last train down from London that night was Pringle. He carried a cricketing-bag, and when safely inside the studio he unpacked first a sailor's jersey, peaked cap and trousers, then a small but powerful spade, a very neat portable pick, a few fathoms of manilla rope, several short lengths of steel rod (each having a screw-head, by which they united into a single long one), and finally a three-inch prismatic compass.

Before sunrise the next morning Pringle started out to commence operations in deadly earnest, carrying his jointed rods as a walking-stick, while his coat bulged with the prismatic compass. The town, a victim to the enervating influence of the visitors, still slumbered, and he had to unbar the door of the hotel himself. He did not propose to do more than locate the exact spot of the treasure; indeed, he felt that to do even that would be a good morning's work.

On the way down in the train he had taken a few experimental bearings from the carriage window, and felt satisfied with his own dexterity. Nevertheless, he had a constant dread lest the points given should prove inaccurate. He felt dissatisfied with the Winchelsea bearing. For aught he knew, not a single tree that now obscured the view might have been planted; the present mill, perhaps, had not existed; or even another might have been visible from the marsh. What might not happen in the course of nearly a century? He had already made a little calculation, for a prismatic compass being graduated in degrees (unlike the mariner's, which has but thirty-two points), it was necessary to reduce the bearings to degrees, and this had been the result:—Rye Church spire SE x S = 146° I5'. Winchelsea Mill SW 1/2W = 230° 37'.

When he reached the field not a soul was anywhere to be seen; a few sheep browsed here and there, and high overhead a lark was singing. At once he took a bearing from the church spire. He was a little time in getting the right pointing; he had to move step by step to the right, continuing to take observations, until at last the church weather-cock bore truly 146° through the sight-vane of the compass. Turning half round, he took an observation of the distant mill. He was a long way out this time; so carefully preserving his relative position to the church, he backed away, taking alternate observations of either object until both spire and mill bore in the right directions. The point where the two bearings intersected was some fifty yards from the brink of the Tillingham, and, marking the spot with his compass, Pringle began to probe the earth in a gradually widening circle, first with one section of his rod, then with another joint screwed to it, and finally with a length of three, so that the combination reached to a depth of eight feet. He had probed every square inch of a circle described perhaps twenty feet from the compass, when he suddenly stumbled upon a loose sod, nearly impaling himself upon the sounding-rod; and before he could rise his feet, sliding and slipping, had scraped up quite a large surface of turf, as did his hands, in each case disclosing the fat, brown alluvium beneath. A curious fact was that the turf had not been cut in regular strips, as if for removal to some garden; neatly as it was relaid, it had been lifted in shapeless patches, some large, some small, while the soil underneath was all soft and crumbling, as if that too had been recently disturbed. Someone had been before him! Cramped and crippled by his prolonged stooping, Pringle stretched himself at length upon the turf. As he lay and listened to the song that trilled from the tiny speck just visible against a woolly cloud, he felt that it was useless to search further. That a treasure had once been hidden thereabouts he felt convinced, for anything but specie would have been useless at such an unsettled time for commercial credit, and would doubtless have been declined by Shipperbolt; but whatever form the treasure had taken, clearly it was no longer present.

The sounds of toil increased around.

Already a barge was on its way up the muddy stream; at any moment he might be the subject of gaping curiosity. He carefully replaced the turfs, wondering the while who could have anticipated him, and what find, if any, had rewarded the searcher. Thinking it best not to return by the nearest path, he crossed the river some distance up, and taking a wide sweep halted on Cadborough Hill to enjoy for the hundredth time the sight of the glowing roofs, huddled tier after tier upon the rock, itself rising sheer from the plain; and far and beyond, and snowed all over with grazing flocks, the boundless green of the seaward marsh. Inland, the view was only less extensive, and with some ill-humour he was eyeing the scene of his fruitless labour when he observed a figure moving over Gibbet Marsh. At such a distance it was hard to see exactly what was taking place, but the action of the figure was so eccentric that, with a quick suspicion as to its identity, Pringle laid his traps upon the ground and examined it through his pocket telescope. It was indeed Mr. Hardgiblet. But the new feature in the case was that the rector appeared to be taking a bearing with a compass, and although he resumed over and over again to a particular spot (which Pringle recognised as the same over which he himself had spent the early morning hours), Mr. Hardgiblet repeatedly shifted his ground to the right, to the left, and round about, as if dissatisfied with his observations. There was only one possible explanation of all this. Cleverer than Pringle had thought him, the rector must have hit upon the place indicated in the parchment, his hand must have removed the turf, and he it was who had examined the soil beneath. Not for the first time in his life, Pringle was disagreeably reminded of the folly of despising an antagonist, however contemptible he may appear. But at least he had one consolation: the rector's return and his continued observations showed that he had been no more successful in his quest than was Pringle himself. The silkworms were still unearthed.

The road down from Cadborough is long and dusty, and, what with the stiffness of his limbs and the thought of his wasted morning, Pringle, when he reached his studio and took the compass from his pocket, almost felt inclined to fling it through the open window into the "cut." But the spasm of irritability passed. He began to accuse himself of making some initial error in the calculations, and carefully went over them again— with an identical result. Now that Mr. Hardgiblet was clearly innocent of its removal, he even began to doubt the existence of the treasure. Was it not incredible, he asked himself, that for nearly a century it should have remained hidden? As to its secret (a punning endorsement on an old parchment), was it not just as open to any other investigator in all the long years that had elapsed? Besides, Shipperbolt might have removed the treasure himself in alarm for its safety. The thought of Shipperbolt suggested a new idea. Instruments of precision were unknown in those days— supposing Shipperbolt's compass had been inaccurate? He took down Norie's "Navigation," and ran through the chapter on the compass. There was a section headed "Variation and how to apply it," which he skimmed through, considering that the question did not arise, when, carelessly reading on, his attention was suddenly arrested by a table of "Changes in variation from year to year." Running his eye down this he made the startling discovery that, whereas the variation at that moment was about 16° 31' west, in 1805 it was no less than 24°. Here was indeed a wide margin for error. All the time he was searching for the treasure it was probably lying right at the other side of the field!

At once he started to make a rough calculation, determined that it should be a correct one this time. As the variation of 1805 and that of the moment showed a difference of 7° 29', to obtain the true bearing it was necessary for him to subtract this difference from Shipperbolt's points, thus: Rye Church spire SE x S = 146° 15', deduct 7° 29' = 138° 46'. Winchelsea Mill SW 1/2W = 230° 37', deduct 7° 29' = 223° 8'. The question of the moment concerned his next step. Up to the present Mr. Hardgiblet appeared unaware of the error. But how long, thought Pringle, would he remain so? Any work on navigation would set him right, and as he seemed keenly on the scent of the treasure he was unlikely to submit to a check of this nature. Like Pringle, too, he seemed to prefer the early morning hours for his researches. Clearly there was no time to lose. On his way up to lunch Pringle remarked that the whole town was agog. Crowds were pouring in from the railway station; at every corner strangers were inquiring their road; the shops were either closed or closing; a steam roundabout hooted in the cricket-field. The holiday aspect of things was marked by the display on all sides of uncomfortably best clothing, worn with a reckless and determined air of Pleasure Seeking. Even the artists, the backbone of the place, had shared the excitement, or else, resenting the invasion of their pitches by the unaccustomed crowd, were sulking indoors. Anyhow, they had disappeared. Not until he reached the hotel and read on a poster the programme of the annual regatta to be held that day, did Pringle realise the meaning of it all. In the course of lunch—which, owing to the general disorganisation of things, was a somewhat scrambled meal—it occurred to him that here was his opportunity. The regatta was evidently the great event of the year; every idler would be drawn to it, and no worker who could be spared would be absent. The treasure-field would be even lonelier than in the days of Brede's gibbet. He would be able to locate the treasure that afternoon once for all; then, having marked the spot, he could return at night with his tools and remove it.

When Pringle started out the streets were vacant and quiet as on a Sunday, and he arrived at the studio to find the quay an idle waste and the shipping in the "cut" deserted. As to the meadow, when he got there, it was forsaken even by the sheep. He was soon at work with his prismatic compass, and after half an hour's steady labour he struck a spot about an eighth of a mile distant from the scene of his morning's failure. Placing his compass as before at the point of intersection, he began a systematic puncturing of the earth around it. It was a wearisome task, and, warned by his paralysis of the morning, he rose every now and then to stretch and watch for possible intruders. Hours seemed to have passed, when the rod encountered something hard. Leaving it in position, he probed all around with another joint, but there was no resistance even when he doubled its length, and his sense of touch assured him this hardness was merely a casual stone. Doggedly he resumed his task until the steel jammed again with a contact less harsh and unyielding. Once more he left the rod touching the buried mass, and probed about, still meeting an obstruction. And then with widening aim he stabbed and stabbed, striking this new thing until he had roughly mapped a space some twelve by eight inches. No stone was this, he felt assured; the margins were too abrupt, the corners too sharp, for aught but a chest. He rose exultingly. Here beneath his feet were the silkworms of Florence. The secret was his alone. But it was growing late; the afternoon had almost merged into evening, and far away across the field stretched his shadow. Leaving his sounding-rod buried with the cord attached, he walked towards a hurdle on the river-bank, paying out the cord as he went, and hunted for a large stone. This found, he tied a knot in the cord to mark where the hurdle stood, and following it back along the grass pulled up the rod and pressed the stone upon the loosened earth in its place. Last of all, he wound the cord upon the rod. His task would be an easy one again. All he need do was to find the knot, tie the cord at that point to the hurdle, start off with the rod in hand, and when all the cord had run off search for the stone to right or left of the spot he would find himself standing on.

As he re-entered the town groups of people were returning from the regatta—the sea-faring to end the day in the abounding taverns, the staider on their way to the open-air concert, the cinematograph, and the fireworks, which were to brim the cup of their dissipation. Pringle dined early, and then made his way to the concert-field, and spent a couple of hours in studying the natural history of the Ryer. The fireworks were announced for nine, and as the hour approached the excitement grew and the audience swelled. When a fairly accurate census of Rye might have been taken in the field, Pringle edged through the crowd and hurried along the deserted streets to the studio. To change his golf-suit for the sea-clothing he had brought from town was the work of a very few minutes, and his port-wine mark never resisted the smart application of a little spirit. Then, packing the sounding-rod and cord in the cricketing bag, along with the spade, pick, and rope, he locked the door, and stepped briskly out along the solitary road. From the little taverns clinging to the rock opposite came roars of discordant song, for while the losers in the regatta sought consolation, the winners paid the score, and all grew steadily drunk together. He lingered a moment on the sluice to watch the tide as it poured impetuously up from the lower river. A rocket whizzed, and as it burst high over the town a roar of delight was faintly borne across the marsh.

Although the night was cloudy and the moon was only revealed at long intervals, Pringle, with body bent, crept cautiously from bush to bush along the bank; his progress was slow, and the hurdle had been long in sight before he made out a black mass in the water below. At first he took it for the shadow of a bush that stood by, but as he came nearer it took the unwelcome shape of a boat with its painter fast to the hurdle; and throwing himself flat in the grass he writhed into the opportune shade of the bush. It was several minutes before he ventured to raise his head and peer around, but the night was far too dark for him to see many yards in any direction—least of all towards the treasure. As he watched and waited he strove to imagine some reasonable explanation of the boat's appearance on the scene. At another part of the river he would have taken slight notice of it; but it was hard to see what anyone could want in the field at that hour, and the spot chosen for landing was suggestive. What folly to have located the treasure so carefully! He must have been watched that afternoon; round the field were scores of places where a spy might conceal himself. Then, too, who could have taken such deep interest in his movements? Who but Mr. Hardgiblet, indeed? This set him wondering how many had landed from the boat; but a glance showed that it carried only a single pair of sculls, and when he wriggled nearer he saw but three footprints upon the mud, as of one who had taken just so many steps across it.

The suspense was becoming intolerable. A crawl of fifty yards or so over damp grass was not to be lightly undertaken; but he

was just on the point of coming out from the shadow of the bush,
when a faint rhythmic sound arose, to be followed by a thud. He
held his breath, but could hear nothing more. He counted up to a
hundred—still silence. He rose to his knees, when the sound
began again, and now it was louder. It ceased; again there was
the thud, and then another interval of silence. Once more; it
seemed quite close, grew louder, louder still, and resolved itself
into the laboured breathing of a man who now came into view.
He was bending under a burden which he suddenly dropped, as
if exhausted, and then, after resting awhile, slowly raised it to
his shoulders and panted onwards, until, staggering beneath his
load, he lurched against the hurdle, his foot slipped, and he
rolled with a crash down the muddy bank. In that moment
Pringle recognised the more than usually unctuous figure of Mr.
Hardgiblet, who embraced a small oblong chest. Spluttering and
fuming, the rector scrambled to his feet, and after an
unsuccessful hoist or two, dragged the chest into the boat. Then,
taking a pause for breath, he climbed the bank again and
tramped across the field.

Mr. Hardgiblet was scarcely beyond earshot when Pringle,
seizing his bag, jumped down to the water-side. He untied the
painter, and shoving off with his foot, scrambled into the boat as
it slid out on the river. With a paddle of his hand alongside, he
turned the head up stream, and then dropped his bag with all its
contents overboard and crouched along the bottom. A sharp cry
rang out behind, and, gently he peeped over the gunwale. There
by the hurdle stood Mr. Hardgiblet, staring thunder-struck at
the vacancy. The next moment he caught sight of the strayed
boat, and started to run after it; and as he ran, with many a trip
and stumble of wearied limbs, he gasped expressions which were
not those of resignation to his mishap. Meantime, Pringle, his
face within a few inches of the little chest, sought for some
means of escape. He had calculated on the current bearing him
out of sight long before the rector could return, but such activity
as this discounted all his plans. All at once he lost the sounds of
pursuit, and, raising his head, he saw that Mr. Hardgiblet had
been forced to make a detour round a little plantation which
grew to the water's edge. The next second Pringle had seized the
sculls, and with a couple of long rapid strokes grounded the boat
beneath a bush on the opposite bank. There he tumbled the

chest on to the mud, and jumping after it shoved the boat off again. As it floated free and resumed its course up stream, Pringle shouldered the chest, climbed up the bank, and keeping in the shade of a hedge, plodded heavily across the field.

Day was dawning as Pringle extinguished the lamp in his studio, and setting the shutters ajar allowed the light to fall upon the splinters, bristling like a cactus-hedge, of what had been an oaken chest. The wood had proved hard as the iron which clamped and bound it, but scarcely darker or more begrimed than the heap of metal discs it had just disgorged. A few of these, fresh from a bath of weak acid, glowed golden as the sunlight, displaying indifferently a bust with "Bonaparte Premier Consul" surrounding it, or on the reverse "Republique Francaise, anno XI. 20 francs." Such were the silkworms of Florence.

# THE AFFAIR AT THE
# SEMIRAMIS HOTEL
## BY A. E. W. MASON

ORIGINALLY PUBLISHED IN 1917

# THE AFFAIR AT THE SEMIRAMIS HOTEL

## BY A. E. W. MASON

A. E. W. Mason's Inspector Hanaud is the very model of a French detective, almost to the point of parody. He was modeled on Mace and Goron, two actual heads of the Paris Surete as well as Gaboriau's Lecoq. In turn, he is said to have influenced Agatha Christie's Belgian detective Hecule Poirot.

In every respect, he contrasts sharply from Sherlock Holmes. He is stout and broad-shouldered rather than thin. He is affable as opposed to Holmes's often sullen and withdrawn manner. He lives and investigates with typical Gallic flair and has a definite appreciation of good food and wine. In his investigations he often is assisted by the retired English financier, Mr. Ricardo.

His methods are to study the psychology of those involved rather than to dwell on the minutia of physical clues, and often spends much of his investigation appearing to do not much of anything. In his investigations he often is assisted by the retired English financier, Mr. Ricardo.

Hanaud first appeared in the 1910 novel *The Affair at the Villa Rose*, and went on to be featured in four other novels as well as a number of shorter stories.

A. E. W. Mason wrote more than twenty novels, including both mysteries and adventure stories as well as a number of plays and short stories. He is perhaps best known for the novel *The Four Feathers* which has been made into a movie on several occasions, as well as *Witness for the Defence* and *The Summons*.

# THE AFFAIR AT THE SEMIRAMIS HOTEL

## I

Mr. Ricardo, when the excitements of the Villa Rose were done with, returned to Grosvenor Square and resumed the busy, unnecessary life of an amateur. But the studios had lost their savour, artists their attractiveness, and even the Russian opera seemed a trifle flat. Life was altogether a disappointment; Fate, like an actress at a restaurant, had taken the wooden pestle in her hand and stirred all the sparkle out of the champagne; Mr. Ricardo languished—until one unforgettable morning.

He was sitting disconsolately at his breakfast-table when the door was burst open and a square, stout man, with the blue, shaven face of a French comedian, flung himself into the room. Ricardo sprang towards the new-comer with a cry of delight.

"My dear Hanaud!"

He seized his visitor by the arm, feeling it to make sure that here, in flesh and blood, stood the man who had introduced him to the acutest sensations of his life. He turned towards his butler, who was still bleating expostulations in the doorway at the unceremonious irruption of the French detective.

"Another place, Burton, at once," he cried, and as soon as he and Hanaud were alone: "What good wind blows you to London?"

"Business, my friend. The disappearance of bullion somewhere on the line between Paris and London. But it is finished. Yes, I take a holiday."

A light had suddenly flashed in Mr. Ricardo's eyes, and was now no less suddenly extinguished. Hanaud paid no attention whatever to his friend's disappointment. He pounced upon a piece of silver which adorned the tablecloth and took it over to the window.

"Everything is as it should be, my friend," he exclaimed, with a grin. "Grosvenor Square, the *Times* open at the money column, and a false antique upon the table. Thus I have dreamed of you. All Mr. Ricardo is in that sentence."

Ricardo laughed nervously. Recollection made him wary of Hanaud's sarcasms. He was shy even to protest the genuineness of his silver. But, indeed, he had not the time. For the door opened again and once more the butler appeared. On this occasion, however, he was alone.

"Mr. Calladine would like to speak to you, sir," he said.

"Calladine!" cried Ricardo in an extreme surprise. "That is the most extraordinary thing." He looked at the clock upon his mantelpiece. It was barely half-past eight. "At this hour, too?"

"Mr. Calladine is still wearing evening dress," the butler remarked.

Ricardo started in his chair. He began to dream of possibilities; and here was Hanaud miraculously at his side.

"Where is Mr. Calladine?" he asked.

"I have shown him into the library."

"Good," said Mr. Ricardo. "I will come to him."

But he was in no hurry. He sat and let his thoughts play with this incident of Calladine's early visit.

"It is very odd," he said. "I have not seen Calladine for months—no, nor has anyone. Yet, a little while ago, no one was more often seen."

He fell apparently into a muse, but he was merely seeking to provoke Hanaud's curiosity. In this attempt, however, he failed. Hanaud continued placidly to eat his breakfast, so that Mr. Ricardo was compelled to volunteer the story which he was burning to tell.

"Drink your coffee, Hanaud, and you shall hear about Calladine."

Hanaud grunted with resignation, and Mr. Ricardo flowed on:

"Calladine was one of England's young men. Everybody said so. He was going to do very wonderful things as soon as he had made up his mind exactly what sort of wonderful things he was going to do. Meanwhile, you met him in Scotland, at Newmarket, at Ascot, at Cowes, in the box of some great lady at the Opera— not before half-past ten in the evening *there*—in any fine house where the candles that night happened to be lit. He went everywhere, and then a day came and he went nowhere. There was no scandal, no trouble, not a whisper against his good name. He simply vanished. For a little while a few people asked: 'What has become of Calladine?' But there never was any answer, and London has no time for unanswered questions. Other promising young men dined in his place. Calladine had joined the huge legion of the Come-to-nothings. No one even seemed to pass him in the street. Now unexpectedly, at half-past eight in the morning, and in evening dress, he calls upon me. 'Why?' I ask myself."

Mr. Ricardo sank once more into a reverie. Hanaud watched him with a broadening smile of pure enjoyment.

"And in time, I suppose," he remarked casually, "you will perhaps ask him?"

Mr. Ricardo sprang out of his pose to his feet.

"Before I discuss serious things with an acquaintance," he said with a scathing dignity, "I make it a rule to revive my impressions of his personality. The cigarettes are in the crystal box."

"They would be," said Hanaud, unabashed, as Ricardo stalked from the room. But in five minutes Mr. Ricardo came running back, all his composure gone.

"It is the greatest good fortune that you, my friend, should have chosen this morning to visit me," he cried, and Hanaud nodded with a little grimace of resignation.

"There goes my holiday. You shall command me now and always. I will make the acquaintance of your young friend."

He rose up and followed Ricardo into his study, where a young man was nervously pacing the floor.

"Mr. Calladine," said Ricardo. "This is Mr. Hanaud."

The young man turned eagerly. He was tall, with a noticeable elegance and distinction, and the face which he showed to Hanaud was, in spite of its agitation, remarkably handsome.

"I am very glad," he said. "You are not an official of this country. You can advise—without yourself taking action, if you'll be so good."

Hanaud frowned. He bent his eyes uncompromisingly upon Calladine.

"What does that mean?" he asked, with a note of sternness in his voice.

"It means that I must tell someone," Calladine burst out in quivering tones. "That I don't know what to do. I am in a difficulty too big for me. That's the truth."

Hanaud looked at the young man keenly. It seemed to Ricardo that he took in every excited gesture, every twitching feature, in one comprehensive glance. Then he said in a friendlier voice:

"Sit down and tell me"—and he himself drew up a chair to the table.

"I was at the Semiramis last night," said Calladine, naming one of the great hotels upon the Embankment. "There was a fancy-dress ball."

All this happened, by the way, in those far-off days before the war—nearly, in fact, three years ago today—when London, flinging aside its reticence, its shy self-consciousness, had become a city of carnivals and masquerades, rivalling its neighbours on the Continent in the spirit of its gaiety, and exceeding them by its stupendous luxury. "I went by the merest chance. My rooms are in the Adelphi Terrace."

"There!" cried Mr. Ricardo in surprise, and Hanaud lifted a hand to check his interruptions.

"Yes," continued Calladine. "The night was warm, the music floated through my open windows and stirred old memories. I happened to have a ticket. I went."

Calladine drew up a chair opposite to Hanaud and, seating himself, told, with many nervous starts and in troubled tones, a story which, to Mr. Ricardo's thinking, was as fabulous as any out of the "Arabian Nights."

"I had a ticket," he began, "but no domino. I was consequently stopped by an attendant in the lounge at the top of the staircase leading down to the ballroom.

"'You can hire a domino in the cloakroom, Mr. Calladine,' he said to me. I had already begun to regret the impulse which had brought me, and I welcomed the excuse with which the absence of a costume provided me. I was, indeed, turning back to the door, when a girl who had at that moment run down from the stairs of the hotel into the lounge, cried gaily: 'That's not necessary'; and at the same moment she flung to me a long scarlet cloak which she had been wearing over her own dress. She was young, fair, rather tall, slim, and very pretty; her hair was drawn back from her face with a ribbon, and rippled down her shoulders in heavy curls; and she was dressed in a satin coat and knee-breeches of pale green and gold, with a white waistcoat and silk stockings and scarlet heels to her satin shoes. She was as straight-limbed as a boy, and exquisite like a figure in Dresden china. I caught the cloak and turned to thank her. But she did not wait. With a laugh she ran down the stairs a supple and shining figure, and was lost in the throng at the doorway of the ballroom. I was stirred by the prospect of an adventure. I ran down after her. She was standing just inside the room alone, and she was gazing at the scene with parted lips and dancing eyes. She laughed again as she saw the cloak about my shoulders, a delicious gurgle of amusement, and I said to her:

"'May I dance with you?'

"'Oh, do!' she cried, with a little jump, and clasping her hands. She was of a high and joyous spirit and not difficult in the matter of an introduction. 'This gentleman will do very well to present us,' she said, leading me in front of a bust of the God Pan which stood in a niche of the wall. 'I am, as you see, straight out of an opera. My name is Celymene or anything with an eighteenth century sound to it. You are—what you will. For this evening we are friends.'

"'And for to-morrow?' I asked.

"'I will tell you about that later on,' she replied, and she began to dance with a light step and a passion in her dancing which earned me many an envious glance from the other men. I was in luck, for Celymene knew no one, and though, of course, I saw the faces of a great many people whom I remembered, I kept them all at a distance. We had been dancing for about half an hour when the first queerish thing happened. She stopped suddenly in the midst of a sentence with a little gasp. I spoke to her, but she did not hear. She was gazing past me, her eyes wide open, and such a rapt look upon her face as I had never seen. She was lost in a miraculous vision. I followed the direction of her eyes and, to my astonishment, I saw nothing more than a stout, short, middle-aged woman, egregiously over-dressed as Marie Antoinette.

"'So you do know someone here?' I said, and I had to repeat the words sharply before my friend withdrew her eyes. But even then she was not aware of me. It was as if a voice had spoken to her whilst she was asleep and had disturbed, but not wakened her. Then she came to—there's really no other word I can think

of which describes her at that moment—she came to with a deep
sigh.

"'No,' she answered. 'She is a Mrs. Blumenstein from
Chicago, a widow with ambitions and a great deal of money. But
I don't know her.'

"'Yet you know all about her,' I remarked.

"'She crossed in the same boat with me,' Celymene replied.
'Did I tell you that I landed at Liverpool this morning? She is
staying at the Semiramis too. Oh, let us dance!'

"She twitched my sleeve impatiently, and danced with a kind
of violence and wildness as if she wished to banish some sinister
thought. And she did undoubtedly banish it. We supped together
and grew confidential, as under such conditions people will. She
told me her real name. It was Joan Carew.

"'I have come over to get an engagement if I can at Covent
Garden. I am supposed to sing all right. But I don't know
anyone. I have been brought up in Italy.'

"'You have some letters of introduction, I suppose?' I asked.

"'Oh, yes. One from my teacher in Milan. One from an
American manager.'

"In my turn I told her my name and where I lived, and I gave
her my card. I thought, you see, that since I used to know a good
many operatic people, I might be able to help her.

"'Thank you,' she said, and at that moment Mrs.
Blumenstein, followed by a party, chiefly those lap-dog young
men who always seem to gather about that kind of person, came
into the supper-room and took a table close to us. There was at
once an end of all confidences—indeed, of all conversation. Joan
Carew lost all the lightness of her spirit; she talked at random,
and her eyes were drawn again and again to the grotesque
slander on Marie Antoinette. Finally I became annoyed.

"'Shall we go?' I suggested impatiently, and to my surprise
she whispered passionately:

"'Yes. Please! Let us go.'

"Her voice was actually shaking, her small hands clenched.
We went back to the ballroom, but Joan Carew did not recover
her gaiety, and half-way through a dance, when we were near to
the door, she stopped abruptly—extraordinarily abruptly.

"'I shall go,' she said abruptly. 'I am tired. I have grown dull.'

"I protested, but she made a little grimace.

"'You'll hate me in half an hour. Let's be wise and stop now while we are friends,' she said, and whilst I removed the domino from my shoulders she stooped very quickly. It seemed to me that she picked up something which had lain hidden beneath the sole of her slipper. She certainly moved her foot, and I certainly saw something small and bright flash in the palm of her glove as she raised herself again. But I imagined merely that it was some object which she had dropped.

"'Yes, we'll go,' she said, and we went up the stairs into the lobby. Certainly all the sparkle had gone out of our adventure. I recognized her wisdom.

"'But I shall meet you again?' I asked.

"'Yes. I have your address. I'll write and fix a time when you will be sure to find me in. Good-night, and a thousand thanks. I should have been bored to tears if you hadn't come without a domino.'

"She was speaking lightly as she held out her hand, but her grip tightened a little and—clung. Her eyes darkened and grew troubled, her mouth trembled. The shadow of a great trouble had suddenly closed about her. She shivered.

"'I am half inclined to ask you to stay, however dull I am; and dance with me till daylight—the safe daylight,' she said.

"It was an extraordinary phrase for her to use, and it moved me.

"'Let us go back then!' I urged. She gave me an impression suddenly of someone quite forlorn. But Joan Carew recovered her courage. 'No, no,' she answered quickly. She snatched her hand away and ran lightly up the staircase, turning at the corner to wave her hand and smile. It was then half-past one in the morning."

So far Calladine had spoken without an interruption. Mr. Ricardo, it is true, was bursting to break in with the most important questions, but a salutary fear of Hanaud restrained him. Now, however, he had an opportunity, for Calladine paused.

"Half-past one," he said sagely. "Ah!"

"And when did you go home?" Hanaud asked of Calladine.

"True," said Mr. Ricardo. "It is of the greatest consequence."

Calladine was not sure. His partner had left behind her the strangest medley of sensations in his breast. He was puzzled, haunted, and charmed. He had to think about her; he was a trifle uplifted; sleep was impossible. He wandered for a while about the ballroom. Then he walked to his chambers along the echoing streets and sat at his window; and some time afterwards the hoot of a motor-horn broke the silence and a car stopped and whirred in the street below. A moment later his bell rang.

He ran down the stairs in a queer excitement, unlocked the street door and opened it. Joan Carew, still in her masquerade dress with her scarlet cloak about her shoulders, slipped through the opening.

"Shut the door," she whispered, drawing herself apart in a corner.

"Your cab?" asked Calladine.

"It has gone."

Calladine latched the door. Above, in the well of the stairs, the light spread out from the open door of his flat. Down here all was dark. He could just see the glimmer of her white face, the glitter of her dress, but she drew her breath like one who has run far. They mounted the stairs cautiously. He did not say a word until they were both safely in his parlour; and even then it was in a low voice.

"What has happened?"

"You remember the woman I stared at? You didn't know why I stared, but any girl would have understood. She was wearing the loveliest pearls I ever saw in my life."

Joan was standing by the edge of the table. She was tracing with her finger a pattern on the cloth as she spoke. Calladine started with a horrible presentiment.

"Yes," she said. "I worship pearls. I always have done. For one thing, they improve on me. I haven't got any, of course. I have no money. But friends of mine who do own pearls have sometimes given theirs to me to wear when they were going sick, and they have always got back their lustre. I think that has had a little to do with my love of them. Oh, I have always longed for them—just a little string. Sometimes I have felt that I would have given my soul for them."

She was speaking in a dull, monotonous voice. But Calladine recalled the ecstasy which had shone in her face when her eyes first had fallen on the pearls, the longing which had swept her quite into another world, the passion with which she had danced to throw the obsession off.

"And I never noticed them at all," he said.

"Yet they were wonderful. The colour! The lustre! All the evening they tempted me. I was furious that a fat, coarse creature like that should have such exquisite things. Oh, I was mad."

She covered her face suddenly with her hands and swayed. Calladine sprang towards her. But she held out her hand.

"No, I am all right." And though he asked her to sit down she would not. "You remember when I stopped dancing suddenly?"

"Yes. You had something hidden under your foot?"

The girl nodded.

"Her key!" And under his breath Calladine uttered a startled cry.

For the first time since she had entered the room Joan Carew raised her head and looked at him. Her eyes were full of terror, and with the terror was mixed an incredulity as though she could not possibly believe that that had happened which she knew had happened.

"A little Yale key," the girl continued. "I saw Mrs. Blumenstein looking on the floor for something, and then I saw it shining on the very spot. Mrs. Blumenstein's suite was on the same floor as mine, and her maid slept above. All the maids do. I knew that. Oh, it seemed to me as if I had sold my soul and was being paid."

Now Calladine understood what she had meant by her strange phrase—"the safe daylight."

"I went up to my little suite," Joan Carew continued. "I sat there with the key burning through my glove until I had given her time enough to fall asleep"—and though she hesitated before she spoke the words, she did speak them, not looking at Calladine, and with a shudder of remorse making her confession complete. "Then I crept out. The corridor was dimly lit. Far away below the music was throbbing. Up here it was as silent as the grave. I opened the door—her door. I found myself in a lobby. The suite, though bigger, was arranged like mine. I slipped in and closed the door behind me. I listened in the darkness. I couldn't hear a sound. I crept forward to the door in front of me. I stood with my fingers on the handle and my heart beating fast enough to choke me. I had still time to turn back. But I couldn't. There were those pearls in front of my eyes, lustrous and wonderful. I opened the door gently an inch or so—and then—it all happened in a second."

Joan Carew faltered. The night was too near to her, its memory too poignant with terror. She shut her eyes tightly and cowered down in a chair. With the movement her cloak slipped from her shoulders and dropped on to the ground. Calladine leaned forward with an exclamation of horror; Joan Carew started up.

"What is it?" she asked.

"Nothing. Go on."

"I found myself inside the room with the door shut behind me. I had shut it myself in a spasm of terror. And I dared not turn round to open it. I was helpless."

"What do you mean? She was awake?"

Joan Carew shook her head.

"There were others in the room before me, and on the same errand—men!"

Calladine drew back, his eyes searching the girl's face.

"Yes?" he said slowly.

"I didn't see them at first. I didn't hear them. The room was quite dark except for one jet of fierce white light which beat upon the door of a safe. And as I shut the door the jet moved swiftly and the light reached me and stopped. I was blinded. I stood in the full glare of it, drawn up against the panels of the door, shivering, sick with fear. Then I heard a quiet laugh, and someone moved softly towards me. Oh, it was terrible! I recovered the use of my limbs; in a panic I turned to the door, but I was too late. Whilst I fumbled with the handle I was seized; a hand covered my mouth. I was lifted to the centre of the room. The jet went out, the electric lights were turned on. There were two men dressed as apaches in velvet trousers and red scarves, like a hundred others in the ballroom below, and both were masked. I struggled furiously; but, of course, I was like a child in their grasp. 'Tie her legs,' the man whispered who was holding me; 'she's making too much noise.' I kicked and fought, but the other man stooped and tied my ankles, and I fainted."

Calladine nodded his head.

"Yes?" he said.

"When I came to, the lights were still burning, the door of the safe was open, the room empty; I had been flung on to a couch at the foot of the bed. I was lying there quite free."

"Was the safe empty?" asked Calladine suddenly.

"I didn't look," she answered. "Oh!"—and she covered her face spasmodically with her hands. "I looked at the bed. Someone was lying there—under a sheet and quite still. There was a clock ticking in the room; it was the only sound. I was terrified. I was going mad with fear. If I didn't get out of the room at once I felt that I should go mad, that I should scream and bring everyone to find me alone with—what was under the sheet in the bed. I ran to the door and looked out through a slit into the corridor. It was still quite empty, and below the music still throbbed in the ballroom. I crept down the stairs, meeting no one until I reached the hall. I looked into the ballroom as if I was searching for someone. I stayed long enough to show myself. Then I got a cab and came to you."

A short silence followed. Joan Carew looked at her companion in appeal. "You are the only one I could come to," she added. "I know no one else."

Calladine sat watching the girl in silence. Then he asked, and his voice was hard:

"And is that all you have to tell me?"

"Yes."

"You are quite sure?"

Joan Carew looked at him perplexed by the urgency of his question. She reflected for a moment or two.

"Quite."

Calladine rose to his feet and stood beside her.

"Then how do you come to be wearing this?" he asked, and he lifted a chain of platinum and diamonds which she was wearing about her shoulders. "You weren't wearing it when you danced with me."

Joan Carew stared at the chain.

"No. It's not mine. I have never seen it before." Then a light came into her eyes. "The two men—they must have thrown it over my head when I was on the couch—before they went." She looked at it more closely. "That's it. The chain's not very valuable. They could spare it, and—it would accuse me—of what they did."

"Yes, that's very good reasoning," said Calladine coldly.

Joan Carew looked quickly up into his face.

"Oh, you don't believe me," she cried. "You think—oh, it's impossible." And, holding him by the edge of his coat, she burst into a storm of passionate denials.

"But you went to steal, you know," he said gently, and she answered him at once:

"Yes, I did, but not this." And she held up the necklace. "Should I have stolen this, should I have come to you wearing it, if I had stolen the pearls, if I had"—and she stopped—"if my story were not true?"

Calladine weighed her argument, and it affected him.

"No, I think you wouldn't," he said frankly.

Most crimes, no doubt, were brought home because the criminal had made some incomprehensibly stupid mistake; incomprehensibly stupid, that is, by the standards of normal life. Nevertheless, Calladine was inclined to believe her. He looked at her. That she should have murdered was absurd. Moreover, she was not making a parade of remorse, she was not playing the unctuous penitent; she had yielded to a temptation, had got herself into desperate straits, and was at her wits' ends how to escape from them. She was frank about herself.

Calladine looked at the clock. It was nearly five o'clock in the morning, and though the music could still be heard from the ballroom in the Semiramis, the night had begun to wane upon the river.

"You must go back," he said. "I'll walk with you."

They crept silently down the stairs and into the street. It was only a step to the Semiramis. They met no one until they reached the Strand. There many, like Joan Carew in masquerade, were standing about, or walking hither and thither in search of carriages and cabs. The whole street was in a bustle, what with drivers shouting and people coming away.

"You can slip in unnoticed," said Calladine as he looked into the thronged courtyard. "I'll telephone to you in the morning."

"You will?" she cried eagerly, clinging for a moment to his arm.

"Yes, for certain," he replied. "Wait in until you hear from me. I'll think it over. I'll do what I can."

"Thank you," she said fervently.

He watched her scarlet cloak flitting here and there in the crowd until it vanished through the doorway. Then, for the second time, he walked back to his chambers, while the morning crept up the river from the sea.

* * * * *

This was the story which Calladine told in Mr. Ricardo's library. Mr. Ricardo heard it out with varying emotions. He began with a thrill of expectation like a man on a dark threshold of great excitements. The setting of the story appealed to him, too, by a sort of brilliant bizarrerie which he found in it. But, as it went on, he grew puzzled and a trifle disheartened. There were flaws and chinks; he began to bubble with unspoken criticisms, then swift and clever thrusts which he dared not deliver. He looked upon the young man with disfavour, as upon one who had half opened a door upon a theatre of great promise and shown him a spectacle not up to the mark. Hanaud, on the other hand, listened imperturbably, without an expression upon his face, until the end. Then he pointed a finger at Calladine and asked him what to Ricardo's mind was a most irrelevant question.

"You got back to your rooms, then, before five, Mr. Calladine, and it is now nine o'clock less a few minutes."

"Yes."

"Yet you have not changed your clothes. Explain to me that. What did you do between five and half-past eight?"

Calladine looked down at his rumpled shirt front.

"Upon my word, I never thought of it," he cried. "I was worried out of my mind. I couldn't decide what to do. Finally, I determined to talk to Mr. Ricardo, and after I had come to that conclusion I just waited impatiently until I could come round with decency."

Hanaud rose from his chair. His manner was grave, but conveyed no single hint of an opinion. He turned to Ricardo.

"Let us go round to your young friend's rooms in the Adelphi," he said; and the three men drove thither at once.

## II

Calladine lodged in a corner house and upon the first floor. His rooms, large and square and lofty, with Adams mantelpieces and a delicate tracery upon their ceilings, breathed the grace of the eighteenth century. Broad high windows, embrasured in thick walls, overlooked the river and took in all the sunshine and the air which the river had to give. And they were furnished fittingly. When the three men entered the parlour, Mr. Ricardo was astounded. He had expected the untidy litter of a man run to seed, the neglect and the dust of the recluse. But the room was as clean as the deck of a yacht; an Aubusson carpet made the floor luxurious underfoot; a few coloured prints of real value decorated the walls; and the mahogany furniture was polished so that a lady could have used it as a mirror. There was even by the newspapers upon the round table a china bowl full of fresh red roses. If Calladine had turned hermit, he was a hermit of an unusually fastidious type. Indeed, as he stood with his two companions in his dishevelled dress he seemed quite out of keeping with his rooms.

"So you live here, Mr. Calladine?" said Hanaud, taking off his hat and laying it down.

"Yes."

"With your servants, of course?"

"They come in during the day," said Calladine, and Hanaud looked at him curiously.

"Do you mean that you sleep here alone?"

"Yes."

"But your valet?"

"I don't keep a valet," said Calladine; and again the curious look came into Hanaud's eyes.

"Yet," he suggested gently, "there are rooms enough in your set of chambers to house a family."

Calladine coloured and shifted uncomfortably from one foot to the other.

"I prefer at night not to be disturbed," he said, stumbling a little over the words. "I mean, I have a liking for quiet."

Gabriel Hanaud nodded his head with sympathy.

"Yes, yes. And it is a difficult thing to get—as difficult as my holiday," he said ruefully, with a smile for Mr. Ricardo. "However"—he turned towards Calladine—"no doubt, now that you are at home, you would like a bath and a change of clothes. And when you are dressed, perhaps you will telephone to the

Semiramis and ask Miss Carew to come round here. Meanwhile, we will read your newspapers and smoke your cigarettes."

Hanaud shut the door upon Calladine, but he turned neither to the papers nor the cigarettes. He crossed the room to Mr. Ricardo, who, seated at the open window, was plunged deep in reflections.

"You have an idea, my friend," cried Hanaud. "It demands to express itself. That sees itself in your face. Let me hear it, I pray."

Mr. Ricardo started out of an absorption which was altogether assumed.

"I was thinking," he said, with a faraway smile, "that you might disappear in the forests of Africa, and at once everyone would be very busy about your disappearance. You might leave your village in Leicestershire and live in the fogs of Glasgow, and within a week the whole village would know your postal address. But London—what a city! How different! How indifferent! Turn out of St. James's into the Adelphi Terrace and not a soul will say to you: 'Dr. Livingstone, I presume?'"

"But why should they," asked Hanaud, "if your name isn't Dr. Livingstone?"

Mr. Ricardo smiled indulgently.

"Scoffer!" he said. "You understand me very well," and he sought to turn the tables on his companion. "And you—does this room suggest nothing to you? Have you no ideas?" But he knew very well that Hanaud had. Ever since Hanaud had crossed the threshold he had been like a man stimulated by a drug. His eyes were bright and active, his body alert.

"Yes," he said, "I have."

He was standing now by Ricardo's side with his hands in his pockets, looking out at the trees on the Embankment and the barges swinging down the river.

"You are thinking of the strange scene which took place in this room such a very few hours ago," said Ricardo. "The girl in her masquerade dress making her confession with the stolen chain about her throat——"

Hanaud looked backwards carelessly. "No, I wasn't giving it a thought," he said, and in a moment or two he began to walk about the room with that curiously light step which Ricardo was never able to reconcile with his cumbersome figure. With the heaviness of a bear he still padded. He went from corner to corner, opened a cupboard here, a drawer of the bureau there, and—stooped suddenly. He stood erect again with a small box of morocco leather in his hand. His body from head to foot seemed to Ricardo to be expressing the question, "Have I found it?" He pressed a spring and the lid of the box flew open. Hanaud emptied its contents into the palm of his hand. There were two or three sticks of sealing-wax and a seal. With a shrug of the shoulders he replaced them and shut the box.

"You are looking for something," Ricardo announced with sagacity.

"I am," replied Hanaud; and it seemed that in a second or two he found it. Yet—yet—he found it with his hands in his pockets, if he had found it. Mr. Ricardo saw him stop in that attitude in front of the mantelshelf, and heard him utter a long, low whistle. Upon the mantelshelf some photographs were arranged, a box of cigars stood at one end, a book or two lay between some delicate ornaments of china, and a small engraving in a thin gilt frame was propped at the back against the wall. Ricardo surveyed the shelf from his seat in the window, but he could not imagine which it was of these objects that so drew and held Hanaud's eyes.

Hanaud, however, stepped forward. He looked into a vase and turned it upside down. Then he removed the lid of a porcelain cup, and from the very look of his great shoulders Ricardo knew that he had discovered what he sought. He was holding something in his hands, turning it over, examining it. When he was satisfied he moved swiftly to the door and opened it cautiously. Both men could hear the splashing of water in a bath. Hanaud closed the door again with a nod of contentment and crossed once more to the window.

"Yes, it is all very strange and curious," he said, "and I do not regret that you dragged me into the affair. You were quite right, my friend, this morning. It is the personality of your young Mr. Calladine which is the interesting thing. For instance, here we are in London in the early summer. The trees out, freshly green, lilac and flowers in the gardens, and I don't know what tingle of hope and expectation in the sunlight and the air. I am middle-aged—yet there's a riot in my blood, a recapture of youth, a belief that just round the corner, beyond the reach of my eyes, wonders wait for me. Don't you, too, feel something like that? Well, then—" and he heaved his shoulders in astonishment.

"Can you understand a young man with money, with fastidious tastes, good-looking, hiding himself in a corner at such a time—except for some overpowering reason? No. Nor can I. There is another thing—I put a question or two to Calladine."

"Yes," said Ricardo.

"He has no servants here at night. He is quite alone and—here is what I find interesting—he has no valet. That seems a small thing to you?" Hanaud asked at a movement from Ricardo. "Well, it is no doubt a trifle, but it's a significant trifle in the case of a young rich man. It is generally a sign that there is something strange, perhaps even something sinister, in his life. Mr. Calladine, some months ago, turned out of St. James's into the Adelphi. Can you tell me why?"

"No," replied Mr. Ricardo. "Can you?"

Hanaud stretched out a hand. In his open palm lay a small round hairy bulb about the size of a big button and of a colour between green and brown.

"Look!" he said. "What is that?"

Mr. Ricardo took the bulb wonderingly.

"It looks to me like the fruit of some kind of cactus."

Hanaud nodded.

"It is. You will see some pots of it in the hothouses of any really good botanical gardens. Kew has them, I have no doubt. Paris certainly has. They are labelled. 'Anhalonium Luinii.' But amongst the Indians of Yucatan the plant has a simpler name."

"What name?" asked Ricardo.

"Mescal."

Mr. Ricardo repeated the name. It conveyed nothing to him whatever.

"There are a good many bulbs just like that in the cup upon the mantelshelf," said Hanaud.

Ricardo looked quickly up.

"Why?" he asked.

"Mescal is a drug."

Ricardo started.

"Yes, you are beginning to understand now," Hanaud continued, "why your young friend Calladine turned out of St. James's into the Adelphi Terrace."

Ricardo turned the little bulb over in his fingers.

"You make a decoction of it, I suppose?" he said.

"Or you can use it as the Indians do in Yucatan," replied Hanaud. "Mescal enters into their religious ceremonies. They sit at night in a circle about a fire built in the forest and chew it, whilst one of their number beats perpetually upon a drum."

Hanaud looked round the room and took notes of its luxurious carpet, its delicate appointments. Outside the window there was a thunder in the streets, a clamour of voices. Boats went swiftly down the river on the ebb. Beyond the mass of the Semiramis rose the great grey-white dome of St. Paul's. Opposite, upon the Southwark bank, the giant sky-signs, the big Highlander drinking whisky, and the rest of them waited, gaunt skeletons, for the night to limn them in fire and give them life. Below the trees in the gardens rustled and waved. In the air were the uplift and the sparkle of the young summer.

"It's a long way from the forests of Yucatan to the Adelphi Terrace of London," said Hanaud. "Yet here, I think, in these rooms, when the servants are all gone and the house is very quiet, there is a little corner of wild Mexico."

A look of pity came into Mr. Ricardo's face. He had seen more than one young man of great promise slacken his hold and let go, just for this reason. Calladine, it seemed, was another.

"It's like bhang and kieff and the rest of the devilish things, I suppose," he said, indignantly tossing the button upon the table.

Hanaud picked it up.

"No," he replied. "It's not quite like any other drug. It has a quality of its own which just now is of particular importance to you and me. Yes, my friend"—and he nodded his head very seriously—"we must watch that we do not make the big fools of ourselves in this affair."

"There," Mr. Ricardo agreed with an ineffable air of wisdom, "I am entirely with you."

"Now, why?" Hanaud asked. Mr. Ricardo was at a loss for a reason, but Hanaud did not wait. "I will tell you. Mescal intoxicates, yes—but it does more—it gives to the man who eats of it colour-dreams."

"Colour-dreams?" Mr. Ricardo repeated in a wondering voice.

"Yes, strange heated charms, in which violent things happen vividly amongst bright colours. Colour is the gift of this little prosaic brown button." He spun the bulb in the air like a coin, and catching it again, took it over to the mantelpiece and dropped it into the porcelain cup.

"Are you sure of this?" Ricardo cried excitedly, and Hanuad raised his hand in warning. He went to the door, opened it for an inch or so, and closed it again.

"I am quite sure," he returned. "I have for a friend a very learned chemist in the College de France. He is one of those enthusiasts who must experiment upon themselves. He tried this drug."

"Yes," Ricardo said in a quieter voice. "And what did he see?"

"He had a vision of a wonderful garden bathed in sunlight, an old garden of gorgeous flowers and emerald lawns, ponds with golden lilies and thick yew hedges—a garden where peacocks stepped indolently and groups of gay people fantastically dressed quarrelled and fought with swords. That is what he saw. And he saw it so vividly that, when the vapours of the drug passed from his brain and he waked, he seemed to be coming out of the real world into a world of shifting illusions."

Hanaud's strong quiet voice stopped, and for a while there was a complete silence in the room. Neither of the two men stirred so much as a finger. Mr. Ricardo once more was conscious of the thrill of strange sensations. He looked round the room. He could hardly believe that a room which had been—nay was—the home and shrine of mysteries in the dark hours could wear so bright and innocent a freshness in the sunlight of the morning. There should be something sinister which leaped to the eyes as you crossed the threshold.

"Out of the real world," Mr. Ricardo quoted. "I begin to see."

"Yes, you begin to see, my friend, that we must be very careful not to make the big fools of ourselves. My friend of the College de France saw a garden. But had he been sitting alone in the window-seat where you are, listening through a summer night to the music of the masquerade at the Semiramis, might he not have seen the ballroom, the dancers, the scarlet cloak, and the rest of this story?"

"You mean," cried Ricardo, now fairly startled, "that Calladine came to us with the fumes of mescal still working in his brain, that the false world was the real one still for him."

"I do not know," said Hanaud. "At present I only put questions. I ask them of you. I wish to hear how they sound. Let us reason this problem out. Calladine, let us say, takes a great deal more of the drug than my professor. It will have on him a more powerful effect while it lasts, and it will last longer. Fancy dress balls are familiar things to Calladine. The music floating from the Semiramis will revive old memories. He sits here, the pageant takes shape before him, he sees himself taking his part in it. Oh, he is happier here sitting quietly in his window-seat than if he was actually at the Semiramis. For he is there more intensely, more vividly, more really, than if he had actually descended this staircase. He lives his story through, the story of a heated brain, the scene of it changes in the way dreams have, it becomes tragic and sinister, it oppresses him with horror, and in the morning, so obsessed with it that he does not think to change his clothes, he is knocking at your door."

Mr. Ricardo raised his eyebrows and moved.

"Ah! You see a flaw in my argument," said Hanaud. But Mr. Ricardo was wary. Too often in other days he had been leaped upon and trounced for a careless remark.

"Let me hear the end of your argument," he said. "There was then to your thinking no temptation of jewels, no theft, no murder—in a word, no Celymene? She was born of recollections and the music of the Semiramis."

"No!" cried Hanaud. "Come with me, my friend. I am not so sure that there was no Celymene."

With a smile upon his face, Hanaud led the way across the room. He had the dramatic instinct, and rejoiced in it. He was going to produce a surprise for his companion and, savouring the moment in advance, he managed his effects. He walked towards the mantelpiece and stopped a few paces away from it.

"Look!"

Mr. Ricardo looked and saw a broad Adams mantelpiece. He turned a bewildered face to his friend.

"You see nothing?" Hanaud asked.

"Nothing!"

"Look again! I am not sure—but is it not that Celymene is posing before you?"

Mr. Ricardo looked again. There was nothing to fix his eyes. He saw a book or two, a cup, a vase or two, and nothing else

really expect a very pretty and apparently valuable piece of—
and suddenly Mr. Ricardo understood. Straight in front of him,
in the very centre of the mantelpiece, a figure in painted china
was leaning against a china stile. It was the figure of a perfectly
impossible courtier, feminine and exquisite as could be, and
apparelled also even to the scarlet heels exactly as Calladine had
described Joan Carew.

Hanaud chuckled with satisfaction when he saw the
expression upon Mr. Ricardo's face.

"Ah, you understand," he said. "Do you dream, my friend? At
times—yes, like the rest of us. Then recollect your dreams?
Things, people, which you have seen perhaps that day, perhaps
months ago, pop in and out of them without making themselves
prayed for. You cannot understand why. Yet sometimes they cut
their strange capers there, logically, too, through subtle
associations which the dreamer, once awake, does not
apprehend. Thus, our friend here sits in the window, intoxicated
by his drug, the music plays in the Semiramis, the curtain goes
up in the heated theatre of his brain. He sees himself step upon
the stage, and who else meets him but the china figure from his
mantelpiece?"

Mr. Ricardo for a moment was all enthusiasm. Then his
doubt returned to him.

"What you say, my dear Hanaud, is very ingenious. The
figure upon the mantelpiece is also extremely convincing. And I
should be absolutely convinced but for one thing."

"Yes?" said Hanaud, watching his friend closely.

"I am—I may say it, I think, a man of the world. And I ask
myself"—Mr. Ricardo never could ask himself anything without
assuming a manner of extreme pomposity—"I ask myself,
whether a young man who has given up his social ties, who has
become a hermit, and still more who has become the slave of a
drug, would retain that scrupulous carefulness of his body which
is indicated by dressing for dinner when alone?"

Hanaud struck the table with the palm of his hand and sat
down in a chair.

"Yes. That is the weak point in my theory. You have hit it. I
knew it was there—that weak point, and I wondered whether
you would seize it. Yes, the consumers of drugs are careless,

untidy—even unclean as a rule. But not always. We must be careful. We must wait."

"For what?" asked Ricardo, beaming with pride.

"For the answer to a telephone message," replied Hanaud, with a nod towards the door.

Both men waited impatiently until Calladine came into the room. He wore now a suit of blue serge, he had a clearer eye, his skin a healthier look; he was altogether a more reputable person. But he was plainly very ill at ease. He offered his visitors cigarettes, he proposed refreshments, he avoided entirely and awkwardly the object of their visit. Hanaud smiled. His theory was working out. Sobered by his bath, Calladine had realised the foolishness of which he had been guilty.

"You telephone, to the Semiramis, of course?" said Hanaud cheerfully.

Calladine grew red.

"Yes," he stammered.

"Yet I did not hear that volume of 'Hallos' which precedes telephonic connection in your country of leisure," Hanaud continued.

"I telephoned from my bedroom. You would not hear anything in this room."

"Yes, yes; the walls of these old houses are solid." Hanaud was playing with his victim. "And when may we expect Miss Carew?"

"I can't say," replied Calladine. "It's very strange. She is not in the hotel. I am afraid that she has gone away, fled."

Mr. Ricardo and Hanaud exchanged a look. They were both satisfied now. There was no word of truth in Calladine's story.

"Then there is no reason for us to wait," said Hanaud. "I shall have my holiday after all." And while he was yet speaking the voice of a newsboy calling out the first edition of an evening paper became distantly audible. Hanaud broke off his farewell. For a moment he listened, with his head bent. Then the voice was heard again, confused, indistinct; Hanaud picked up his hat and cane and, without another word to Calladine, raced down the stairs. Mr. Ricardo followed him, but when he reached the pavement, Hanaud was half down the little street. At the corner, however, he stopped, and Ricardo joined him, coughing and out of breath.

"What's the matter?" he gasped.

"Listen," said Hanaud.

At the bottom of Duke Street, by Charing Cross Station, the newsboy was shouting his wares. Both men listened, and now the words came to them mispronounced but decipherable.

"Mysterious crime at the Semiramis Hotel."

Ricardo stared at his companion.

"You were wrong then!" he cried. "Calladine's story was true."

For once in a way Hanaud was quite disconcerted.

"I don't know yet," he said. "We will buy a paper."

But before he could move a step a taxi-cab turned into the Adelphi from the Strand, and wheeling in front of their faces, stopped at Calladine's door. From the cab a girl descended.

"Let us go back," said Hanaud.

## III

Mr. Ricardo could no longer complain. It was half-past eight when Calladine had first disturbed the formalities of his house in Grosvenor Square. It was barely ten now, and during that short time he had been flung from surprise to surprise, he had looked underground on a morning of fresh summer, and had been thrilled by the contrast between the queer, sinister life below and within and the open call to joy of the green world above. He had passed from incredulity to belief, from belief to incredulity, and when at last incredulity was firmly established, and the story to which he had listened proved the emanation of a drugged and heated brain, lo! the facts buffeted him in the face, and the story was shown to be true.

"I am alive once more," Mr. Ricardo thought as he turned back with Hanaud, and in his excitement he cried his thought aloud.

"Are you?" said Hanaud. "And what is life without a newspaper? If you will buy one from that remarkably raucous boy at the bottom of the street I will keep an eye upon Calladine's house till you come back."

Mr. Ricardo sped down to Charing Cross and brought back a copy of the fourth edition of the *Star*. He handed it to Hanaud, who stared at it doubtfully, folded as it was.

"Shall we see what it says?" Ricardo asked impatiently.

"By no means," Hanaud answered, waking from his reverie and tucking briskly away the paper into the tail pocket of his coat. "We will hear what Miss Joan Carew has to say, with our minds undisturbed by any discoveries. I was wondering about something totally different."

"Yes?" Mr. Ricardo encouraged him. "What was it?"

"I was wondering, since it is only ten o'clock, at what hour the first editions of the evening papers appear."

"It is a question," Mr. Ricardo replied sententiously, "which the greatest minds have failed to answer."

And they walked along the street to the house. The front door stood open during the day like the front door of any other house which is let off in sets of rooms. Hanaud and Ricardo went up the staircase and rang the bell of Calladine's door. A middle-aged woman opened it.

"Mr. Calladine is in?" said Hanaud.

"I will ask," replied the woman. "What name shall I say?"

"It does not matter. I will go straight in," said Hanaud quietly. "I was here with my friend but a minute ago."

He went straight forward and into Calladine's parlour. Mr. Ricardo looked over his shoulder as he opened the door and saw a girl turn to them suddenly a white face of terror, and flinch as though already she felt the hand of a constable upon her shoulder. Calladine, on the other hand, uttered a cry of relief.

"These are my friends," he exclaimed to the girl, "the friends of whom I spoke to you"; and to Hanaud he said: "This is Miss Carew."

Hanaud bowed.

"You shall tell me your story, mademoiselle," he said very gently, and a little colour returned to the girl's cheeks, a little courage revived in her.

"But you have heard it," she answered.

"Not from you," said Hanaud.

So for a second time in that room she told the history of that night. Only this time the sunlight was warm upon the world, the comfortable sounds of life's routine were borne through the windows, and the girl herself wore the inconspicuous blue serge of a thousand other girls afoot that morning. These trifles of circumstance took the edge of sheer horror off her narrative, so that, to tell the truth, Mr. Ricardo was a trifle disappointed. He wanted a crescendo motive in his music, whereas it had begun at its fortissimo. Hanaud, however, was the perfect listener. He listened without stirring and with most compassionate eyes, so that Joan Carew spoke only to him, and to him, each moment that passed, with greater confidence. The life and sparkle of her had gone altogether. There was nothing in her manner now to suggest the waywardness, the gay irresponsibility, the radiance, which had attracted Calladine the night before. She was just a very young and very pretty girl, telling in a low and remorseful voice of the tragic dilemma to which she had brought herself. Of Celymene all that remained was something exquisite and fragile in her beauty, in the slimness of her figure, in her daintiness of hand and foot—something almost of the hot-house. But the story she told was, detail for detail, the same which Calladine had already related.

"Thank you," said Hanaud when she had done. "Now I must ask you two questions."

"I will answer them."

Mr. Ricardo sat up. He began to think of a third question which he might put himself, something uncommonly subtle and searching, which Hanaud would never have thought of. But Hanaud put his questions, and Ricardo almost jumped out of his chair.

"You will forgive me. Miss Carew. But have you ever stolen before?"

Joan Carew turned upon Hanaud with spirit. Then a change swept over her face.

"You have a right to ask," she answered. "Never." She looked into his eyes as she answered. Hanaud did not move. He sat with a hand upon each knee and led to his second question.

"Early this morning, when you left this room, you told Mr. Calladine that you would wait at the Semiramis until he telephoned to you?"

"Yes."

"Yet when he telephoned, you had gone out?"

"Yes."

"Why?"

"I will tell you," said Joan Carew. "I could not bear to keep the little diamond chain in my room."

For a moment even Hanaud was surprised. He had lost sight of that complication. Now he leaned forward anxiously; indeed, with a greater anxiety than he had yet shown in all this affair.

"I was terrified," continued Joan Carew. "I kept thinking: 'They must have found out by now. They will search everywhere.' I didn't reason. I lay in bed expecting to hear every moment a loud knocking on the door. Besides—the chain itself being there in my bedroom—her chain—the dead woman's chain—no, I couldn't endure it. I felt as if I had stolen it. Then my maid brought in my tea."

"You had locked it away?" cried Hanaud.

"Yes. My maid did not see it."

Joan Carew explained how she had risen, dressed, wrapped the chain in a pad of cotton-wool and enclosed it in an envelope. The envelope had not the stamp of the hotel upon it. It was a rather large envelope, one of a packet which she had bought in a crowded shop in Oxford Street on her way from Euston to the Semiramis. She had bought the envelopes of that particular size in order that when she sent her letter of introduction to the Director of the Opera at Covent Garden she might enclose with it a photograph.

"And to whom did you send it?" asked Mr. Ricardo.

"To Mrs. Blumenstein at the Semiramis. I printed the address carefully. Then I went out and posted it."

"Where?" Hanaud inquired.

"In the big letter-box of the Post Office at the corner of Trafalgar Square."

Hanaud looked at the girl sharply.

"You had your wits about you, I see," he said.

"What if the envelope gets lost?" said Ricardo.

Hanuad laughed grimly.

"If one envelope is delivered at its address in London to-day, it will be that one," he said. "The news of the crime is published, you see," and he swung round to Joan.

"Did you know that, Miss Carew?"

"No," she answered in an awe-stricken voice.

"Well, then, it is. Let us see what the special investigator has to say about it." And Hanaud, with a deliberation which Mr. Ricardo found quite excruciating, spread out the newspaper on the table in front of him.

# IV

There was only one new fact in the couple of columns devoted to the mystery. Mrs. Blumenstein had died from chloroform poisoning. She was of a stout habit, and the thieves were not skilled in the administration of the anaesthetic.

"It's murder none the less," said Hanaud, and he gazed straight at Joan, asking her by the direct summons of his eyes what she was going to do.

"I must tell my story to the police," she replied painfully and slowly. But she did not hesitate; she was announcing a meditated plan.

Hanaud neither agreed nor differed. His face was blank, and when he spoke there was no cordiality in his voice. "Well," he asked, "and what is it that you have to say to the police, miss? That you went into the room to steal, and that you were attacked by two strangers, dressed as apaches, and masked? That is all?"

"Yes."

"And how many men at the Semiramis ball were dressed as apaches and wore masks? Come! Make a guess. A hundred at the least?"

"I should think so."

"Then what will your confession do beyond—I quote your English idiom—putting you in the coach?"

Mr. Ricardo now smiled with relief. Hanaud was taking a definite line. His knowledge of idiomatic English might be incomplete, but his heart was in the right place. The girl traced a vague pattern on the tablecloth with her fingers.

"Yet I think I must tell the police," she repeated, looking up and dropping her eyes again. Mr. Ricardo noticed that her eyelashes were very long. For the first time Hanaud's face relaxed.

"And I think you are quite right," he cried heartily, to Mr. Ricardo's surprise. "Tell them the truth before they suspect it, and they will help you out of the affair if they can. Not a doubt of it. Come, I will go with you myself to Scotland Yard."

"Thank you," said Joan, and the pair drove away in a cab together.

Hanaud returned to Grosvenor Square alone and lunched with Ricardo.

"It was all right," he said. "The police were very kind. Miss Joan Carew told her story to them as she had told it to us. Fortunately, the envelope with the aluminium chain had already been delivered, and was in their hands. They were much mystified about it, but Miss Joan's story gave them a reasonable explanation. I think they are inclined to believe her; and, if she is speaking the truth, they will keep her out of the witness-box if they can."

"She is to stay here in London, then?" asked Ricardo.

"Oh, yes; she is not to go. She will present her letters at the Opera House and secure an engagement, if she can. The criminals might be lulled thereby into a belief that the girl had kept the whole strange incident to herself, and that there was nowhere even a knowledge of the disguise which they had used." Hanaud spoke as carelessly as if the matter was not very important; and Ricardo, with an unusual flash of shrewdness, said:

"It is clear, my friend, that you do not think those two men will ever be caught at all."

Hanaud shrugged his shoulders.

"There is always a chance. But listen. There is a room with a hundred guns, one of which is loaded. Outside the room there are a hundred pigeons, one of which is white. You are taken into the room blind-fold. You choose the loaded gun and you shoot the one white pigeon. That is the value of the chance."

"But," exclaimed Ricardo, "those pearls were of great value, and I have heard at a trial expert evidence given by pearl merchants. All agree that the pearls of great value are known; so, when they come upon the market——"

"That is true," Hanaud interrupted imperturbably. "But how are they known?"

"By their weight," said Mr. Ricardo.

"Exactly," replied Hanaud. "But did you not also hear at this trial of yours that pearls can be peeled like an onion? No? It is true. Remove a skin, two skins, the weight is altered, the pearl is a trifle smaller. It has lost a little of its value, yes—but you can no longer identify it as the so-and-so pearl which belonged to this or that sultan, was stolen by the vizier, bought by Messrs.

Lustre and Steinopolis, of Hatton Garden, and subsequently sold to the wealthy Mrs. Blumenstein. No, your pearl has vanished altogether. There is a new pearl which can be traded." He looked at Ricardo. "Who shall say that those pearls are not already in one of the queer little back streets of Amsterdam, undergoing their transformation?"

Mr. Ricardo was not persuaded because he would not be. "I have some experience in these matters," he said loftily to Hanaud. "I am sure that we shall lay our hands upon the criminals. We have never failed."

Hanaud grinned from ear to ear. The only experience which Mr. Ricardo had ever had was gained on the shores of Geneva and at Aix under Hanaud's tuition. But Hanaud did not argue, and there the matter rested.

The days flew by. It was London's play-time. The green and gold of early summer deepened and darkened; wondrous warm nights under England's pale blue sky, when the streets rang with the joyous feet of youth, led in clear dawns and lovely glowing days. Hanaud made acquaintance with the wooded reaches of the Thames; Joan Carew sang "Louise" at Covent Garden with notable success; and the affair of the Semiramis Hotel, in the minds of the few who remembered it, was already added to the long list of unfathomed mysteries.

But towards the end of May there occurred a startling development. Joan Carew wrote to Mr. Ricardo that she would call upon him in the afternoon, and she begged him to secure the presence of Hanaud. She came as the clock struck; she was pale and agitated; and in the room where Calladine had first told the story of her visit she told another story which, to Mr. Ricardo's thinking, was yet more strange and—yes—yet more suspicious.

"It has been going on for some time," she began. "I thought of coming to you at once. Then I wondered whether, if I waited— oh, you'll never believe me!"

"Let us hear!" said Hanaud patiently.

"I began to dream of that room, the two men disguised and masked, the still figure in the bed. Night after night! I was terrified to go to sleep. I felt the hand upon my mouth. I used to catch myself falling asleep, and walk about the room with all the lights up to keep myself awake."

"But you couldn't," said Hanaud with a smile. "Only the old can do that."

"No, I couldn't," she admitted; "and—oh, my nights were horrible until"—she paused and looked at her companions doubtfully—"until one night the mask slipped."

"What—?" cried Hanaud, and a note of sternness rang suddenly in his voice. "What are you saying?"

With a desperate rush of words, and the colour staining her forehead and cheeks, Joan Carew continued:

"It is true. The mask slipped on the face of one of the men—of the man who held me. Only a little way; it just left his forehead visible—no more."

"Well?" asked Hanaud, and Mr. Ricardo leaned forward, swaying between the austerity of criticism and the desire to believe so thrilling a revelation.

"I waked up," the girl continued, "in the darkness, and for a moment the whole scene remained vividly with me—for just long enough for me to fix clearly in my mind the figure of the apache with the white forehead showing above the mask."

"When was that?" asked Ricardo.

"A fortnight ago."

"Why didn't you come with your story then?"

"I waited," said Joan. "What I had to tell wasn't yet helpful. I thought that another night the mask might slip lower still. Besides, I—it is difficult to describe just what I felt. I felt it important just to keep that photograph in my mind, not to think about it, not to talk about it, not even to look at it too often lest I should begin to imagine the rest of the face and find something familiar in the man's carriage and shape when there was nothing really familiar to me at all. Do you understand that?" she asked, with her eyes fixed in appeal on Hanaud's face.

"Yes," replied Hanaud. "I follow your thought."

"I thought there was a chance now—the strangest chance— that the truth might be reached. I did not wish to spoil it," and she turned eagerly to Ricardo, as if, having persuaded Hanaud, she would now turn her batteries on his companion. "My whole point of view was changed. I was no longer afraid of falling asleep lest I should dream. I wished to dream, but——"

"But you could not," suggested Hanaud.

"No, that is the truth," replied Joan Carew. "Whereas before I was anxious to keep awake and yet must sleep from sheer fatigue, now that I tried consciously to put myself to sleep I remained awake all through the night, and only towards morning, when the light was coming through the blinds, dropped off into a heavy, dreamless slumber."

Hanaud nodded.

"It is a very perverse world, Miss Carew, and things go by contraries."

Ricardo listened for some note of irony in Hanaud's voice, some look of disbelief in his face. But there was neither the one nor the other. Hanaud was listening patiently.

"Then came my rehearsals," Joan Carew continued, "and that wonderful opera drove everything else out of my head. I had such a chance, if only I could make use of it! When I went to bed now, I went with that haunting music in my ears—the call of Paris—oh, you must remember it. But can you realise what it must mean to a girl who is going to sing it for the first time in Covent Garden?"

Mr. Ricardo saw his opportunity. He, the connoisseur, to whom the psychology of the green room was as an open book, could answer that question.

"It is true, my friend," he informed Hanaud with quiet authority. "The great march of events leaves the artist cold. He lives aloof. While the tumbrils thunder in the streets he adds a delicate tint to the picture he is engaged upon or recalls his triumph in his last great part."

"Thank you," said Hanaud gravely. "And now Miss Carew may perhaps resume her story."

"It was the very night of my debut," she continued. "I had supper with some friends. A great artist. Carmen Valeri, honoured me with her presence. I went home excited, and that night I dreamed again."

"Yes?"

"This time the chin, the lips, the eyes were visible. There was only a black strip across the middle of the face. And I thought— nay, I was sure—that if that strip vanished I should know the man."

"And it did vanish?"

"Three nights afterwards."

"And you did know the man?"

The girl's face became troubled. She frowned.

"I knew the face, that was all," she answered. "I was disappointed. I had never spoken to the man. I am sure of that still. But somewhere I have seen him."

"You don't even remember when?" asked Hanaud.

"No." Joan Carew reflected for a moment with her eyes upon the carpet, and then flung up her head with a gesture of despair. "No. I try all the time to remember. But it is no good."

Mr. Ricardo could not restrain a movement of indignation. He was being played with. The girl with her fantastic story had worked him up to a real pitch of excitement only to make a fool of him. All his earlier suspicions flowed back into his mind. What if, after all, she was implicated in the murder and the theft? What if, with a perverse cunning, she had told Hanaud and himself just enough of what she knew, just enough of the truth, to persuade them to protect her? What if her frank confession of her own overpowering impulse to steal the necklace was nothing more than a subtle appeal to the sentimental pity of men, an appeal based upon a wider knowledge of men's weaknesses than a girl of nineteen or twenty ought to have? Mr. Ricardo cleared his throat and sat forward in his chair. He was girding himself for a singularly searching interrogatory when Hanaud asked the most irrelevant of questions:

"How did you pass the evening of that night when you first dreamed complete the face of your assailant?"

Joan Carew reflected. Then her face cleared.

"I know," she exclaimed. "I was at the opera."

"And what was being given?"

"*The Jewels of the Madonna.*"

Hanaud nodded his head. To Ricardo it seemed that he had expected precisely that answer.

"Now," he continued, "you are sure that you have seen this man?"

"Yes."

"Very well," said Hanaud. "There is a game you play at children's parties—is there not?—animal, vegetable, or mineral, and always you get the answer. Let us play that game for a few minutes, you and I."

Joan Carew drew up her chair to the table and sat with her chin propped upon her hands and her eyes fixed on Hanaud's face. As he put each question she pondered on it and answered. If she answered doubtfully he pressed it.

"You crossed on the *Lucania* from New York?"

"Yes."

"Picture to yourself the dining-room, the tables. You have the picture quite clear?"

"Yes."

"Was it at breakfast that you saw him?"

"No."

"At luncheon?"

"No."

"At dinner?"

She paused for a moment, summoning before her eyes the travellers at the tables.

"No."

"Not in the dining-table at all, then?"

"No."

"In the library, when you were writing letters, did you not one day lift your head and see him?"

"No."

"On the promenade deck? Did he pass you when you sat in your deck-chair, or did you pass him when he sat in his chair?"

"No."

Step by step Hanaud took her back to New York to her hotel, to journeys in the train. Then he carried her to Milan where she had studied. It was extraordinary to Ricardo to realise how much Hanaud knew of the curriculum of a student aspiring to grand opera. From Milan he brought her again to New York, and at the last, with a start of joy, she cried: "Yes, it was there."

Hanaud took his handkerchief from his pocket and wiped his forehead.

"Ouf!" he grunted. "To concentrate the mind on a day like this, it makes one hot, I can tell you. Now, Miss Carew, let us hear."

It was at a concert at the house of a Mrs. Starlingshield in Fifth Avenue and in the afternoon. Joan Carew sang. She was a stranger to New York and very nervous. She saw nothing but a mist of faces whilst she sang, but when she had finished the mist cleared, and as she left the improvised stage she saw the man. He was standing against the wall in a line of men. There was no particular reason why her eyes should single him out, except that he was paying no attention to her singing, and, indeed, she forgot him altogether afterwards.

"I just happened to see him clearly and distinctly," she said. "He was tall, clean-shaven, rather dark, not particularly young— thirty-five or so, I should say—a man with a heavy face and beginning to grow stout. He moved away whilst I was bowing to the audience, and I noticed him afterwards walking about, talking to people."

"Do you remember to whom?"

"No."

"Did he notice you, do you think?"

"I am sure he didn't," the girl replied emphatically. "He never looked at the stage where I was singing, and he never looked towards me afterwards."

She gave, so far as she could remember, the names of such guests and singers as she knew at that party. "And that is all," she said.

"Thank you," said Hanaud. "It is perhaps a good deal. But it is perhaps nothing at all."

"You will let me hear from you?" she cried, as she rose to her feet.

"Miss Carew, I am at your service," he returned. She gave him her hand timidly and he took it cordially. For Mr. Ricardo she had merely a bow, a bow which recognised that he distrusted her and that she had no right to be offended. Then she went, and Hanaud smiled across the table at Ricardo.

"Yes," he said, "all that you are thinking is true enough. A man who slips out of society to indulge a passion for a drug in greater peace, a girl who, on her own confession, tried to steal, and, to crown all, this fantastic story. It is natural to disbelieve every word of it. But we disbelieved before, when we left Calladine's lodging in the Adelphi, and we were wrong. Let us be warned."

"You have an idea?" exclaimed Ricardo.

"Perhaps!" said Hanaud. And he looked down the theatre column of the *Times*. "Let us distract ourselves by going to the theatre."

"You are the most irritating man!" Mr. Ricardo broke out impulsively. "If I had to paint your portrait, I should paint you with your finger against the side of your nose, saying mysteriously: '*I* know,' when you know nothing at all."

Hanaud made a schoolboy's grimace. "We will go and sit in your box at the opera to-night," he said, "and you shall explain to me all through the beautiful music the theory of the tonic sol-fa."

They reached Covent Garden before the curtain rose. Mr. Ricardo's box was on the lowest tier and next to the omnibus box.

"We are near the stage," said Hanaud, as he took his seat in the corner and so arranged the curtain that he could see and yet was hidden from view. "I like that."

The theatre was full; stalls and boxes shimmered with jewels and satin, and all that was famous that season for beauty and distinction had made its tryst there that night.

"Yes, this is wonderful," said Hanaud. "What opera do they play?" He glanced at his programme and cried, with a little start of surprise: "We are in luck. It is *The Jewels of the Madonna.*"

"Do you believe in omens?" Mr. Ricardo asked coldly. He had not yet recovered from his rebuff of the afternoon.

"No, but I believe that Carmen Valeri is at her best in this part," said Hanaud.

Mr. Ricardo belonged to that body of critics which must needs spoil your enjoyment by comparisons and recollections of other great artists. He was at a disadvantage certainly to-night, for the opera was new. But he did his best. He imagined others in the part, and when the great scene came at the end of the second act, and Carmen Valeri, on obtaining from her lover the jewels stolen from the sacred image, gave such a display of passion as fairly enthralled that audience, Mr. Ricardo sighed quietly and patiently.

"How Calve would have brought out the psychological value of that scene!" he murmured; and he was quite vexed with Hanaud, who sat with his opera glasses held to his eyes, and every sense apparently concentrated on the stage. The curtains rose and rose again when the act was concluded, and still Hanaud sat motionless as the Sphynx, staring through his glasses.

"That is all," said Ricardo when the curtains fell for the fifth time.

"They will come out," said Hanaud. "Wait!" And from between the curtains Carmen Valeri was led out into the full glare of the footlights with the panoply of jewels flashing on her breast. Then at last Hanaud put down his glasses and turned to Ricardo with a look of exultation and genuine delight upon his face which filled that season-worn dilettante with envy.

"What a night!" said Hanaud. "What a wonderful night!" And he applauded until he split his gloves. At the end of the opera he cried: "We will go and take supper at the Semiramis. Yes, my friend, we will finish our evening like gallant gentlemen. Come! Let us not think of the morning." And boisterously he slapped Ricardo in the small of the back.

In spite of his boast, however, Hanaud hardly touched his supper, and he played with, rather than drank, his brandy and soda. He had a little table to which he was accustomed beside a glass screen in the depths of the room, and he sat with his back to the wall watching the groups which poured in. Suddenly his face lighted up.

"Here is Carmen Valeri!" he cried. "Once more we are in luck. Is it not that she is beautiful?"

Mr. Ricardo turned languidly about in his chair and put up his eyeglass.

"So, so," he said.

"Ah!" returned Hanaud. "Then her companion will interest you still more. For he is the man who murdered Mrs. Blumenstein."

Mr. Ricardo jumped so that his eyeglass fell down and tinkled on its cord against the buttons of his waistcoat.

"What!" he exclaimed. "It's impossible!" He looked again. "Certainly the man fits Joan Carew's description. But—" He turned back to Hanaud utterly astounded. And as he looked at the Frenchman all his earlier recollections of him, of his swift deductions, of the subtle imagination which his heavy body so well concealed, crowded in upon Ricardo and convinced him.

"How long have you known?" he asked in a whisper of awe.

"Since ten o'clock to-night."

"But you will have to find the necklace before you can prove it."

"The necklace!" said Hanaud carelessly. "That is already found."

Mr. Ricardo had been longing for a thrill. He had it now. He felt it in his very spine.

"It's found?" he said in a startled whisper.

"Yes."

Ricardo turned again, with as much indifference as he could assume, towards the couple who were settling down at their table, the man with a surly indifference, Carmen Valeri with the radiance of a woman who has just achieved a triumph and is now free to enjoy the fruits of it. Confusedly, recollections returned to Ricardo of questions put that afternoon by Hanaud to Joan Carew—subtle questions into which the name of Carmen Valeri was continually entering. She was a woman of thirty, certainly beautiful, with a clear, pale face and eyes like the night.

"Then she is implicated too!" he said. What a change for her, he thought, from the stage of Covent Garden to the felon's cell, from the gay supper-room of the Semiramis, with its bright frocks and its babel of laughter, to the silence and the ignominious garb of the workrooms in Aylesbury Prison!

"She!" exclaimed Hanaud; and in his passion for the contrasts of drama Ricardo was almost disappointed. "She has nothing whatever to do with it. She knows nothing. Andre Favart there—yes. But Carmen Valeri! She's as stupid as an owl, and loves him beyond words. Do you want to know how stupid she is? You shall know. I asked Mr. Clements, the director of the opera house, to take supper with us, and here he is."

Hanaud stood up and shook hands with the director. He was of the world of business rather than of art, and long experience of the ways of tenors and prima-donnas had given him a good-humoured cynicism.

"They are spoilt children, all tantrums and vanity," he said, "and they would ruin you to keep a rival out of the theatre."

He told them anecdote upon anecdote.

"And Carmen Valeri," Hanaud asked in a pause; "is she troublesome this season?"

"Has been," replied Clements dryly. "At present she is playing at being good. But she gave me a turn some weeks ago."

He turned to Ricardo. "Superstition's her trouble, and Andre Favart knows it. She left him behind in America this spring."

"America!" suddenly cried Ricardo; so suddenly that Clements looked at him in surprise.

"She was singing in New York, of course, during the winter," he returned. "Well, she left him behind, and I was shaking hands with myself when he began to deal the cards over there. She came to me in a panic. She had just had a cable. She couldn't sing on Friday night. There was a black knave next to the nine of diamonds. She wouldn't sing for worlds. And it was the first night of *The Jewels of the Madonna!* Imagine the fix I was in!"

"What did you do?" asked Ricardo.

"The only thing there was to do," replied Clements with a shrug of the shoulders. "I cabled Favart some money and he dealt the cards again. She came to me beaming. Oh, she had been so distressed to put me in the cart! But what could she do? Now there was a red queen next to the ace of hearts, so she could sing without a scruple so long, of course, as she didn't pass a funeral on the way down to the opera house. Luckily she didn't. But my money brought Favart over here, and now I'm living on a volcano. For he's the greatest scoundrel unhung. He never has a farthing, however much she gives him; he's a blackmailer, he's a swindler, he has no manners and no graces, he looks like a butcher and treats her as if she were dirt, he never goes near the opera except when she is singing in this part, and she worships the ground he walks on. Well, I suppose it's time to go."

The lights had been turned off, the great room was emptying. Mr. Ricardo and his friends rose to go, but at the door Hanaud detained Mr. Clements, and they talked together alone for some little while, greatly to Mr. Ricardo's annoyance. Hanaud's good humour, however, when he rejoined his friend, was enough for two.

"I apologise, my friend, with my hand on my heart. But it was for your sake that I stayed behind. You have a meretricious taste for melodrama which I deeply deplore, but which I mean to gratify. I ought to leave for Paris to-morrow, but I shall not. I shall stay until Thursday." And he skipped upon the pavement as they walked home to Grosvenor Square.

Mr. Ricardo bubbled with questions, but he knew his man. He would get no answer to any one of them to-night. So he worked out the problem for himself as he lay awake in his bed, and he came down to breakfast next morning fatigued but triumphant. Hanaud was already chipping off the top of his egg at the table.

"So I see you have found it all out, my friend," he said.

"Not all," replied Ricardo modestly, "and you will not mind, I am sure, if I follow the usual custom and wish you a good morning."

"Not at all," said Hanaud. "I am all for good manners myself."

He dipped his spoon into his egg.

"But I am longing to hear the line of your reasoning."

Mr. Ricardo did not need much pressing.

"Joan Carew saw Andre Favart at Mrs. Starlingshield's party, and saw him with Carmen Valeri. For Carmen Valeri was there. I remember that you asked Joan for the names of the artists who sang, and Carmen Valeri was amongst them."

Hanaud nodded his head.

"Exactly."

"No doubt Joan Carew noticed Carmen Valeri particularly, and so took unconsciously into her mind an impression of the man who was with her, Andre Favart—of his build, of his walk, of his type."

Again Hanaud agreed.

"She forgets the man altogether, but the picture remains latent in her mind—an undeveloped film."

Hanaud looked up in surprise, and the surprise flattered Mr. Ricardo. Not for nothing had he tossed about in his bed for the greater part of the night.

"Then came the tragic night at the Semiramis. She does not consciously recognise her assailant, but she dreams the scene again and again, and by a process of unconscious cerebration the figure of the man becomes familiar. Finally she makes her debut, is entertained at supper afterwards, and meets once more Carmen Valeri."

"Yes, for the first time since Mrs. Starlingshield's party," interjected Hanaud.

"She dreams again, she remembers asleep more than she remembers when awake. The presence of Carmen Valeri at her supper-party has its effect. By a process of association, she recalls Favart, and the mask slips on the face of her assailant. Some days later she goes to the opera. She hears Carmen Valeri sing in *The Jewels of the Madonna.* No doubt the passion of her acting, which I am more prepared to acknowledge this morning than I was last night, affects Joan Carew powerfully, emotionally. She goes to bed with her head full of Carmen Valeri, and she dreams not of Carmen Valeri, but of the man who is unconsciously associated with Carmen Valeri in her thoughts. The mask vanishes altogether. She sees her assailant now, has his portrait limned in her mind, would know him if she met him in the street, though she does not know by what means she identified him."

"Yes," said Hanaud. "It is curious the brain working while the body sleeps, the dream revealing what thought cannot recall."

Mr. Ricardo was delighted. He was taken seriously.

"But of course," he said, "I could not have worked the problem out but for you. You knew of Andre Favart and the kind of man he was."

Hanaud laughed.

"Yes. That is always my one little advantage. I know all the cosmopolitan blackguards of Europe." His laughter ceased suddenly, and he brought his clenched fist heavily down upon the table. "Here is one of them who will be very well out of the world, my friend," he said very quietly, but there was a look of force in his face and a hard light in his eyes which made Mr. Ricardo shiver.

For a few moments there was silence. Then Ricardo asked: "But have you evidence enough?"

"Yes."

"Your two chief witnesses, Calladine and Joan Carew—you said it yourself—there are facts to discredit them. Will they be believed?"

"But they won't appear in the case at all," Hanaud said. "Wait, wait!" and once more he smiled. "By the way, what is the number of Calladine's house?"

Ricardo gave it, and Hanaud therefore wrote a letter. "It is all for your sake, my friend," he said with a chuckle.

"Nonsense," said Ricardo. "You have the spirit of the theatre in your bones."

"Well, I shall not deny it," said Hanaud, and he sent out the letter to the nearest pillar-box.

Mr. Ricardo waited in a fever of impatience until Thursday came. At breakfast Hanaud would talk of nothing but the news of the day. At luncheon he was no better. The affair of the Semiramis Hotel seemed a thousand miles from any of his thoughts. But at five o'clock he said as he drank his tea:

"You know, of course, that we go to the opera to-night?"

"Yes. Do we?"

"Yes. Your young friend Calladine, by the way, will join us in your box."

"That is very kind of him, I am sure," said Mr. Ricardo.

The two men arrived before the rising of the curtain, and in the crowded lobby a stranger spoke a few words to Hanaud, but what he said Ricardo could not hear. They took their seats in the box, and Hanaud looked at his programme.

"Ah! It is *Il Ballo de Maschera* to-night. We always seem to hit upon something appropriate, don't we?"

Then he raised his eyebrows.

"Oh-o! Do you see that our pretty young friend, Joan Carew, is singing in the role of the page? It is a showy part. There is a particular melody with a long-sustained trill in it, as far as I remember."

Mr. Ricardo was not deceived by Hanaud's apparent ignorance of the opera to be given that night and of the part Joan Carew was to take. He was, therefore, not surprised when Hanaud added:

"By the way, I should let Calladine find it all out for himself."

Mr. Ricardo nodded sagely.

"Yes. That is wise. I had thought of it myself." But he had done nothing of the kind. He was only aware that the elaborate stage-management in which Hanaud delighted was working out to the desired climax, whatever that climax might be. Calladine entered the box a few minutes later and shook hands with them awkwardly.

"It was kind of you to invite me," he said and, very ill at ease, he took a seat between them and concentrated his attention on the house as it filled up.

"There's the overture," said Hanaud. The curtains divided and were festooned on either side of the stage. The singers came on in their turn; the page appeared to a burst of delicate applause (Joan Carew had made a small name for herself that season), and with a stifled cry Calladine shot back in the box as if he had been struck. Even then Mr. Ricardo did not understand. He only realised that Joan Carew was looking extraordinarily trim and smart in her boy's dress. He had to look from his programme to the stage and back again several times before the reason of Calladine's exclamation dawned on him. When it did, he was horrified. Hanaud, in his craving for dramatic effects, must have lost his head altogether. Joan Carew was wearing, from the ribbon in her hair to the scarlet heels of her buckled satin shoes, the same dress as she had worn on the tragic night at the Semiramis Hotel. He leaned forward in his agitation to Hanaud.

"You must be mad. Suppose Favart is in the theatre and sees her. He'll be over on the Continent by one in the morning."

"No, he won't," replied Hanaud. "For one thing, he never comes to Covent Garden unless one opera, with Carmen Valeri in the chief part, is being played, as you heard the other night at supper. For a second thing, he isn't in the house. I know where he is. He is gambling in Dean Street, Soho. For a third thing, my friend, he couldn't leave by the nine o'clock train for the Continent if he wanted to. Arrangements have been made. For a fourth thing, he wouldn't wish to. He has really remarkable reasons for desiring to stay in London. But he will come to the theatre later. Clements will send him an urgent message, with the result that he will go straight to Clements' office. Meanwhile, we can enjoy ourselves, eh?"

Never was the difference between the amateur dilettante and the genuine professional more clearly exhibited than by the behaviour of the two men during the rest of the performance. Mr. Ricardo might have been sitting on a coal fire from his jumps and twistings; Hanaud stolidly enjoyed the music, and when Joan Carew sang her famous solo his hands clamoured for an encore louder than anyone's in the boxes. Certainly, whether excitement was keeping her up or no, Joan Carew had never sung better in her life. Her voice was clear and fresh as a bird's—a bird with a soul inspiring its song. Even Calladine drew his chair forward again and sat with his eyes fixed upon the stage and quite carried out of himself. He drew a deep breath at the end.

"She is wonderful," he said, like a man waking up.

"She is very good," replied Mr. Ricardo, correcting Calladine's transports.

"We will go round to the back of the stage," said Hanaud.

They passed through the iron door and across the stage to a long corridor with a row of doors on one side. There were two or three men standing about in evening dress, as if waiting for friends in the dressing-rooms. At the third door Hanaud stopped and knocked. The door was opened by Joan Carew, still dressed in her green and gold. Her face was troubled, her eyes afraid.

"Courage, little one," said Hanaud, and he slipped past her into the room. "It is as well that my ugly, familiar face should not be seen too soon."

The door closed and one of the strangers loitered along the corridor and spoke to a call-boy. The call-boy ran off. For five minutes more Mr. Ricardo waited with a beating heart. He had the joy of a man in the centre of things. All those people driving homewards in their motor-cars along the Strand—how he pitied them! Then, at the end of the corridor, he saw Clements and Andre Favart. They approached, discussing the possibility of Carmen Valeri's appearance in London opera during the next season.

"We have to look ahead, my dear friend," said Clements, "and though I should be extremely sorry——"

At that moment they were exactly opposite Joan Carew's door. It opened, she came out; with a nervous movement she shut the door behind her. At the sound Andre Favart turned, and he saw drawn up against the panels of the door, with a look of terror in her face, the same gay figure which had interrupted him in Mrs. Blumenstein's bedroom. There was no need for Joan to act. In the presence of this man her fear was as real as it had been on the night of the Semiramis ball. She trembled from head to foot. Her eyes closed; she seemed about to swoon.

Favart stared and uttered an oath. His face turned white; he staggered back as if he had seen a ghost. Then he made a wild dash along the corridor, and was seized and held by two of the men in evening dress. Favart recovered his wits. He ceased to struggle.

"What does this outrage mean?" he asked, and one of the men drew a warrant and notebook from his pocket.

"You are arrested for the murder of Mrs. Blumenstein in the Semiramis Hotel," he said, "and I have to warn you that anything you may say will be taken down and may be used in evidence against you."

"Preposterous!" exclaimed Favart. "There's a mistake. We will go along to the police and put it right. Where's your evidence against me?"

Hanaud stepped out of the doorway of the dressing-room.

"In the property-room of the theatre," he said.

At the sight of him Favart uttered a violent cry of rage. "You are here, too, are you?" he screamed, and he sprang at Hanaud's throat. Hanaud stepped lightly aside. Favart was borne down to the ground, and when he stood up again the handcuffs were on his wrists.

Favart was led away, and Hanaud turned to Mr. Ricardo and Clements.

"Let us go to the property-room," he said. They passed along the corridor, and Ricardo noticed that Calladine was no longer with them. He turned and saw him standing outside Joan Carew's dressing-room.

"He would like to come, of course," said Ricardo.

"Would he?" asked Hanaud. "Then why doesn't he? He's quite grown up, you know," and he slipped his arm through Ricardo's and led him back across the stage. In the property-room there was already a detective in plain clothes. Mr. Ricardo had still not as yet guessed the truth.

"What is it you really want, sir?" the property-master asked of the director.

"Only the jewels of the Madonna," Hanaud answered.

The property-master unlocked a cupboard and took from it the sparkling cuirass. Hanaud pointed to it, and there, lost amongst the huge glittering stones of paste and false pearls, Mrs. Blumenstein's necklace was entwined.

"Then that is why Favart came always to Covent Garden when *The Jewels of the Madonna* was being performed!" exclaimed Ricardo.

Hanaud nodded.

"He came to watch over his treasure."

Ricardo was piecing together the sections of the puzzle.

"No doubt he knew of the necklace in America. No doubt he followed it to England."

Hanaud agreed.

"Mrs. Blumenstein's jewels were quite famous in New York."

"But to hide them here!" cried Mr. Clements. "He must have been mad."

"Why?" asked Hanaud. "Can you imagine a safer hiding-place? Who is going to burgle the property-room of Covent Garden? Who is going to look for a priceless string of pearls amongst the stage jewels of an opera house?"

"You did," said Mr. Ricardo.

"I?" replied Hanaud, shrugging his shoulders. "Joan Carew's dreams led me to Andre Favart. The first time we came here and saw the pearls of the Madonna, I was on the look-out, naturally. I noticed Favart at the back of the stalls. But it was a stroke of luck that I noticed those pearls through my opera glasses."

"At the end of the second act?" cried Ricardo suddenly. "I remember now."

"Yes," replied Hanaud. "But for that second act the pearls would have stayed comfortably here all through the season. Carmen Valeri—a fool as I told you—would have tossed them about in her dressing-room without a notion of their value, and at the end of July, when the murder at the Semiramis Hotel had been forgotten, Favart would have taken them to Amsterdam and made his bargain."

"Shall we go?"

They left the theatre together and walked down to the grill-room of the Semiramis. But as Hanaud looked through the glass door he drew back.

"We will not go in, I think, eh?"

"Why?" asked Ricardo.

Hanaud pointed to a table. Calladine and Joan Carew were seated at it taking their supper.

"Perhaps," said Hanaud with a smile, "perhaps, my friend—what? Who shall say that the rooms in the Adelphi will not be given up?"

They turned away from the hotel. But Hanaud was right, and before the season was over Mr. Ricardo had to put his hand in his pocket for a wedding present.

# AVAILABLE FROM RESURRECTED PRESS!

## GEMS OF MYSTERY
## LOST JEWELS FROM A MORE ELEGANT AGE

Three wonderful tales of mystery from some of the best known writers of the period before the First World War --

A foggy London night, a Russian princess who steals jewels, a corpse; a mysterious murder, an opera singer, and stolen pearls; two young people who crash a masked ball only to find themselves caught up in a daring theft of jewels; these are the subjects of this collection of entertaining tales of love, jewels, and mystery. This collection includes:

In the Fog - by Richard Harding Davis's
The Affair at the Hotel Semiramis - by A.E.W. Mason
Hearts and Masks - Harold MacGrath

## JOURNEYS INTO MYSTERY

A collection of three novels of travel and mystery from some of the best known writers of the Edwardian Age

A man is mysteriously murdered on the night express from Rome to Paris. Which one of the passengers is the murderer. The Countess? The General? The clergyman? The maid who disappeared?

A sapphire necklace stolen from a cab in the London fog. A ship's steward who is either more or less than he appears to be. A jewel thief who criss-crosses the Atlantic in search of victims.

A grand London hotel. A missing German prince. A murdered man whose body disappears from the hotel. These are the challenges facing an American millionaire and his daughter after he buys The Grand Babylon Hotel.

*The Rome Express* – Arthur Griffiths
*The Voice in the Fog* – Harold MacGrath
*The Grand Babylon Hotel* – Arnold Bennett

# RESURRECTED PRESS CLASSIC MYSTERY CATALOGUE

**E. C. Bentley**
*Trent's Last Case: The Woman in Black*

**Ernest Bramah**
*Max Carrados Resurrected:*
*The Detective Stories of Max Carrados*

**Agatha Christie**
*The Secret Adversary*
*The Mysterious Affair at Styles*

**Octavus Roy Cohen**
*Midnight*

**Freeman Wills Croft**
*The Ponson Case*
*The Pit Prop Syndicate*

**J. S. Fletcher**
*The Herapath Property*
*The Rayner-Slade Amalgamation*
*The Chestermarke Instinct*
*The Paradise Mystery*
*Dead Men's Money*
*The Middle of Things*
*Ravensdene Court*
*Scarhaven Keep*
*The Orange-Yellow Diamond*
*The Middle Temple Murder*
*The Tallyrand Maxim*
*The Borough Treasurer*
*In the Mayor's Parlour*
*The Saftey Pin*

## R. Austin Freeman

*The Mystery of 31 New Inn from the Dr. Thorndyke Series*
*John Thorndyke's Cases from the Dr. Thorndyke Series*
*The Red Thumb Mark from The Dr. Thorndyke Series*
*The Eye of Osiris from The Dr. Thorndyke Series*
*A Silent Witness from the Dr. John Thorndyke Series*
*The Cat's Eye from the Dr. John Thorndyke Series*
*Helen Vardon's Confession: A Dr. John Thorndyke Story*
*As a Thief in the Night: A Dr. John Thorndyke Story*
*Mr. Pottermack's Oversight: A Dr. John Thorndyke Story*
*Dr. Thorndyke Intervenes: A Dr. John Thorndyke Story*
*The Singing Bone: The Adventures of Dr. Thorndyke*
*The Stoneware Monkey: A Dr. John Thorndyke Story*
*The Great Portrait Mystery, and Other Stories: A Collection of
Dr. John Thorndyke and Other Stories*
*The Penrose Mystery: A Dr. John Thorndyke Story*
*The Uttermost Farthing: A Savant's Vendetta*

## Arthur Griffiths

*The Passenger From Calais*
*The Rome Express*

## Fergus Hume

*The Mystery of a Hansom Cab*
*The Green Mummy*
*The Silent House*
*The Secret Passage*

## Edgar Jepson

*The Loudwater Mystery*

## A. E. W. Mason

*At the Villa Rose*

## A. A. Milne

*The Red House Mystery*

## Baroness Emma Orczy

*The Old Man in the Corner*

**Edgar Allan Poe**
*The Detective Stories of Edgar Allan Poe*

**Arthur J. Rees**
*The Hampstead Mystery*
*The Shrieking Pit*
*The Hand In The Dark*
*The Moon Rock*
*The Mystery of the Downs*

**Mary Roberts Rinehart**
*Sight Unseen and The Confession*

**Dorothy L. Sayers**
*Whose Body?*

**Sir William Magnay**
*The Hunt Ball Mystery*

**Mabel and Paul Thorne**
*The Sheridan Road Mystery*

**Louis Tracy**
*The Strange Case of Mortimer Fenley*
*The Albert Gate Mystery*
*The Bartlett Mystery*
*The Postmaster's Daughter*
*The House of Peril*
*The Sandling Case: What Would You Have Done?*

**John R. Watson**
*The Mystery of the Downs*
*The Hampstead Mystery*

**Edgar Wallace**
*The Daffodil Mystery*
*The Crimson Circle*

**Carolyn Wells**
*Vicky Van*

*The Man Who Fell Through the Earth*
*In the Onyx Lobby*
*Raspberry Jam*
*The Clue*
*The Room with the Tassels*
*The Vanishing of Betty Varian*
*The Mystery Girl*
*The White Alley*
*The Curved Blades*
*Anybody but Anne*
*The Bride of a Moment*
*Faulkner's Folly*
*The Diamond Pin*
*The Gold Bag*
*The Mystery of the Sycamore*
*The Come Back*

**Raoul Whitfield**
*Death in a Bowl*

**Mildred A. Wirt**
*The Clock Strikes Thirteen*
*Clue of the Silken Ladder*
*The Cry at Midnight*
*Ghost Beyond the Gate*
*Guilt of the Brass Thieves*
*Hoofbeats on the Turnpike*
*The Secret Pact*
*Saboteurs on the River*
*Signal in the Dark*
*Voice from the Cave*
*Whispering Walls*
*The Wishing Well*

*And much more!*
*Visit ResurrectedPress.com for our complete*
*catalogue*

## About Resurrected Press

A division of Intrepid Ink, LLC, Resurrected Press is dedicated to bringing high quality, vintage books back into publication. See our entire catalogue and find out more at www.ResurrectedPress.com.

## About Intrepid Ink, LLC

Intrepid Ink, LLC provides full publishing services to authors of fiction and non-fiction books, eBooks and websites. From editing to formatting, from publishing to marketing, Intrepid Ink gets your creative works into the hands of the people who want to read them. Find out more at www.IntrepidInk.com.